AS
GOOD
AS
TRUE

AS GOOD AS AS TRUE

Cheryl Reid

LAKE UNION
PUBLISHING

Published by Lake Union Publishing, Seattle

www.apub.com

Amazon, the Amazon logo, and Lake Union Publishing are trademarks of Amazon.com, Inc., or its affiliates.

ISBN-13: 9781542049733 (paperback)
ISBN-10: 1542049733 (paperback)
ISBN-13: 9781503949546 (hardcover)
ISBN-10: 1503949540 (hardcover)

Cover design by PEPE *nymi*

Printed in the United States of America

First edition

For William, Reid, Grant, and Nathaniel

Death

Any other day, the shrill alarm would ring at four thirty and I would dress in cool darkness and start the day's baking for the store. By five, I would be leaning against the oven, its heat ticking up, while I sipped my first cup of coffee and cooked his breakfast. By six, he would have eaten and left to open the grocery. But I had failed to set the alarm and I woke startled at nine a.m. with the bright sun in my eyes and sweat beading on my neck. The heat was already at a high pitch and the cicadas had begun their deep drone outside my window.

At the doorway of Elias's room, morning light filtered through the sheer drapes. Across the bed, on top of the sheets, his body lay stiff. The stench of vomit and shit still lingered. I opened windows and turned on the fan. No breath. No movement. Only the whir of hot air pushing across my cheek. The house was quiet with a dead man in it.

The night before, he had scratched around and pried at my door until the small hours, when all he could do was say my name, at first begging, then with rage. But I stayed locked in my bedroom, the highboy pushed against the entrance, and I listened for him to be still.

When finally I stood over him in the dark, his body was contorted, his knees drawn inward, his head crooked sideways, and his eyes fixed on the north-facing window.

I did not turn on lights in the wee hours as I cleaned his mess with vinegar and baking soda to kill the odor. I turned his body to change the dirty sheets. The deadweight was heavy and unwieldy, but I straightened his limbs and ran my fingers over his eyelids. His dying had not been easy.

In the bright morning light, I searched for any signs he might have left behind, anything I might have missed in the dark. His pants lay crumpled on the floor by his bed. In his pockets were small change and bills, about two hundred dollars, bound by a silver clip our son had given him. He had kicked off his work shoes—black wing tips, polished to a high shine, the hard ridges of leather gleaming and clean. His thin black socks had been peeled off, and the shapes of his toes were molded in them. I looked in his bureau for anything out of the ordinary but found only the white T-shirts, the underpants and socks, all of which I had washed, folded, and put away.

I picked up the dirtied sheets on the floor. From them fell a piece of paper, a wadded receipt from our store. I smoothed it and saw Orlando Washington's name and address. I studied the paper in my hand and knew Elias had intended him harm.

My chest constricted as if someone were binding me in a corset. I'd had similar spells of pain over the years, finding it hard to catch my breath, as if my ribs were too small to contain my heart and lungs. I told myself Elias was no longer a threat, just an empty shell. I wiped my palms against the cotton of my gown.

My fingers found the fresh bruises on my arms where he had held me down and tried to press the life out of me. I wanted his body out of my sight. My eyes landed on the old crucifix, carved of olive wood, hanging between the bedposts. His father had brought it with him on the boat from Beirut. The Christ figure's head hung sideways and the suffering wooden eyes gazed down on Elias. We had been married twenty-seven years and I felt relief to have him gone.

Mourning

A piercing ring disturbed the silence of the house. I knew who was calling. The store had not been opened, and she would be worried. I folded the paper with Orlando Washington's name and slipped it in the pocket of my gown. I gathered the dirtied sheets and Elias's pants and socks and hurried down the stairs to answer the telephone. My hand shook as I put the receiver to my ear.

"Mother," Marina's voice demanded. "Michael went by the store on his way to the office and no one was there."

"I was about to call you." She loved her father, and the news of his death would strike her hard.

"What's wrong? Is Daddy sick?" I heard a splinter of uneasiness in her tone.

"I just found him." I tried to speak gently. "He's gone."

"What do you mean you just found him?" Her usual unflinching voice broke like a scratched record.

"I overslept and he didn't wake me," I said. I cradled the receiver on my shoulder and fingered the paper in my pocket. "I woke up and he was still in bed." My chest shook from the inside out. I wondered if she could hear the shaking in my voice. "He died."

"How?" She sounded small, weak.

"I don't know. In his sleep."

She held her breath for a moment. Then the sobbing came. From early on, she had been Daddy's girl, something about his deep voice or his bright-green eyes or the smile he could not drop when she was near. From the time she could reach for him, he had held her. When she had bad dreams he sat with her at night, and he left the store in my charge so that he could drive her to piano or dance lessons. He gave her anything she wanted. He never said no, not even when I caught her smoking at sixteen and, raging mad, sent her to him for punishment. She stayed calm and baited him: "You smoke, everyone smokes. So why can't I?" And he let her have her way. She shot me a look, one of her perfect eyebrows raised and a smirk on her lips, to let me know my place.

"I haven't called Eli or anyone," I said.

"I will." I listened to her cry for a respectful amount of time.

"Let me come to get you." She was too far along to drive.

"That will take too long." Marina's voice shuddered from the sobs.

"If you go into labor and wreck, it could kill the both of you."

"I'm getting dressed and coming over," she said.

"Okay." I knew better than to argue with her, especially the past few days. She had been frustrated with me over Orlando Washington.

Elias liked to say Marina and I were like oil and water, but it was his fault, always doting, spoiling her, and treating me like the whipping boy whenever things did not go his way. He never hit me in front of the children. He tried to keep his cruelty hidden, but they must have known.

I hung up the receiver and hurried to make the house presentable. I ran to the basement and put his sullied sheets and clothes in the washer. I opened windows and turned on fans to move the hot air. Already I was sweating, and it would matter to Marina, to others, how I looked, how the house looked. My father's Old World and Riverton, Alabama, were the same in that respect. Family duty and pride were tied to honor and shame, how a person was seen, how things appeared, whether a person was respectable or not. All efforts to save face must be made.

I should have stayed awake longer after he died, should have forgone the comfort of bed when I usually began the day's baking. I should have worn myself out getting the house ready for what was to come. There was my bed to make, and back downstairs to clean the kitchen counters. He'd been sick here in the early-morning hours, and my hands shook as I wiped and rinsed all the spots I had missed in the dark. In the corner, my crock of bread starter was bubbling from the heat.

At this time any other day, I would have already taken the leaven to start the bread. I would have fed the rest with water and flour, the counters would have been covered with proofing loaves, and the ripe, sweet smell of bread would have filled the air. But this day, the flour, bowls, and bread baskets were put away. I took the crock of starter from the counter and put it in the icebox, and as soon as duty would allow, I would come and care for it.

I ran back upstairs to my closet to find a dress to cover the bruises Elias had left on my arms. All of my long-sleeved dresses would be too hot. The only dress near appropriate, a black gabardine with a high collar and dolman sleeves, was too heavy to wear all day. I'd come back, find something cooler and lighter when I had a moment, once Marina and Eli came and after the funeral home took the body away.

I transferred the paper with Orlando Washington's name to my dress pocket, and then lipstick, a brush through my wild hair, stockings. My face was slick with sweat. Powder, a handkerchief. A clean sheet over Elias and shut his door. Marina would care what others saw when they looked at me. I'd been born and lived my whole life in Riverton, but I was a Syrian immigrant's daughter who'd grown up on the Negro side of town. My features were odd to most people in town—the olive skin that darkened with one day of sun, the heavy eyebrows, the curly hair too stubborn to tame, and the Arab nose, like my father's, that curved down toward my lips. A few times that I had stayed in the sun too long, whites had mistaken my race. I was alien, even though my family had been here for fifty years. I needed to be circumspect in everything I did now.

I was on the bottom step and blotting my face when Marina pushed through the front door. The screen slapped behind her. Her stomach and rear protruded. Her thin, angular face was now full and plump. She was so big. It was painful to see. The baby could come any minute. For days she'd complained of aches and pains and stiff, swollen legs, but she glided to the base of the stairs because her beloved father was up there.

I was shocked to see my beautiful Marina in such a mess, no makeup and her green eyes bloodshot. Her ebony hair, usually smooth and swept up in a French twist, was disheveled and damp. She wore one of Michael's button-downs and rolled-up blue jeans, not one of her smart and tidy dresses. To my surprise, she wrapped her arms around me and held tight. Heat emanated from her body.

I was dazed to have her holding me. It was not the normal thing for Marina to be close or give affection. She was independent. There were times she wanted me, like the day I taught her to float on her back in the river. At first she'd clung to me out of fear and held my arms and legs in a death grip, though she was only waist deep. My gentlest coaxing loosened her grasp, and once she floated, her hands released. Part of me wanted her to grab hold again, to need me, and then a small comfort came, her delicate fingers brushed my arm, my side, to check that I was near.

The day her father died, I held on to her and pitied her to be nine months along in August. I hoped that grief would churn inside and the baby would come and distract her from thoughts of Elias, and that all her attention and love would flow to the newborn. I wanted Elias buried, and then I would have Marina to myself, never to deal with him again. And when the time came, I would listen to her grief and keep my mouth shut. I could forgive her for her complicity, for all those times it was them against me. My jealousy could float away.

Elias saw me as little more than the one who did his laundry and cooked, the one who worked in his store and raised his children. I had dwindled to nothing in his eyes, and I worried that was how she saw me too. Maybe now that he was gone, she could see me untainted, that I was her mother who loved her. For now, I would keep secret my happiness that he was gone. I would give her that.

I touched her hair and she pulled away. Her long, delicate fingers rubbed her eyes. "I called Father McMurray and Eli. He'll telephone the funeral home and Grandpapa." My father. She sniffled. "Grandmother is on the way."

At the mention of Nelly, Elias's mother, I lost my breath. My mind had skipped over all the people who'd be involved in his death—his mother and those who would mourn him. Marina would busy herself with details of what should happen and how it should go. I had forgotten all the *shoulds* that Marina would demand, and the hell of kneeling and praying and nodding politely to strangers before he was in the ground.

"Go see him if you want," I said.

She began a slow climb upstairs. Marina would not be still for long, nor would she lean on me.

My fingers skimmed the hem of her shirt. I went up with her, maybe to stop her. "Don't, if it's too much."

She looked back at me. Her face wrenched, and a stream of tears rolled down her cheeks. I tried to hold her again. She waved me off and stepped inside his room.

I waited and listened to be sure she had not broken down. My stomach tightened with hunger, and after a few minutes, I left my post outside his room and went downstairs to the kitchen.

I took the starter from the icebox and scooped out the usual amount of leaven, and though I hated to waste it, I threw it in the trash. There would be no flatbread or popovers made with the discard. I fed the remaining leaven with flour and water and stirred it with my hand. Marina loved my bread, but she hated the sticky feel of dough, so she never made it. I rinsed my hands and placed the starter back in the icebox. I put the flour away and looked at the shelves of baskets and pans and wondered how long before I would bake again. I should have baked some quick bread to comfort her and get my mind off what was about to happen, but that would not look right. My house would soon be full, and there could be no questions about why I was baking at this sorrowful time. For all anyone needed to know, our house was peaceful, I was in mourning, and his death was an ordinary one.

I had known Elias my entire life—his parents and mine were two of three Syrian families in town. I had begged my father to let me marry him. The summer after I graduated high school, he came to Papa's store, not to talk the usual business with my father or ask Gus to do a day's work at Nassad Grocery, but to talk to me. He smelled good, of cloves and spice, and I liked when he stood close and leaned on the counter so that his forearm brushed against mine. I liked the way his long fingers tapped a cigarette on his lighter before he put it to his lips. One Sunday, after a few months of his attention, he walked me home from Mass and we spent the afternoon sitting on the bank of the river, holding hands and kissing, after surveying to be sure my father was not watching. That was the day he reached into his shirt pocket and pulled out a gold ring with a square emerald. He proposed to me, and I was giddy and full of nerves.

I showed Papa the ring on my finger. He stared at it as if I held a rat in my hand. "You are too young." His kind voice was gruff and hard.

"I'll be nineteen in a month," I said.

He thought he could say no once and I would listen. His body stiffened and his head shook as he looked at me with pity. "The Nassads are hard on their women." I did not understand his meaning, then, but he had known Elias's father and what kind of man he was. He had watched Elias grow up and seen what he'd had to take.

For months, I argued and I wept. I insisted to my father, to myself, that if I married him it would be a step up, away from the colored section of town. My father's store was a half mile west of the railroad track. People in Riverton called it Blacktown or worse, but the neighborhood people called it Mounds for the two flat-topped hills where the Cherokee had buried their dead. My brother and I had crossed the tracks each morning to go to school and later to come home. We crossed them to go to church or the movies or town, and I had the notion that I would marry Elias and cross into Riverton proper, elevate myself and never look back.

Elias came to convince Papa what a good match we would make. He shook Papa's hand and smiled. Elias swore he wanted to marry me, that our marriage would be an opportunity, and his store and Papa's store would benefit each other.

In private, Papa pleaded with me, "You can go to school or we can arrange a better marriage for you." But an arranged marriage would mean leaving him and Gus, and leaving Riverton. I was nineteen years old and thinking how smart I was to position myself for a better life with Elias, ten years older and handsome and rich. His store was on Main Street in the middle of town. I would be moving across the tracks and up in the world.

Elias whispered in my ear how wonderful our life would be, and I believed him. The words sounded nice, like a dream. I liked the salty smell of his breath, his clove aftershave, his bright-green eyes. A bird in the hand, I thought. I stared at the bright-green emerald and knew that no one else in Riverton would give me such a prize and marry me, the Catholic Syrian girl from across the tracks.

I dug my heels in, refused to eat, and stayed in bed. I tormented Papa with threats that I would run off and elope. The thought that I would marry outside the Church shamed him. He was still broken from his wife long dead, and being his only daughter, the only female he loved, I confounded him. Papa gave in to me because he wanted me to be happy, but he should have told me, then, that Elias's father beat Nelly and abused his boys. Papa should have heeded his worries that brutality seeped down through generations. I did not know. Maybe Papa second-guessed his worries and told himself it was history, dead and buried. Elias seemed earnest and hopeful, and maybe Papa convinced himself that Elias would not repeat his father's sins. Maybe Papa thought I was too delicate for the truth, and that if he told me what he feared, if he said it out loud, that if I married Elias, then the beatings would become prophecy for me. Not until years later, when Elias first hit me, did I know what my father meant when he'd said, "The Nassads are hard on their women."

~

My back was turned, but I could feel Nelly's presence. She entered the kitchen from the hallway. She called out in her thick accent, *"Sahira."* *Witch.* She lapsed into a flurry of Arabic that I could not follow. Papa had refused to teach my brother Gus or me. We were to grow up American, and Arabic was of no benefit to us here. But we gathered what scraps we could.

I turned to face Nelly, and when she saw that her words were wasted on me, she spoke in English. "You never cared for my Elias." Her glasses were as thick as bottle bottoms. They magnified her ancient eyes to the size of ripe plums. "You killed my baby."

"Nelly," I said, "Elias was a long way from 'baby.'"

"You feel nothing." She leaned on her cane and pointed a shriveled finger in my face.

When I married Elias, Nelly had been a fat woman, gluttonous, but now her black dress hung on her like a dress on a wire rack. Just as Papa had begged me, she had pleaded with Elias not to marry me. *Anna is too young,* she said. *She is too frail. She will end up like her mother, dying in childbirth, and where will that get you, a dead wife and a dead baby?* Nelly wanted to decide Elias's bride, and she was irate that he would choose for himself. She wanted a better marriage for him—one that would connect them to a rich Lebanese family from Birmingham or Mobile, not me, the scrawny girl from across the tracks.

She tolerated me for a few years, until Marina was born, and when I was not the kind of mother she thought I should be, her frustration with me festered.

Marina pushed through the swinging door from the dining room in time to hear Nelly's words: "You never cared for him. If you did this in the old country, you would be stoned." Marina said nothing to admonish her grandmother, who had belittled me all of Marina's life. Instead, Marina trudged across the room with her belly like a lead weight and embraced Nelly.

When Marina was born, I thought I would die. The birth had been traumatic—my body torn by forceps and stitched back up. My milk did not come and she wailed with hunger. My breasts were swollen and hard like stones, and my mind was in bad shape. I worried that no one—not Elias, not the baby—loved me. For four days, the nurses brought me food and I refused it. They asked me if I wanted to see her, and I said no. I knew I should hold her, but I was afraid I would never be a good-enough mother for her. All I wanted to do was sleep, to close my eyes and shut the world out.

Elias drove us home, slowly, nervously. I held the baby in the car, and I fought the urge to lay the bundle on the seat between us. But I knew better—that would have been wrong. When he opened my car door, he took her so I could get out, but I did not wait to take her back. I hobbled to my room and shut the door.

At home, Nelly appeared in my room, the baby wailing in her arms. "You will feed her," she informed me. "It is the best way." She undid my gown and took my breast in her hand, squeezed, and put the baby's mouth to it, again and again. The baby cried. I cried. Nelly was trying to help us, but I cringed at my nakedness and her closeness. Marina sucked, and the pulling felt like nails shooting through my breast. The pain became too much, and finally I cried, "Take her. Take her and go." I thought, then, she would be better off without me. "Just take her."

"What is wrong with you?" Nelly nestled Marina in her own bosom, cooed to her and looked at her with eyes full of love. I knew I should want to hold the baby and feel attached, to feel love for her, but in my gut and head, there was only despair. Nelly clicked her tongue. "A mother who refuses a newborn is unnatural."

If they had made me hold her, I would have laid her down and slunk away. I thought, *The baby will suffer because of me.* I thought, *I have nothing to give her.* Nelly shushed Marina's cries, and soon, she held a bottle in Marina's mouth. The baby's slurping carried down the hall. I rolled over and thought she was better off with Nelly.

For the next week and weeks after, I lay in my room, which smelled of blood, my sour breath, and thick sleep. I could hear that Marina was safe and being cared for. I limped to the bathroom and the kitchen only when I would not see them—not Elias, not Nelly, not the baby girl whose cries disturbed my sleep.

I felt betrayed by them all—by Elias, whom I wanted to love but who did not love me; by his child who cried in the night, but softened and cooed when Nelly took her. I felt alone, with no mother of my own. My father and brother were not able to tend me, nor would they know what to do. For almost too long, I chewed on that lonely feeling like a bitter root and let the taste wash through me like the tide coming in.

On the day Elias died, I watched the two wailing women claim my house. Nelly, feeble with age and wrinkled like a vine, pointed at the cuckoo clock over the kitchen sink. Marina raised her swollen arm to stop the pendulum. The ticking ceased. Then Nelly led Marina to the buffet in the dining room for tablecloths. Nelly had Marina drape one over the mirrored hat rack near the front door. Then Nelly pointed to the mirror above the mantel. Marina pushed a chair toward it.

I stopped her. "I don't want you climbing." I took the cloth from her. "You could hurt yourself and the baby." Elias had been dead since one thirty in the morning, and if his spirit was to be caught in mirrors or clocks, it was too late.

"I can do it."

My daughter had always done what the old woman wanted, but I had not suffered Elias for so long to have Marina suffer now. I pulled her back and stepped up in the chair to cover the mirror. "I won't have you fall over this nonsense."

Seeing what she had asked Marina to do, Nelly said, "Your mother is right. You should not be up there." Her voice was gentle, full of motherly concern. I could not fault her for loving Marina. "Soon you are to be a mother. Blessed be God that I will see my great-grandchild."

"What else would you like done, Nelly?" I would be helpful to the old woman in an effort to soothe Marina.

Nelly swatted the air as if my voice were a droning fly. She hobbled across the living room to the dining-room table and took two candles in her withered hands. She spoke to Marina. "Take me to him."

Marina wrapped her arm around the old woman's waist and they climbed the stairs. She loved her father, and now was her time to mourn him. She loved her grandmother too, and I knew better than to come between them.

I looked out the screen door for any signs of my son, my father, or the priest, but saw no one. I leaned against the wide wooden door and turned my eyes to the rooms of the house. We were rich to most people. To the left, the dining room with its mahogany panels and coffered ceilings. The buffet, the china cabinet, the long table, and the piano Marina played to delight her father. To the right, the living room, its massive stone fireplace, the Persian rugs and fine furniture and beautiful lamps, as good as any in Riverton. I had Wedgwood china and Roseville pottery. I had silver trays and cutlery and nice things that could be bought. But nice things only went so far. We were oddities in Riverton—my

father got off the boat with thirty-eight dollars in his pocket and peddled from New York to Nashville. Elias's father's experience had been
similar, and both men had saved and prospered. But money could only
raise you so high. We were curiosities, and we had to be extra careful
what we did or didn't do.

Yesterday, Elias had walked in our door and stood in the same spot
I was now standing, between the dining and the living rooms, the heart
of the home. He noticed nothing of the furniture or the fine things we
had. His eyes lit on Orlando Washington, a glass of water in his hand,
sitting at our dining-room table, and me across from him.

In my pocket, I fingered the paper on which Elias had written
Orlando Washington's name and address. Elias had accused me of more
than I had done, but now the accusations were dead with him.

Soon, the funeral men would carry Elias's body down the wide
stairs and out the front door. I would have no reasons to dread life here.
I had itched to have Elias and this house, finer than my childhood home
with its rough edges, cracked plaster walls, and beams of wood showing
from the ceiling. The furniture was hard and the windows leaked. The
odors of the store drifted up to the bedrooms and clung to the curtains
and bedsheets. The spices, the onions, the tobacco from the cigarette
shelf, blood from the meat counter, and the earthen smell of silk fabric
and wool carpets stacked in the store's back room. When my mother
lived, the smell of burning wood from her brick oven woke me in the
morning, and in the afternoon, the smell of white ash and hot bread
comforted me. There was nothing soft or fancy about that place, but
I remembered feeling safe. Now that Elias was gone, I hoped I would
have that feeling again.

The floor above me creaked where Nelly and Marina moved. Then
I heard steps on the porch. Eli opened the screen door and stood, pale
and young, in the black dress of a priest. He looked like his father thirty
years ago, tall and thin, the angular face framed by jet hair, cropped
short. The difference between the two: Eli stood with his shoulders

slumped, his head hanging low, as if he did not feel worthy of his height or the power of a man's body. His father had always stood straight and moved with confidence—or false confidence, unsuspected by anyone, even me. Elias's expression had been intense, no matter the emotion, whether he was speaking kindly to a customer or glowering at me. Eli's gaze was soft, forgiving, so unlike his father's, but their eyes were the same.

"Mama," he said. He hugged me. His dark shirt was damp with perspiration. He must have sped from the seminary, thirty miles south. Eli looked at me with boyish eyes, full of sorrow. That was how his father had seen him: as a boy, not a man. Elias loved Eli, I knew, because he never raised a hand against him, but Elias hated that his son wanted to be a priest. He had never shown Eli that he was proud of him in the way he had Marina, and I realized how difficult his father's death would be for him. My throat stung.

"Anna, Eli." Father McMurray stood on the opposite side of the screen door. "I am sorry." He was a bald, fat Irishman with a thick brogue, pale skin, and a pink tip of a nose. At times, in conversation, his words would ramble and trail off, and I would notice the sweet odor of alcohol hanging around him and understand that he was drunk. That morning, I prayed he'd had a shot or two in his coffee.

He carried what looked like a doctor's bag. Inside it were his holy instruments—a censer and incense, holy oils and balms, holy water. He had come to bless the dead.

"Go up with Eli, Father." I pointed to the stairs. "Marina will be glad you are here." The two men ascended in their somber clothes. The ceiling creaked above. I hesitated before I walked the stairs and stood outside his room, where my family gathered to pray the Rosary.

Father McMurray recited scripture. "As Saint Paul tells us in the Corinthians: 'The trumpet shall sound, and the dead shall rise again incorruptible: and we shall be changed. For this corruptible must put on incorruption; and this mortal must put on immortality. And when this mortal hath put on immortality, then shall come to pass: Death is swallowed up in victory. O Death, where is thy victory?' May our prayers for Elias deliver his soul incorruptible before Jesus Christ, our Lord."

Marina and Nelly made the sign of the cross. Marina had combed her hair and pinned it in a French twist. She had rinsed the redness from her face. The windows had been shut and the heavy curtains pulled over the sheer drapes, so that only a dim light bled from the edges of the windows. Vigil candles burned on either side of the bed. The air was humid and heavy with the warm odors of melting beeswax and sulfur from a match. Small flames licked the air as the ceiling fan spun round and sent shadows dancing across the dead man's face. A trick of light made Elias blink. I looked away to keep from falling down.

The priest continued: "Our prayers for Elias show our love for him. Though he has lived a good life, no one can know the temptations his soul has suffered on earth. May our prayers help purify him and excuse him from purgatory, so that he can reach his destiny with our Lord in heaven." The priest swung the censer and ribbons of smoke trailed around the room. "May our prayers float heavenward to God on this sweet smoke." The odor of incense mingled with the rose water that Nelly used to wash her son.

The priest began his first invocation of Mary, and familiar voices followed. I got lost in the sounds, especially Eli's deep voice breaking in sorrow. For nine months, since last Thanksgiving, Eli had been praying at the seminary for every living person on earth, and now he prayed for his father's soul. I felt a sting in the pit of my stomach—my son, his father, Nelly's voice warbling in prayer, her son, my husband, my daughter—and then a lightness in my head. *This will pass.* My own quiet prayer. *It will be better now.*

Elias's body was covered with the linen sheets Nelly had given us when we married. She found them on the highest, farthest shelf in the hall closet. Somehow, with a mother's touch, she had manipulated the shape of his mouth and the arch of his forehead to look peaceful. She had laid his hands, long and delicate, over his heart, and entwined a rosary through his long, thin fingers, the same long fingers of his children.

Across the room, Nelly hung on Marina's arm, and Marina's shoulders drooped with the extra weight. Her legs and feet must have throbbed. I wanted to lead her out of the room, away from his body and Nelly and into a comfortable chair. But if I tried, she would protest and Nelly would cling more. I prayed Marina's water would break to loosen Nelly, who clung like a vine winding around a great tree, grounding Marina to that place to pray for her father.

Elias's skin had grown gray. The coarse black hairs on his body seemed darker in death against his pale skin. The holy oil that Father McMurray smeared on his forehead gleamed in the candlelight. Soon he would be in the ground. The thought soothed the pressure in my chest. Familiar rhythms of prayer filled the room. I swayed to the sound. It was the duty of the living to pray for the dead, but I did not pray for Elias. The last thing I wanted was to help him. God was straight with the facts. If I prayed for anyone that morning, it was for myself.

Midway through the Rosary, I heard voices in the kitchen, then heavy shoes clomping up the stairs. Elias's brother, Ivie, brushed past me into the room. Nelly saw him and fell into a fit of wailing. *"Ibni,"* she screeched. *"Ibni!"* It meant *my son.* "He is gone," she squalled. She pulled at Marina to go with her to Ivie, but Marina did not budge. Marina distrusted him, the same as her father and me.

The old woman's gnarled hands gripped a handkerchief, and she flapped her thin arms like a wounded bird. Nelly disappeared in Ivie's arms. He was tall like Elias, but thicker in the chest and shoulders from years of manual labor and his time in the army. He'd been back six months now without a bender, and Elias had succumbed to Nelly's pleas to give Ivie odd jobs—painting, cleaning, and stocking at the store. They had fallen into roles—Elias had the money and called the shots, and Ivie, who was a down-and-out drunk, took what he could get.

Instead of calming Nelly, Ivie's touch seemed to inspire her grief. She'd lost Ivie to drink so many times, too many to count, and now her good son was dead and laid out in front of her. If she could have sacrificed Ivie to raise Elias, I swear she would have. Ivie must have sensed his mother's feelings, because he stared at me across the room, as if blaming me for his mother's pain.

I left the scene and went downstairs to find Nelly's sister, Louise, in my kitchen. She was putting on coffee and hiding the sugar, for the coffee must be bitter—*murrah*—on such a sad occasion. Her English was broken and she spoke little, having depended first on her husband, Joe, to speak for her, and now that he was gone, on Nelly, whom she loved and served. But Louise had always been kind to me, her one rebellion against Nelly. She put her damp hands on my cheeks and said a prayer—something about Jesus blessing those who suffered most—and gave the sign of the cross. I kissed her powdered cheek, and she wrapped her soft, fleshy arms around me. She smelled of rose water and Pond's Cold Cream. I wanted to rest on her shoulder, to sink down into the loose flesh of her neck and pretend she was my own mother, raised from the dead to comfort me. But I pulled away, because indulging in that thought would only hurt. Louise spoke in Arabic, something about my mother, and her words in that familiar yet strange language were all the comfort I could afford.

"I don't think we should move him." Eli's voice fell from the top of the stairs. "We should let the funeral home do that."

From my vantage in the kitchen, I saw Ivie begin to step backward down the stairs. At first I thought he was moving furniture.

Ivie appeared with Elias's shoulders in his grip, Elias's head resting on his forearms. Then Eli came around the corner with his father's legs. Eli knew his father would have spit in anger to have Ivie's hands on his body, moving him, standing over him. A procession followed: my stunned daughter, Father McMurray, Nelly. They trailed through the kitchen over my freshly waxed linoleum. Ivie's work boots left black marks. Louise scurried ahead of Ivie and held open the swinging door into the dining room.

Father McMurray paused beside me. He held his black case in one hand and shoved the other deep into his pocket. He was older than me and took no pause at the laying out of the dead at home. I'd had no intention of that, but I kept quiet as Ivie and Eli placed the body on my mahogany table, the one I had dusted earlier, the one that we used for special occasions like Christmas and Easter or Marina's wedding party two years before.

His pale bare feet poked out of the linen sheet. His toes pointed to the coffered ceiling and the crystal teardrops of the chandelier. The room was crowded with bodies and furniture. Eli stared at Ivie, and I could see that my son was figuring how to stand up to his uncle without his father's protection.

When Eli was fifteen, he had screamed from the alley, and I ran out of the store to find my husband with bloody knuckles and Ivie's face smashed. Elias had shouted at Eli, "Don't let me catch you alone with him! Not a walk. Not behind the store. Not alone in your grandmother's house. He's crazy. Do you hear me?" Elias's red face and the veins popping in his neck spoke of what would happen if Eli did not obey. Elias said to me, "The bastard had a knife on Eli." Ivie skulked off and was gone for weeks. All I could imagine was that Ivie wanted to hurt Eli because he was a gentle boy, and after all the terror that Ivie had suffered in the war, he was jealous of Eli's innocence. I made ice packs for Elias's knuckles, and we spoke nothing more of it.

Nelly stood over Elias's body. She looked to Ivie, Marina, and Eli, and cupped her hands around Elias's cheeks. "We will prepare him for the wake," she said, half asking, half demanding.

"No, Grandmother." Eli took Nelly's hands from his father's face.

"He should be here." She looked hard at Eli and reprimanded him with her pointed finger. "He should be mourned at home with his family."

"It's 1956, for goodness' sake." Eli's voice sounded small and boyish. He was a child in Nelly's eyes. Even as smart as he was, he was not capable of dissuading her from what she wanted.

"Listen to Eli." I stepped toward them. "The funeral home will take him."

She turned her ancient face toward me. Her eyes loomed large behind her Coke-bottle glasses and she wagged her finger at me. *"Yishghal balak,"* she said. *May your mind be troubled.* "You think you got away with something." Nelly spoke evenly.

Eli stepped between us. He knew how unkind she could be.

"Grandmother," Marina whispered. "Stop it." She looked at Father McMurray and placed a hand on Nelly's shoulder.

Ivie stood close behind his mother. They gave me the evil eye. She had been giving it to me for years. In her eyes, I could do nothing right. I was the scapegoat that she pinned every sorrow to, never good enough for her son. She never missed the chance to say how I brought him misery, how I was weak or lazy, how unfit a mother I was.

Marina's dark, groomed eyebrows knit together. I could see her mind was turning, trying to decide how to handle the situation, how she might convince her grandmother one way or another that it was best to send him to the funeral home—or, if Nelly got her way, what excuses Marina would tell her friends and her husband about having the wake at home. She looked like the little girl at the piano trying to please her father, only now it was Nelly, it was everyone who would come to pay their respects.

"Look at her." Nelly poked Eli and pointed at me. "She is happy he is gone."

Eli wiped tears from his eyes. He had heard her venom before, but I sensed it was his grief, not Nelly's words, that affected him as he stood over his father's body. He had wanted to prove himself to Elias, and now that chance was gone. "There's no need for this." Eli's voice trembled. "The funeral home should take him."

Father McMurray's blue eyes grazed the floor. He cleared his throat and stepped through the swinging door, now propped open. He asked Nelly's sister for a cup of coffee.

Marina took her hand from Nelly's shoulder and touched her belly. She stared out the dining-room window, and I regretted the closeness of Marina and Nelly. She would not go against her grandmother.

"I won't leave him in a funeral house." Nelly was insisting on an old-fashioned wake, laying his body out for three days before the funeral. "We will sing *Ginnazat* for him." She tapped Eli's chest with her gnarled fingers. She sang in her old, warbling voice. The words sounded soft and thick, familiar from my mother's vigil, when Nelly and Louise had sung them, as had my father and my mother's sisters, Elsa and Mayme.

Nelly pointed at Eli, then Marina, then Ivie, as if the words would come to them like a forgotten nursery rhyme if she kept on singing and pointing. We did not know the traditions of the Maronite Catholic Church, as she and my father did, both from Mount Lebanon in what was once Syria. My children knew only English, only the Roman Church, the Latin Mass.

Louise shuffled in and took Nelly's hands.

Nelly cried to her sister, "They do not know how to sing for the dead."

Father McMurray crossed the room to Nelly. He balanced a steaming cup of coffee in one hand, unable to place it on the table by Elias's body. With the other hand, he touched Nelly's arm with his thick pink fingers. "We will pray. The Lord will take care of him."

Her words shot like arrows. "I won't have him in a funeral house." Her eyes glared at the priest. "He should be mourned at home with his family." She wailed. "It was not his time." She buried her face in her old hands, knotted and twisted like an aged rope. "It should have been me."

Eli lowered his voice. "The coroner will need to examine him." He had regained composure. "They have to embalm. It's summer and it's not sanitary otherwise."

"That is best," the priest tried to reassure Nelly.

"So long as they bring him home," Nelly whimpered, then she turned to Ivie and broke into another fit of tears.

The doorbell rang. Nelly quieted as if the sound were a warning to her. Relieved, I left them and walked the ten steps to the door. Maybe it was the hearse come to take him. I should have insisted then that there would be no old-fashioned wake, but as long as he was dead and buried, it made no difference to me how it occurred. I would live my life without him standing over me, reminding me of my failures.

With my back to the dining room, I took the paper with Orlando Washington's name from my pocket, tore and wadded it into small pieces. Even in his death, I wanted Elias to have nothing to do with him.

Ayb

My brother Gus's wife, Lila, stood on the top step of the porch. Sophie, my five-year-old niece, danced in the shade of the pecan tree a few yards away. Parked on the road was my brother's truck, the words *Khoury's Best Groceries and Dry Goods* stenciled in white on the black door. I opened the screen and stepped onto the porch. The river breeze cooled my forehead, and I was happy to be out of the swelling heat in my house. Cicadas buzzed, the songbirds called, and the sounds soothed me.

Lila wrapped her arms around me. "I came right over." The sharp smell of ammonia rose from her hands. She had been cleaning that morning. The odor made me stand straight and come to attention.

Lila stood out in our family. She had blue eyes, and fair skin that burned and freckled from working in the sun. She was different also because she had no pretense. Her father was a farrier and she worked horses. She had rough hands and strong arms. She was loud and she'd stand up to a bucking horse without flinching. She wore whatever was comfortable to do her day's work, sometimes Gus's clothes, and she didn't worry if her hair fell out of her braid or looked crazy.

Gus had eloped with Lila more than twenty years ago, even though Papa had arranged a marriage to Zada, a beautiful Lebanese girl from Mobile. Zada was visiting us when Gus came home married to Lila, who was not Lebanese, Catholic, or even a believer. Lila had a bad reputation. She'd run off with a traveling musician and returned alone a year later, somewhat tarnished, but Gus had been so smitten with her, this pretty woman who loved a hard day's work, that he did not care how angry Papa was. Gus was salt of the earth himself, and he loved Lila, who was grace and power on top of a horse.

That morning, though, Lila was in a dress and stockings, not denim for the farm or my brother's grocery business. She wore nude-colored pumps, not boots. Her ash-blonde hair was pinned in a neat bun at the nape of her neck. She wore pale lipstick and a thin gold necklace. She had dressed for me on account of Elias.

"Aunt Annie," Sophie called and glided up the steps. She hugged my legs and looked up, revealing a row of perfect baby teeth. She was dark like her father and looked more like a child of my own than Lila's. Long and loose brown curls framed her face. Two heavy, dark eyebrows crowned her light-blue eyes, the only clue that she belonged to Lila. Her face reminded me of Marina's as a child, and my heart beat fast thinking Marina's baby would be as beautiful as this girl.

Sophie held up her left arm. "See my watch?" Her voice was gleeful. She had no idea of the somber occasion.

I nodded.

"Mama gave me it so I could get us to my dance lesson on time."

I took her hand in mine and admired the new treasure. "Can you read it?"

She shook her head, and the dark curls bounced around her face. "When it's twelve thirty." She pointed to the watch face. "The little hand is here and the big one there. That's the one I have to know. That's when my lesson is."

When Gus was her age and I not much older, children heckled us as *dirty Turks* or *white niggers* or *dagos* or *sheeny*. They did not know what we were, and Gus fought them to make them leave us alone. Still, people asked, "Where are you from?" I would say, "Mounds," and they would laugh. Papa told us, "You must say, 'Our parents were born in the Holy Land—the same as Jesus,' and that will silence them." I wondered what children said to Sophie and what she said in return.

Nelly's words carried onto the porch through the screen door and the open windows. "This is *ayb*." It was Arabic for *shame*, but it meant something worse than shame. It meant that our family honor had been smeared, that someone had been wholly disgraced.

If Sophie looked in a window or the screen door, she would see him lying on the dining-room table. There was nothing to shield her from the sight.

I shut the door.

Eli begged from the dining room. "Grandmother, please."

Nelly's words flowed out of the open windows: "Your mother disgraced him. This *ayb* caused his death." Nelly knew *ayb* and how to hide it. She knew what Elias had done over the years. She had been the one to stand at my bread counter when he left a mark on my face. She gave me advice, how to submit and please him, how to beg, how to save myself. Instead of correcting him, she worked to bend me and to protect her son's honor.

Sophie's head perked in curiosity toward the open windows. Lila laid a firm hand on Sophie's shoulder to keep her from bounding inside. Lila had a strong, balanced presence. Nothing could throw her off, not wild horses, not flaming torches or what was happening inside my house.

"We should have a modern funeral, Grandmother." Eli spoke softly. "This is not what he would want."

"Why do you take your mother's side?" Nelly's voice needled him. "Your father belongs in his home."

"He was her son," Ivie said to Eli. "She knows better than you."

Nelly moaned her agreement.

Marina opened the front door and whispered to me through the screen. "Mother, can you stop them?" Her eyes narrowed. She was embarrassed. "I don't want Father McMurray to hear this."

Sophie's face beamed when she saw Marina.

"You'll do better with Nelly than I will," I told Marina. Blood was thicker than water.

Marina stepped onto the porch and shut the door behind her. She acknowledged Lila, who leaned against the porch rail. "Eli should let Grandmother have her way."

Sophie's blue eyes tracked Marina's every move.

Marina stood close to me and I touched her protruding belly. She shifted away from my hand. "This could kill her."

Before I could answer, Sophie's voice chirped, "Marina." She hooked her arms around Marina's legs.

Lila stood back, silently watching her daughter's infatuation with Marina.

Marina noticed Sophie, and the worry on my daughter's face vanished. "My sweet girl. Aren't you a pretty ballerina?" She touched Sophie's curls.

Sophie held Marina's hand like it was a fragile china doll. She ran her small brown fingers over the pale-pink nails and the soft knuckles, no doubt a wonder to Sophie, in comparison to Lila's rough hands.

Sophie picked at the jeans on Marina's legs. "Where is your dress?" Sophie was always captivated by what Marina wore, the folds of her beautiful clothes, the silk blouses, the flowing skirts. Before she was pregnant, Marina's tall, thin body moved like a ballerina's, and I could see similarities between Sophie and Marina, their long legs and short torsos. Their slightness, their grace. Both of them moved with ease, like my mother pulling bread from the oven or rolling out piecrust and placing the fragile discs gingerly inside the tins.

I was thankful Sophie distracted Marina, if only for a short while. I was scraping together minutes and hours to add up to the three days when he would be in the ground. I nudged Marina to a chair. The porch was large and wide and shaded by the pecan tree. I pulled the cord of the ceiling fan. The stone floor was cool, and the air from the fan was like a baby's breath on my neck. Marina's swollen fingers gripped the rocking chair in her effort to balance to sit. I wanted to keep her outside, away from Nelly. I begrudged Marina for loving him and not me, and I wanted to start over with her. He was gone now. I could have her to myself, change the way she saw me. Soon her baby would be in my arms on this porch and I would hold the newborn like I had not held her.

Marina heard Nelly crying inside and worry knotted on her face.

Sophie noticed Marina's distress and looked to Lila. "Mama's taking me to class," she said. "We're practicing for recital."

"Let me know when." Marina touched the girl's chin. "I want to come."

Sophie nestled her cheek against Marina's arm. "When is the baby coming out of your tummy?" She whispered, knowing this was a private matter.

"Very soon." Marina held Sophie at arm's length to have a look at her. "And this baby will be as big as you before I know it. I remember when you were a tiny baby."

Sophie glowed at her words. "You want to see me dance?" Sophie posed for her. She reminded me of Marina at the piano playing for her father, trying to calm the unhappiness she sensed. Children knew when things were wrong.

"Yes." Marina nodded and smiled. The wind of the fan kissed her hair.

Sophie moved in graceful waves across the porch, her body plumb and her legs taut, disciplined, beyond her years.

"Allegro! Allegro!" Sophie twirled and shuffled. She bounded into the air. "That's what my teacher says. I think it means 'Big! Big!'" Her voice boomed.

Sophie curtsied, and Marina clapped. "Brava!"

Lila's face beamed with pride as Sophie's chest rose and fell with heavy breaths from her dance.

"That was so beautiful." Marina would soon have her own child to care for, and I was jealous of what she had. She would be a good

27

mother, better than me. Michael loved her. He was from an old family—Catholic, but moneyed enough that people forgot his religion.

"I have a tap solo in the recital too." With eager eyes, Sophie begged her mother. "Can I get my tap shoes to show Marina?"

Lila shook her head no. "We need to be quiet now."

Sophie's face fell and we could feel her disappointment.

Again, I heard Nelly's voice from inside invoke *ayb*.

"I'll see your tap dance later." Marina touched Sophie's curls and looked at me with a worried expression.

My whole life, *ayb* had been used as a threat, a control. The notion of it had kept me in line, married to Elias and raising our children when I suspected things might be better otherwise. When I was first pregnant with Marina, he had not yet raised his hand against me, but by then I knew he did not love me. I was sad and lonely and I walked to the train depot and read the names of cities—Birmingham, Nashville, Mobile, Memphis, New Orleans, Louisville, Charlotte. On the map I traced the lines of railroads that went all the way to New York, Chicago, San Francisco, or Seattle. I imagined what I would pack in my suitcase and how to pull enough money together to pay rent for a month or two, long enough to find a job. But threat of *ayb* tainted my thoughts, how my father and Elias would be humiliated from my leaving, how I would have to lie the rest of my life about who I was, who my child was, and there was shame in that too.

After they were born and the beatings started, I did not desert my children. My mother had died and left me, and I loved them too much to orphan them willingly. If I had left, his rage might have one day rested on them, and the shame of that would have broken me. So I obeyed my vows, and I hoped for better, swimming in the happy moments that I could find. I hid the sorrow of my life as best I could and retreated so as not to draw attention from Elias or anyone else, to save face, to protect our good honor.

Nelly's wailing dribbled out onto the porch. "Oh, Eli!"

Marina's head turned toward the open window. Duty would not let her ignore the old woman any longer. "I wish I could watch you dance all day." Marina held her arms open for Sophie to hug her. Then she shifted her weight, huffed, and began the process of rising from the chair. I wanted to stand between her and the door. I wanted to cast everyone out, but I knew better than to come between her and her father.

The front door opened. "Marina?" Nelly's face, a map of wrinkles, peered through the mesh of the screen. "Marina?" she called.

"I'm here, Grandmother."

Sophie watched Marina's slow, labored movements, and gloom fell across her face to see Marina going inside. So delicate and small, she had her mother's eyes, light blue, like a September sky, so incongruous against her olive skin. I had the urge to lift and hug her, to make her smile again, to hold something good for a minute. I reached for her, but she bounded off the porch. A blur of pink and well-worn ballet slippers into the bright sunlight, she spun like a top on the green grass.

Marina opened the screen and guided Nelly back inside the house. "This is what we're going to do," Marina said. She had worked it out, what was plausible to appease Nelly and to stay socially acceptable. Her instructions included everything—the funeral home, the visitation, the Rosary, the funeral.

"If you say so," Nelly conceded.

My watch read noon. The river breeze died and the air grew thick. I was anxious to have his body out of the house.

Lila, who had been observing Marina, came close by me. "You look terrible."

I gazed into her steady, sunburned face. The night before had been hellish—Elias scratching about and banging on my door. He would have killed me if he had not died.

"Annie?" Lila's voice was deep like a cold current in the river.

"I found him this morning after I woke up." I searched her cool blue eyes to see if she sensed my untruth. I had waited thirty minutes, until two a.m., listening for any movement or sounds of life before I dared open my door and peek out. If Eli and Marina found out, they would never forgive me.

"Gus doesn't know he died," she said. "He was already out on the rolling store when your father called." Monday through Saturday, Gus drove a school bus stocked with groceries from our father's store into the country to sell to people who couldn't come to town. "He won't be back until late."

"There's nothing he can do," I said. My eyes returned to the dark girl in pink.

Lila took my arm and led me down the porch steps toward Sophie. "You're burning up," Lila said.

I was hot from the dress, the heat, the worry.

An old mockingbird I'd been feeding for years flew down and landed on the porch rail. He called to me in notes, *short, short, long.* "Go on, now." I waved my hand. Back up into a low branch he went. He held his tail feathers high. He expected the raisins and breadcrumbs I threw out every morning. People said, "You can't feed a mockingbird," but my mother had kept one caged in her Nashville hat shop when she was new to America. Its chirping reminded her of the songbirds back home, and she hung fruit in its cage to keep it singing. She'd find crickets or dig worms from her garden.

"Mama," Sophie bellowed. She was a tiny, dark-headed sprite. "We have to go or we'll be late."

Lila looked at her watch. "In a minute."

Sophie skipped across the green grass, and with her slippered feet on the running board, she hung from the truck's door handle. She looked at us, her eyes squinting in the sun. A fly buzzed near my ear.

"Mama," Sophie demanded from the truck. "It's hot."

"Hold your horses, little girl." Lila took my hand. "That damn watch of hers." She laughed. "She's going to get us there, one way or another."

I smiled. "She's growing up."

She knew better than anyone how I felt to have him gone. She had seen the marks he'd left before. More than once, she had said, "I'd kill the bastard if he did that to me." But what she didn't know was how Elias had come home early yesterday, how he had seen Mr. Washington at the dining-room table with a glass of water in his hand, how Elias had cursed him, how Mr. Washington ran to save himself, but then Elias caught me, flung me down and pinned my arms to the floor, his knee pressing into my chest. How he had accused me, "Did you bed him in this house?" Or how I spit in his face. She didn't know he pushed the air from my lungs, how he said, so eerily calm, "I could kill you and no one would fault me." She didn't know how his eyes bulged and how he wanted to press the life out of me, how my last hiss of air sounded, or how he said, "You would humiliate me to have your way." She didn't know I had almost died, that I could not breathe against his weight, or how he argued with himself, his face bright red, "I have every right." He got off of me, not for my life, but because he knew the trouble he'd have if he killed me so blatantly. He knew that his daughter, who loved him without hesitation, even she would shame him for the black stain on his heart. Before he walked out the front door, he had said their names. "What about Eli and Marina?"

I had been surprised because for almost a year he had not laid a hand on me, not since Marina told us she was to have a baby. I had thought he was sorry for beating me in the past, or that he hoped for better with our grandchild, or that he'd lost the urge to fight and had resigned himself to his station with me. I should have known he would hurt me over Mr. Washington.

Lila squeezed my hand. "I have to get Sophie to her lesson. You okay for now?"

I nodded.

"I'll come back this evening." Lila walked to the truck. She moved awkwardly in the dress, and with each step, her heels sank in the pea gravel. I felt honored she had dressed up for me. She opened the door for Sophie. I forced a smile and waved.

They drove off and the hearse pulled up. Two men in dark suits stepped out of the car. One was tall, with a long neck and large Adam's apple, the other short and squat. They shut their doors with little noise and walked solemnly toward the house. They removed their summer straw-brimmed hats from their heads.

"Ma'am," the tall, pale man said.

"We're sorry for your loss," his partner, the shorter, fat man said. His eyes were a cloudy hazel color.

"He's inside." I motioned toward the front door and followed them. I wondered if they would be able to tell what had happened to him. My legs felt heavy, as if I were treading through thick mud and not the green grass of my lawn.

Inside, my vision blurred in the dim light. The yellowed soles of his feet stared at me. Coffee, milky breath, and the musty odors of bodies and death mingled in the air. Nelly propped her elbows on the table and bowed her head near his head. Eli stood beside Nelly. His shoulders slumped and his lips moved in prayer. I could see the sadness in his body. Ivie flanked the other side of Nelly. Both men stood close in case she collapsed. She refused to leave him, afraid, maybe, that if she did, his body would disappear altogether.

I retreated to the far corner of the living room by the stone fireplace, away from his body and the long, dark faces of his kin.

The undertakers glanced my way. I gripped the collar of my dress and wished I could loosen it. I wanted to change out of it, put on something loose and flowing, but the bruises would show and everyone would know what he had done.

Soon they would take him out. Nelly would go. Father McMurray would leave, and then, some peace. I could take off this dress and the stockings and lie in my bed with the fan spinning above.

Eli's eyes appeared as hollow as mine felt. With a clenched jaw, he said to Nelly and Ivie, "I'll take care of this." He looked antsy, the same as when he was a teenage boy, helping me with the baking when he could have been out doing fun things—paddling the canoe we bought him, or reading, or lying in a hammock. Partly he stayed near because he enjoyed the ritual of baking, the same as me, but also to protect me from his father. The worst Elias would do around the children was grumble and scowl, but Eli sensed the violence in his father, so he stayed near to watch over me.

The funeral men spoke in low voices. "We will take him, and the coroner will examine to determine the cause of death. Then, we will embalm."

Nelly's voice boomed. "You bring him back."

Marina opened the swinging door from the kitchen and stood behind Nelly. She did not want her grandmother to do or say anything to cause alarm.

The funeral men eased out the front door as silent as monks.

Father McMurray spoke to Nelly. "Come with me to the church and we will pray."

"No. I will wait for my son to come back." With her cane, she walked into the kitchen.

Marina said, "I'll go, Father. We need some things from the Fellowship Hall." She had begun to plan the particulars, unlike me, who had not thought past the moment he died. Marina, though she never worked in the store, could run it from a stool behind the counter. She never lifted a finger, but told her father and me what needed to happen, how to arrange the fruit or how to stack the bread in the glass counter. When she was little, Elias would smile at me and say, "What did we do, Anna, before our little dictator arrived?"

The funeral men returned, quietly opening the screen door. With soft steps they pushed a gurney inside. The wheels hummed against the hardwood floor. With reverent movements, they pulled the chairs away from the table and set to their work.

Marina, Eli, and Father McMurray joined Nelly and her sister, Louise, in the kitchen so as not to see the undertakers move him. Ivie crossed the dining room to me. He stood too close and the heat swelled around us.

The men worked like priests preparing the Eucharist, folding and unfolding, lifting and placing. Soon he was on the gurney and the gurney was outside.

I inched away from Ivie, but he was broad and tall and leaned in, filling the space around me. Shadows hid his expression. He had been looking over his brother's body all morning. He put his lips near my ear. "Elias told me he was in the house." It was a whisper, a threat.

"What?" I asked. It was the one mistake I had made—inviting Mr. Washington in—the one thing I would change, that impulse, that moment of familiarity that I should have warded off. Afraid Marina might hear, I pushed past Ivie and out the front door, out of the thick, stale air of the house. There would be trouble for me, and worse for Mr. Washington, if people knew that I had asked him in, that he stepped through the front door of our house, that I had given him a glass of water, that I sat with him at the table. If Marina heard, she would be furious, and if Nelly knew, she could make my life more miserable than I could imagine. She would see to it that the rumors never stopped.

Ivie followed me outside. "Does Marina know you had him inside?" He sucked his teeth.

I stepped away toward the porch rail, but he pressed close to my side.

"Elias came by, picked me up last night," he said. "We drove to Mounds to talk to that Washington fellow." The smell of tobacco seeped from his clothes.

"Did you hurt him?" My legs felt hollow. Ivie had been hanging around Elias more the last week, since I had told Elias about Orlando

Washington. In the past few days, Elias had allowed Ivie to sit behind the counter at the store. I wondered if the news of Mr. Washington had brought them together, if somehow they had found a common thread of hatred against him, against me. If Ivie knew he'd been inside, Orlando Washington was in worse danger now that Elias was no longer here to restrain his brother.

"You worried about that old spade?" Ivie took a flask from his shirt pocket with shaky hands. He'd been a drunk so long, he had to sip it like medicine to keep from dying. He unscrewed the cap and the sweet smell of whiskey sifted out. He took a swig. Licked his lips. "Strange my brother's dead the morning after he catches Washington with you." He screwed the lid back on his flask. He leaned near and his warm breath landed in my ear, like a snake slithering out of the river onto the muddy bank. "I think Mama's right. I think you killed him, and I'll be damned if you get away with it." He smiled, showing his stained teeth. He raised his eyebrows up and down like he was in the catbird seat.

The undertakers reached the back of the hearse and pushed the stretcher in like bread into an oven. They removed their hats, wiped their foreheads with handkerchiefs. They took in the beauty of the front yard, an excuse to stand still and catch their breath. Then, with the same care with which they'd arrived, they were gone.

"You two worked like field hands in this yard." Ivie took another sip and put his flask away. "I guess it was the one thing you could agree on." He had nothing like my house or my yard, only a servants' quarters behind his mother's. "Shame it will go to shit." Ivie glared down at me. His gloating made me sick, how he reveled in his newfound position, having his mother's full attention now that his overbearing brother was dead. Recently, Ivie had come home broke and drunk from a yearlong bender. He had cried to Elias that he'd been in love with a woman in New Orleans, but that she'd come to her senses and kicked him out. Always the prodigal son, the ne'er-do-well, and Nelly always took him in, patched him up, and sent him begging to Elias for work.

Ivie's boots clapped on the limestone steps and crunched the gravel drive as he lumbered away. The silhouette of his shoulders, the nape of his neck, the same as Elias except thicker. He drove off in his truck, maybe to the funeral home, maybe to Elias's store, maybe to rouse more trouble against me or Mr. Washington.

I left the porch and stood in the shade of the pecan tree. A stranger passing by might think happy people lived here, for it was a lovely house, a big, brick, Craftsman-style home with a green tile roof and wide porch with limestone steps broad enough to lie across and gaze at the sky. My father had bought the lot and a Sears and Roebuck house plan for my mother's Christmas, two years before she died, but after her death, he put the deed and the plans in a drawer until my engagement to Elias, when he built it for my wedding gift.

Ferns hung from the porch ceiling, and petunias cascaded down from pots. On the second floor were two large windows—one to my room, the other to Elias's. On the backside of the house were two more that had been Eli's and Marina's rooms. Our lot was wide and long, larger than any other on the street because Papa had bought the land before people built so near the river.

Elias had planted rows of cedars along the east and west property lines. Folks assumed he planted them because of where our people were from—they'd heard of the cedars of Lebanon in the Bible—but Elias wanted them for privacy. He lived in public view at the store, where he had to smile, be friendly, and shake people's sweaty hands when what he wanted was to be left alone.

Only Verna, across the street, had a good view of our house. Early on, she'd watch and wait until we were working in the yard. She'd make some excuse to walk over, make polite small talk, until eventually she'd ask, "Now, exactly where are your people from?" Elias knew she disliked having us across the street, and he would answer her differently each time. Once he said, "The Levant," and she'd asked, "Where is that?" He'd said, "You don't know?" Other times, he'd answer, "the

36

Holy Land," or "Mount Lebanon," or "the former Ottoman Empire," or "Syria," or "just east of the Mediterranean." Each time he would wink at me, and I ducked my head to hide my laughter. She looked confused and his eyes danced with glee. A few years in and Verna had had enough of him. She avoided us altogether, which was what he wanted.

I looked up into the pecan tree. The branches kissed the roof. The pale-yellow drapes hung straight without the breeze. The night before, I'd studied the branches for a way to escape. Goose bumps rose on my skin. To which the old woman inside would say, *Someone is walking on your grave.*

The mockingbird swooped down again. His dark sliver of beak parted with sound. He cocked his head in my direction.

"I have nothing for you, old man." I put my hands in my pockets.

He flew up and swooped down twice more. His chest rose with the sound coming from his beak. *Short, short, long.*

"Go on," I said.

The screen door slapped shut. I turned to see Eli helping Marina down the steps. Father McMurray came behind her. He had his arms outstretched to break her fall if she slipped.

"We're going to the church, Mama." Her voice sounded thin and tired. Her face was flushed from the heat and the blood pulsing through her swollen body.

"Let me go instead," I said.

Marina dismissed me with a wave of her hand as she walked to the car.

"Marina, you go home and rest," I called after her.

"No, Mama." Her voice deepened, gaining strength to offer the litany of reasons why she must be the one to go. She ignored my pleas as I had brushed off the bird's pestering for his morning's handout.

"There's no arguing with her," Eli said.

I wanted to grab Eli, tell him that Ivie and Elias went to Mounds to talk to Mr. Washington. My son could find out what Ivie meant by *talking.* Eli had been my one ally when I found out Mr. Washington was to be given the job to deliver mail to white houses, that he was to deliver on our street. I had told my family that I planned to allow it, but Eli had been the only one to say it was the right thing to do. He could find out now if Mr. Washington was okay. But I had to quiet the worry. I could not ask about him near Marina. I would have to find another way.

"Let me," I argued and trailed after her. "You go home, put your feet up."

"No, no, Mama," she said. "I'm fine. I'd rather be busy. Father McMurray and I are talking about the Mass, and there's no need to go over that again. Besides, I know where the ladies keep the big coffee maker and the plates." She ran her fingers across an eyebrow and then to her temple. She would supervise her father's funeral as she saw fit, with or without me, asserting her independence as she always had.

"I'll keep up with her." Eli rolled his eyes and opened her door. "Don't worry."

Marina skimmed my dress with her graceful hands. She raised her arched eyebrows and her green eyes scoured over me. "Find your pretty navy dress, Mama. That one is too heavy in this heat."

"What does it matter?" The bruises would peek out the sleeves of the navy dress.

"People might come by to pay their respects." She sat in the passenger side of Eli's car. "You're sweating like a pig."

I ignored her. "You're not driving. That's good." I shut the door.

She rolled down the window. She knew nothing of Orlando Washington coming inside the house. She would have chastised me. She would be angry that I had done damage to our family, to her. She was like Elias, worried I might smear us, discredit us, when she worked so hard to climb to the highest ranks, a female college graduate, the president of her sorority, married to an up-and-coming lawyer in his daddy's firm, and now the secretary of the Junior League, the one of us that no Junior League lady would dare look down on.

Eli started the engine.

She turned her eyes on him. "First, take me by home," she said. He backed out and I could hear her rattling off all they must accomplish.

Father McMurray drove off in his black Chevrolet.

At the front door, I opened the screen, and the rooms met me hard. The house smelled of him, his death, his mother. I had lived in the house for twenty-seven years, and still I felt out of place. I pulled the tablecloth from the mirror over the fireplace. I folded it, crossed to the dining room, and picked up the old linen sheets that Nelly used to shroud him. I tossed them down into the basement to be laundered.

From the kitchen doorway, I watched Louise move a dishrag in long, quiet strokes, stopping only to shift canisters from one spot to the next.

Nelly had stopped her carrying on. With only me and her sister here, she had no easy audience. Her wrinkled face and dour eyes were hard like stone.

"Why don't you go home, Nelly?" I tried to speak kindly. She was suffering the loss of her child.

"This is my son's house." Her tone was sour. Her glasses slipped down her nose. "I am home."

"Go to your house," I said as charitably as I could. "Marina will call you when she gets back."

With her crooked index finger, she pushed her glasses to the bridge of her nose. Her eyes grew in size. "If Marina had a decent mother, she'd be resting."

I ignored her insult and went to the pantry for raisins to feed the mockingbird. I would not be cooped up in the house with Nelly.

As I passed, she sucked her dentures. "Ivie's gone to speak to your father." Her magnified eyes looked like black marbles. What image she saw of me I did not know—if my nose, eyes, mouth appeared clearly, or if I was patches of light and dark.

"Why?" I suspected she sent Ivie to deal for her, so worried was she about Elias's store, about this house, so afraid I might have something she thought belonged to her. Nelly was a shrewd businesswoman. Neither she nor my father had left the clannish ways of the Old World. Her son's property she claimed as her own, and because I was her son's wife, she wanted to rule over me. In the old country, they hoarded what they earned. They held it close and guarded its safekeeping. At times I had to remind myself how Nelly had begun life, a poor farmer's daughter who, as soon as she could carry a bucket of mulberry leaves, fed the silkworms in the morning, and for the rest of the day gorged the spring lambs, leaf by leaf, fattening them for fall slaughter. Everything she had was fruit of her toil, and I knew the memory of poverty haunted her. She would not allow me or any interloper to take what she believed was hers or her children's.

Louise placed a cup of hot coffee in front of her sister. Louise gestured, asking silently if I wanted one.

I held the box of raisins against my chest. I shook my head no.

"If you killed him, I will find out." Nelly's shriveled lips moved with calm, not with the hysterics of the morning. Her large, dark eyes, behind the thick glasses, bored into me. If she knew Mr. Washington had come inside, she kept it to herself. I would not be surprised if she were keeping quiet now to hurt me later. Nelly curled over the cup and it steamed her glasses. "You were never good for him. You disobeyed him. You broke him with your misery, and I blame you that he's gone. I don't want you here."

"Nelly, my father built this house for me." She had stirred my anger, and I could hear it in my voice. "Leave, if you want to."

Louise was on her hands and knees, her head down, scrubbing the black marks left by Ivie's boots.

"You let that man come here, and Elias told you no." Nelly blew the black coffee to cool it. Her glasses fogged. "I think you killed my son, and when I tell the children, they will have nothing to do with you."

"You have lost your mind." I sounded indignant, but her words crept across my skin like a cold wind.

"You can leave on your own, or I can tell the sheriff what you did and you can rot in jail, or they can string you up in a tree." Nelly slurped from the cup. "Makes no difference to me."

"You're an old fool." I tried to sound calm, to call her bluff, but my voice broke. She could raise doubt in Marina's mind. I felt as if Elias's knee were pressing into my chest again, squeezing the breath out of me. She could do what she threatened, but then the same *ayb* she threatened for me would fall on her. The store would fail. Eli and Marina would be shunned. She loved them too much to hurt them.

She spoke solemnly. "In the old country, when the town must rid itself of evil, they take a she-goat and put a silver ring around her neck. They pray and confess and then chase her into the wilderness to carry away all the sins. You are the she-goat that must go."

"You are a crazy old bat." I clamped the raisin box to my chest as if it were a Bible, and I headed to the front door.

Her words followed me outside. "Maybe your papa will send you someplace nice."

The bright sun burned my eyes, and I blinked until they adjusted to the white glare. The heat had risen and the cicadas' high-pitched hum droned on.

Elias had worked here, the same as me. This garden was our one thing together. Ivie was right about that. Outside, the world had seemed big and open, with no roof over our heads trapping us in our misery and mistakes. Elias pruned vines and rosebushes, plowed the garden in the spring. He and my father had planted the fig tree before Marina was born. Now it was ten feet wide and taller, shoots coming up all around. In the shade of the cedars grew our snowball hydrangeas, Marina's favorite. Elias cut back the deadwood in the spring, and we had planted a new one each year on her birthday. The day Elias died, the heart-shaped leaves were singed by the August heat.

We had won a beautification prize from the city for our garden. Our picture was on the front page of the People section of the Riverton paper. His arm wrapped around my shoulder and both of us smiled. I wore the three pearl necklaces he had given me over the years and the navy-blue dress Marina had spoken of. My arms looked thin and strong.

I held a spade and he a rake. He wore his usual starched shirt and tie, the sleeves rolled to the elbows. The headline, *Bringing the Plants of the Holy Land to Riverton*. The article took half the page, detailing our sunny front lawn with its roses, the fig and lavenders, the rows of cedars to the east and west. I planted swaths of low-growing purple queen, also called "wandering Jew." The name reminded me of my parents, how they had come from that far-off Holy Land and spread across America. "In the backyard near the river," the article went on, "the garden winds with grapevines and sumac trees, with lovely rhododendrons and large ferns toward a trail of white mulberry that ends by the water."

The mockingbird settled in the fig tree. I flung a handful of raisins into the air. The bird glided above the green grass. He flew high and dove down. He found one, flew up again, and screeched, as if to tell other birds to stay away. Maybe he was thanking me, even though the daily ritual was long in coming. "Sorry I'm late, old bird," I said. I watched him peck the grass with his wings open. He flicked his tail and then flew up into the pecan tree. A hot breeze blew from the river.

For a moment, in the shade of the tree, my eyes burned with sweat or tears. I was not sure which. I wasn't sure of anything but the pressure in my chest. Orlando Washington would not dare deliver our mail that day. Then, a shrill ring pierced the air. I wiped my eyes. The ringing did not relent. I remembered Marina's state, that she might need me at the hospital, and I hurried inside.

I ran the length of the house to get it. It was Papa. He said to come immediately. "Immediately," he repeated.

"Are you sick?" I asked.

Nelly cupped her hand to her ear. I turned my back and said little.

Papa swore, a mixture of English and Arabic. He said the word *ayb*, and I knew Nelly had made good with her threat. Ivie had been to see him.

The Path

I wanted to walk the two miles to Papa's house on the path along the river that connected his home to mine. Walking it promised to calm me, better than driving through town, where I felt out of place. On the path, there was the water, the cover of trees, the birdsong and the dusty red earth, and I could forget Elias while I walked. The path was a place that comforted me—no dividing line between white and black, only a line between land and water. But Papa had said *immediately*, so there was no time to walk the path.

The first time I had walked it was a Christmas morning when Papa told us, "Bundle up. We're going on a long walk through the trees." Gus was toddling around and likely to head for the cold water, so Mama strapped him to her chest with a long piece of material. He squirmed and cried to be put down, but she shushed him, wrapped herself and him in a heavy shawl, and placed a rose-colored hat, a treasure from her old shop, neatly on her head.

We stepped out into the winter morning, and Gus settled his cheek against her chest and his black hair peeked from beneath his cap.

Mama moved slow and I ran after Papa, already halfway to the water.

"Binti," Mama called. *Binti* was *my daughter* in Arabic. "Faris, slow down." But we could not be harnessed, and I rushed to him by the steel-blue river.

Papa and I could walk side by side on the path that led into what seemed like a thick and dense forest. I had never followed the path into the canopy of trees. "Where does this go?" I asked.

He said, "This path goes east toward town. They tell me this was once an Indian highway." He pointed ahead through the trees. "We will pass the bridges and then the big courthouse and a little bit farther we will come to my surprise."

The bare trees were alive with a thousand birds, and the branches were like black lines drawn against the gray winter sky. Ducks and geese floated across the water. So many I could not count. Papa stopped and pointed to the cranes and the herons, their long legs like stilts rising out of the shallows. A tree full of black birds rustled as our steps approached. Papa made a sign for me to be still, and when the birds settled, he clapped his hands together and the slap of his leather gloves echoed like a shotgun. A curtain of black whirled out of the trees and a hundred black wings fluttered and rippled into the air like a heart beating.

When we arrived at an empty lot on the water, Papa told Mama he had bought this land and showed her the house plans. She held them like a fragile piece of glass and stared at the rendering of a brick house with a green tiled roof. She did not disappoint him, for she laughed and smiled. "Oh, Faris," she said over and over. "It is all so fine."

Mama loved the water. That was why Papa built the store on the river. That was why he bought the property where my house stood. She wanted to live where she could see any water—a river, a lake, or the sea. In her childhood village, a river ran down from the mountains and through the center of town. "Water is life," she liked to say. "It reminds us we are always moving, that we are alive."

She walked every inch of the lot, with Papa talking in her ear and baby Gus sleeping against her chest, his legs hanging like deadweight, her arms wrapped protectively around him. Down the path on the way home, with the cold air on our faces, the winter birds and black tree limbs that seemed to touch the sky above us, I felt content and thought that no matter where we lived, if we were together, we would be happy.

After Mama died, Thea knew to get me outside, where Mama had loved to be with me and where I had loved to be with her. Thea knew what to do, because she had been my mother's friend, the woman to whom my mother spoke her last words.

It felt good to be outside beneath the blue sky and away from my brokenhearted father and our sad Aunt Elsa, my mother's sister who had come to care for us after Mama died.

Elsa never married, she said, because she did not like children, or the noises they made, but she tolerated Gus and me for the love of my mother. Nor did Elsa like outsiders or Negroes in her home, and because Papa was in his mournful state, he did not argue when Elsa relegated Thea to the store, the garden, and the wash. But because Elsa could only take so much of Gus's energy and noise, she allowed Thea to take us outside.

The four of us—Thea, her son Orlando, Gus, and I—took long walks down the path. Orlando was a few months younger than Gus. They played and ran, and Thea prodded me to run with them. On our walks, Thea took us to the river bridges to watch the cars and trains go over. It was great entertainment for the boys, and I liked it too, because when the trains rumbled over the steel frame, the vibrations filled me, and the shaking and the blare of the horn would make the grief inside me recede. The boys would scream at the tops of their lungs, and I would too, and at the end of the screaming, I felt purged of sadness, at least for a while.

Thea did not feel safe walking us into town, and so we turned back west at the bridges and headed toward home. If there was still daylight, Thea would pass Papa's store and we would head to the Indian mounds.

Each of the mounds was about ten feet tall with gently sloped sides. I could make fifty large steps across the grassy, level top. Mama had told me ancient people had built the mounds by bringing baskets of dirt, one by one. The three of us children scrambled up the steep edge and looked out over the river. Thea stood halfway up the slope as Gus and Orlando rolled their bodies down. They scrambled back up, laughing, and slid down again. Thea stayed put in case she needed to reach out and slow their descent. They rolled until they were too dizzy to climb again. When the boys began to dig by the trail in search of an arrowhead, Thea climbed up to me.

I stared off at Riverton Bridge and the rail bridge beside it. I could see the river shore by Papa's store and the old courthouse rooftop just beyond. Thea pointed off in the distance, across the water to the line of trees on the southern shore. "Look how small those trees are," she said. The river was wide and deep, and across the way the trees were miniature lines of bark and leaves. She held her thumb up and took mine to do the same. She squinted, showing me how to measure the size of the trees. "See how small they look," she said. "But they're as big as these." She pointed to the trees, the tulip poplars and grand old oaks, one hundred feet tall, growing near the trail, and I could see perspective, how something so large looked smaller the farther away you got from it.

"That feeling you have, how sad you are about your mama, won't ever go away," she said. "It's not supposed to. But one day it'll be like those trees over there, not like these here."

I pulled my knees to my chest and hid my face. The hot tears streamed down my cheeks. She placed her warm hand on my back. The hand steadying me was the same one that had touched Mama. Thea's hands had brushed the hair from Mama's face and washed her body when she was gone. Thea didn't hurry me or shush me but sat quietly, calm and patient, as my mother would have done.

When my face was dry and my breathing still, I looked again at the water, the trees, the sky. I could take comfort in the view I had shared with Mama. Thea and I walked down the mound and gathered the boys to go back home.

Orlando Washington

Five days before Elias died, the name of Thea's son, Orlando Washington, was in the *Riverton Daily*. I was in the store, wrapping a loaf of bread for a customer. The lunch rush had begun. Businessmen and secretaries bought a Coke and a pack of peanuts, or cheese and crackers, or a flatbread rolled with meat. The aisles were busy with housewives and maids in uniform buying groceries for the week.

The bell above the door tinkled. A man from Rotary Club, who liked to talk numbers with Elias, walked in with an air of disgruntlement around him. "I told you, Elias. It was bound to happen." He slapped a paper on the counter by the register. "Civil rights has come to Riverton." He spoke loud and clear, so that the whole room of people turned their heads.

I picked up the paper and read the offending piece.

> On August 1, Orlando Washington, decorated war veteran of the Tuskegee Airmen, son of Thea and Odell Washington from Mounds, will be the first black postman to deliver mail to white residents in Riverton, Alabama. Mr. Washington, who has

worked for the United States Post Office since 1947, will be transferring from his route in Brooklyn, New York, to a carrier position in Riverton.

The article went on to say that Poplar Street and the Negro section of town were to be his route and gave instructions to concerned citizens to file a form if they preferred to pick up their mail at the post office in person.

"Reads like an obituary to me," someone said, and all day long, the conversations went on and on, the complaints in the aisles and at the counter—the boycotts in Montgomery, King and Parks in the newspaper every day. *It will not happen here,* they said. *We'll tape our boxes shut and walk to the post office, by God.*

I kept the paper near my counter the rest of the day. I read his name a hundred times. I wondered why he wanted to put himself in harm's way.

I listened to the ramblings of customers. *They're taking over . . . Goddamn boycotts . . . instigators . . . They can deliver their own mail in Mounds . . . Separate but equal . . . Have to deport them before we get any peace . . . Poplar Street, that's your street, ain't it?*

Elias's back stiffened with all the talk and stirring of emotions in his store, yet he nodded and grunted in affirmation. He rolled his eyes when he turned his back to one old lady saying over and over, "What will we do? Oh, what will we do?" He didn't want to be in the middle of it or make any claims that could be used against him, one way or another.

I saw no harm in Orlando Washington doing the job. The complaints made no sense to me—many white people in town had Negro maids raising their children, dealing in intimate parts of their private lives, cooking meals, cleaning their houses, some of them running their households. White people bought the same foods in Elias's store as black people bought in Papa's store. Hams at Christmas, black-eyed peas and turnip greens for New Year's Day, chicken to fry and watermelon to cut on Fourth of July. What harm was there in a war veteran, a law-abiding man, bringing their mail? When Thea had died ten years before, my father and my brother had shaken Orlando Washington's hand at her funeral.

I clipped the article and took it home, as if I had someone to save it for, but Thea was gone and I did not know who else would want it, maybe Gus. I laid the clipping on the piano.

That night at dinner, I told Elias, "We should let him deliver." I expected him to say no. I expected some rumbling, but he had been reasonable with me for months, since Marina had given us the news of her expectancy. I thought if I gave him my reasoning, he might agree.

I told him, "White families have people working in their homes, holding their babies, feeding their children. Why can't he deliver mail? I've known him his whole life. I knew his mother. She cared for us. If we help him, others will too, and we'll be doing a good thing."

Elias gave no reply. His gaze was fixed on his plate.

"I called Eli and told him about it."

"What did he say?" Elias looked at me with calm green eyes.

"He said it was right." It was strange to hear my voice outside my head, speaking firmly to Elias. As a young woman, I had doubted he or anyone else would take me seriously. Later in our marriage, when Elias became violent, I stayed quiet to preserve myself. But I felt it was time to say what I needed to say.

"That's about what I expected." Elias put his fork down. He smiled like a wolf and that old spiteful look came into his eyes. "Did you tell Marina?"

I was silent and looked at my untouched plate of food. I had called her and before I could finish my sentence, before I could tell her who Orlando Washington was and why I wanted to help him, she said, "Don't do that, Mother. You won't be helping him or yourself."

"But I will help him," I told her. I could hear tapping, her nails or a pencil on a hard surface. I was afraid to speak, that if I did, she would hang up and I would turn to salt. So I waited.

Finally, she said, "I will talk to you about this in person." The line was dead before I could say another word, and all I could hope was to persuade her with my actions. I would tell her of my connection to the man, and how his mother had been the one to care for my mother on her deathbed, had been the one to console my grief, when everyone else—Papa, Aunt Elsa, Gus—was too consumed in their own sorrow to notice mine. Since she was soon to be a mother, she might understand.

"Well, what did she say?" Elias barked, still chewing the food in his mouth.

"She did not think it was a good idea."

"That's what I thought," he said. "She knows better."

"It's not Marina's decision." I heard the conviction in my voice. I stood to clear the plates. "I'm going to allow it." My mother had whispered her dying words into Thea's ear. I owed it to Thea's memory to help her son.

"All I've heard today is this race business." He rubbed his forehead as if to soothe a headache. "All I want is quiet and I come home to you yammering on about it too."

"I don't see any harm in him doing the job." I felt like Lila must feel on a horse, racing around barrels, catching speed in the straightaway. I could not stop myself.

"That's because you grew up around them." His anger seemed to surface like an itch, and his voice grew harsher by the moment. "You do that, and you'll regret it."

I had twisted my thinking to believe he would hear me, that things had changed, that maybe we were approaching a return to the early days of our marriage, when he had restraint, when he tolerated me, when kinder words flowed between us. I thought his anger had softened because of the coming grandchild. I thought the pressure he felt must have eased now that the children were out of the house and the business was strong and money was good. But when I spoke up, I scraped the surface of an old wound.

I had decided when I saw his name in print—Orlando Washington—that I would help him. I was soon to be a grandmother. My son was studying to be a priest, and his voice on the other end of the telephone line had sounded like Elias's voice, but kind and soft. He'd said, "It's the right thing to do." My son agreed with me, despite knowing his father and what he was capable of. I replayed Eli's words in my head. He was smart and kind, an authority on what was right and what was wrong. *It's the right thing to do.* I worked on Marina's layette. *It's the right thing.* I prepared dinner. I waited for Elias to come home. *It is the right thing to do.* In my gut, I knew that if I did not do what was right, if I did not stand up to Elias and all the talkers at the store, I would die a coward.

"Hit me if you want," I said to Elias.

He was a handsome man, his dark hair, his long face, and his bright-green eyes. He had aged well. Distinguished. I had wanted him to love me, but he had not. Out of his mouth came a gravelly, low laugh. "You have lost your mind."

"All you can do is hurt me," I said. "You've done that before."

"I won't have to," he said. "If you do this, you'll hurt yourself."

In the afternoon two days later, on the first of August, Orlando Washington stood outside our front door. He wore a new starched uniform, and across his shoulder hung a heavy mailbag. He clutched our mail in his hand. "Hello, Mrs. Nassad." I recognized the boy from my memory. He stood on the other side of the screen a grown man with Thea's calm, serious eyes.

My neighbor Verna, ever vigilant, came down her drive to the street and watched us. She had a sign in her yard, the same as others on the street: *No nigger mailman.* But he was not that.

"Your street and the Negro section are my route," he said. No doubt he had been given this street to satisfy the law and to ensure his failure. He shifted from one foot to the other, clearly nervous but determined to stand where he stood, at the front door of a white man's house. "Would you and Mr. Nassad allow me to deliver your mail?"

He spoke nothing of his familiarity with my brother, of the two of them running ahead of me down the river trail or playing in the field behind my father's store, or when he and Gus jumped a train to Nashville in the middle of the night to run away to the World's Fair. He spoke nothing of his mother's place in my family's life.

Nor did I. "How are people treating you?"

Deep lines ran across his forehead and at the corners of his eyes. The help did not ring the front bell or walk up the front steps of a white man's house. The lift of his chin reminded me of Thea. On my last visit to her before she died, she had been angry with me. She turned away from me, like a petulant girl. "You got too busy, too big, to come see me."

I took her scolding. "I'm sorry," I said. "I'm here now." I waited for her to forgive me.

She scowled and shook her head against her pillow. "You got uppity like your Aunt Elsa." She stared at me for several minutes, deciding what she would say or do, if she was angry with me or glad to see me. "You look like your mama," she said. "She was a good woman." She closed her eyes and dozed off. When she woke and saw that I was still there, she talked about Orlando. He had gone to Tuskegee and then flown an airplane in France. "He lives in New York." She spoke with pride and wonder. "Wants me to come up there and be with him."

Mr. Washington gripped the envelopes until they bent. "Most folks—this is as close as I've gotten today."

I looked across the street and saw Verna with her hands cocked on her hips and her eyes glowering like hot coals.

"People don't want me up on their front porch every day," Mr. Washington said.

The talk at the store went round and round like a stuck needle on a record.

World's been turned on its head.

Stealing a white man's job.

Can't be trusted with money and checks and documents.

It's not his place to come to the front door of a white man's house.

If he sees something he wants, and he don't take it, someone he knows will.

Keep them in their place.

I felt deliberate. "Yes," I said. As easy as that, I cracked the screen door and opened my hand. He placed the envelopes in my palm. The paper was warm and damp.

He stepped backward toward the steps, as if the second he took his eyes off of me, I would disappear, his one victory, the only victory he would have. No other white person in Riverton would allow him to deliver.

"Thank you, ma'am." He tipped his cap.

Pea gravel crunched under his feet. I opened the mail. I stood tall behind my screen door. From the corner of my eye I could see Verna, red faced, standing like a statue, in shock, in disbelief of what I had done.

Verna drove off in a hurry, and not long after, Elias pulled in. He rushed in the house and stood over me where I sat at the dining-room table working on the baby's layette. "That heifer came in the store yelling that you let him deliver our mail today." He meant Verna. He pulled me from my chair and pushed me against the wall. "If you want to go back to Blacktown, you have my permission. But he's not delivering mail to this house."

As calmly as I could, I said, "I'm working on Marina's baby's clothes."

At the mention of Marina's baby, he dropped his grip on my dress.

I walked back to the table and resumed my work.

"Tape the mailbox shut." He stood over me. He snorted like a mad bull. He smelled of cigarettes. His temple throbbed. He stared at the baby clothes and I could see he was holding himself back.

I continued the whipstitch around the baby blanket. My heart beat fast in my chest, but I did not show him any fear.

He pushed my forearm on the table and his knuckles went white from the pressure. "You do what I say. Think of your children, for God's sake."

The next morning, he hammered one of the neighbors' crude signs in our yard and he assumed I would obey. All our years together, I had succumbed to his shouting and pushing. I had done what I had to, to keep peace and be with my children, but they were gone now.

I began the day's baking and he watched me as he ate a breakfast of cold leftovers from the icebox.

"Anna," he said, and touched my arm gently as if he had an audience. "Remember what I said." He brushed my cheek with his hand. "You let this go. It's for the best, for the kids, for us." My blood curdled that he would try to move me with charm. Too many times he had hit me or belittled me or ignored me.

He left for the store, and while my bread proofed on the counter, I kicked his sign down.

Growing up over my father's store, I was never accepted into the fold of things. In high school, I ate alone and kept my nose stuck in a book to avoid the girls whose parents warned them against socializing with me, the foreign one who lived across the tracks. Later, around white women at church, at Elias's store, there was an air of politeness, but when I joined the ladies' conversations, the tone changed or the talk would cease altogether, lose its breath, as if a foul odor hung around me. I was the Syrian storekeeper's daughter, then another's wife.

That second day, after I kicked down Elias's sign, I brought my bread to the store. Customers scoured me with their eyes. News of

Verna's rant and my allowing him to deliver had spread all over town. One customer politely said to me, "We need to be together on this. Make them understand where they belong." Elias shook his head in apology to the man.

I left the store early and rushed home to be sure I saw Mr. Washington. My children were grown—Marina was in a fine position, married to a bright and good-looking lawyer who came from a good family. Eli was joining the priesthood. I could not lose Elias's love or respect. I had never garnered those—not by my work for the store, or trying to make a good home, or raising the children we had made. I had no stake in him. I had risen as far as I could, and there was nothing left to gain between us.

That was my thinking when Orlando Washington walked up the porch steps that second day. He was my brother's old playmate, my beloved Thea's son, and he stood in front of me. When I took the mail from his hand, he stood taller. He smiled. I felt kinship to him, though I did not imagine he knew the feelings his presence conjured in me. To him, I was probably just another white lady—though a strange sort. He couldn't have known what his mother meant to me, eight years old and hidden in the corner, as I watched her clean my mother's crumpled, lifeless body. She had held that last baby and sung to him while he lingered. What harm could Orlando Washington do? It was a job, and if I did not do something on my own accord, would I ever?

When he was gone down the gravel drive, I saw Verna leave again. I readied myself for Elias's outrage. He would not come home the man who had touched me softly that morning. The Elias coming home would be the one who used his fists or the back of his hand or a belt or the weight of his body as he forced me down on the bed. It would be the Elias who stalked me through the house, who jimmied open locks, who shoved open doors when chairs were pushed against them.

I picked up a white gown I was making for the layette and decided that I would not cook for him or bake for his store. With each stitch on the soft cotton that was to clothe our grandchild, I told myself that what I had done I would not undo, not for his threats or his temper, not for his hitting. I steeled myself against his worst and promised myself to show Marina whatever he did. I would make her look at my face, my arms, my back, whatever mark he left, and show her, because it was time for her to learn what her father was.

The sun was setting when he pulled into the driveway. The sky a deep cerulean blue. I sat still and waited. My heart banged in my chest. He got out of the car, shut the door, and lit a cigarette. The sweet tobacco smell drifted through the open window. A few minutes later, Marina's car pulled in behind him. He had called her or she had called him, and now they were working together against me. I listened to their sweet talk: "Hello, Daddy," and "How you feeling, darling?" Back and forth, with kindness dripping, they made their way up the drive and onto the porch to devour me.

Across Town

Papa had said *immediately*, so I drove fast up Poplar Street and west on Water Street. I slowed as I crossed Main and saw the post office and wondered if Mr. Washington might be there.

My hands gripped the wheel. I felt sick that I had put him in harm's way by asking him inside the house. I wanted to go in and get word to him of the trouble Ivie was stirring, but he already knew, better than me. Ivie and Elias had been to his house. He might not even be at the post office, and no good would come for him or me if I searched him out. A lynch mob could come in the day as well as the night.

Across the street from the post office, the old courthouse sat on a hill overlooking the river. The old beacon of money and cotton and the river had survived the War because of its position on the hill, a lookout over the river, first for the Confederates and then the Union soldiers. I had run my fingers over the bullet holes in the stone columns.

Next to the courthouse, the soda fountain was busy with men on lunch break, kids and teenagers out of school for summer, and mothers with their young children. A sign in the store window said *Whites Only: Maids in White Uniform Allowed.* Elias had put a similar sign in our storefront in reaction to the bus boycotts. I had not wanted the sign because it reminded me how people liked to put me in my own place.

A customer of ours came out of the soda fountain and headed to the courthouse. His eyes landed on me and he nodded in recognition as I passed. Lawyers, officers, secretaries came and went. People I knew saw me driving by. They looked at me with cross expressions and I felt uneasy. Every person in town knew that Orlando Washington delivered my mail.

I was not where I should have been on the day of my husband's death. I might have to explain myself, why I was where I was, just as my brother and I had to explain why we crossed the train tracks every morning and afternoon to go to school, or how my father went into too many details when the census taker came and wanted to mark us as *Y* for yellow. Papa argued too long with the man about how the Supreme Court said Syrians were white, like Jesus, because both were from the Holy Land. So Papa made sure the census taker wrote *W*, not *Y* or *Neg*. Papa was an *O*, owner, not an *R*, renter, like most of the *Neg* on the list before us. The census taker did not care that we were immigrants from the Holy Land, or that Papa came from the part of Syria that was now Lebanon, or that Papa called his native language *Syrian*, or that Papa came from the city of Deir al-Qamar, in Mount Lebanon, a city of stone houses and palaces with a history more ancient than Christ, or that my mother came from a city named Zahlé, a beautiful town famous for its wine and poetry. The census taker knew well enough we were oddities, and no amount of explaining would make us anything else.

I continued west on Water Street toward the railroad crossing and Mounds. A fool to think I could help Mr. Washington, then or now. I could not understand my own thinking. Maybe Marina had been right—maybe Elias too—that it was cruel to allow him hope, with everyone and everything against him. He would have been better off if I had kept to myself and refused him as Elias and Marina had wished.

Two bridges—one for the train, one for cars—spanned south across the wide river. A half mile farther and across the tracks, Papa's store stood along the riverbank. The car bobbed over the timber and metal of the tracks like a sailboat over a barge's wake. I had been naive to think I'd cross them one last time on my wedding day. My connection to Papa and his store kept me coming back.

The wind was dead and the river was still. It looked dark and peaceful, like a sheet of black glass, but lurking beneath the surface was a current, cold and deep, with snakes and tangles of vegetation that could be your end. People could be the same. They could smile to your face with hatred in their heart while they pulled you down.

Papa

The sight of Papa's store eased my nerves. Sunlight dappled the red brick through the breaks of tree branches. It was home, this two-story building with *Khoury's Groceries and Home Goods, Oriental Silk and Rugs* painted in decorative letters on the brick wall. The rugs and the reams of lace and silk in Papa's back room saved us from complete isolation in Riverton. Papa imported them from his old country and had them shipped by train from New York. White ladies with a maid in tow came to buy them. They'd brag of their big adventure to the colored grocery to buy one, how they bartered my father down, what a good deal they made, though he always got what he wanted out of it.

This day, cars and trucks lined the street in front of Papa's store and the AME church across the way. A white hearse sat on the lawn. The roller shades covered Papa's windows like dead eyelids. A *Closed* sign hung in the glass door.

I turned into the alley between Papa's store and the low brick storefronts he'd built and rented to a barber, a dress shop, a dentist, and a doctor. On a bench outside the barbershop, a man with short white hair peered in my direction. He was Brewster, my father's employee since I was a girl, but an argument could be made that he was my father's best friend, the one who sat with him at night and played cards or talked with him about the weather or the news. He knew me, as every person in Mounds did. My father's store was a meeting place. I acknowledged him, but Brewster did not wave or nod. He looked the other way, and I guessed he knew Elias had been at Mr. Washington's house last night.

The hot breeze died when my car halted behind Papa's store. I got out and the sky above was blue and bright, but storm clouds were forming across the river to the south. In an hour's time, the river would be choppy, angry with the storm.

The back door of my father's store was bolted shut. I knocked and called for him but he did not answer. I looked out over the back field and orchard and walked toward the path, thinking he might have come out, as he liked to do when his fruit trees were in season.

This was the place I came, my safe ground, where I brought my children for an afternoon. Marina would run and Eli would play with the orchard cats, and together we would step out into the river, the tiny rocks and bits of mussel shells biting at our feet. It was the one place Elias could not hurt me, but this day, being summoned by Papa, I felt exposed.

I passed the fig tree, and the limbs were heavy with fruit. Hungry from not eating all morning, I pulled a fig, split open the purple skin, and ate. Papa had planted it for my mother when she was expecting twins. In her old country, a woman told her, "Figs for prosperity. Plant a fig as an offering to God." So Mama badgered him until the spring morning he planted it. Their muffled voices had floated through my open window and woken me. I went to the balcony and watched as the hem of her sky-blue skirt snapped like a sail in the spring wind and the thick silver bracelets on her wrists jangled. He dug and planted the fig. The smell of cool earth drifted up in the morning breeze. Overhead, honking geese made a great V, twenty or thirty, and they curved northward in their spring migration. Her face turned up to watch them, and then her eyes fell on me. How beautiful she looked. *"Binti,"* she had called to me. "Come help me water the new tree."

When I saw no sign of Papa in the garden, I walked around to the front of the store.

Across the street, the church doors were propped open and a mournful song rolled out. Silhouettes of women in hats and men in their Sunday suits swayed. From the size of the crowd, someone important had died. My father's friend Brewster was gone from the barbershop bench. I looked up and down the street for signs of him. He would know if Mr. Washington was at work, if he was home, or if he was safe, but Brewster was nowhere to be seen, and I could not go looking for him.

I opened the door of Papa's store, the bell above it rang, and I found him standing behind the register. He was a broad-faced man with jowls, and everything about him seemed solid—his face, his body, his mind. Papa no longer worked in the sun, like my brother, so even my skin, tanned from gardening, was darker than his. In his old age, his black hair was gone and his skin had grown pale, and he looked as white as anyone in town. His hands were shoved deep in his pockets and his eyes narrowed. "It's about time," he said.

"The back door was bolted." My voice was small like a girl's. I had always felt safe near him, but that day his expression unnerved me. "Are you feeling okay?"

"Yes," he said. He moved around some clutter behind the counter. Cigarette cartons lay torn open, and the penny singles were strewn about.

"I'm here," I said. "You said to come immediately."

"You know why my store is closed today?" Papa wore a tie. Elias wore one every day, but Papa's store was less formal, and I thought he must be wearing it because of Elias's death or because he planned to pay his respects to the people across the street.

"Because of Elias?"

"Not because he's dead." His voice sounded agitated. "Come with me." He locked the front door and headed toward the back room. "I need to give you something." He seemed unsteady and his steps were labored as if pebbles filled his shoes. I wanted to help him, but I worried if I touched him he might reject me.

The store was no longer the tidy shop of my youth, when Mama baked bread in the brick oven and the warm smell filled the whole building. Now the place smelled of aging produce. Empty crates, waiting to be taken out, stood in the corners. Dust lined the shelves, and they sagged in the middle. Perhaps he could not see it or perhaps he no longer cared.

We passed the back room where the Oriental rugs were stacked. Across the hall was my mother's old baking room. He pushed the door to his office and it creaked open. Usually he kept it locked, because he hid money in there. The air was hot and stale in the room. I turned on a fan to move the air and reached for the pole to crank open the high windows, but he said, "No, leave it. The birds will come in."

He moved slowly around his cluttered desk and lowered himself into his chair. "Sit," he said.

I had been in that room before, whenever he had business with me, like the day I learned of my new responsibilities after Mama died, or the day he finally agreed to my marriage. I thought he would tell me what to do about Mr. Washington. I thought he would have the answers.

"I know Ivie came to talk to you," I said. "I know he wants the store. So tell me what you want to say."

He stared at me with his lively eyes. "Ever since Elias came sniffing around after you, it's been nothing but trouble, and nothing to stop him or you."

"*Abb,*" I pleaded, *father* in Arabic. "Say what you want to say. God knows what Nelly is doing at my house." I worried Marina might need me. I worried what Ivie was doing.

"A bunch of men, including your husband and his brother, burned a cross and threatened Washington last night. Everybody in Mounds is torn up about it."

"Ivie and Elias?" I could not believe Elias would burn a cross. It was the others with him. "Elias would not do that."

He shrugged at that. "You didn't know?" he asked. He took a hand-kerchief from his pocket and blotted his forehead.

"No," I said. "Ivie said they talked to him. He didn't say anything about burning a cross or a mob." The talk of *ayb*, the paper with Orlando Washington's name, Nelly's accusations and Ivie's threats, the thought of Elias pressing down on my chest with his knee—all of it weighed on me.

"Brewster says they going to boycott me for that mess," he grumbled under his breath. He was in trouble for what I'd done and what Elias had done in response.

"Do you know if Mr. Washington is safe now?"

"Hell." He grunted and waved his hand as if shooing a fly. "I'm not worried about him. Worried about you."

"Don't worry about me," I said, not trusting my own voice.

"Anna, what I'm telling you, you going to do." Papa's English was a mix of Southern speech, both Negro and white, and the quick tempo of his mother tongue. He stared at me and was quiet for a long time. "I know what you did." The wooden desk creaked as his weight shifted. "You should know better."

"I haven't done anything wrong." He had said nothing when I told him I would allow Orlando Washington to deliver my mail, and I had taken his silence as acceptance.

Papa dug out a canvas bag from his desk. From the drawer, he pulled stacks of fives, tens, twenties, some fifties, and a few hundreds. He hoarded money in the house in cigar boxes and metal tins and under loose floorboards because he did not trust banks. He arranged it on the table and fingered the bills. His breathing had grown strained.

Disgust covered his face. "Ivie says you messed with the *abeed*."

"You believe that?"

"No," he said, "but it don't matter what I believe." He wheezed, then broke into a spell of coughing. His face reddened with each cough.

The *abeed. The slave.* It was his and Elias's way of saying *nigger* without saying it. My heart rattled in my chest to hear his words. I had heard him say *abeed* a thousand times, and it had never bothered me in the same way. Now he was saying it about Orlando Washington.

"What matters," he said at last, his voice ravaged, "is what people think, and then, what they do once they think it." Again he doubled over in a coughing fit. He pulled a handkerchief from his pocket and spit into it.

"Papa, you're not well."

His face was crimson. "It's not me you need to worry about." He wheezed again. He loosened his collar and tie.

I thought Papa had understood why I wanted to help Mr. Washington, because Papa came from a world that dealt in factions, where people lived among different groups—Catholics, Protestants, Jews, Druze, and Muslims—in business and on the street. The Europeans and the Arabs mixing. After all his years living in Mounds, I thought Papa saw color the same way, a difference to be tolerated.

"You let the *abeed* in your house, with you alone." He put the money on the table and counted through it.

The hair on my skin stood up. I had been alone in his store count-less times serving his customers, but moving across the tracks had made my being alone with a person of color a problem. "Why are you count-ing money?"

"I'm giving you money to leave." His expression was hard like the wood of the desk.

"This is craziness. This is Nelly talking." I stood to walk away, to go back home and cast Nelly out. I would stop at the funeral home and have them keep Elias there. But my legs would not obey. My knees shook like I was caught in a nightmare, and it was all I could do to grip the chair.

"There will be more talk," he said.

"There is already talk."

"It's worse now, and it means trouble for you. If you leave, you'll have no trouble."

"He came in for a glass of water. It was ninety degrees."

"You think he took that job for comfort?" Papa asked.

"He's Thea's son."

"Do you think Thea would approve how you put him in harm's way?"

I had to shake my head and wished again that I had never invited Mr. Washington inside.

"You better listen to me now if you never did before." The look on his broad, pale face held the same look of pity as twenty-seven years before when I sat across from him, insisting that I would marry Elias. "Ivie don't think it's coincidence Elias came in on Washington and you, and Elias dead the next day."

I watched his lips move and understood that I had left the protection of my father twenty-seven years before, and he had none to offer now.

"Take this." He dropped the stacks of cash back in the canvas bag. He leaned forward with the money in his outstretched hand. When I did not take it, he moved with forced steps and dropped the bag on my lap. "That's twenty thousand. It's enough to buy a house and get you started." A trickle of sweat rolled off his forehead. He wiped it away with a folded handkerchief.

"Keep your money, Papa. I'm not going anywhere." Elias had almost killed me, but I had stood up to him. I would get through this too. I would hold my grandchild; Nelly and her threats wouldn't stop me. The money sat heavy on my lap. My heart pounded and I wanted fresh air.

His eyes seemed wet. He had been a good father to me. He began to cough. He braced himself and gripped the desk through another fit of wheezing. "Round here, Anna, you don't do what you've done and just go on like things are normal." His words were slow and determined, and they had the ring of truth in them. "If Ivie talks to anyone else, they're bound to go after you, put you in jail."

The word *bound*—I had been bound to Elias, bound to my place, my job. Marina was having her baby, and soon I would hold it. I would not let them take it so easily. I placed the canvas bag in front of him on the desk as if I were serving him a plate of food. "They won't disgrace themselves." Shame on me equaled shame on them.

"Take it. Take it!" He yelled like in his peddling days when growling dogs got in his way. He held the bag of money in my face until I took it. "You have no idea what they will do."

"Who are 'they'?"

Papa didn't answer. He bellowed instead a flurry of words: *shame, dishonor, craziness.* I could not detect a complete thought, a sentence, any direct statement, but the idea was clear. His face flushed from pale to red. I tried to hush him by waving my hands, as if I were a soldier waving a white flag to surrender. If he went on, he would surely have a stroke. But I could do nothing to stop him.

I mustered the strength to say, "I've got my own. The baby is coming and I won't go." I tried to keep my voice cool and stern, forceful. But I had lost control. I was shrieking. "I won't let them push me out. I've got the store. My house. I don't need your money."

"No. No, *binti*." His voice broke and I thought I saw tears welling in his eyes. "You got nothing." His skin went slack and sallow. "You got nothing."

The rough canvas bag had raised letters stamped on it, *The Bank of Riverton*.

He wiped his eyes and regained control of himself. "I made a deal with Ivie for you. He'll take your part in Elias's store. The other half will go to the children. You can stay for the funeral. It won't look right otherwise. Then you leave and we bury this."

"You have no right." I forgot myself and raised my voice to him. "No right to deal for me. That store belongs to me—my husband." My mind was working around everything that had happened: meetings between Ivie, my father, Elias. "Marina's baby," I said. Mr. Washington had slipped from my thinking. I clung to what I loved. "I'm not going anywhere. This is my home."

"Don't be a fool, Anna." He hit the desk in frustration. "You are too headstrong."

"No," I said. "Nelly won't risk it."

He shook his head. "I should have moved you across town. If I had done that, you would not have grown up here. You would be better off. I should have built the house I promised Vega." He had not said her name since shortly after she died. "Vega," he said again.

My given name, *Vega*, the same as Mama's, and the sound of it was like a long-forgotten song. He said it over and over in a tender voice. The sound of it affected me as if she stood in the room with us. No one had called me Vega since Mama died. After her death, Papa said carrying the name of the dead was bad luck and he changed my name to Anna. He told me, "Vega means *the fallen one*, like the star that falls from the sky, like your mother." But superstition was not the reason he changed my name. He could not bring himself to say those two syllables. Her memory pained him too much, and to ease his pain, I never questioned being called Anna, even though the sound *Anna* broke my heart. I missed *Vega*, as I missed her. But I gave it up for our heartaches to ease.

"If you don't go, Ivie will ruin you." The red had drained from his face. "He'll ruin all of us." His last words were like a death sentence coming down from a judge: "He knows everything."

"What?" I was lost in the day, in Elias's death, in the hope for a grandchild, in Papa's office, in the danger. "What does Ivie know? That I've worked for twenty-seven years in that store, the hell his brother and mother gave me?" Sweat had collected on my temples. "He knows nothing."

Papa hung his head. He looked pale and weak and old.

"I'm not going anywhere." I held the bag and felt the ridges of money beneath the canvas. There was the house, the store, bank accounts, and money squirreled away. All of it was profit from my toil as well as Elias's. I would stay and I would have my share. I would have my daughter to myself.

Papa coughed. When he caught his breath, he cast his eyes upward at the light coming through the window, like he was praying in church. With a closed fist, he rapped the desk with his knuckles—a nervous tic he had when a customer had gone on too long and Papa did not know how to end the conversation. "I've bought you three days from Ivie. Get yourself in order. The Nassads want you gone."

"What have I done so bad as this, Papa?"

"I don't know what to believe. That's between you and God." His eyes were cold and golden-brown like the river shallows in winter. Looking into them made me feel like a stone sinking.

I listened for a trace of love in his voice and looked for a sign of gentleness across his face. My father had never said he loved me. I'd taken it for granted in the past, but he was telling me to go and I was not certain.

"What harm is there in a man delivering mail?" My knuckles grew white from my grip on the canvas bag. "He is Thea's son."

Papa had watched them, Gus and Orlando, playing by the river, shooting marbles and swimming, throwing rocks at geese. Papa drove to Nashville in the middle of the night to retrieve the boys from the train station after their failed attempt to stow away to the World's Fair.

At some point, Aunt Elsa had told my father, "Anna needs to play with white girls," and then I was no longer allowed to join my brother and Orlando. But no white girls invited me to play at their homes, and no white girl would come to Mounds to play with the motherless daughter of immigrants. No Riverton mother would think of allowing it.

"Are you going to take their side over mine?" I asked.

"Ivie said you killed Elias." Behind his large, square head, the sun radiated and the room floated in heat.

"You believe that?" My words sounded hollow in my ears. I wondered how they sounded to him.

"He says you poisoned him." His voice broke. "I pray you did not." His temple throbbed. He spoke softly, but his words hit like a hammer at a nail. "If you don't go, Ivie will tell his story to a judge or a lynch mob. It sounds suspicious—Elias walks in on you, Elias goes to Washington's house, and that night Elias is dead. No one will believe you."

I had been naive to think Elias's death would free me.

I felt the weight of the money in my lap. I remembered Nelly's words—"You killed my baby"—in front of Marina. "Nelly won't let Ivie do that," I said. "Nelly won't hurt Marina."

He shook his head. "I am afraid for you."

I stuffed the bag into my purse as best I could.

I somehow found the strength to move away from him.

I thought of Mama the day he planted the fig tree. She wore her blue dress the color of the sky, and a white scarf held her black hair. A camera bulb flashed late in the afternoon when Papa took a break from the store. Somewhere in my father's house there was a photograph, and in it she is kneeling down with her face close to mine. Her dark almond eyes, flecked with gold, unabashed and full of love for me, Papa, Gus, and her coming children, looked into the camera.

He had framed it and hung it on the wall. When she died, he took it down. For a while, I knew where he kept it, and when the pain of missing her was too much, I would pull it from its drawer and stare at that image of her face—the sleek nose, the curve of her cheekbones, the deep-set eyes, the white scarf against her dark hair. Then one day, the photo was not in its spot and I could not bring myself to ask him for it. I had not seen it in over thirty years, and I wanted it.

No other person had loved me the way she had. Being in my father's house always brought back the feeling that once in my life I had been safe, that long ago there had been someone who adored me. I wanted some remembrance of that time. The photo had to be nestled away in a room upstairs in some drawer. If what he said was true, if Ivie planned harm against me or Orlando Washington, I would never be welcomed in Riverton or Mounds. Marina would be shunned. If Orlando Washington was harmed because of me, the people of Mounds would reject my father, and his store would fail. If I left, I'd save him and I'd save Marina shame.

I left his office and went across the hall to Mama's baking room, where she'd made daily bread on a long table and in a brick oven. Empty cardboard boxes littered the floor. Papa had brought in his yard tools and leaned them against the wall—a rake, a hoe, a spade, clippers. The table that once held her cooling pies had long been covered with his papers and old invoices. I shuffled through the papers to see if the photo of her was hidden there.

I ran up the back stairs in my black pumps. The sound on the wood floors echoed and clapped. My feet tripped over floorboards. Papa yelled, "Anna, listen to me. You must go." He sounded broken. He walked slowly but deliberately behind my tripping path. I stumbled from room to room, going through drawers and boxes for the picture. I scratched through old clothes, jewelry, cigar boxes of coins and bills, drawers full of old letters written in Arabic and French, piles of yellowed *Al-Hoda* and *Syrian World* papers. He never taught me Arabic because, he said, "You are an American girl. We are not going back." With his words, a dark sadness crossed his face and his voice gave away that he missed his homeland. But he had decided what he had in America was more, and because it was more, it was better, and we would sacrifice our past.

For the hope of a better future, Papa assumed his new country's prejudices, that foreigners were suspicious, Jews were untrustworthy, and Negroes deserved no respect. He wanted us to be Americans, but by "Americans," he meant the ones who lived in Riverton across the tracks, and he was not them. He learned to play at being white, a part that did not fit a foreigner like him. The best sense he could make of it was: "You will go to school in Riverton, you will be an American girl, and if people ask you, you say your parents come from the Holy Land."

His steps came closer to me in his room. "Anna." I scrounged through drawers on my hands and knees. "I want you to go. For your sake, for the children."

"I want the photograph of her and me." My voice shook.

"Go. You must go." His voice was hard. He did not want my mother's memory sullied by this. He held my purse full of money.

"No."

I stumbled over the *kashshi*, his old peddler's box that he had worn strapped to his back. As a child, I had played in it, opened its empty drawers, and breathed in the smell of spices that once filled them. At one time, he had displayed it proudly, but now the *kashshi* sat beneath the bed, an edge poking out like a scolded dog's nose. My hands grew clumsy as I searched it. I wanted that photograph of my mother. I remembered our faces looked hopeful, like something good was about to happen, like grand possibilities awaited this mother and her child. But there was nothing inside the box. Those days were long over. If I managed to survive their threats, if I stayed, my father might have nothing to do with me, and if he took their side, I would ask nothing from him.

"God forbid it is true." He grabbed my arm where Elias had bruised me. My father pulled and pushed me toward the door to the balcony. "Go." His voice was like a storm wind. "Your mother would die a second death if she had thought this shame would fall on her daughter." He ranted on. "God forbid. Tell me it is not true."

I flinched at his doubt. Ivie had convinced him that it was possible that I had killed Elias, and I feared if my father could not believe me, no one would.

He shoved the purse into my arms and led me to the balcony. He pushed me out the door. Tears rolled down his cheeks. I had seen Papa cry once, on the day she died, and now I was dead to him too. "Take the money and go." His voice was muffled and weak.

I stood outside on the balcony. "I won't leave," I said.

I hoped he would say that I should stay, or that he was sorry, or that I should ignore Nelly's threats. I hoped he would say he loved me. Why, I don't know, because my father never said those words. At the very least I wanted him to say, *This will pass*, as he always did when there was trouble. I waited, but nothing.

I searched his face for a trace of faith in me. "This flame will die down."

"No, *binti*." He looked away from me to the river. His voice was resolute. "You're my daughter, always be my daughter. That money is what you have from me. That's all I can give you." He shut the door in my face. That's how I remembered my father. He called me his daughter in one breath and banished me in the next.

The First Time

The first time Elias beat me, the children were sleeping. He stumbled into my room past midnight. By the smell of him he'd been drinking. His shoes hit with a thud by my bed. He undid his belt, and the pants fell with a clatter. He crawled into my bed and wrapped himself around me, warm and gentle at first. But then he said, "You will be Zada."

"No," I said, angry that he would call me her name. I put my elbow into him. The alarm clock read *1:00*. Only four hours before I started the baking for the day. I had waited up for him already and listened to Marina pining for him. "I want Daddy. Let me stay up 'til he gets home." She had begged and cried and carried on until ten, two hours past her bedtime.

Elias was back from one of his fishing trips to Mobile, those trips he awaited eagerly twice a year, when he would see Zada. He had been on ten such trips, two a year, since Marina was in my belly. As the days got closer to these trips, his anticipation grew like a kid's at Christmas. He'd go for a week and return happy to see the children, to embrace them and give them the presents he bought, but then he would slink down into despair, spending his days in the back of the store and staying late each night, drinking the bourbon he kept hidden in his desk. By the fourth or fifth night, he'd have finished the bottle and life would slip back to normal. He'd work full days and come home to the children in the evening. This trip was to be the last one, and his bout of self-pity had gone on longer than usual.

He pulled at my gown.

"It's too late," I said. "I need to sleep."

He reeked of cigarettes and whiskey. It was the first time I had denied him.

"What did you say?" His voice was loud and his words slurred.

"Shhh," I said. "The children are sleeping."

"Are you shushing me?" His eyelids hung low with drink, and he removed his hand from my thigh.

"I have to get up soon," I said. "And bake." My voice sounded apologetic. "Go," I said as gently as I could. "Get some rest."

His body tensed. The muscles in his arms, his chest, his face, flexed in anger. His eyes opened fully and he stared at me in the dark. Gripping my face, he pushed my head to the pillow and climbed on top of me. He breathed heavily and the day's growth of beard scratched my neck. He grabbed my wrist and twisted my arm behind my head.

I tried to pull away, but the more I fought, the tighter he wrenched my arm. He turned me over and pulled at my gown. His weight pressed me against the mattress and my gown was tangled around my neck, pulling tighter and choking me as he wrestled to get between my legs.

He did not relent with my arm, twisting as if it were a rope. I feared he would snap it in two.

When he was done, he climbed off the bed and stood shakily. He pulled his pants up and looked down at me on the bed. "Get up," he said. "Get up." His voice was loud. He held the bedpost for balance.

"The children," I said. I tried to cover myself as I stood before him.

He slapped my arms away from my chest. "I'll wake them if I want to. They're mine too." His voice was grit and drink and hate. He took my breasts in his hands and he squeezed until I flinched. He buried his face in my neck, then bit my shoulder in anger.

I was cold and his mess was running down my legs. I tried to inch away.

"I want you to hurt." He pulled me close to him and grabbed my hair on the back of my head. His chest was warm and strong. He yanked my hair and he said, "She won't see me because of you."

My father had said the Nassads were hard on their women. Until then, I had thought the hardness Papa spoke of was the void of feeling I lived in with Elias. He loved his children, was kind to his customers, but to me he was withdrawn and sullen and every smile or bit of kindness was like a drop of precious water in the desert.

"You're crying?" He grabbed my arms and shook me. "I'm not good enough for you? I'm not good enough for Zada." He said it again and again. *Not good enough*—that's what he had been thinking as he drank in the back of the store that night. He was not good enough for her, and I was not good enough for him. I was not what he wanted. He wanted her, and now he said she was done with him. He staggered around the room as if he were looking for the door to leave.

That would have been the end of it, if I had kept my mouth shut. He would have walked out of my room and into his and I could have gone to sleep. In the morning, I would have made excuses for his behavior and let the night fade in my memory. But I opened my mouth. For the past week, I had done everything without him, and I was angry that he had treated me so poorly. I wanted him out of my room. "You're drunk," I said. "You can't even find the door."

He tripped toward me and swung. The back of his hand and his knuckles kissed my cheekbone. I felt the flare of heat beneath the skin. He grabbed my shoulders and pushed me to the floor.

"Stop," I said. "Please." I tried to keep my voice low. I did not want to wake the children. I did not want them to see. Marina was five and Eli three.

He stood over me and rubbed his face, as if he were waking from a bad dream. I expected he was done, and I started to move, but he stomped his foot into my thigh. I balled up and his foot landed again on my leg and then in my side. I winced in pain and moaned. And he left me and staggered across the hall to his room.

I listened for the children, but they did not stir. I found my robe and went to the bathroom. I washed myself in the tub and splashed cold water on my face. I tried not to look in the mirror. Blood seeped through the bite mark on my shoulder and I poured iodine in the cut. In the kitchen I made an icepack for my cheek. I tried to sleep with it resting on my face, but the cold burned my skin and my thigh throbbed. I floated in and out of a painful sleep, never letting myself completely go, not trusting that he would stay in his room. When the alarm went off, I was thankful the night was over.

I dressed and went to the kitchen to make coffee and begin the baking for the store. Coming down the stairs, his footsteps dragged. He carried his shoes, which he'd had to retrieve from my room. I wondered if he remembered what he had done. When he saw my face, he looked startled to see the dark bruise.

"Anna," he said. "Did I do that?" He held his hand close to my cheek. I could slap it or take it and kiss it. When I did nothing to reproach him, he took me in his arms and mumbled apologies into my hair. "I'm sorry," he said. "I was out of my mind." He smelled of alcohol, and I imagined he was still drunk. I rested my good cheek against his chest and listened to his heart beating through his shirt. I wanted to believe him, to trust his soft touch, the pleading words, the warmth of his chest. I could not help myself.

The morning was still dark and it was easy to give myself over in the dark. I wanted to forget the humiliation of the night before and have his arms around me. But by falling into that embrace, I silently agreed that what he had done had no consequence.

He kissed my head like I was the one seeking forgiveness. When he left for the store, I felt disgust at my weakness. He had treated me like an animal and I had folded so easily into him.

The children slept late into the morning, well after the loaves were proofing in baskets on the counter. The commotion must have disturbed them the night before. I spent the morning drinking coffee and thinking what I should do. I could stay and pretend all was fine. I could hope he would come home as he had a thousand nights before and sit at the table, eat dinner, and smile at Marina, who hung on his every word. But when I imagined sitting at the same table and looking at him, having him look at me, I wanted to run away.

Marina came down first. She saw the bruise and she gasped. "Mama, what did you do?"

"I'm okay," I said. "Just a little bruise."

"No, it's big." She had me sit so she could see. She gently touched it with her fingertips.

It hurt and I winced. I lied to her, told her what a clumsy mule I was, that I tripped and fell into my bed.

"You must be more careful," she said. She took her seat at the table while I made her a late breakfast. Eli came down with his pants in his hands. He laughed at first when he saw me. He must have thought I had on clown's paint, but Marina explained I had hurt myself. She explained, too, how he must be careful and not trip and hurt his face like Mama. He nodded with frightened eyes and sat to eat.

I scored the bread and had put eight loaves in the oven when Nelly walked through our front door unannounced.

"Hello," Nelly called out. Marina and Eli ran and latched on to her legs, so happy to see their grandmother.

"This is for your cheek," she said to me. She held up a brown paper bag as she labored into the kitchen. Her girth had only expanded since I married Elias. "You must sit." She led me to a chair. She took the raw steak from the bag and held it on my face. The light pressure of her hand and the cold meat felt good, and for the first time since it happened, I felt how tired and sore I was. I let my body relax.

He must have called her, confessed to what he'd done, or else he told her I'd had an accident. He must have said how bad I looked and told her to bring my loaves to the store so that no one would see me.

"This will stop the swelling," she said. "Believe me. I've raised two boys." Nelly looked in my cabinets and took out the aspirin. She was fat and slow and with every step she seemed breathless. She drew a glass of water. "You are tired," she said, as if the bruise on my face came from a sleepless night. "Go rest, and I'll watch the children."

"The bread." I motioned to the oven. I wanted to go to my bed and let sleep erode the heavy feeling of shame, but the timer was ticking down. "I'll wait until the bread is done."

"I can take it out." Eli hung on her skirt. She crouched down to his height, kissed his cheek, and pulled out two lollipops from her pocket. She presented one to Eli, and Marina scurried over to take possession of hers.

I took the steak into the living room and lay on the couch. I listened to her singing and playing with the children. The timer buzzed and then the oven door creaked. Her breathing strained as she pulled the pans from the oven. "Hot! Hot!" she said to Eli. "No touch!" She rustled and moved and I smelled the lovely warm bread.

When the steak was no longer cool, I took it to the refrigerator. Eli played on the floor with toy soldiers and Marina colored at the table.

"Go rest." Nelly fanned herself, hot from the stove.

"I have to deliver the bread." I decided not to hide behind the bruise on my cheek. Marina had believed my story and I thought others would too.

"I am here. Take advantage and go to bed. Shut the door and sleep." Her insistence for me to stay out of view struck like a match inside me.

"I want to get out of the house," I said.

"No, no." Panic filled her voice. Nelly ushered me to a chair. "You will rest. You will stay home. Until you are better."

"I'm not sick." Pride swelled in my chest like heat in the oven. "I want to go."

"People will see you. What will they think?" Her voice took on an edge that gave her away.

I touched the bruise. It would be days or weeks before I could cover it with makeup.

Nelly moved nervously around the kitchen, washing the bread pans and laying them out to dry.

I thought how easily I had forgiven him. I had laid my head on his chest and let him pet me. I had lowered myself like a cowering dog.

Marina watched me. "Grandma says to keep the meat on your face."

"It won't make the bruise go away." I patted her hand and she looked at me with pity. I felt angry that she was seeing me bruised and hearing her grandmother tell me to hide away. I wondered what she had heard the night before, if the noise had colored her dreams. I wondered if he would do it again.

Nelly touched the bread to see how much longer it needed to cool before she wrapped it.

I crossed the room to shoo her away from my bread. "Nelly," I said. "You go home and I'll take the bread as usual."

She looked at me keenly. "Go upstairs," she told the children. "If you stay in your rooms and let Mama rest, I will bring you some candy."

They knew her promises were good and they gathered their things and hustled up the stairs. When they were gone, Nelly led me back to the table. She laid her fat hand on my arm. "You must be careful. His father was the same." She made the sign of the cross.

I could not trust Nelly any further than I could throw her. She was trying to cover his actions.

"When I was a young woman, I would say something to my husband, what he should do or what he shouldn't, and it was enough." She slapped her hands together in the air and made a popping noise. She knew how I felt, and I could not bring myself to be cruel to her. She was trying to help me, even though it was in her son's interest. "I learned to keep my mouth shut." She leaned forward as if she were imparting a great wisdom. "Make myself small."

The more she said, the more my face throbbed and stung. I wanted to take the bread to the store to embarrass him. "I was sleeping in my bed," I said. "He came in and dragged me out."

She sucked her teeth and shook her head. "None of them can handle the drink." She patted my shoulder. "Not Ivie. Not Elias. Not their father. I tell you, stay out of the way when he is drinking. You come to me. You bring the children." Her breathing strained as she stood.

"It was past midnight." He had ambushed me in bed. I could not have gathered the children and left when I was naked and he was raging.

"You can come to me in the middle of the night." She left me at the table and busied herself packing the bread in paper and into a large box. "I will make sure Elias is home tonight. I will make sure he is good to you."

I wanted to cry, but I would not cry in front of her.

"Let me take the children, so you can rest," she said.

"No," I said. "They can go with me to the store." I did not want them with her. I wanted them close to me.

"No, I say no to that." Her patient tone turned sharp and she wagged her finger in my face. "You think you are something, but you will not bring shame on him or this family. If you show your face, people will know." She yelled, and I knew the children could hear. "Of course he is angry with you. I see how stubborn you are. You had no one to teach you. You are a stupid girl. You go to the store, and people talk, and no one buys, and then you have no roof over your head. You think he will be easy on you if you make it hard on him?" She wiped her hands on her dress, picked up the big box of bread loaves, and headed toward the front door. "No. You stay here. The best thing for you is to heal and to please him. I'll bring you dinner tonight."

The screen door shut behind her, and I listened as the pea gravel crackled under her tires. The oven ticked as it cooled and the children were quiet. A few minutes after Nelly left, I went upstairs to gather our things. I did not trust that Elias would return calm and remorseful. He had betrayed me with Zada and now this. Even if he did come home soft and kind, I did not want to see him or him to see me. I had been humiliated, and the thought of sitting at the table with him, pretending I had fallen, that I was the clumsy mule and that he was the good father whom they loved and adored, would be another degradation. Marina would tease me about falling and he would laugh at whatever she said. I could not suffer that. I did not trust that Nelly could make him be good, or that she cared what happened to me. She only cared about her son. I could not trust anything. Elias had never hurt me before, and I had no sure footing to know what would come next.

The children played in their rooms while I packed bags of clothes and toys into the trunk of my car. I told them we were going to visit their grandpapa. I pulled a hat low on my head to shield the bruise from sight. On the drive through town, I cupped my hand over my cheek as if I were pondering a deep and important question. Marina asked, "Why are you holding your face like that?"

"I don't want anyone to see the dumb bunny who falls on her face," I said.

She laughed at my expression. "You are a dumb bunny. Tripping and falling." All the way to Papa's backyard, she and Eli sang, "Dumb bunny. Dumb bunny. Mommy's a dumb bunny." I could not help but smile at their glee, their freedom to laugh at me.

"I'll try not to be a dumb bunny anymore. I promise." And by that, I meant I would try to be strong and not forgive him. I would try to stay away from him, but even as I said that to myself, I knew that leaving him would be difficult. Where would I go and what would I do? As I drove across the tracks, I had to stop thinking what was to happen. For the moment, all I wanted was to feel safe. I pulled behind my father's store and felt a twinge of relief.

I sent Marina in to get Papa from the store so no one would see my face.

Papa hurried out, wiping his hands on his apron. "What is this?" He touched my cheek. "Marina said you fell."

I nodded.

He took me by the hands and searched my arms for other marks, as if I were a child who'd fallen on the playground. Papa's large forehead wrinkled in concern. "Let me finish up with the customers." He tousled Eli's head of curly black hair. "Thea is here," he said.

"I don't want to see her," I said.

"Why not?"

"I'm embarrassed." I opened the trunk and got out the bags.

"Of a fall? So, you were clumsy." When he saw my bags, his expression clouded over. He must have realized that the marks were not caused by an accident and that I had arrived seeking refuge. "Maybe Thea can help you." He spoke low, his voice full of worry.

"Please don't send her out," I said, but he was gone.

I put the bags of clothes by the back door. "Let's go to the water," I said to the children. They ran across the field and their shoes were off by the time I reached them. I took off mine and we stepped into the cool river water. I held tight to Eli to keep him from going too far. The hem of Marina's skirt hung wet, but I didn't care. I was happy to be outside with them. We gathered stones and built a tiny dam in the shallows by the shore. We threw rocks and watched the surface splash. We sat under the trees by the water and made dandelion chains. I was grateful to be out of my house, away from Nelly and Elias and not working in the store.

Marina pointed east to the opening in the trees. "Let's take the trail home," she cried.

"No. We're here to visit with Grandpapa." I wondered how long I could keep her satisfied away from her father, and I imagined her anger if we left town and she never saw him again.

"I want to go home now."

Already I could feel the pull Elias had on us. Marina would demand him.

"I want to eat dinner with Daddy." Since his return, Elias had stayed late at the store, alone, drinking and wallowing, and Marina had missed him. "Grandmother is bringing us candy."

I had to distract her. "Grandpapa has candy too," I said. "And Coca-Cola. Go inside and ask politely."

She pivoted away from me and ran across the field as fast as she could. Eli heard "candy" and "Coca-Cola" and he knew to follow her, that at the end of her run would be treats from Grandpapa.

As soon as they disappeared inside the door, Thea emerged from beneath the balcony. I imagined she had been biding her time, waiting for me to be alone so she could see the damage Elias had done. Thea had worked for my father two days a week since Aunt Elsa had died shortly after my wedding. Thea cleaned the store and his rooms and cooked him a few meals. Facing her was not what I wanted to do. She would know what had happened. I covered my cheek and turned away from her.

"Your daddy said you don't want to talk to me." Her voice was rich with concern.

"I'm not feeling well." I stared at the river instead of looking at her.

"Why not let me put my eyes on you?" she asked. "It's been a while."

"I don't want to get you sick."

"That kind of sick won't catch me." She touched my arm, but I pulled away. I did not want her to see me like this, and I was angry at my father for sending her out. "Your babies look good. Growing fast."

"I'm tired. I want to sit out here and be quiet." It was true. The long night, the morning of coffee, Nelly's presence, and packing had worn me out. "I've been working too much at the store and I need a rest."

"If you say so." She stood by, waiting for me to give in and face her. "Your daddy never raised a hand to your mama, so I know you know it's not right."

"That's not what happened." I felt like a coward, hiding Elias's misdeeds from her, when she already knew.

"You brought all this luggage to your daddy's door, and you won't look me in the eye." She sounded irritated. "Some men think they can rule their house with their fists." Certainly she had seen this before, not in her own home, but she was a trusted woman in Mounds, a midwife, a caregiver. "He ever done this before?"

"No," I said. "It's not going to happen again." I did not believe my own voice. I doubted Thea was convinced either.

"It will if you go back," she said.

I took a step away from her toward the water. "I'm here," I said, as if it were a consolation. "I'm not going back."

"You strong enough to stay away?" Her words landed the challenge at my feet. "I hope so. For your sake. For those babies."

"I don't know," I said, angry that she would ask it, angry that I might not be.

"Look at me, Anna."

But I walked away. "You can go home, Thea. I'll be here now. You can take some days off."

"All right." I heard the frustration in her voice. "I'll check in with Mr. Faris next week." She walked back toward the store, and I was sorry I had turned away. But I was ashamed for her to see what he had done, and I worried she might be right, that I would not be strong enough to stay away.

I sat on the ground by the river. Papa came outside and scanned the field for me. He saw me and waved, as if to signal, *Stay, take your time.*

He carried our bags inside and shut the door. I had no energy to move from that spot near the water.

The sky dimmed and the crickets began to chirp. The volume of animals increased as the sun dipped. The noises of river frogs and birds, of water lapping on the shore, made me happy. I had sat in this spot with Mama, watching the geese land and honk as they arrived in fall.

Papa could feed the children whatever they wanted. I did not care if he let them eat packaged cookies and cheese and candy by the fistful. They were safe with him and I was outside alone. I was thankful to be free, away from the stove, away from my house or any house. I was proud I had been brave enough to drive my children across town, brave enough to walk away from Elias. Lightning bugs flashed over the water and the sun dipped completely below the horizon.

That he had hit and kicked me seemed unreal, but all I had to do was touch my tender flesh for the truth. No one had ever raised their hand against me. I wondered if Elias was home, if Nelly had made good on her promise to bring us dinner and make him behave. I remembered his tenderness this morning and wondered if it was still in his heart, and if he felt guilty, or if his frustrations had simmered all day. I imagined him in the back room of the dark store, sitting alone, penned in by shelves of groceries, sipping a new bottle of bourbon and counting up the disgruntlements of his life—how he did not want to keep the store or the books or the employees, how he wanted to work with his hands and sleep past sunup, how I was not the woman he wanted and how he missed Zada. If he was drinking in the store, he would not even know we were gone.

If he had gone home, he would walk into a silent house, empty of the chatter of the children, devoid of the smell of dinner cooking, and absent of me waiting to serve him. I wondered how still the house must be without us in it and if he hated the sight of me so much that he basked in the quiet. I wondered if he felt regret.

My solitude was cut short as the children rushed out of the house with glass jars in their hands. My father moved slowly after them. They shrieked as they caught their first lightning bugs and each time after. When Marina counted more bugs in Eli's jar, I could hear the jealousy in her voice. She demanded he give her some and did not relent, even with Eli crying out, "No. Mine." My father tried to settle it. "Marina, Marina. Leave him be." His deep voice counseled her and settled their fussing. Soon they were squealing with delight again.

He walked up to me, and I worried what he would say. With grunts and adjustments, he made his way to the ground to sit beside me. He said nothing about the mark on my face or my husband. He said, "I wish your mother could see them." I wished so too. I ached from sitting on the hard ground all day, but I had no will to move.

"Funny how the boy is like you and Marina is like Gus," he said. It was true that Eli was like me, quiet and watchful. Marina was loud and adventurous like Gus, but I did not correct him that she most favored Elias. A force of will. Even then, she watched me and knew what I felt. She knew what to do to make me react, and then she played coy to get her way.

"The time has flown," he said. "I remember when you and Gus were their age. And your mother"—he made the sign of the cross and kissed his fingers—"she was here with you then." Papa ran his hands over his face, maybe to clear away mosquitoes or to mask his emotions.

I let the children play in the field behind my father's house long past bedtime, and I was happy watching them flit around, sprites with jars of glowing bugs. I expected Elias to drive up any minute and ask us to come home. Part of me hoped he would come and promise he would never hurt me again, say that he had been a fool and a beast and he would make our life good, but he did not. Around ten o'clock Eli ran to me and collapsed in my lap on my sore leg. Marina soon dragged herself to Papa and leaned heavily against him.

After much bartering with Marina, Papa opened the jars, and the lightning bugs flew out in a swirl of light. "Now they can see their friends." Papa pointed to the stars.

Marina laughed. "Those are stars, not lightning bugs, Grandpapa."

"You don't know," he said. "You never know."

My eyes burned, staring after the bugs as they spread out and diminished against the dark. Marina's eyes blinked heavily with sleep. I carried Eli, and Papa carried Marina, into the store and up the stairs and into my old bedroom. The bed was made and the room had been cleaned. A small lamp burned next to the bedside. Thea must have straightened the room for me, and I felt a wave of remorse for being cold with her. She cared for me, and I had pushed her away to protect him. What he had done made me small and weak, and in turn, I had belittled her.

I went to bed that night in my old room and felt the comfort of my mother's memory around me. I thought I could make it better with Thea, once the bruises were gone, once I had my pride back. Marina and Eli lay on either side of me. My arms worked as their pillows. I stared up at the ceiling and followed the trails of cracked plaster. Marina snuggled close like a cat and tucked her head against my side. It was unlike her to want to be close and touching. She knew I needed her comfort, or else she needed mine.

The next morning, I woke stiff and aching from the bruises and from where Elias had wrenched my arm. Papa was in the kitchen making eggs and frying country ham. He had learned to cook a few meals since he had no woman waiting on him daily. He poured me a cup of coffee and took my chin in his hand, as if I were still a little girl. "Looking better today," he said. "You will rest and I will keep the children. The store can close."

But I did not want to rest, or lie in bed, or be trapped by four walls. I had packed the children's swimsuits. "Why don't we drive to the springs and take a picnic?" Ten miles away was a swimming hole made from a warm spring bubbling up in a limestone canyon.

It was Saturday, and we decided to go by Gus and Lila's and invite them too. From the store, Papa gathered peaches, a watermelon, chocolate candy, and pickles from a gallon jar. I fried a chicken and wrapped up the leftover cornbread. We packed it all in a basket, and Papa put a case of Coca-Cola in a cooler.

The children and I put on our swimming clothes. I checked to see if my shoulder strap covered the bite mark Elias had left. It did not, so I took a button-down shirt to wear in the water. Marina and I wore summer dresses over our suits. We piled into Papa's Oldsmobile, and on the way to Gus and Lila's place, the children looked out at the farms and kitchen gardens with rows of canna lilies and sunflowers and corn shoulder high. They counted horses and cows in the pastures.

When Gus saw my cheek, his face twisted with confusion. "When did you take up boxing?" His Adam's apple bobbed in his throat as he chuckled.

"Oh, that," I said, trying to sound flippant. "I fell."

Lila had gone to her father's farm to work for the day, but Gus came along. He sat between the children and played peekaboo, hiding his face behind his straw fedora. I wanted to tell him they were past the age of playing peekaboo, but they were in a fit of giggles, laughing until they almost cried.

"You have to stop, Gus," I said. "They'll get the hiccups."

"You worry too much, Grandma." Gus rolled his eyes and the children laughed harder still.

When we got to the spring, we parked at the side of the road and followed a path through spindly pine trees and dogwoods. We came to a clearing and the place was as I remembered it, the giant limestone boulders jutting out of the water on the far end, and close by, large stepping stones along the shallows. Marina and Eli could climb one to the next.

I took off my dress and quickly covered up in the button-down shirt. The water was warm, but a chill ran through my whole body. Papa saw the bruises on my leg and looked away. I sank low in the water. Gus did not see because he had scampered off to climb the large boulders at the far end of the spring. He got to the top of one, whooped to get our attention, and plummeted fifteen feet into the water. He swam beneath the surface toward us and popped up in front of the children. Marina screamed with delight. Eli clung to me and his face froze in a state of surprise.

We spent the day playing in the warm water. Eli could not swim, so I held him close and pulled him like a motorboat. We bounced and splashed, and he adored my attention. Marina, whom I had taught to float and kick, had Gus tossing her in the air so that she could fly like a bird. She bobbed up, the water dripping from her thick eyelashes, kicked back to him, and begged, "Again, again."

He threw her a hundred times, and a hundred times I said, "Be careful. Not so high." She must have tired of my nagging, because she soon contented herself humming and floating on her back near me in the shallows. I was proud of her, such a big girl and floating on her own, her arms wide and her legs long. I gave her a lesson, how to use her arms to move through the water. She fluttered around and then floated on her back, singing and staring at the blue sky. She was happy and peaceful. Eli watched her too, from his seat on a stepping stone, his feet dipping in the water.

Gus grabbed me in a brotherly way and said, "Your turn now." I laughed and struggled against him, but he was able to dunk me under. I came up grinning. I caught sight of Papa smiling at us. Eli and Marina stared, mesmerized, as if my brother and I were a movie on the screen. They had never seen me so happy or free as I was playing with my brother. I hoped Marina and Eli would share the good feeling Gus and I had always had.

Gus wrestled me under again, and this time when I came up, the shoulder of the shirt fell aside. Gus looked at the dark blue circle on my shoulder. He looked away, probably uncertain how I got it, embarrassed to mention it. I pulled the shirt up and started toward the shore.

"Ready for lunch?" I combed my hair with my fingers. Gus and the children followed me toward Papa, where he had begun to lay out our food. As my leg emerged from the water, before I could grab a towel to wrap myself, Gus noticed the bruises. He grabbed me and halted my progress.

"You didn't get that from a fall." His voice was raw. "Or that." He pointed to my shoulder. He was loud, with no regard for the children. "Did Elias do that to you?"

"No." I motioned to the children. "Be quiet. I fell."

Marina stared as if she could sense my lie. "She got that because she's a dumb bunny." Marina made a silly face to make Gus laugh.

"No, she's not," he snapped. "Be respectful of your mother."

Marina's eyes widened at his stern tone. She looked as if she might cry.

"You're lying," he said to me under his breath. He glared at me and Papa, and then Gus walked off into the woods.

"I'm fine." I took Marina's hand. "I fell and got a few bruises, but I'm okay."

She questioned me with her big green eyes. She pulled away and climbed onto the large, flat boulder where Grandpapa was opening Coke bottles. Eli had his and was sucking it down. Marina nestled against my father and tucked her head into his chest. I put on my dress to cover up my leg.

The boulder was enormous and smooth, warmed from the sun. We ate cold chicken and saved some for Gus, who returned with a subdued temper. Everyone was quiet. Papa cut the watermelon and I watched the children and Gus as they climbed along the low stepping stones. "Be careful of Eli near the water," I yelled to Gus. He waved his hand in recognition of my voice, but he was no longer joyful or playful with the children.

When they were out of earshot, Papa said, "You will stay with me."

His words felt like a balm, but moving back home with him would not be so easy. Everyone in town would know that I had left my husband. I had thought of driving to another town and telling only Papa and Gus. That idea was full of loneliness, and I could not bear to face Marina and her anger on my own. She would never accept my leaving her father.

If I took them away, Elias would find us. He would be angry that I had taken his children, and even if his anger wore off, his pride would kick in, and he would want them back home where they belonged. I made excuses. What he had done was not all of who he was. He was a good father and loved his children. His children loved him, and I had begun to waver. I remembered Thea's challenge to me—would I be strong enough to stay away? My heart felt tight in my chest. My father and brother wanted me safe, but I did not know how to say no to Elias.

On the way home the children sang and played a counting game Marina invented to teach Eli his numbers. Gus sulked, no longer their lighthearted uncle. He stared at the back of my head and I could feel his eyes burning a hole in me.

"I'm okay, Gus."

"Have you looked in the mirror?"

Marina stopped singing and her eyes bore down on him. She understood his meaning.

Papa held his arm outside of the window to let the air flow over his skin. I looked at the emerald on my finger and wondered what it meant, the good times and the bad.

The sun was a brilliant gold and low on the horizon when we dropped Gus at his house. Lila opened the door and smiled. I heard her tease, "Looks like I missed the fun." Gus whispered in her ear and the smile dropped from her lips. She stepped onto the porch to come to the car, but Gus grabbed her arm to stop her. She waved goodbye, a frown on her face, and went inside. He would tell her about the marks on my body and I did not want him to.

We pulled into the alley by Papa's store. Eli had fallen asleep. His head rested on Marina's lap. "That was a fun day," I whispered to her.

She scowled, shushed me, and pointed to Eli. She was troubled by the bruises on my leg, my swollen cheek, by what Gus had said. She was smart enough to put all the pieces together. She was angry at Gus for blaming her father, in shock to imagine Elias hurting me, and doubly angry at me for lying.

She looked out the window of the parked car and her face brightened. Before she said the word *Daddy*, I knew who she was looking at. She bolted out of the car with little care for Eli's head.

Papa let out a long sigh. "I had a feeling," he said. He took my hand in his. "Anna, don't go. Stay here with me."

The pressure in my chest hurt. No matter what I did, I had to face Elias. "Okay, Papa," I said, but seeing Elias standing by his car, our little girl in his arms, I was not sure I was strong enough to stay true to my word.

I got out of the car, and Marina babbled, "Mama took us to the warm springs with Uncle Gus, and we had a picnic with Grandpapa."

"That sounds like a perfect day," he said. His voice was deep and throaty. He had not shaved and the stubble on his face was thick and dark. "I'm so glad to see you." He spoke to Marina, but he was looking at me, and goose bumps ran over my arm.

"Mama taught me more swimming," she said.

Elias put Marina on the ground, but she clung to his leg. "You got a good mama," he said.

I opened the back door of the car and scooped Eli up.

Elias rushed to my side. "I'll get him for you."

"No." His closeness sent a hot rush through me, but I moved to Papa's back door. "Marina, come with me."

"No," she whined. "I want to see Daddy."

"Marina." I heard anger in my voice that was intended for Elias. "Come with me. Now."

Elias patted Marina on the back. "Go with Mama. Do what she says."

Marina dragged her feet across the ground, and once I felt her close to me, I hurried up the back stairs. I was short-winded at the top. Eli was heavy, almost too big to be carried. I tucked him into bed. Marina pouted and moaned to punish me. "I want to go with Daddy. I can go and you stay here." She stomped her foot. "He won't hurt me."

I gave her a hard look and pointed my finger in her face. "You go get a bath. Not another word."

She marched down the hall and slammed the bathroom door.

I went to the windows and eavesdropped on Elias and Papa. My heart pounded in my chest.

"I was wrong," Elias said. "I drank too much. I don't know why I did it." He sounded sincere.

"You did it," Papa said. "You can't take it back."

"I will never do that again." Elias hung his head. "You have my word, Faris."

"Your word is nothing to me," Papa growled. "I never hit my wife." Papa spit at the ground and left Elias in the backyard. Papa slammed the door and turned the lock.

I watched Elias standing there with his hands in his pockets. He looked up and saw me in the window. *I'm sorry,* he mouthed. He dug out his keys, slunk into his car, and drove away.

I got into bed with Marina, and she pulled away from me. I touched her cheek and she lifted my hand like a dirty rag and let it go. I turned over and lay on my bruised thigh. I snuggled against Eli and closed my eyes.

The next morning, Marina woke with a cross face and her lips pouting. "I don't know why we have to stay here. Daddy wants us home."

All day she scowled. The florist delivered flowers from Elias, and I could only stare at them and set them aside. Marina looked at me as if I had failed a test.

That night Elias knocked on the back door. He wore a tie and a wrinkled shirt. It was six thirty. He'd come from closing the store. He held a jewelry box in his hands. I had put him and his image in jeopardy, and he would not let me go easily.

"Go home," I said. "I'm not coming with you."

"I want to see my kids." He put the jewelry box in my hands. "Can't I see them?" He took me by the waist and pulled me close to him. He whispered in my ear. "I want to see you too. I want you home."

My stomach fluttered. He smelled of cloves and coffee, not whiskey. I wanted to rest against him and pretend nothing bad had happened.

"It's not right," he said. "Without you home."

"No, nothing is right," I agreed. "But you did this, and I can't pretend you didn't."

"Give me another chance." He touched my cheek. "The bruise is better," he said, as if he had not been the one to cause it. "Please, let me show you." His breath, warm and soft, fell against my forehead.

I stepped away from him, because if I had not, I would have gotten in his car and told him to take me home. His eyes were beautiful, bright green. His face strong and angular.

"My mother is at the store with me every day, and she wears me out. I want you there."

He took the box from me and opened it. Inside was a necklace with a locket. He had placed a photo of Marina and one of Eli in the oval frames. He clasped the necklace around my neck. "I'll do better."

I felt myself pulling away from my father's house, from my anger at Elias, from my own pride. Elias knew the power of telling people what they wanted to hear. He did it at the store to boost sales, he'd done it with my father years before, and again last night. Now he was making promises so I would fall in line.

"People ask where you are. I tell them you are helping Faris." He looked humble and tired. His greatest talent was shifting gears, from anger to kindness, from calmness to frustration. "It's true. You're helping him. But it's my fault."

My resolve melted with each word that flowed like honey from his lips, and that night I played his words over in my mind as I lay sleepless beside Marina and Eli.

The next day, Elias called. "Come home. I want to see the children." His voice was deep and calm.

"No," I said.

"I miss them." I could hear his sadness, and I rationalized that yes, he should see his children. He had done nothing to hurt them, and at my invitation, Elias came to dinner.

Papa turned red when I told him he was coming to dinner. "He is a snake, Anna," he yelled. "Slinking through the grass, working his way to you." It had been four days since I had left my house and the bruise was a sickly yellow-green.

At dinner, Papa did not touch his food. He sat like a statue with stone eyes fixed on Elias.

Marina bubbled with questions, asking her father if had he missed her while she was on vacation. Who had come into the store that day? Had Grandmother remembered the candy she promised? Finally, she noticed Papa fuming at the end of the table. With a mouth full of green beans, Marina said, "Why are you mad, Grandpapa?"

Papa turned his face to hers. "I'm not."

"You look mad," she said.

He placed his hand on top of her head as if he could contain her in that safe place next to him. "I am not mad, little one. I am concerned."

She raised her eyebrows and returned to her food, chattering to her father about her new pet ducks she'd been feeding on the water, and how if she left a trail of crumbs along the shore and down the path, they might follow her home.

I took the dishes from the table.

Papa said to Elias, "Let's go outside."

Marina hung close to me as I washed the plates. The men's voices carried inside. She could hear them talking.

"What you did is a sin," said my father.

Elias sighed. "You're right."

"I talked to the priest. She can get an annulment." Papa spoke loudly.

"She won't do that to the children," Elias said. "And the Church won't allow it. You know that. I know that."

"How can I let her go with you?" Papa paused. "Imagine Marina with bruises on her whole body." Papa choked on his words.

"I hear you, Faris." Elias sounded calm and smooth, compared to my father's emotion. "It won't happen again."

"I don't believe you," Papa said. "I never believed you."

"I respect you." Elias controlled the anger in his voice, but I felt it creeping beneath the surface. "But she's my wife. They're my kids. They belong with me."

Marina grabbed my legs. She could hear everything. "Mama," she cried. "I want to go home." Her tears streamed down her face. I wiped her warm cheeks and brushed the dark hair from her forehead.

I felt a knot in my stomach.

"I want to go home," she bawled.

"I know you do." I knelt down and took her in my arms. Eli saw Marina getting attention and he began crying too. I touched the necklace Elias had given me.

I heard Papa yelling, "Go home!"

Elias said, "Faris, please understand."

"No," Papa barked. "Go. Get out of here."

"Please, Faris," Elias pleaded. "Let me say goodbye."

Papa slammed the door. I heard the bolt lock in place. Papa charged up the back steps. He walked past me and to his bedroom. He shut the door and I could hear his grumbling. I was left alone in the kitchen, my children in hysterics, bawling and begging for their father. Elias started his engine and the lights flashed on the ceiling as he turned his car around in the back field.

The next morning, I awoke with Marina standing over me and staring hard. She watched me dress. She was in her church clothes. It was Sunday, and Papa planned to take the children to Mass to let me have a quiet morning.

"I'm going home now," Marina said resolutely.

"No," I said. "You're going to Mass with Grandpapa." I looked at my watch. It was eight, and Mass started in an hour.

"I'm tired of your vacation, and I'm going home." In her hand, she held a pillowcase of her possessions. I threw on a blouse and skirt as she walked out of the room, scampered down the steps and out the back door.

When her feet hit the green field she started running. I grabbed my shoes and slipped into them. "Marina, stop!" I yelled, but she did not relent.

Her nimble body and long legs moved gracefully across the field toward the path. Her long black hair bounced and flipped. She stayed in my sights but I never got close. She had youth and slightness on her side. "Marina," I called after her. She was wondrous to watch, running, never doubting, never looking back. She was fierce in her determination.

She ran beneath the bridges and I had to walk up the small hill behind the courthouse. She flew off the trail at the point where our yard met the water. She flung herself past the garden and up the back stairs of our house. I stopped in our backyard to catch my breath. I had no idea I could still run so far, but I had not caught her, that beautiful sprite who tested me in every way, and now she was inside, out of reach.

From the vegetable garden, Elias said, "Good morning." He held the small clippers in his hand. He was trimming back the suckers on the tomato plants. He smiled at me and tipped his straw-brimmed hat. A sheen of sweat glistened across his forehead. "She decided to come home?" A chuckle ran beneath his words. Outside, in the morning light, he was not the man who had attacked me. He was their father, the friendly shopkeeper, the young man who had once courted me.

"She's a determined child," I said.

"I'm glad." He threw the handful of vines aside. He took several long strides toward me, and I felt nothing of the fear I had felt in my room that night. "You are here too. That's good."

My resolve slipped as he walked two steps closer and then got down on his knees and held his arms out. He looked at me in the way I had always wanted him to, as if he desired me, as if he needed me. I imagined he had looked at Zada this way.

"Get up." I turned to go. That was the only way I could be strong, to walk away from him, but he grabbed my wrist in his hand.

"Please forgive me," he said. "I made the worst mistake of my life." He pulled me close and placed his damp forehead against my stomach. "I was wrong. I won't touch a drink again."

I wanted to believe it was the drink that had made him cruel. I wanted to quiet the thoughts that he hated his marriage to me, because I was not enough.

"I've been to confession. I'll do my penance." He looked up at me with his green eyes and his dark brows arched high on his forehead. "It's over, what I did." I wondered if he meant seeing Zada or hitting me or both.

"Why don't you take Marina to Mass, and then bring her back to Papa's after?"

He pulled himself to standing and let go of me.

I headed toward the path to walk back to Papa's.

"Please, don't go," he said. "We have this life. We have the store and the children." He seemed near tears. "I was wrong." He sounded true. He was convincing.

"You don't love me," I said. "If you did, you would not have done that."

"We can't just quit." He did not contradict me about his love.

Some part of me hoped he would.

"I have thought of leaving, but you're the one who left me, and here we are." His words felt like acquiescence—this is who we are, this is the straw we drew. He pulled me toward him. "Our daughter wants to be home where she is happy."

I let him embrace me, even though he did not love me. There was truth in what he said. I was settling for less, but I liked his closeness. I wanted to hold him. I wanted to feel his weight and his skin and find some forgiveness for him. I was tired of being alone. I was tired of fighting him off and fighting with Marina.

Elias sensed my body giving in to him and he led me to the side of the river beneath the mulberry trees we had planted. "We made vows. We are bound together." He kissed me as he had probably kissed Zada. He touched my face and kissed the bruise. He had his business, his reputation, his pride at stake. He needed me more than I needed him. He undid my blouse and kissed the bruise of his bite mark and he ran his fingers along my arms and my back. He said, "Never again."

I returned to Papa's without Marina. Papa and Eli were dressed for Mass, but they had not gone. They stood waiting in the doorway, and Papa figured what had happened. "Don't go back," he pleaded. "You don't have to go." He followed me to my room and Eli played with his toy soldiers as I gathered our things in our bags.

I could smell Elias on my skin. "He won't do it again." I did not want to hurt my father. I did not want to be a fool.

"You can't trust him," Papa said.

I squeezed past Papa, and Eli followed me like a duckling.

"If you go, he will do it again." Papa's voice was gruff.

"We have the children." I had blind hope that Elias would be true to what he said, that he would be satisfied and we could move on and one day remember this episode as a dark stain on a long marriage. If he could learn to feel for me the way I felt for him, then we would be fine. "I have to trust him."

"He'll never be what you want." Papa took me by the arms. "I cannot help you if you go back to him. You will be on your own." My father looked broken, and I wanted to fix him and Elias and make the children happy too. "You can go to my brother in Connecticut. Or we can find a place for you to start over."

"Elias promised he would never do it again." I sounded weak in my own ears.

Papa shook his head. "It will get worse."

I wanted Papa to understand. "He is contrite. He's been to confession." My father was a religious man, and if anything would persuade him to give Elias another chance, holy forgiveness would.

"When he gets drunk and hurts you again, *binti*, where will the priest be?" Papa pleaded. "Will the priest come and rescue you and those children? Will his prayers shield you?"

My skin burned red.

"The priest won't help you." Papa hung his head. "If you go back, I can't protect you. I can't stop him. You will be on your own. But if you are strong, if you stay here with me, you will get through it and you will be safe."

"We will be fine." I passed Papa several times as I loaded the car. I put Eli in the back seat and I kept saying to myself, as I pulled out of the alley and east on Water Street, *We will be fine.* Eli looked out at the river as we drove toward home. My father's words—*You will be on your own*—burned like a hot stamp against my skin.

I imagined Elias's green eyes looking into mine as he kissed my face and ran his fingers gently over my hair. We were married. I had lowered myself into a dark well and tossed the rope back to the surface. He was the father of my children, and he had persuaded me that it was my duty to forgive him. *I am on my own,* I thought as the car bounced over the railroad timbers. I looked out over the water, peaceful and dark on that summer afternoon, and I wished I could be sure I had done the right thing.

Where I Belong

I stood on my father's balcony and looked south over the river. To the east, the path disappeared beneath the trees. Over the treetops peeked the bridges and the slate roof of the old courthouse. I took the bag of money from my purse. I had the urge to walk to the riverbank, toss it in the air, and let it flutter to the water's surface, like geese lighting on a fall day, but that would have been shortsighted. I went to my car and put it under the seat.

"This will pass." That was Papa's philosophy when something bad happened—tell yourself, *This will pass.* This night will pass. This illness will pass. This beating will pass. Maybe that was how he saw happiness too, and so he took happiness with care and caution, because it would all pass.

In the distance, a wall of gray rain fell. Lightning struck far off, but overhead, blue sky. The storm was coming. I stared at the dark water, so deep and cold, churning now from the hot wind. The wide, deep river was always changing, but always the same. The river had become the one constant solace after Mama died. The dark liquid movement swirled and lapped and reminded me of the comfort and goodness of Mama and gave me the hope that comfort and goodness would come again.

On the day Elias died, I looked in the rearview mirror and tried to remember my mother's face by looking at my own. I could not see her in me or remember her voice or her smell. She had been young, thirty-two, and I was almost old. My black hair, streaked with gray, curled with the humidity. My eyes were red. I wiped away the sweat from my forehead. I imagined Mama would have looked like me had she lived to be my age. She would never have let me go back to him. Mama would have shooed Old Lady Nassad out of my house. She would have acted differently than Papa the day he lost faith in me and disowned me.

I pressed my fingers to my temples. No. Mama would never have allowed me to marry a man like Elias in the first place. She would have saved me from that. She would have seen me for what I was, nineteen and naive and jumping at the first thing that came my way. But I had no way of knowing, and no business wondering what might have been. I stared at the river. I missed my mother. I looked at the river bridges and believed I could drive away.

I turned my car around and sat idling at the end of Papa's alley.

Across the street, mournful singing still flowed out of the AME church. Men and women in dark clothes spilled out of the white door-frame onto the steps. I knew the sounds of that church as well as I knew the Catholic Mass. After early Mass on Sundays, we'd arrive home and Papa would work in the store. On her way to church, Thea would see us on the front bench and know we were hiding from Papa as he cleaned the store, counted inventory, and restocked. We needed to stay out of his way, or else he would give us chores. Upstairs Aunt Elsa cooked Sunday dinner, and she didn't like us or anyone else underfoot. We distracted her, she said, with all the little noises we made, and if her things were not in their right place, she blamed us, grumbling that little imps hindered her every progress. Gus and I learned to stay away.

On those Sunday mornings, Thea walked by and she was happy to see us. She knew how starved we were for a mother's love. She'd walk up in a bright dress, a hat, and white gloves in spring or summer. Orlando tagged behind her and she would call to us, "Come on," as if we were slowing her down.

Gus and I sat in the pew with Thea and listened to the preaching and singing, so different from solemn Mass. Thea's church was loud and passionate. There were heaven and hell and rapture and damnation. One time, the preacher locked his eyes on me and ranted about the sins of worshipping Mary and praying to idols and saints. He was letting me know I did not belong in his congregation—a Catholic girl, a white girl. Thea put her arm around me. "Don't you mind that," she whispered in my ear. After the service, she went up to the preacher and had her say. She rejoined me and we watched Gus and Orlando run circles in the churchyard, where the hearse was parked now.

The back door of the white hearse was open, reflecting the glare of sunlight. The hats of the women clustered together like a bouquet of flowers. From the top of the steps, the women's eyes bore down on the pallbearers as they strained under the weight of the coffin.

A woman's eyes caught mine. Thea had been one of those church ladies. Lips moved across the street. One woman informed the others of my presence in Papa's alley. Their eyes turned toward me.

I thought of Orlando Washington and the lies Ivie intended to spread. I wanted to know if he was safe now, if he had abandoned his job or left town as Elias and the others wanted him to do, or if he was defiant and back at work. My heart pounded. I wanted to know what exactly had happened, if a cross had really been burned or what threats had been made. I wanted to know how many others were involved, if Elias had been one of a small handful of men or a body in a crowd. Surely, Mr. Washington would know to avoid my house. Those women could tell me.

I turned the engine off and stepped out of my car. My foot touched the road and I hurried across. My dress stuck to my damp back. They could see my dishevelment, my wet face and undone hair. I stepped on the gravel of their drive, and one woman shook her head, *No*, and then the next, and the next did the same. Ten women shaking their heads, *No*, shooing me off like a beggar. They looked at each other and then turned their backs to me. My presence did more harm than good. If the wrong person saw me, Mr. Washington's worries would grow.

My help had been no help to him. I was not a friend. I had grown up across the street from their church, but I was no more a part of their world than they were of mine. I was "Mrs. Anna" to them and I had no place walking across the street and up the hill to their church. I was just another woman from Riverton, only I had put Orlando Washington in real danger. I stood in the middle of the road for a moment more. One woman turned to see if I had retreated back across the road.

The night before, when Elias attacked me, he accused me of bedding Orlando Washington.

I answered, "What if I did?" Not because there was any truth to his accusation, but I wanted to stoke his anger.

Those women could not know what I had said or that my words caused Elias to cross town and do whatever he had done. Maybe they did not even know that Elias was dead. I told myself, *This will pass. Elias is dead now, and his deeds will pass with him.* I felt a weight in my stomach like a sinker on a fishing line. I wondered what Thea would think of me, trying to help her son and then being the fool that hurt him.

I got back in my car, and without looking for traffic, I pulled out across Water Street. A man in a delivery truck screeched his brakes to keep from hitting me. I looked back in my rearview and saw his angry hands waving.

Up ahead, the red lights at the railroad crossing flashed and the rails jolted down. The train horn bleated low and long. The three o'clock. It chugged past slower than usual. The driver behind me was ranting, beating his fist on his horn, still angry that I had pulled out in front of him and cut him off. In my rearview mirror, I saw the veins in his neck popping. Even the driver ahead turned to see what the commotion was about.

The long train snaked across the rail bridge and the caboose was not yet in sight. I bowed my head onto the steering wheel. The motion of the train vibrated through my hands, arms, and neck, and into my skull. My breath was sour and my stomach churned from hunger.

"Good family, good business," Elias used to say. I had to trust that Nelly would think of Marina's and Eli's futures and keep her mouth shut. She loved them. Marina was as much her baby as she was mine.

A clearing spread green and wild toward the river beneath the train tracks. The train rumbled over the bridge. Dark clouds hung low in the southern sky, and the river chopped and brooded. Lightning flashed far off. Ivie could have the store. Fine by me.

Yesterday morning, instead of baking, I drank my coffee at the table. After Elias and Marina intervened, I decided I would no longer help him in any way. I did not make his breakfast or start the baking for the store.

Elias came down and asked, "Why do you want to help the *abeed*? Is it because you grew up over there?" A flash of hate or jealousy crossed his face, and he leered at me. "You want to be with him?"

Calmly as I could, I repeated, "Thea helped me and she cared for my mother. I want to help her son."

His green eyes narrowed. "You know that Thea was paid help?" He poured himself a cup of coffee and slugged it down. "She never cared for you. She did not love you or your mother. It was her job."

"No," I said. "That's not true."

Elias looked in the icebox for his breakfast. He opened the cold oven door. "That's what they do. They are servants. They serve."

"How was it for our fathers?" I said. "They got off the boat with nothing, no trust, only a little English." Our fathers were shooed off farms and doorsteps until they proved themselves trustworthy to customers.

"Not the same." Elias must have realized then that I was not baking or lifting a finger to help him. He slammed the oven door and the crash of metal made me jump. He put his face near mine. His green eyes darted back and forth in their sockets. "Do you think I like all those people at the store? I'm their servant. Paid to serve and say, 'Yes, ma'am' and 'No, sir' and get them what the hell they want when they want it."

I did not cower. I returned his gaze. "Then you should understand and want to help him."

He ground his teeth, and his voice, eerie and calm, slithered out. "My mother always said you were a white nigger."

"Maybe she was right," I said. "Maybe that is what I am. Maybe that's what you are too."

He threw his coffee cup in the sink and it crashed. "Goddamn it." He stormed out and made a big show of taping the mailbox shut.

He left for work and I removed the tape. The house was hot, but I wanted to be busy. I missed the smell of bread rising and the loaves cooking in the oven, but I would not lift a finger for him anymore. I worked on baby clothes for Marina and thought of the child who would wear them.

I would wait to meet Mr. Washington and give him warning. I would tell him Elias did not want him to come, but that I wanted him to continue delivering our mail. The heat stood in the house like an army. I opened the front and back doors to get a cross breeze and had a fan blowing on me.

When his shoes scraped the limestone step, I looked up from my stitch. I stood. The lid of the mailbox creaked. I opened the screen door, and he greeted me, "Ma'am." He removed the mail from the box. The lid clapped shut. He handed me the envelopes.

I took them. "My husband wants you to stop delivering our mail."

"Yes, ma'am." He nodded and stepped backward as if he were bowing out after a dance. Standing on my front porch, he must have been wary, more so than I could imagine, but he held my gaze. I saw Thea's likeness in his face.

That day his uniform was heavy wool, too hot for summer. The earthy scent of his perspiration hit me. Maybe the white postman wanted to make him miserable and had switched out his locker, stolen the correct uniform and made him wear this winter one.

Had Verna, my neighbor, been watching that day and seen us standing there on my front porch, with the door open and us looking at one another, she would have been shocked at our closeness, at his proximity to the heart of my home.

"But I do want you to go on delivering to us," I said. The cicadas buzzed from the trees. Both of us were weighed down by the thick heat, him especially, in wool with the mailbag slung over his shoulder. I imagined his mailbag was similar to the peddler's box that had once burdened my father. "You can keep us on your route, but I thought I should warn you."

"I understand," he said. The creases at the corners of his eyes deepened. "I'll think about what to do."

I wiped my brow. "Okay." I felt defeated.

"I took this job for a purpose." He took another step backward. A bead of sweat rolled down his forehead into his eye. He blinked it away.

Mr. Washington's skin was darker than my brother's, who stayed in the sun day in and day out on the country roads, selling goods to farmers from his rolling store. My father, when he was young and peddling on foot, stayed dark from the sun too, until he opened his store and worked indoors. Mr. Washington was bold to walk up my front steps, the first Negro to ring the bell on our front door. I thought how it would have been for my father, a dark foreigner with an accent and poor clothes, a box strapped to his back, returning to a house after he'd been told to go on.

I felt a surge, probably the same as a soldier feels when gunfire starts popping around him, before he pulls his own trigger—half panic, half nerve. I could not let him walk away. He had won something, and I felt I had too.

"I want to help you," I said. It was true. But I also wanted to punish Elias for the years he'd punished me and had no feeling or understanding.

"My mama thought highly of you." It was the only acknowledgment he made of our connection.

"Come in," I said. "Do you want a glass of water?"

I held the screen wide and motioned for him to come inside.

"Thank you, ma'am." He looked over his shoulder. He knew better than to take another step. "I'll wait here."

"No." The sound of my voice vibrated in my ear, as deliberate with him as I had been when I told my father that I would marry Elias. "Come inside. I insist."

The delivery-truck driver blew his horn. In my rearview, I saw him stick his head out the window and yell, but his voice was muffled. I could not hear him because I had not opened the windows. The air inside the car sweltered. I rolled it down and the outside air rushed over my damp face. I could hear his shouting now. "Damn it, what in the hell's wrong with you?"

I looked forward again. The guards had been up long enough for the car ahead to cross the next intersection. The man in the delivery truck revved his engine and crossed the yellow line to pass me. I hit the gas and lurched over the tracks, but I had to slam the brakes to keep from hitting the truck as it cut in front of me. The bag of money jolted and spilled on the floorboard. With my foot on the brake, I leaned over to rake the money under the seat. When I sat up, sheriff lights reflected in the rearview. I pulled over near the old courthouse.

"Hey, gal," the deputy hollered. He scowled as he walked toward my window. "You going to kill somebody the way you're driving."

People on the sidewalk stared in my direction. Blood rushed to my cheeks. I tried to smooth my hair. I was not where I should be, at home mourning, waiting on my family. Even if they didn't know my husband was dead, they would soon know, and they would wonder why I was out when I should have been home. I peeked to see if the money was hidden or littering the floor. The canvas bag stuck out from the seat.

Up close, I knew the deputy from my lunch counter. His face softened when he recognized me. "Mrs. Nassad," he said.

"Yes, sir," I said. My father had taught me to be cautious of the law. He'd been bullied in his days of peddling, and he'd lived in Mounds long enough to know that when the sheriff came, it was not a good sign.

"You need to be more careful." He placed his golden forearm on top of the car and his face hung in the window.

"I'm sorry," I said. My eye caught a young man who looked like Marina's Michael, with blond hair and dressed in a suit, going into the courthouse.

The deputy leaned closer into the window. "I thought it was a drunk colored gal in front of me." He whispered as if he were letting me in on a joke.

"No, sir." I looked at him squarely.

"Because you're coming from Blacktown." The deputy cleared his throat. His face blushed. "That's why."

"I was checking on my father."

"Everything okay over there?" He tried to show concern.

"Yes," I said and wondered if he knew about Elias's visit to Mr. Washington.

"Let me call in." He tapped the roof of my car and sauntered back to his. He opened the door, sat, and talked on his radio.

I looked for Michael. He went to the courthouse every day, but I saw no sign of him. People gawked at me pulled over with the blue lights flashing behind my car. Surely some of them knew by now that Elias was dead.

The officer stood over me again. "Heard you been having some troubles." He would know I allowed Mr. Washington to deliver our mail. Everyone knew.

I started to refute him, but then I remembered my precarious position. Elias was dead. "This morning." I paused. "My husband passed away."

He stood tall and placed his hand on his belt. "But I just saw him last night."

My chest tightened. He had been party to the group at Mr. Washington's.

"No wonder you're driving crazy," he said.

"I need to get home," I said. "Now that I checked on my father."

"At least that ape won't bother you no more." He grunted and leaned on the roof of the car. His face came close to mine. "We took care of that for you."

I covered my eyes. The air felt trapped in my chest. I wanted to ask if Mr. Washington had been harmed, but I did not know how to ask without more trouble.

I wondered what Elias had said about Orlando Washington to this man and the others. Had he merely gone along with the town's anger or had he added his own, about me allowing Mr. Washington to deliver and inviting him inside for water? Surely he had not told them Mr. Washington was inside the house with me. If he had, Elias would have lost face and Mr. Washington would be in jail or worse.

"Next thing, they'll want to be sheriff," the officer said. "Or mayor."

I looked up at him. "Is that man all right?" As soon as the words were out, I feared they might put Orlando Washington into further harm. But I needed to know.

He looked at me sideways. "I guess that depends. He got fair warning."

"Fair warning?"

He smirked. "Didn't Elias tell you?"

I shook my head. "No," I said. He had told me nothing of what he'd done. "I was asleep when he came home." But that was a lie.

Wind from the south blew thick and hot. The storm was getting close.

"I guess he didn't want to worry you. He was a good man." He tapped the top of my car again. "Storm's coming," he said. "You get on home, where you belong, and settle down. My condolences to you."

I did not know what he thought of me or what Elias told him. I pulled away, left him standing in the middle of Water Street. I crossed over Main. I was not paying attention, and I had to slam the brakes to keep from hitting a woman and her child crossing in front of me.

The woman's white-gloved hand jerked her little girl's arm. The mother looked back, her face enraged and at odds with her perfectly coiffed hair and pink lipstick. "Slow down," she yelled.

I felt sick at my carelessness.

The little girl stared at me as if she could see through me. She reminded me of Marina, how watchful she was, waiting for something to happen, waiting to intervene. Marina was always so wise and could give me a look and break my heart. My chest tightened, because Papa wanted me gone, away from my home and my children, but I had worked as hard as Elias. All of it was as much mine as his.

I looked down into the floorboard. The money had spilled again. I pulled over on the side of the road and reached down to clean it up. I did a quick count, as I had all my years in the grocery business. It was more than twenty thousand. That was a lot of money. Enough to start over. All that money, but it was not all that was mine. My father and Elias were both rich men. A daughter and wife's inheritance should be more. I was owed more. I tucked the bills back in the canvas and then into my purse.

I knew where Elias kept money in the store. If I did not get it now, Ivie would have it. I would be damned if Ivie got it. I wanted to get what I was after and find my children. I needed to move on, like the people on the sidewalk—the lawyers heading to the courthouse, the mothers with strollers, the secretaries going home. That money was for Marina, for Eli, for my grandchild. It was for me too, so I could stay near them where I belonged.

The Store

I turned left onto Main Street and the old courthouse loomed in my rearview mirror. I crossed Maple and then Sycamore Street. One block away, the sign—a large porcelain disc, *Nassad's Lion Grocery* with the image of the lion in the center—hung over the sidewalk. The familiar sight of it aroused a feeling of dread, as if Elias himself stood in the middle of the road. I turned left on Oak and into our lot. I passed the painted brick wall promising *Coca-Cola, Ice Cold and Refreshing*.

I pulled around back to the alley, past the bars of the metal cage where Elias had kept the lion, years before we married. Leona the lion. Ivie had traded with the Gypsy circus, food for the cub. When Elias saw it, he threatened to drown it in the river, but Ivie guarded the cub, and in a short time Elias began to value the curiosity she stirred in his customers. She was to become his best draw ever. He had posters made: *Come to Nassad's Lion Grocery and see Leona the Lion*. He plastered them all over town. Gus and I, ages three and eight, hand in hand, watched Elias weld the cage. We had witnessed the cub ride in the cab of his delivery truck. "Crazy," my father had said under his breath as they drove by. Then she got too big and Elias locked her inside that cage. She moaned and roared from that day forward, and her groaning and grumbling carried for five miles. The noise became as familiar as the train horn blaring.

I turned the engine off. My mouth was dry, and I smelled musty and damp. I hoped no one noticed me. If someone saw me here, asked me why I was at the store, I'd tell them I was gathering food for the wake. I locked the money and my purse in the trunk of the car.

A chill ran over me as the hot wind hit my sweat-soaked dress. The storm was close. Over half my life had been spent in this store. It was where I belonged, bringing the bread, cleaning the shelves, working behind the counter. Here, I smiled at customers and accepted their compliments, and Elias would touch my shoulder or nod in a proud way. It was an act, but I played along because I liked the feeling that people wanted something I had made, and the feeling made me smile. In her teenage years, Marina held it against me, called me two-faced. She said I was never so friendly at home, that I had one face for the store and a sour face for home. She said, "Maybe if you smiled at Daddy like you do at the store, he'd be happy to see you."

Notes were lodged in the crevice of the storeroom door. Four crates of milk, spoiled from heat by then, blocked my way. I pushed them out of my path. I unlocked the bolt and the notes cascaded to the ground. One from the clerk, one from the bread man, one from the milkman . . . *Nobody here,* they wrote. *I waited. Where are you?*

"He's dead, of course," I answered aloud. "That's the only reason he would not be here." I pushed open the large wooden door on its metal track. It rumbled and the sky thundered.

The dark stockroom smelled of concrete and earth, of potatoes and onions, of overly ripe cantaloupe in damp cardboard. There was money hidden in that back room. I closed the track door and locked it from inside.

A shot of sunlight beamed through a high window on the far wall and streaked across the concrete floor. Then, dark clouds covered the sun and the sky opened up. The rain rushed down in sheets and pounded the flat roof. The storm had arrived.

Up high, on the tallest shelf and in the farthest corner, Elias kept money in oatmeal tins. He hoarded cash, the same as my father. I rolled the ladder along the wall of shelves and climbed up. I dug past the boxes and brought down two at a time. I found six tins.

Behind two loose concrete blocks in his office were cigar boxes with cash. I pulled out nine. There was the safe. I turned the code, the children's birth months and days, but it would not open. I tried again. My hands shook. In my absence the last two days, he had changed the combination.

There was also the register. I pushed through the swinging door into the store proper. The gray rain pounded the street outside and the roof above. The humming noise of the drink coolers greeted me. My hand reached to switch on the dozen milk-glass pendants hanging from the tin ceiling. I fingered the switch, but decided no, turning on the lights would draw attention to my presence.

The heels of my shoes echoed in the empty room as I crossed the floor to pull the shades down over the door and windows. The heavy rain cast a gloom through the plate-glass windows. Smudges covered the glass where the morning and lunch customers pressed their faces to see in. Elias would have cleaned the marks right away. Appearances meant everything, and he'd go behind people, straightening products on shelves and cleaning smudges. I pulled the shades and the place went dark like it was twilight.

The large room smelled of him, or as he had always smelled—a mixture of cigarettes, cloves, and coffee, of blood from the meat counter, the excess juices wiped on a rag looped to his apron, the sour odors of olives and pickles kept in glass jars on the back counter. We used vinegar to clean the glass cases and to mop the floors at the end of each day. The musty smell of money was there too.

I had worked here beside him. An entire section of counter devoted to my pies, baked goods, and breads, a baker's case full of my labor. The case was empty—he would have sold the day-olds and then thrown the rest out. I wondered how, yesterday, he had explained my absence, how he had answered the customers asking for me and why there was no fresh bread. People must have suspected a rift between us—they'd heard Elias say we wouldn't help the colored postman, but I had allowed him to deliver our mail.

Behind my counter on the brick wall, like a banner, the words regarding me were painted: *Mrs. Anna's Delicious Fruit Pies, Breads, and Savory Treats*. A surprise when we returned from our trip to the beach. An idea that Nelly had conjured, something to keep me busy until the children arrived, and it had. She liked my baking because she saw profit in it. The one sweet thing—my cooking, my baking, the attention I got. I could get lost in the rhythms, the silky mess of the flour, the feel of the dough on my hands in my kitchen, and I answered to no one while I baked.

Marina did not like baking, but she would watch me work. She salivated and begged as the bread cooled, but I held out to keep her attention. I told her I wanted to be sure I had enough to fill the counter, even though I knew there was plenty. She helped me carry the boxes of bread to the car and rode with me as the car filled with the smell of yeast and warm bread. We carried it in—the mountain bread, the loaves, and often pies or savories—and the end reward would be mine, watching her eagerly choose a treat and thank me for what I had made. Having her close gave me a pleasure I felt no other time. I thought, I had done that, had made that with my hands and made my daughter proud.

Those first years, the town women came in and asked, "Aren't you Mr. Khoury's daughter?" Puzzled that I was out of place, as if I were a prop in their world, not an actual, unfixed human, who lived and felt and dreamed as they did. They would whisper to each other and their eyes would fall on me.

"Yes, ma'am," I would say. Still surprised to be in Elias's store, so bright and ordered, so full of white faces, unlike my father's place. I knew them all, and learned quickly their preferences, if they had bought carpets from Papa or if their husbands were important or if their children had attended school with me. I knew the gossip that surrounded them and where they lived, the names of their maids. They knew nothing about me except I had come from one side of town to the other. That kind of crossing was unheard of and made me a lesser person in their eyes. Not black, but not wholly white—an Arab, a Catholic, like a coffee stain on a white tablecloth. "Elias and I married," I answered.

"Of course you did." They smiled as they put it all together. "Bless your heart," they said, unsure, because I was Khoury's daughter, the girl whose mother had died, the one who lived with her father and brother above the colored store across the tracks, the dark girl who had gone to school with their daughters or sisters. "Welcome," they said, as if I were standing on the thresholds of their homes and not in my husband's store. And sometimes they said, as an afterthought, "I bought rugs from your daddy."

"Thank you," I would say. Gratitude, so important to my father, to Elias, to our business. *Be deferential to the customer,* Elias would say, but I knew he wanted me to be deferential in all matters. Their maids in white uniforms moved in and out of aisles. White shadows of the women they were—not as I had known them in my father's store in their own clothes, moving and talking with ease, their children, or a man, or both, buzzing around them, doing as they said.

"Now, did you bake all this yourself?" the white ladies would ask.

"Yes." I could read their faces, uncertain that I was clean enough to cook for them.

"My goodness," they would say. "That's a lot of work. I'll have to try something." Their lips puckered as they studied the mountain bread, the tabbouleh or hummus. They'd choose a pie or half a dozen rolls, something familiar, because they were not sure of me. But they came back for more or sent their maids. Their husbands, less restrained, asked for the stuffed grape leaves or the mountain bread rolled round Elias's deli meats.

The women smiled to my face, but I heard what they said to each other behind my back. "He works her like a nigra. She doesn't know any better, growing up over there." They scared their children with warnings: "If you don't mind me, Mrs. Anna will get you." My looks frightened them. My olive skin, my thick eyebrows, and my large, curved nose. To those children and their parents, I resembled a Halloween witch. The warnings heeled them to their mothers like obedient dogs, and they dared only to peek round their mothers' skirts. Those frightened looks would send me to the bathroom to powder my nose and escape their gaze. Sometimes, instead of seeing what they saw, by some trick of light, I saw my mother, and I felt whole again.

"It's good for business if you look like something," Elias said. "Impressions go a long way." So I wore nice dresses from the best dress shop. The same dress shop the ladies frequented. I wore gifts of pearls and gold brooches he gave me. His gifts flattered me for a few years until I understood the nature of our marriage and the reasons for the gifts. They were not gifts to show his love. They were investments in my appearance and a show of our status. The gifts were an attempt to distract me from the fact that he did not love me and he never would.

We had money and things, when most people had nothing. With our store on Main Street, we had a good position in Riverton, and Elias walked into places like he belonged, like no questions could be asked. He was the secretary in the Knights of Columbus and was a member in the Rotary Club. The way he carried himself, no one would have known he felt inferior. He knew we'd never be invited to the country club, but if we worked hard enough, if people saw us in a good light, maybe Eli and Marina would.

The words on the wall lurked over me—*Mrs. Anna's Delicious Fruit Pies, Breads, and Savory Treats*—and I could hear Elias's voice in my head. *You're late*, or *You're short on goods today*, or *The spinach pie didn't go over*, or *Where's mine?* Always, his voice filled this place. He yelled orders to one of the boys working in the back or he crooned sweetly to a customer.

I remembered the times he was not here—when he'd gone to Mobile to see Zada, the woman that my father had arranged for Gus to marry. When Gus did not marry her, Elias gave her his sympathies. A few months passed, my belly grew, and unbeknownst to me, Elias and Zada were making their own arrangement through an exchange of letters. They planned a rendezvous and the first time he went to her, I was six months along with Marina. He told me he was going on a fishing trip to Mobile, but I suspected that he was going to see her. He denied it. I asked to go along, but he said I needed to stay put for the baby's sake and he needed me to watch over the store. Hours after he left, I found the letters tucked in a box in his closet. I sat on the floor, the baby kicked inside me, and I cried reading her words to him. I hoped he would not submit, that he would return and our marriage would be intact, that he was only fighting a natural curiosity, but when he returned so happy and jubilant, I knew the truth.

On his subsequent trips, I could have taken his absence as another humiliation, but I tried not to care that he was gone. I had no power to change the fact that he loved another woman. I tried to relax and be happy in my own skin. I looked for the silver lining in his absence—I was my own boss and free of him for a week. I told people he was fishing, and that was partly true—he brought back pictures of himself holding up fish.

Nelly suspected he was up to something with his trips. "What does it mean when a man leaves his wife?" she asked pitilessly. "It reflects badly on you, that's what." She worried what would happen if he ran away like Ivie. What would happen to her and the business and the shame it would bring. But even with all her theatrics, I persuaded myself I did not care that he was gone. At least my home and the store were my domains, if only for a few days.

The first time Zada had come to meet my brother, she stepped off the train and mesmerized us—Gus, Elias, and me. Besides English she spoke Arabic and French, was just back from a trip to Beirut, and so beautiful, her smooth sable hair and straight nose. Unknown to my father or me, my brother had no intention to marry Zada, because as Gus later said, Zada reminded him of me and he felt brotherly toward her. Besides that, he was already in love with Lila. This did not stop me or Elias from falling for Zada.

Her voice carried the same cadence as my mother's when she spoke of Beirut: "Everyone has a fruit tree. The olives, the wine, the cafés— and the people are from every religion: Jews and Muslims, Druze, Catholics and Protestants." She'd been visiting her grandparents and cousins. When she spoke of the sea and the air and the land my parents came from, I felt happy. At last, here was proof that I was not an oddity, that I had people and that the world was full and greater than Riverton. I thought, *When Zada marries my brother, we will have children who will be cousins, we will have each other, and life will be better.*

I took her to bridge at church, to Mass, to the dress shop and the soda fountain. We went to the movies and walked all over town so that people would see me and know I was not alone. Zada was like my brother, friendly and outgoing, and she could talk to anyone. She told me that although I was not a stylish person, there was something interesting about me, and I was not insulted. "Your eyes, especially," Zada said. "They are so odd—a mixture of gray and brown and green, like the bark of an olive tree." She plucked my eyebrows and rouged my cheeks. She made me try on every dress in the dress shop. "You must always belt your waist to show off how small it is," she said. The shopgirls all nodded and agreed. She took me to the hairdresser and, without my permission, said, "Cut it to the nape of her neck and let the curls fall along her jawline to the tip of her chin." I liked being her art project.

As a child, the other children had called Gus and me *dirty Arabs*, but that would no longer matter if I had someone like her at my side. She was more worldly than any other woman in Riverton. She had just returned from a tour of Lebanon from Tyre to Beirut and she had seen the ancient ruins of the Phoenicians. She showed me her travel album and promised I would love it there. She seemed to be thinking of our future together.

For fun one day, Zada and I baked using my mother's brick oven. My father rose early to build the fire, so the coals would turn to ash at the right time. He was happy to look at her and listen to travel stories. He nodded as Zada spoke of the mountain bread in Lebanon, how the women patted out rounds of dough in their hands and placed them for only a minute, maybe two, on a hot metal dome until they blistered. Papa liked having her there and I was happy to be connected to that world, his and my mother's, happy to take Zada's instructions, how she'd seen her mother and aunts make the bread, how she'd seen the women in Lebanon do it. She must have reminded him of Mama, and for that, I was thankful.

We took the breads to Elias's store. She stood behind the counter next to me, teaching me things my mother would have taught me, how the crisp mountain bread was different from the fluffier *laffa*, how to strain the *labneh*, and what were the best proportions of sumac, thyme, and sesame in *za'atar*. She told me how her mother cooked down grapes to make *dibs* to put on bread or ice cream, all that Aunt Elsa had not the time or the need to teach me. Aunt Elsa, who, above all things, had been practical and American with no use for passing on her knowledge of the old country.

Zada brought a gift of Arabic coffee and ground cardamom. From my china cabinet she got the *rakweh*, the Arabic coffeepot that had belonged to my mother, with its long wooden handle and flat, rimmed spout. She reached for the demitasse cups. The set had been my mother's, put away after she died because Papa drank only the instant coffee he sold in his store.

"The coffee set," Zada said, "is a symbol of hospitality." She paused to make her point. "Hospitality is the most important thing for the Lebanese. Generosity and hospitality. Offer coffee to the eldest first, men before women. *Helweh* is sweet. *Murrah* is bitter. *Mazbootah* is in the middle. You drink one cup and that's all. More is gluttony." She mixed the sugar and the cardamom and added scoop after scoop of very finely ground Arabic coffee into the pot of water. "Today, we will make it sweet—*helweh*. The sweeter the occasion, the sweeter the coffee. Now, if it were a funeral, we would make it *murrah*."

The water boiled. I watched her carefully.

"Arabic coffee is strong," she said. The mixture foamed to the top of the pot. She cut the heat and raised the pot by its long handle. The foam reduced. "See what I did?" she asked, and then let the coffee boil up twice more. On the third boil, she ran to the sink and added a few drops of cold water. "Pour it now before it completely settles," she said. "After we drink it, I will read your fortune at the bottom of your cup." The coffee was strong for my taste, but I made it for her every morning and evening of her visit.

On the night before she and Gus were to sit with the priest and discuss their marriage, I filled the table for Zada and Gus and Elias. Elias had driven two counties over to buy gin, and he tried to make cocktails with mint and lime. I drank a sip and felt sick. I ran to the bathroom to vomit, and Zada checked on me. She touched my hair and blotted the sweat from my temples. In the kitchen she made me a concoction of orange-blossom water and sugar to ease my stomach, and while I sipped it, I counted my days and knew I was pregnant. Everyone ate and drank. Elias smiled and praised my efforts. I picked at my food, afraid of being sick again. But I was happy and burning with my secret knowledge. I was charmed to watch them, Gus, Elias, Zada, the four of us a family. Gus seemed in fine spirits, not once revealing that he would elope with Lila the next day.

Zada and I sat up late on the porch despite the autumn chill in the air. She told me, "When you come with me to the old country, you will see the mountains from the sea and the sea from the mountains. You will know your mother then. You will know why she wanted to be close to the water." She looked off into the dark night. "Every summer we will go to Mobile. We will bring our children and stay with my family. We will watch the sea roll in and not lift a finger to work." In her presence I felt as if I belonged on earth.

The next afternoon I made another feast for the evening. It was to be her last night with us before the marriage and I wanted to celebrate, but then Zada arrived alone and distraught. Gus had not shown at the rectory to meet with the priest. He was nowhere to be found, and then the phone rang. Gus was on the other end. He called to say he had eloped with Lila. His giddiness the night before had been the mask of his love for Lila. Elias closed the store early, and we sat—Zada, Elias, and I—around the table and watched the food go cold. Zada and Elias drank gin from the bottle, but I could not.

When the drink took hold, Zada cried. Elias stood and opened his arms. She went to him and cried on his shoulder. How beautiful they looked together. They took the bottle to the front porch, and I did the dishes. The windows were open. She sobbed, but he had soft words for her. "You are young and beautiful. You will find better." I sat on the couch and listened. I did not want her to go. I felt the same regret that I heard in his words, but his voice oozed with comfort, and then charm. I saw his hand reach across and touch her shoulder, and then she scooted close to him and rested her dark, beautiful head on his shoulder. He stroked her hair with his long fingers and my stomach rolled.

I awoke the next morning on the couch. Elias had left me there. I imagined he and Zada stood over my sleeping body. They would have been drunk and laughing at me as they passed. The next morning, she asked me to take her to the train station.

But I could not drive. I heaved all morning. I called Elias and he left the store without complaint. I heard them speaking in bits of Arabic. His voice was gentle, sad. He left me, alone and sick in the bathroom, without a word.

That night, after Zada left, I waited eagerly for Elias to come home. He had been a different man, happier in her presence, and I thought he might give me some comfort. I cooked our meal and lit candles on the table. I sat in the glow of my home and knew it was up to me to make it happy now that she was gone. I would tell him that I was expecting our first child. I waited for him until the candles were puddles of wax.

I wrapped his dinner in foil and left it in the warm stove. He came in and fished around the kitchen. A chair dragged across the floor. He kicked off his shoes. Not long after, he was standing in my doorway. He was drunk.

He undressed. The hall light glowed behind him. He climbed on top of me.

"You stink," I said.

He touched my hair. At first gentle. Then he covered my face with his hand.

"What are you doing?" I asked.

He turned my face away from his. He raised my gown.

"Stop," I said.

He whispered in my ear, "I wish you were like her."

I had wished the same.

"If you could be like Zada." He moved on top of me. "Beautiful Zada."

I flinched. My eyes hot with tears.

"I will have a child," I said, in the hopes he would have some feeling and stop the cruel words.

"No, you can't," he said. "I told her I would leave you and go to her."

"I will have a baby," I said.

"I begged her to run away with me. But she won't because of you."

"Please," I said. "Don't be cruel."

He covered my mouth with his hand. "Shut up. You are ugly and skinny, and when I touch you, I close my eyes and think of her." Only, he glared at me when he said it.

My whole being was hot with sorrow.

He finished and then collapsed beside me. He moaned and I saw tears on his cheeks. His arm lay across my swollen, sore breasts. The weight of his arm reminded me who I was—an immigrant's daughter from the store across the tracks. I should be grateful to Elias for what I had. A marriage. A position in town in a good house away from my father's store. I was to have a child and become a mother, and that was what I was supposed to do. I should be full. I should not expect more, not love, not happiness, but I wanted his love.

And then, his arms softened and his face was wet. He held me. We cried together. He was warm and there was some comfort in that. We had slept in the same bed on vacation, but this was the only night of our marriage that he stayed in my bed in our home. Every fiber of me was grateful to have him there. I never wanted him to leave that place beside me.

When I awoke, he was gone. I knew he did not love me. He never would. Instead of facing him and seeing the look in his eyes that I was not Zada, I thought I would leave. I could give him that. It was not too late for me either. I could board the train like Zada, and Elias could go to her. My mother and her sisters had crossed the ocean. My father too. I could go to New York, where my father had started, or New Orleans like my mother, or to Gulf Shores, where Elias and I had once gone. I thought life would be better without him, even with a child in tow. I imagined he would not look for me. But, like a dutiful daughter and wife, I dressed and started the baking for the day. I delivered it to the store before lunch. He did not glance at me when I filled my counter. He thought if he ignored my presence, I would not exist.

Instead of going home, I walked to the train station and stared at the board. I read the list of places I could go. I thought of the money I would need, of the jewelry I could sell, but then I thought of Papa and Gus and never seeing them again. I thought of starting over in an apartment or an empty house and giving birth all alone, and the nausea swept through me, and I ran to the side of the platform.

Now Elias did not exist. He was dead and gone, and I had survived him. I stood in his store. I felt a moment of victory, but then I remembered the choice before me—to move on like a Gypsy or stay put and suffer the punishment his family wanted for me.

I crossed the room to the bread counter. My shoes clapped against the wooden floors. The rain continued to pound the roof. I looked out over the five long, neat aisles of groceries with their bright labels, the red cans of tomatoes, the white sacks of flour and sugar, Tony the Tiger staring back at me from the boxes of Frosted Flakes. The tables of produce—the yellow lemons, the white and green melons, the apples and oranges—were stacked in careful rows. I could live without this place and the work, but I could not live without my daughter. She and my son were my home. I got to the business I came for.

I opened the register. There was enough money to fill a small paper bag. Beneath every dollar was another dollar and another and another. I rummaged through the drawers behind the candy counter, through the boxes of papers and bills, the pocket watches, the rings, the things factory and dock workers left behind to hold their credit. I would leave that for Ivie.

All in all, six tins, nine cigar boxes, and a small paper bag. I stacked the money down in three grocery bags. I unlocked the back door and, with my arms full, opened the trunk of the car and made two trips. The rain pounded my hair flat, my dress flatter. I ran back inside, rolled the door shut. Water dripped from me onto the concrete floor.

The dark storeroom felt like a grave swallowing me up. I should have left then, but that place held my blood and sweat, and I was greedy to get what was mine. I could not stop pushing boxes to the side and looking beneath the shelves. I thought I should have whatever was hidden away. I found three Folgers jars filled with change. I held them against my chest with one arm and scavenged through with the other. My chest grew tight at the thought of Marina and Eli and what they would think if they found me gathering up money. If Ivie and Nelly knew, they would call me a thief. They'd charge me, and in the paper the headline would read, *Store Owner Robbing Her Own Store.*

A tree branch scraped the high window. The wind was picking up.

I turned to go, and in the doorframe stood Ivie. Behind him the rain beat down. Gray light outlined his barrel chest. A toolbox hung from his hand.

"Here I am to change the locks and keep you out," Ivie said. His voice was raspy from years of heavy drinking.

"This is my store." I shivered, soaked to the bone.

"Not anymore." He placed the toolbox at his feet.

"You can't just take my husband's property."

"You're a drowned rat looking for a lifeboat," he said. "Get out." He took a step toward me. His clothes hung wet and disheveled on his large frame.

"I came to get food for the wake." I hugged the jars against my chest.

"Like hell you did." Another step toward me and I could see his face in the dim light. He smirked.

"This is my property." My voice sounded thin. I shuffled around him.

Again he said, "Not anymore." The smell of alcohol seeped from his pores. He had always been the whipping boy. First their father beat him for his careless mistakes, and later Elias would not give him a chance unless Nelly pestered.

"Go or I'll call the sheriff," I said.

He laughed. "You do that." He touched my chin in a gentle way that unnerved me. His hands were rough like sandpaper.

I tried to get around him, but he was tall and broad. He hovered above me in whatever direction I moved, as if we were dancing without touching. Buttons were missing from his worn work shirt.

"I've waited a long time to have this chance," he said. Did he mean me or the store or both?

I looked him in the eye. "What's here is mine," I said.

He gripped my arm in the same place Elias had bruised me the day before. "I know your daddy told you it ain't yours, or you wouldn't be here trying to get what you can." He grabbed a jar of the coins and threw it on the floor. The glass shattered and the coins rolled and clanged against the wet concrete.

"Let go of me!" I yelled, hoping someone might hear, and then I regretted calling out. If someone witnessed this and gossiped, Marina's opinion would turn against me.

His grip tightened on my arm. "I'll do what I want."

I knew how he looked at me. I had ignored his inappropriate words in the past. I had overlooked a brush of his hand on my skirt. I had felt sorry for Ivie and said nothing. One word to Elias and Elias would have laid him out, but Elias wasn't here to protect me from his brother. "You have no right here." My voice was hard. "I'll call the sheriff."

His breath was hot and stale. "I'll call the sheriff myself." He grabbed another jar and then the last and threw them against the wall.

My arms were suddenly empty and I flinched as the glass shattered and the coins rolled across the floor.

He stared down at me. His eyes were wild like when he came back from the war and people had called him "Crazy Ivie." For a year he walked the streets late at night, despite Nelly's protests and the sheriff picking him up, keeping him overnight, and calling Elias to come get him early in the morning. The doctors said he was in a fugue, not knowing his name, standing outside houses staring like he didn't know where he was or who he was, or what was appropriate. He didn't move, no matter if dogs nipped at him, no matter if people called out, "Go on home, Ivie." He was stuck there, all of him frozen, except those wild eyes.

"I believe you're shook up." He pulled me close to him.

"Let me go." I struggled against his grip.

"We took care of that nigger." His mocking tone, cool and quiet, sent a shiver down my neck. "That postman."

"You said you talked to him." I knew what my father had said, what the deputy said, but I wanted to hear Ivie's version.

His skin was sallow. His features, though thicker, took on his brother's likeness.

"We took care of him." He boasted big and loud. "Walked him through the woods, took in the scenery, showed him how a rope felt around his neck." The smell of alcohol, sweet and rank, came from his breath.

"Who is 'we'?" I needed to know my enemies.

"Just some friends."

"You put your hands on him?" Part of me believed he was exaggerating, trying to make himself look big. The other part of me knew he was capable.

"Sheriff didn't seem to think it was a problem." Ivie smirked, revealing his stained teeth.

"Why'd you take Elias and get him involved with a mob?" I asked.

"Why'd you kill him?" He dropped the smirk and widened his eyes.

"You are crazy," I said.

"Yes, I am." He tightened his grip on my arms.

I had a sick feeling to think of what they'd done and what Ivie would do to me given the chance. I needed to know if Orlando Washington was safe. The danger was real for him and for me too. I did not have only Nelly to worry about. She would protect Marina, but Ivie had no compulsion to save face or help my children. He'd burn me down and the rest of us too, even if he had to burn with us.

He put his lips close to my ear and whispered, "How are we supposed to protect our women with some spook walking up, coming inside?"

"You're what I need protection from." I tried to push him off, but he pulled me close against his chest. I felt sick that I had put Mr. Washington in harm's way, sick that Ivie had me in his grip. I had asked Orlando Washington into my house. I had insisted. I had thought my connection to his mother mattered more than his color and mine, that I could have some influence on helping him and his cause.

"I see you're upset." Ivie held me as if we were dancing.

"Who else?" I tried to turn away from the stench of his clothes and his breath.

"Who else what?" he asked.

"You, Elias, the sheriff. Who else?" If I could find out, I could know better my situation and Mr. Washington's.

His jaw clamped tight like a steel trap. He spoke through his teeth. "All you need to worry over is where you're going day after tomorrow."

The peaceful feeling I had standing over Elias had long since disappeared, and in its place, the familiar tug in my chest, as if Elias had not died at all.

Ivie swayed with me in his arms. He whispered, "Strange, how Elias died on the same night he walked in on you two, the same night he went to tell that coon to stay off his porch and out of his house."

"Strange things happen," I said.

"Elias didn't understand you." He gently took my head in his hands. His face hovered over me and in a quiet voice he said, "He didn't understand me either. I worked for that bastard as long as I could. Now it's my turn."

"Your mother gave you land. Money." I pushed against his chest. "You had every chance he did. You fouled it up."

He twisted my hair. "You can go to hell." His voice was low, intense.

"I'm not leaving because you tell me to," I said.

"I could hang you in a tree tonight." His hot breath fell on my face. His thick hair fell across his forehead.

"You don't have the nerve," I said.

"You don't belong here no more." He shoved me toward the door.

My shoes slid on the coins and the wet concrete, and I fell. The heel of my hand caught broken glass. Shards covered my stockings.

"You will get your comeuppance. Marina too."

Warm blood flowed out of my hand. I swallowed to keep from yelling in pain.

"I'm tired of being the grunt." Glass crunched under his boots. He stood over me where I'd landed.

"You'll run this place into the ground." I pulled myself up, careful not to cut myself again.

"You're not as smart as you think you are," he hissed. He tried to grab me, but I slipped from his reach.

When Elias beat me, I would submit until it passed, because if I did not, the beating would go on and on. If I gave in, the sooner I could go back to what was good, watching the children, the garden, my work. That was my life, surviving the bad so I could relish the good. But this was not Elias and I had nothing to lose.

I scratched at his face and left a trail of blood, mine or his, I did not know. I scrambled past him to the open door.

"Hellcat!" he screamed as he touched his cheek, stunned at the blood.

I rushed through the rain to the safety of my car and locked the doors.

"Stay out," he hollered. His voice penetrated the pounding rain. "Don't come back."

He hit the trunk of my car with his fist. He was still yelling as I drove down the alley to the street. The glass trapped in my stockings scratched at my skin. The wipers screeched against the windshield. I stopped when I was safely away from the store and picked the glass from my stockings. I dropped the shards out the window in the pouring rain.

I searched my glove box for something to stop the bleeding at the base of my palm. I found a blue silk scarf Marina had given me. When she was twelve, she picked it out herself and paid her own money. She had given it to me for my birthday and I treasured it. I wound it tight around the gash. Whiskers of wine-red blood spread across the silk and I knew it was ruined.

Maple Street

The rain stopped as quick as it started. Steam rose from the pavement as I headed east on Oak and turned down Church Street. I wanted to find Marina. Ivie had rattled my nerves, and I wanted my daughter. I drove past the Episcopal church and the Methodist and slowed in front of St. Patrick's. No one moved about the rectory or on the lawn. All was quiet. Marina's car was nowhere to be seen.

I turned on Maple Street, Marina's street. The sky had a green-and-purple cast like a bruise waiting to erupt. The storms were not over. The wind blew the top branches of the oak trees. I wanted to find her and tell her what her father had done and how he and Ivie had gone after Mr. Washington. She would argue that the postman overstepped his boundaries, and I'd admit to her that I should not have let him in. I'd let her rail at me over that, but then I'd show her the bruises her father had given me and I'd tell her how he tried to press the life out of me.

The wind blew into the car, but the air was thick with heat and I could not cool off. My hand bled through the scarf. On my dress was a slick of blood, black like the wet pavement outside.

On Maple Street, the canopy of trees trapped the smells of rain and cut grass. Marina's car was not in sight. I parked and took the stone path to her porch. Michael's family came from old money, and only the most magnificent Victorian would do for him and Marina. It was a beautiful house, grand in scale, with stained glass and woodwork that rivaled any church in town.

I knocked on the door and called her name. No one answered. Lights glowed through the leaded glass. I crossed the porch and looked in the turret windows. The large windowpanes rippled with light, and white roses floated in a crystal bowl on a mahogany table. Inside the large curved windows, the cradle I had used for her and Eli waited for her child. Soon, Marina would sit with her newborn and rock the cradle with her well-heeled foot. She could forget the sadness of her father and me, and no worries, no heat, no dirt or death would reach her then. I wanted her to sit with the baby and be happy, and if Marina had happiness, I could be happy too.

I walked around to the back of the house and knocked on the kitchen door. "Marina," I called out.

"Hello, there," a voice chimed from the yard next door. Over the hedge, I saw the pert nose of Peggy Simms. We had been classmates and I had warned Marina not to trust her. She had been an unkind child, one who treated me as if I were dirty and low. I hid my hand and the bloody scarf behind my back.

"Oh, it's you," Peggy said. Her blue eyes studied me. "I thought it was Marina." Her pink nails flashed in the grim light. "Quite a storm we had there."

Her maid, Mabel, swept sticks and leaves from the back steps. The three of us were the same age. I had slipped pennies beneath Papa's side door to Mabel so she could buy candy from his shelves. But in Elias's store, she simply nodded at me with her eyes cast down.

Peggy squinted to get a better look at me. My bloody hand was hidden behind my back, but she could see the ripped stockings and the dust covering my wet dress. Mabel did not look up but kept on sweeping the brick steps. I wanted away from Peggy's scouring gaze. My eyes felt hollow and dark from no sleep. I wanted to brush my hair, wash my face, and change out of the damp, bloodied dress.

"Have you seen Marina?" I asked.

"I saw her this morning. She was a mess, and oh, poor thing, the tears. I thought she might be in labor." She touched her hair with her pink talons. "She was worried about you. She kept saying, 'My mother needs me.' She was so distraught. Bless her heart." Peggy meant no such thing. She was gathering gossip.

I stepped away to end the conversation, but she kept on.

"She's been fretting over your dealings with that mailman." Her voice dripped with sweetness. "I told her to be patient, that you must have some history with him. You know his people." Peggy glanced sideways at Mabel, who pretended not to hear.

People had said this behind my back, but Peggy was bold to say it to my face. Worse, she had said it to Marina. I understood that Peggy had intended to offend Marina—*Your mother grew up in Mounds. Your family is fresh off a boat. Stay in your place.* Marina hated people looking down on her, and my past brought her shame.

I walked toward the iron gate to get away from her.

Peggy called after me, "You should stay close to your girl now."

Her tone raked my skin, and I wondered if her husband had been with Elias and Ivie the night before.

I waited for Marina on her grand front porch. She wanted prestige from this house. She was ambitious like Elias, wanting people to know what she had and what she was worth. She wanted to belong here, but I felt out of place on her rich street.

When they bought the house, Marina had carried on about paint colors, if she should use gold or brass for the ormolu or which blue—turquoise or teal—for the lapped siding. I could not help her with the correct colors, but I pulled the best rugs from Papa's store. I worked in her garden and wrestled the evergreen clematis vine on the veranda and brought her roses back to life. She snipped, "You don't have to do this. We have a man."

The hot wind blew the clematis leaves, and the vine shimmied with light. Marina appeared on the bottom step. She huffed and I hurried to her. She had not changed her clothes. Michael's shirt blossomed with a wealth of life under it. Her skin was slick with perspiration. She gripped the rail to pull herself up. I reached with my good hand to guide her.

"Oh, Mother," she said, matter-of-fact. She waddled to the door, not paying me any attention, and stuck the key in the hole. "What are you doing here?"

"I wanted to see you."

She turned the brass key and the lock clicked. "I tried calling you, but you weren't at home."

"Grandpapa called me to come over," I said.

"Is he all right?" Her groomed eyebrows knit together. She fumbled getting the key out of the lock. "Don't tell me he's sick."

"He's fine." A lie, considering how worried he was. "He wanted to talk to me."

"We needed a suit for Daddy. Aunt Louise answered and said you were gone, so she and Grandmother brought one to the funeral home." She was out of breath as she stepped inside. "I went to the men's store and got a new shirt and tie." She looked at herself in the mirror by her front door. "Would you look at me? I've been all over town like this."

I knew that was hard for Marina to do. She took great stock in how she looked, wishing she was blonde and blue-eyed, often saying sarcastically, "I'm an exotic beauty," but knowing full well people liked to look at her for that very reason.

I stood on the threshold and the cool air of the house flooded over my skin.

"Well, come in." She turned her keen eyes on me.

I stepped inside and could smell myself, sour from the rain and the sweat on the wet gabardine.

"Who has seen you like that?" The circles under her eyes were dark, like my own.

"Your neighbor Peggy." I was a crumpled mess—no makeup, my hair in knots, the dress wet and dark with blood. Traces of dust remained where I had hit the storeroom floor. There was a large run in my stockings and little pricks of blood along my leg. I tried to smooth the skirt of my dress and run the fingers of my good hand through my tangled hair.

"You look like you've been to war." Her gaze burned my skin. Her eyes landed on the dark spot of the skirt. She touched it and red stained her finger. "Is that blood?" She raised an eyebrow. "Your dress is ruined." If she knew what Papa had said or what Nelly accused me of, she would never forgive it. She unwrapped the bloody scarf. "That's more than a cut. Come into the kitchen." She supported the small of her back. Her fingers were the size of sausages and ruddy too. If she swelled any more, her rings would have to be cut off.

I followed her around the baby grand Michael had given her for a wedding present, past the staircase and the stained-glass windows of weeping willows, into the large dining room with its crystal chandelier. The rooms held her scent, a distinct mixture of soap and coffee, bread and vanilla, the same as it had been when she was a baby—her scalp, her warm breath, the same as her wedding day when I leaned near her face to pin the veil in her dark locks. I could almost smell milk on the baby's breath.

If she would have me, I would serve her, live quietly in the attic rooms and care for the baby. I could be the night nurse, the baby's grandmother, nothing more. I could care for the house, the garden. I could bake her daily bread and cook for them. I could do anything so long as I did not have to leave them. I breathed deeply as she pulled me into the kitchen at the back of the house.

"What happened to your hand?" Her face was dark with concern. "Did that man bother you?" She meant Orlando Washington.

"No, no." I should have told her then, Ivie had done this, and then shown her the bruises her father had left. But I could not. I could not upset her in her state, and I wanted to protect her from the shame of it all. She would want to fix it, protect me from Ivie, and then he and Nelly would spew their accusations. Being face to face with her, I feared her knowing the truth. I could not burden her with more of it. She had lost her father, and she was going to give birth any moment. I could not tell her that Orlando Washington had been inside my house or that Nelly and Ivie accused me of her father's death. I needed to prepare myself for her reaction and what I should say. "I slipped on some broken glass."

She shook her head in disbelief.

Beneath the rolled hem of her pants, her ankles and calves looked unnaturally swollen. With each step, she let out a whispered moan.

"Sit down." I touched her belly. It was hard like a melon. "Are you hurting?"

"Yes." Her lips pursed. She pushed my hand off. She was self-reliant to a fault, maybe because of me. I had not coddled her. I never babied her the way I had Eli.

"How long has your belly been tight?" I asked.

Her fists clenched the seat of her chair. "It's not time," she said. "The doctor said to wait until my water breaks."

"What does he know? He's never had a baby." If she gave birth, it would distract her from Elias and Nelly. The thought eased the pressure in my chest. "I'll take you to the hospital. Let them check you."

"No." She was as tough as a nutshell. "After the funeral."

"You can't cross your legs and hold it in." I heard frustration in my voice, and arguing would not help.

"Don't be crass," she said.

I poured a glass of water for her.

She drank and then took my hand. She could read people. She knew how to read her father as well as me. Calling "Daddy" when she saw his mood was foul, or if he started in on my mishandling of a cus-tomer, or if I'd baked too little or too much. She'd change the subject or play a chirpy song on her piano.

"Don't worry about the cut." I tried to pull away, but she *tsk*ed me and held my fingers firm, my palm flexed upward, as if she were an experienced nurse.

"Tell me what really happened." Her voice was tender. She had a way of getting what she wanted. She led me to the sink and ran water over the wound.

It stung like madness. My fingertips turned white. "It's simple," I said. "I dropped a glass and I slipped on it. Then I got caught in the storm on my way here."

She wrapped a clean dishcloth around my hand. "Hold it tight to stop the bleeding. You need iodine on that." She waddled out of the kitchen. "When I was little, Daddy called it 'red medicine.' Remember?"

I followed her. My hands reached after her as if she were a toddler taking stairs for the first time.

She gestured for me to stop. "I'll just be a minute."

The house was still and quiet except for her feet padding across the ceiling. Everything was in order. The walls were crisp yellow and cheerful blue. There was no trace of death or weariness. I slid off the torn stockings, found a dishcloth, and wiped the dots of blood from my legs. I dusted off my dress and tried to make my hair more presentable.

I wanted to leave behind all the commotion of that day and the night before. I wanted to be close and forget the old injuries I'd given her. I wanted it to be like the day I pinned her veil and she looked at me full of hope. I wanted the baby to come so I could hold it, swaddle it, and hand it to her like the most precious gift. I wanted this mournful dirge to end. But she was taking care of me, and even if her tenderness came from mourning her father, I would take it.

~

Two days before, on the second day of August, Marina had entered my house with Elias. She said she had come to see the baby's layette, but she and her father wanted the business with Orlando Washington to stop.

She spoke as if she were the mother and I were the child. "You're going to tape your mailbox shut and go to the post office like a respectable person."

"You're the only one," Elias said calmly. "He won't last another day if we shut him out."

Marina fingered a baby gown.

I said, "He's doing a job. It's no different from your gardener."

Marina rubbed her forehead. "He'll handle important papers and know your business." Then her eyes locked with her father's. "They can't be trusted. You give them an inch and they'll take a mile."

Elias nodded, nudging her on.

"He's taking a good man's job." She folded the gown and patted the stack of white cotton clothes.

"I don't want him on our front porch every day," Elias said. "Especially when I'm not home." He stood to leave us. "It's not right." That was how he operated when Marina was present. He seemed reasonable until we were alone. He walked out on the porch and lit a cigarette. The smell drifted in.

"Listen to Daddy," she said. She shifted in her chair to balance the weight of her belly. "It's not safe here by yourself."

"Marina, I have lived in this town my whole life." Elias listened from his spot on the porch. "No one is going to walk in and rape or murder me, especially not Orlando Washington. Your gardener comes in your basement every day."

"It is different. My gardener knows his place." She was cool and collected, like a trial lawyer working through each position. "That Washington crossed a hundred boundaries when he walked on your front porch. If he wants something, what's to stop him?"

"Nonsense," I said. "He's not a criminal."

"Maybe he is. Suppose they gave him the job to slip him up." She raised her dark eyebrow like a question mark.

"I know him," I said. "He's Thea's son."

"It does not matter that he's your maid's son." She smirked. "My gardener has a son. Should Michael get him a desk job at the firm?"

"She cared for me," I said. "I want to do good by her."

She looked at me thoughtfully. She ran her long, swollen fingers over the baby's things. "Ever since you said you were going to do this, I've been trying to understand." She leaned in and took my hand. "Mama, you are the only one. She's gone, and you're not helping her. You are hurting him by making it seem possible. The town is not going to let this go on."

Elias turned his ear toward the open window, like a cat sensing prey in the bushes.

"He's a good person," I whispered.

"I know you have lived on both sides of this town and you feel familiar with his people." Marina's voice was stern. "But your affiliation will embolden him and others. They will take advantage of you."

I hated her embarrassment of me and where I was from.

"Daddy's store will suffer." Her voice hit a shrill tone. "Michael's law partners worry this could hurt the business. Our livelihood is not worth that man and his pipe dream."

There was truth that the store could suffer, that people would gossip about me and it would affect her and Michael. "Eli said this is the right thing. He said people will come around."

She shook her head. "Mama, you are stirring up a hornet's nest." Irritation mounted in her voice. She did not want to deal with any of this, not Orlando Washington or her father or me.

I said, "It will pass." The same as my father said. "He'll show them he can do the job."

"You don't know what's being said." Her green eyes widened. She lowered her voice. "You don't know what they'll do."

"You are smart, Marina," I said. "You must know these people are wrong to deny him a job that he's earned."

Marina whispered. "Things have been good lately." She looked out the window at her father's silhouette and then at me. She touched her belly. "Don't make more trouble for yourself." She raised her eyebrows and looked at me sternly. "That is the only thing you've accomplished." She stood slowly and her voice resumed its normal volume. "I hope you decide to listen to reason."

She was warning me against her father and the town. I wanted to make her sit and admit what was right.

"I have to go now. Michael will be worried." She gathered the layette and gave me a tentative smile. "The baby's things are beautiful."

She stepped outside and I listened to her and Elias. She said, "Be patient, Daddy. Let her sleep on it and she'll come around." She kissed him on the cheek, goodbye, and I was jealous because she had not kissed me.

~

Marina's front door opened and shut. "Mama?" Eli's deep voice resonated through the grand rooms. He entered the kitchen with a stack of table linens in one hand and a golden-tipped meringue pie in the other. One of the church ladies must have given it to him.

Eli's long face looked weary and his shoulders slumped. He put the linens and the pie on the counter and walked toward me. "I saw your car out front."

I reached out for him. My face was hot and wet from tears.

He took my hand and unwrapped the bloody dishtowel. "Are you all right?" Dark circles ringed his eyes, the same as Marina and me. We were all so tired.

"It's nothing." I touched his hair with my free hand. "A cut." No good would come if Eli knew Ivie had pushed me around. Eli would defend me to the end and that would put him in harm's way. Eli was still a boy in some regards, innocent and soft, and Ivie was a cold-blooded snake.

Eli led me to a kitchen chair. His green irises, the same as Marina's and his father's, darted back and forth. "I know what Ivie and Grandmother are saying." His voice was tender, forgiving.

I felt a pang of guilt.

Eli said, "I know they threatened Washington last night. I know Dad was there."

I felt sorry for him to know his father's actions. It would be a stain on Eli's heart, when Eli had hoped to show his father what good he could do. "Who told you?"

"Ivie," he said. "Marina doesn't know, not about Washington in the house or about Dad going there." It was clear she did not, how kind she was being to me. She hated that I allowed Orlando Washington to deliver. If she knew he'd come inside my house, that her father had gone there, she would blame me for causing her father grief and maybe his death.

I wiped the tears from my cheeks and tried to calm the shaking feeling that Ivie might have told my son I harmed Elias. "Was Mr. Washington hurt?"

"Not physically. Not yet." His deep voice was tentative, but he looked indignant. "I don't know what that does to your spirit."

I bowed my head. Soon Marina would be down and she would want to know why I had been crying. In her gut, she must know I would never shed so many tears for him. But I was in distress and I could not tell her why.

At the sink, Eli ran cool water over a dishcloth and wrung it out. "I told Ivie to leave her out of it for the baby's sake." He ran the damp cloth across my face as if I were a sick child. "He said he would, for now."

"They can't leave her out of it." I wanted to protect him from their ugliness, but he was a man in the world's eyes, one who would become a priest. I took the cloth from his hand. "If they want to run me out of town, Marina will know."

"Your trouble will blow over." His words were matter-of-fact. "But Mr. Washington's won't. He has a choice to make." Eli sounded worried. Unlike Marina, he always shied away from fights.

"Eli?" Marina hollered down, her voice muffled from the top of the stairs. "Is that you?"

"It's me," he called out. His eyes did not leave mine.

"I'll be down in a minute." Marina's feet padded across the floor upstairs. "Since you're here with Mother, I'm going to freshen up."

"Take your time," he yelled.

I wanted her to come down, make her sit and rest. I wanted to tell her in my own words what Nelly accused me of. Maybe, with Eli beside me, I could be brave. If she heard it from me with Eli near, if I showed her the bruises and she saw what her father had done, maybe she would side with me. "Nelly and Ivie are not to be trusted." I went to the sink to change the blood-soaked cloth on my hand. "If it benefits them, they'll do anything."

Eli leaned against the counter. He sighed a long breath and hung his head in worry.

"What did Ivie say to you?" I was angry they would try to turn my child against me.

Eli straightened his shoulders. He ran his long fingers through his bristly, cropped hair. "What Ivie said is a lie." He scowled. "Ivie's no good, like Pop always said. He's chomping at the bit to get his hands on the store. Marina knows that. He'll go off again."

"I should talk to Marina before they do." I wanted to have been a better mother, the way I was with Eli, to have held her and bonded with her early on. But when she was born, when she was little, my mind was dark and I could not feel what I was supposed to. I let Nelly mother her, and when I realized what I had done, when I had Eli and my body and mind set back to right, it was too late. Marina knew my failure, not in words or actions, but in feeling. She had known in her small being that I had betrayed her. And now, I wanted to have her love me the way I should have loved her. "I want to stay here and help her with the baby."

"They can't make you leave," Eli said.

I shook my head. "They can make it impossible for me to stay." The water gurgled as it ran down the pipes from the bathroom upstairs.

He looked like a tall child, too innocent to know what his grandmother or Ivie would do. "I know you didn't love him." He spoke low and carefully and fixed his gaze on me. "But I know you didn't hurt him."

I studied my son's eyes to see if he had a trace of doubt, if he were thinking, *Did you kill my father?* He stared back and gave no clue. He would make a good priest and confessor—someone calm, trustworthy, someone to tell one's deepest sins.

"But I did love him," I said. "If he ever loved me, I don't know." I sounded bitter, and I wanted to say, *I'm sorry*, but what would he think I was apologizing for?

"For what it's worth, Mama," he said, "your heart was in the right place. It's the law that Washington can have that job." Eli was an honest soul. "I know it wasn't anything more." His cheeks blushed. Eli touched the shining chrome trim of the kitchen table.

"I didn't help him for the right reason," I confessed. "Part of me did it to spite your father."

"Don't doubt yourself." He touched my arm and looked at me earnestly. "Whatever reason—it was the right thing to do."

"I should never have asked him in." I felt uncomfortable sitting before Eli so disheveled. "I've always done what I was supposed to do." I had not worried about the news of the bus boycotts or the arrests or the petitions on either side. I did not argue with Marina when she complained that Autherine Lucy had tricked the University of Alabama to accept her and had caused the white riot that followed.

Eli had taken notice of the injustices, and I'd read his papers from seminary and listened to his positions. He'd been incensed by the daily news and the rules holding people down. He did not hide behind the popular feelings, but Elias had no patience for his son's views and the fact he was studying to be a priest. He said to us all, "He could do anything he wanted. He's wasting his life."

But Eli had told me he saw his father's disdain for what it was— regret that Elias had been afraid to live the way he wanted. So Eli had taken pity on his father's failures and withstood his father's slights.

I said, "I should not have married your father. I should never have stayed."

"Mama, let's don't go down this road." He grabbed my good hand. "You cannot question your whole life. What about Marina and me? Surely we were the good that came from your marriage."

I saw the pain on his face. I kept hurting them when I wanted to be a source of love. The wounds ran so deep that I could not help myself. "He was not always bad to me, but he did not love me. Not *me*."

"I'm on your side, Mother." Eli's wide eyes stared at me with pity. "This will pass."

I had said it to Marina. Papa said those words whenever trouble came. *This will pass.* When crosses were burned. *This will pass.* When Mama died, I relied on the notion. *This beating will pass, this loneliness and this marriage too.* And now, from Eli's lips.

"You know what your father did to the postman," I said. My face was hot. Eli did not know all that his father had done to me. The toll had been more than physical, forcing me to play this strange game with my life, watching him for signs of his boredom or displeasure to keep myself safe, until finally I could play it no more.

The cut seeped warm blood. What I had expected with Elias gone—a quiet, peaceful house, my children around me, no worries, a chance to give them love and live without fear—was slipping like sand through my fingers. I was lonely and tired of being hurt, not in my body, but in my spirit. I had accepted my place and the place of others, but I was tired of the low regard in which Elias held me. That was why I had helped Mr. Washington. He was tired of his position and he was doing something about it. "This won't pass," I said.

"I won't let anything happen to you," he said. He squeezed my good hand and straightened his shoulders.

My Two Children

Marina stepped into the kitchen. She wore a dress and had fixed her hair in a chignon. Before her, I had thought beauty was the creamy white skin of blue-eyed blondes, not what I saw in the mirror. But Marina had reminded me of my mother's beauty, and even in Marina's swollen state, the flesh of her feet spilling over the edges of her ballet flats, I was amazed at the loveliness of my child.

She eyeballed us. "Are you two plotting to save the world again?" Sarcasm dripped from her big voice.

"The world needs saving," Eli said.

Marina waved him off and placed an iodine bottle and bandages on the table. She steadied herself to sit. "I figured I should put on a proper dress in case someone drops by." She reached for my hand and unwound the bloody rag. "Now, you said you cut yourself on a piece of glass?" She arched one eyebrow in disbelief.

"Yes," I said.

"Looks like you were thrown on glass." She huffed. "Was it that man you are *helping*?"

"No," I said, frustrated that she was hounding after Mr. Washington again.

Eli's brow furrowed. "I am concerned for him." His face looked like Elias's when Elias was angry. I lost my breath, as if it were Elias, wily and tough, standing before me. I told myself, *This is the son and not the father. The father is gone forever.* He asked, "Do you know what our father did?"

She took my palm, dropped the iodine in the gash, and ignored his temper.

"He was part of a group," Eli said. I could hear the restrained edge of anger in his voice. "They threatened to lynch that man unless he left town."

I watched Marina's face. Placid like still water.

I felt the urge to tell them their uncle had pushed me into broken glass at the store, but then I would have to tell them I was there to get money and explain why I needed it. I would have to tell her the accusations, that Grandpapa told me to go, and then it seemed tawdry that I had stolen my own money. Marina would never understand.

"They did not lynch him," she said in a defensive tone and squeezed the dropper again. She looked coolly at Eli. More iodine rolled into the open flesh.

"No," Eli said. "But he was threatened." His voice shook.

"Let's not jump to conclusions." Marina sounded matter-of-fact. "Those people exaggerate. Maybe the Riverton people went to voice their honest concerns."

"Honest?" Eli huffed and ran his fingers over his lips. "I'm sitting vigil at his house tonight and I'll be witness to any more of their 'honest concerns.'"

She blew on my palm to ease the burn. "Do you see what you've started?" She accused me with her eyes.

I felt the guilt she intended, but for different reasons. The more I thought about it, the worse my story sounded, that if I said one thing about her father beating me, then everything would flow like water out of a dam. Then everything I had hoped for—a chance to love my daughter and hold her child, a chance to live in peace—would be gone.

Her eyes fell on Eli and she deftly changed the subject. "Did you take the things from the church hall to Mother's?"

"Of course," he said. "Your directions were very clear." He turned his back and slammed the counter with his fists. "It amazes me that you care more about dishes than a man's life." He hung his head. He was praying, maybe for us or Washington or his father's soul.

"Eli, would you mind making some coffee?" Marina asked, giving him something to do, to take his mind off the unpleasantness she did not wish to discuss.

He let out a long breath and then filled her percolator with water. "What about Daddy's soul?" he asked. "If he did that, his soul is in jeopardy." The worry on his face aged him. He scooped the grounds and turned the pot on and the water bubbled up. The room filled with the warm, gritty smell of coffee.

"I have faith our father's soul was clean." Marina looked as if she might cry again. "I don't believe that mumbo jumbo anyway."

Eli's pale face was red with frustration.

I did not want them to argue, but I could not settle it.

Marina blinked away tears and turned her attention to me. "You're going to need stitches, Mother." Her warm hand cradled mine.

"I'll have it looked at when we go to the hospital for you." It felt good being so close to her, even though she refused to see her father for what he was. I would bend to her will if she would forgive me.

She tightly wound gauze around my hand and it went numb. She released me and screwed the medicine dropper back onto the bottle. My fingers pulsed in time with my heart.

"Hold it high." She held her hand in the air to demonstrate.

I cradled my arm like a baby and rested the hand on my shoulder.

Eli was agitated. "Doesn't the injustice of a man being threatened over his job bother you?" He did not stammer. He stood straight.

Calmly, she said, "No."

"I'm going to Washington's house," he said. "He won't be alone if they come again."

I said, "I don't want you to go. It's not safe."

Marina stared at Eli and her jaw pulsed. "Why must you worry us over this, with Daddy's funeral?"

"Father McMurray's going too," he said.

"You're putting yourself in danger," I said.

"It's my calling," he snapped at me. He looked like Elias with his anger ticking up. He turned to Marina. "You should be ashamed of what he did. We should right the sins of our father."

Marina touched her belly. "You're making things worse for that man and for us." She bit her lip, it seemed to keep from saying more. I could tell she did not want to be involved any deeper.

"What our father did was wrong!" Eli yelled. He had never raised his voice to her or me.

"I'm not so sure about that," Marina said. Her expression was hard, but she did not flinch at Eli's show of temper. "The best thing to do is to let things settle and see where they lie."

"Mama did the right thing." Eli's voice broke. I had never seen him so passionate.

"Maybe Daddy did the right thing. Maybe that man will take the warning and move on and leave us alone." She sounded adamant. "I'm not sure what any of this Negro business matters when our father is dead."

"You don't recognize the horror of this?"

"I cannot fix that man's life. I cannot right the wrongs of the world." She stood with much effort and packed up the bandages. "I won't talk about it anymore. Tomorrow is the visitation and the Rosary." With much exertion, she stormed out of the kitchen.

Eli stared at me with dark eyes and shook his head. I wanted to tell him not to go to Mr. Washington's that night, but that would have been wrong.

When Marina returned, her emotions seemed settled. She reached for some plates and cut the pie Eli had brought.

Eli stared at the wall as the percolator steamed. He reached for three cups. His skin was flushed and his expression was tangled like the brambles by the river.

"Eli dropped off some things at your house," Marina said. "The big coffee urn from church, the plates, and cups." She placed a plate in front of me. She gave a weary smile and took in a deep, shuddering breath. "Come on, Eli. Eat something. We have a lot to do before tomorrow."

Eli poured the coffee and placed a cup before Marina.

Marina held the cup between her palms.

My chest felt hollow. Here was one child struggling to do right and another lost in appearances. I had given birth to them, raised them, watched them, and yet I did not understand either of them. By the way they traded looks, they did not understand each other either. Marina was not very religious. She would skip Mass any chance she got. She pitied Eli. She thought it was simpleminded to devote his life to the Church. Eli looked at her and saw everything he hated—ambition, status, materialism. He thought she turned a blind eye to problems he saw with clarity. I could tell he wanted to make her see.

I blamed Marina's shortcomings on her father, but I had done the same as her, plowed through what was expected of me. The only difference between us, I had ducked my head down while she held hers high without apology.

"I'm bringing over my silver and the large servers in the morning." Marina took a bite of the pie.

Eli rolled his eyes. "She has thought of everything," he said, "except what it means to be Christian or human."

Marina shot him a look. "Give it a rest, Pope Eli." She took another bite of the pie and said, "Mother, you need to go home and get yourself ready. There will be a houseful tomorrow."

I took a bite. It was coconut, thick and sweet, but I could not enjoy it. My chest constricted as if Elias was sitting on top of me again, crushing the breath out of me.

I watched them eat. Both were tired and worried. I wanted to go back to the day after Elias beat me for the first time and I took them to Papa's. That night, I lay between them in my childhood bed. I stared at the cracked plaster and listened to my father snore across the hall. The night train rumbled over the bridge, and when it was gone, I could hear the night birds, the loons and the owls shouting over each other. I felt grateful that my children were close and quiet and still and lovely. Their hot breath brushed over my arms and I marveled how they could sleep through the noise. I had a strange sense of peace and I wanted it to last forever. Maybe because I was in my mother's house, maybe because I felt free of Elias, but mostly it just felt so good to be close to them. I was their mother, and thanked God and my luck that I'd had the strength to stand up for myself and leave him.

But I loved Elias and I was hopeful he would come to his senses and miss us. Those little creatures beside me were so beautiful, so mesmerizing. I knew he would feel the weight of our absence and want us back. He loved the children, and because we had made them together, maybe he could see me in them and come to love me too.

"Mama," Marina said. "I'm craving your bread. After the funeral, I want you to make me a loaf a day."

I smiled and nodded. I wanted to go home and bake for her then, but I had no energy.

Eli's eyes met mine. I thought this could be the last time the three of us sat together in peace, for what I had done and what I had failed to do. My stomach turned. I told myself it was the rich pie on an empty stomach. It was the long night and a longer day.

My heart pounded in my chest. "I want to tell you something." Now, before Nelly tried to make a case against me, was my chance to show her the marks her father had left. I was willing to tell Marina he'd hurt me because I had invited Mr. Washington in. If she knew that, and with Eli there to bolster me, Marina might have empathy for me.

"Oh, no more talk," she said firmly. That girl of mine was the eye of the storm, calm when everything else went to pieces. She was the child who could change the course of an evening with a tinkling song on the piano, not once giving away what she knew. Her silver fork clinked against the china plate. "That was so good."

I gathered their dishes. I would let her have her way for the time being. Knowing her, she probably guessed what I was hiding—the bruises, the fact that Mr. Washington had been in our house, her grandmother's accusations that I killed Elias. Marina would never want to hear it pass from my lips. Maybe she thought, if everyone stayed silent, the problems would go away and she could be relieved of scandal. She could defend herself against the truth by ignoring it. She must have known her father hurt me, because she had played interference in the past, but she had never condemned him or spoken of what she knew. I began to wash the plates.

"Don't get your bandage wet," Eli said. He took my place. "I'll do that." I watched his hands move in circles over the plates. I had gathered food, cooked for them, filled the house with the good odors. They would eat, and then I would wash it all away, the dishes, the crumbs, the grease, the smell. I had stayed for them and raised myself out of bed every morning, put one foot in front of the other, done my duty, but still, they did not know how much of myself I had sacrificed for them. I felt I was drowning in the circumstances. Eli would go to Mounds and put himself in danger. Marina would have her baby, Nelly and Ivie would spew their accusations, and I would be cast out or worse. I would sully Marina and her new family.

"Have you had any more pains?" I asked Marina.

"No," she said. Her fingertips kneaded her thighs as if she could stop the swelling.

"Why don't you lie down and rest?" I asked. "I'll stay here with you."

She stared across the kitchen at Eli's back as he finished drying the plates.

Eli paid us no attention. His mind no doubt turned on how to help the postman and what to do for me, now that his father was dead and his family wanted to put the blame on me.

Marina looked at the clock, then at me. "I want you to go." Papa had said those same words earlier. Her deep voice was firm.

"I want to stay with you." I dreaded driving to the house where her father had died, afraid of the quiet waiting there for me, afraid of the memory of the night before with his scratching around and calling my name. If Nelly was correct that his soul was caught in the house, I wanted never to set foot through the door again.

She sat straight in her chair. She breathed in deeply, her face full and flushed. She touched her belly. "No, Mother." Her voice had an edge to it. "Michael doesn't need to see you like this."

It was clear that Marina did not like seeing me so tousled and wild, but part of me wanted her to recognize the awful situation I was in. The kitchen light dimmed. More dark clouds had rolled in. I felt helpless against Marina and her wishes.

"Another storm." I looked at Eli. "Will you stay here with her until Michael comes home?"

He nodded.

"Will you call me if you go into labor?" I was afraid the baby would come and they would leave me out.

"Yes." She looked around her kitchen, taking inventory of what to bring to my house. Probably trying to get her mind off me and the scandal surrounding us. "You will have a houseful tomorrow and then the funeral the next day. Go home and roll your hair. Get a nice long bath. I'll call Mitsy's shop to gather a few summer suits for you."

Her directions frustrated me, as though all would be well if I looked pretty and neat. But I had to be patient. "I don't need a suit. My closet is full."

"You need to cover your arms." She spoke as if I had no propriety and didn't know that women covered their arms in church. There would be gloves, a hat, a sheer black veil. She knew nothing of the marks her father had left.

"I've been going to Mass longer than you've been alive." I looked to Eli, but he was lost in thought and staring out the window. "Will you be careful tonight?" I touched his arm.

He nodded. The kitchen lights flickered.

"You know, storms bring babies," I said to her.

She ignored me. "Tomorrow the partners and the mayor will pay their respects."

"You and the baby are more important than what I wear or who comes tomorrow or the next day." I could have said, *Your father would want you to take care of yourself and the baby.* If I had invoked him, she would have listened and taken it easy, but for my own selfish reasons I did not want her thinking of him. "My mother came here with nothing and built a business with her sisters. No husbands, no connections except her own parents." My skin burned. "I can help you. You don't need those people and all their trappings."

"Don't lecture me." Her voice was calm, disengaged. She stared at her swollen fingers. She looked tired and her emotion was spent. "Time to go before it storms again." Slowly, carefully, like a circus elephant trying to balance on a stool, she stood. She took my arm and led me through the hallway. The storm clouds hung low in the sky and the stained-glass windows were dark as night. Marina's grand house felt like a cave.

"I wish you would let me stay." I felt close to begging. If I stayed, I would find the way to tell her, prepare her for what was coming, but nothing could prepare Marina for Nelly's accusations. My chest tightened as if Elias were squeezing my heart.

Eli walked close. "Stay until Michael gets here," I said.

"Don't worry," he said—did he mean not to worry about her, about himself, about Orlando Washington? This young man was not a boy. He was a man protecting everything he cared about.

Soon, I stood by my car on Maple Street and looked back at my grown children. The shade of the grand porch fell across their faces. The dark shadow of clouds hung over us. I could have been looking at myself and Elias twenty-three years ago. Eli cut the figure of his father, and Marina's silhouette was the same as mine the night I gave birth to her.

That night, Elias had driven me to the hospital. I lay sprawled across the back seat because I could not sit upright. My bowels felt like they were being ripped out. I thought I would die, like my mother, and he knew my fear. He tried to comfort me. He was so kind to me that night. His hand reached over the seat and stroked my hot arm. "Almost there. The doctors will keep you safe." He drove carefully over bumps. "Close your eyes," he said. "Think of blue skies."

My daughter was ignorant of the changes that would consume her, not only the pain of childbirth, but also the uncertainty of being a mother. I wished I could change something, anything, to make this point in time different. Marina stared past me. She was counting silver forks and china plates in her head. I wanted to cry out to Marina like a wailing woman and see if she felt any connection to me, her mother, banged up, a few steps below in a stained dress and stockingless. She turned and wobbled into the house past Eli. He waved goodbye and shut the door.

The wind spit hot out of the sky. I was afraid I had walked the last time down her stone path. Afraid she would choose her grandmother over me. If my father could believe I killed Elias, surely Marina would believe the same. Who but she had witnessed more clearly the bitterness between us?

The wind sounded like a stiff new broom on the sidewalk. The keys rattled in my hand, the engine rumbled, and the hot air blew in the car windows. I drove home, one half block east and a few blocks south toward the river under an angry sky.

Sophie and Lila

In the gloom beneath the pecan tree, Sophie bounced like a firefly. She had not changed out of the pink leotard from earlier that day. The mockingbird perched on a low branch, and as Sophie ran with her arms stretched out, cawing like a crow, the bird swooped down at her. She squealed, unbothered by the bird's charge, and ran another loop around the tree.

Lila's truck was parked close to the house. Lila emerged from the shadow of the porch and stood at the top step. "We've been waiting on you." She'd changed out of the proper dress into a worn western shirt and blue jeans rolled at the ankles.

"Have you been here long?" I retrieved my purse and the money from the trunk and tucked the canvas bank bag so she could not see it.

"No." Lila ambled down the stairs and opened the door to her truck. She craned her neck to see what I was doing.

I shut the trunk and held my purse close to my heart.

Lightning flashed in the sky and then the dark clouds rumbled with thunder. The wind blew hot, like tornado weather, and the cedar trees along the property lines bent in the heavy wind.

"I brought food." Her arms laden with dishes, she shut the truck door with a kick.

A white rose wreath hung on the screen door. Marina would have ordered it.

Sophie bounded across the grass and hurled herself into my legs. Up close, I saw the trails of dirt on her leotard from a day of playing. She no longer wore the ballet slippers from earlier, but had changed into black patent tap shoes with wide ribbon laces. Her face pressed against the crusty bloodstain on my skirt. She released me quickly. "Your skirt is sticky."

"I had an accident." I showed her my bandaged hand. She looked puzzled, not connecting the bandage with the soiled skirt. She thought I had an accident of a five-year-old sort.

Lila's brow creased. "What happened?"

"A piece of glass happened." I felt calm in Lila's presence, like every worry had its place and I could keep going and things would right themselves. Gus must have felt that, her horses too. She had no pretense, no worry about what people thought, and she steered straight in the line she wanted to go.

A hot gust of air whipped through the pecan tree. The wind felt good and cleansing after the day, but then a large branch crashed six feet from us and Sophie jumped against me.

"Let's get inside." I tucked the bulging purse under one arm and picked Sophie up. She was heavy and I was weak from the long day, dizzy from the lack of food. I put her down on the top stair and rain fell like bullets from the sky. Hail bounced onto the ground and pinged against the cars. I fumbled with the key, but the door was not locked. I held the screen and door open for Lila. The rich smell of fried kibbe and cabbage rolls came from the pans in her arms and mingled with the perfume of the roses on the wreath, more than two dozen. Marina had spared no expense.

I laid the screen door gently to rest and hooked the latch. Sophie clung to my leg.

Lila headed for the kitchen. The swinging door flapped in her wake.

The closed windows trapped air thick with Pine-Sol and furniture polish. Louise had been heavy handed in her cleaning. With Sophie clutching to me, I opened the windows and the cool, wet air flooded the house. The rain, thick and gray, pounded the hydrangeas. Limbs and leaves littered the yard. I turned on the dining-room light. The table was crowded with glass plates, coffee cups, and saucers, and the enormous electric coffee urn from the church hall. I placed my purse amidst Marina's preparations.

The living room had been turned into a chapel. My furniture lined the walls to make room for three rows of folding chairs facing the limestone fireplace. An empty space awaited his casket. On the mantel, Nelly had propped a large framed photograph of him as a young man, standing with his arms crossed, a head of dark hair, and his cheeks tinted pink. Nelly loved her son with a vengeance. She loved him as I loved my children, but she burdened us with the depth of her love. It went as deep as misery.

I made my way through the maze of chairs and turned on a lamp. Lightning popped near us. Thunder rolled over the surface of the river and seemed to shake the house. Sophie whimpered and gripped tighter to my legs. Rain pounded down. The lights flickered off and then back on.

"Good Lord," Lila called from the kitchen. I picked up Sophie and went into the kitchen. Lila's head was tucked in the refrigerator door, and light from inside it glowed around her silhouette. I flipped the switch and yellow light flooded down from the ceiling. "Louise has not left an inch."

She clattered dishes and muttered her annoyance as she moved pans from the refrigerator to the counter and back again. Odors of her food filled the room—the cinnamon and the mint of the kibbe, the sour smell of the cabbage rolls, the savory scent of okra stewed in tomatoes and coriander. Twenty years ago, my brother begged me to teach Lila Lebanese cooking so that she could make his favorite foods—the fried kibbe, the tabbouleh salad, the stuffed grape leaves. I had refused his wish because their marriage was stormy with drinking and leaving, one miscarriage after the next. I blamed it on her hard ways. Then Sophie was born and my feelings for Lila softened and I taught her what I knew about the food.

Rain fell in sheets outside the window. The sky was black with the storm.

"There's no room." Lila slammed the refrigerator shut. The glass dishes clanked inside. "Let's eat some of this while it's hot."

She gathered plates and filled them. She worked the kitchen like it was her own. "Where have you been?"

"I had to go see Papa," I said.

"Why?" She had not heard the news of the almost lynching or Nelly's threats because she had not spoken to Gus. He would know as soon as he checked in with my father at the end of his day.

"He said he needed to see me."

The white linoleum floor gleamed with light. Louise had scrubbed away any trace of Ivie's boot marks.

Lila put the plates of fried kibbe and cabbage rolls onto the table. She returned to the stove to cover the pans. "What do you want to eat, little girl?" Lila asked Sophie, and the sound of her voice eased the tension in Sophie's body. She pushed off me to be set down.

Sophie tap-danced around and then moved to the plates of food set out on the yellow Formica table. Her chin cleared the chrome edge of the table. She popped one kibbe ball after the other into her mouth until her mother's plate was clean. She shuffled out of the kitchen into the hallway.

"Step, ball, step. Step, ball, change." Her voice started small and grew with intensity as did the clapping of her shoes on the wood floors, making music with the thunder and the rain.

"She won't take those off." Lila refilled her plate. "All blessed day long."

"You'll miss it one day." My hand throbbed as I thought of Marina.

"Want the stew?" Lila asked.

"Yes." I cradled the bandaged hand.

She placed a bowl in front of me. Her hands and forearms were muscled, sinewy from her work with the horses. She started back to the sink, but took notice of blood seeping through the bandage. "That is some cut. Let me see it."

"No, it's nothing." With my left hand, I spooned the stew to my mouth. "I'm fine."

She raised her eyebrows in doubt. She sat near and ate.

The lamb was tender. The tomatoes were warm comfort going down. She refilled her plate and mine with kibbe balls. She made the kibbe the way I liked it, the way I taught her, with the right proportions of lamb and bulgur, with roasted pine nuts, with more cinnamon than allspice, with mint instead of basil. I ate slowly.

The taste of it reminded me of the work of cooking, holding me comfortably in place, my purpose to do daily good for my children. Cooking had been my meditation. Cutting, chopping, measuring, mixing, the precise moments of the rise and fall of dough, the sweet and sour smell of leaven; too vinegary and the bread was sour, too sweet, no flavor. All of my cooking ended with a tangible thing but it was also my silent prayer of love for them. I loved seeing Marina and Eli come home from school and eat a popover or an almond cookie that I had made. I loved hearing them ask for more bread at dinner. Elias liked my food, and I could please him with that, if nothing else. I wondered if he knew I did it to please him, to anchor him to me, to us, to try and make our life bearable, like Lila was doing for me now. She was giving me love and the energy to face what was to come.

I had not kneaded dough in two days. I had fed the starter, and I would have to remember it tomorrow. It was older than Marina, and I wanted to keep it alive. All the daily vigilance gone in a single day, how I had kept my hands busy in the garden, in the kitchen, in the store, so I did not have to stop and think, what would please or displease him? What would I say or what look would I give that would remind him that his life was not enough, that things would never add up to make him happy?

Lila leaned back in her chair and lit a cigarette. She crossed her arms. Her body was taut with strong curves. She watched me eat. "I left a note for Gus. It's his late night. I figured we'd stay a while."

I was happy she was with me, and for that moment, she did not know all the trouble. Sophie tapped into the kitchen with a box of crayons and sheets of butcher paper in her arms. She huddled on the floor on her knees and elbows and began to draw.

"What did your father want?" Lila knew how he was. She had once been on his bad side, a thief, in his view, stealing Gus from a proper marriage.

I took my plate to the sink and looked out. The rain had stopped suddenly. Hail and fallen branches had knocked the garden down. Any other day, I would be mending the garden, even in the dark, to escape the confines of the house and Elias's presence. "He said come over 'immediately.' I thought he was having a heart attack."

"Was he okay?"

"Wait here." I retrieved my purse from the dining-room table. Outside the front window, the storm had caused cedars to bow like old men with broken backs. Pecan limbs littered the yard. Back in the kitchen, I handed the purse to Lila. "Look inside."

She peered in and fingered the canvas bag. Her mouth gaped open. She touched the bills with the tips of her fingers, then pulled the money from the purse. Her fingers worked swiftly and her lips moved with the counting.

"He gave me that money so I would leave town," I said.

The kitchen's light was warm and yellow against the dark night sky. In her hands was proof of Papa's rejection of me. She knew what that money was. I fingered the chrome edge of the table.

Sophie stood at my side and presented her drawing. A tree, a girl, a bird. She climbed in my lap and I nestled my face into her deep-brown ringlets. Sophie's eyes followed her mother's nimble fingers, the snapping bills and her counting lips. Holding Marina had never been so easy. Marina pulled away, fickle, never at ease, as if we were strangers.

I nudged Sophie to tear her eyes from the money. She would remember sitting at my table, the storm, the money. "You been helping Mama today?"

Her head brushed up and down against me.

"Or have you been a dancer?" I tickled her ribs. She squirmed against me and giggled. "You are a sweet girl." It was what I always said to her. I waited for her usual response.

"You a sweet girl too."

When I stopped tickling, she pleaded, "More, Aunt Annie."

I kissed her billowing hair and breathed in the smell of salt and sweat, like cut green grass. I put her down. "Be good, now." She flashed a perfect row of small white teeth. Soon I was to be a grandmother, and at the thought of a grandchild, my arms felt empty. I wanted Sophie back in my lap. She tapped away, so full of energy, so excited to be in my house and out of her normal routine. She disappeared in the hallway and her dancing echoed through the empty rooms.

Lila stacked the bills and placed them back in the bag. "More than twenty thousand." Her voice sounded like a judge delivering a guilty verdict. The lines across her forehead deepened. "He offered me half that for Sophie when I left Gus."

"I know." I had carried the letter from Papa to her, when she and Gus were separated. I had not known its contents, that it was from Papa's lawyer offering payment for custody of Sophie. "I still feel terrible about that."

She had been working horses on her father's farm. Sophie was a year old, and Papa was incensed that Lila had left Gus. I drove out, walked up to her, handed her the letter like it was a glass of iced tea.

She read it as I held her baby on my hip. When she finished, she thrust the paper in my face so that I could see, in neat typed rows of legal language, an offer of ten thousand for custody and the cold reasoning that Sophie would be better off with us—how Gus, Papa, and I could provide stability, family, money. The language was biting about Lila—an unfit mother, prone to drink. Attached were the custody papers.

Lila's fair skin had turned red with fear and anger.

"I'm sorry," I had said, but it sounded easy, like a lie, like the way Elias touched my arm in public for show. I was sorry for having delivered it, for blindly obeying my father, for having treated Lila poorly, when in fact Lila was my family, my brother's wife.

"He's not going to take her," I had said. With my free arm, I had pulled Lila close to Sophie and me. "I won't let Papa do that."

She had smelled of earth and horse. I imagined it was one reason Gus loved her, the way she smelled, how she had no pretense toward anything more than what she knew.

"We're past that," she said now. The wrinkles around her eyes deepened. A disapproving shake of her head. "That man's gall."

"It's Nelly," I said.

"But he's your father." Lila handed me the purse. "Why would he turn his back on you?"

"They're boycotting him for what Elias did." I placed it on the table.

"What exactly did Elias do?" Her face looked puzzled.

From the dining room, Sophie's steps were accompanied by a chant: "Step, ball, change. Shuffle, shuffle, kick. Heel, toe, heel, toe. Step, ball, change." She was dancing around the table where he had been laid out. There was a nice rhythm to it, and I wanted to be lulled by it, but Lila watched me like a hawk. My hand throbbed and I cradled it in my arm. Heat came from it, like it was infected.

Her piercing blue eyes were like ice. I held the bandaged hand against my cheek to gauge its heat. She pushed back from the table. The chair legs dragged across the floor. "You are the same as your brother and father." She stood. Her voice was even, steady. "All of you, stubborn as the day is long. Tell me what Elias did."

I felt hot, steaming, like the grass and garden outside.

Sophie's shoes tapped into the room and she piled onto my lap. Her chest moved with every breath and the musky odor of her sweat filled my nose. Sophie wrapped herself around me. Her weight was a conciliation for the sadness and guilt.

Lila sat. "Tell me."

Without regard for Sophie, I answered her. "He and Ivie and some others went over there to scare him. Ivie says they put a rope around his neck. Papa said they burned a cross. Then Elias is dead. Ivie and Nelly think I killed him and Nelly wants me gone."

Sophie did not flinch. Her body was still and I regretted the words she heard.

"Eli and Father McMurray are sitting vigil at his house tonight," I said.

Lila was silent. The lines in her face did not waver. A tendril of dark-blonde hair fell across her forehead. Lila knew that if anybody had reason to kill him, I did. Through the years, she saw the evidence of his anger.

I was grateful she did not ask if what Nelly said was true.

I told her, then, what had happened the day before, that I asked Mr. Washington in for a glass of water and Elias found us sitting at the dining-room table. I could see Lila was thinking of Gus and what he would do in that situation. "You should have let him drink from the hose," Lila said.

I put Sophie down and pushed up the sleeves of my dress to show Lila my arms. I whispered in her ear, so Sophie would not hear, how Elias had pressed his knee into my chest and wrenched my arms by my head. I told her what he said, that he could press the life out of me and no one would care.

Her fingertips skimmed my swollen and purple arm. "I would have killed him," she said. Lila's blue eyes darted from the window to me and back.

Sophie climbed into my lap again and I buried my nose in her curls and bounced her on my knees. She might remember this and make sense of it all. I should have sent her out, but her weight on my lap fortified me. Soon, I might have to leave, maybe not come back, and I prayed she would forget this night. Sophie turned her face up to mine. She whispered, as if her mother could not hear. "Is Uncle Elias dead?"

"Yes," I said.

"Is he in heaven?" Sophie's blue eyes were intent on mine.

I nodded, yes. No good would come of scaring her. Better for her to be ignorant of the truth.

"He was nice," Sophie said. "He always gave me peppermint." Elias had welcomed this child. She reminded him of Marina. "He played Chinese checkers with me." Often, Sophie stayed at the store while Lila worked the horses on her father's farm and Gus worked the route. Elias doted on Sophie like she was his own, and he would be kind in her presence. He'd wink at me and say, "What do you think, Anna, do you think Sophie could have an ice cream?"

Sophie's mouth opened to ask another question about her uncle.

Lila cut her short. "That's enough." Lila left the room and returned with her purse. From it she pulled out a pint of amber-brown whiskey. "I thought we might need this." She took two glasses from the cupboard, cracked ice from a tray, and poured the whiskey. She opened a Coke and mixed mine to weaken the spirits.

I was afraid to drink it. I did not know how it would affect me because I never drank.

Sophie slid from my lap and took up coloring again.

Outside, the sky was pitch black. The first sip burned my throat. Dark clouds hid the moon and stars. Noises of cicadas and tree frogs spilled inside. I told her about the scene earlier, how Nelly wanted an old-time wake, and how at Papa's, he told me Ivie would have the store and I would leave town after the burial.

She sipped her drink and stared out the black window over the sink. Her jaw clenched and her temples pulsed. She narrowed her eyes, so that I could barely see the blue. "Tell me that Nelly doesn't know about him and that water, alone with you in the house."

I took another sip. The burn in my chest gave some relief. I looked over her shoulder out the dark window. "If Ivie knows, she must know."

She closed her eyes, as if to get a clear picture in her mind of what Nelly and Ivie thought they knew. "And they went to Faris about this glass of water?" She opened her eyes. "And Faris believes them, that you and he—?"

"I don't think Papa believes that." I studied her eyes. "He seems to think I'm capable of the other." I did not want to mention Elias's death in front of Sophie again. "He's worried I'm in danger if they talk."

Lila shook her head. Both Lila and my father had witnessed the cruelties he had done to me. I imagined neither mourned his loss, but they did not want me to suffer any more because of him.

Eli and the priest would be at the postman's house by now. "What do you think will happen to Mr. Washington?"

"Who's Mr. Washington?" Sophie did not look up from her artwork.

Lila's eyes cut through me. She took a deep breath, but no words came.

"Is he coming here?" Sophie looked up from her drawing, a smile on her face, excited that we might have a visitor.

"No," Lila said. "Be quiet, now." Lila gave Sophie a hard look. "And don't repeat what you hear."

Sophie tucked her head and took up drawing again.

"Eli is there now." I placed my throbbing hand on the cold glass. "He's not safe."

"Eli has God on his side." She swirled the liquid and swallowed down the last of her drink. "But you don't have a leg to stand on."

I went to the sink to pour mine out but forced it down instead. The dark clouds separated. A waning sliver of moon, barely visible, peeked from the separating clouds. The moon was tilted as if it were a scoop holding more rain.

"Your papa is right. You're not safe here." Lila cursed under her breath and walked out. She paced the length of the hall, returned, and whispered in my ear, "They're liable to finish him and come here for you."

I sat stone still. My hand throbbed on the cold glass. "Maybe I should go there with Eli and save them the trouble."

She slammed her glass on the table. "You're going to get yourself killed."

"He's in trouble because of me," I said. "And now Eli is in harm's way."

"Are you love-struck? You are so worried about that man." Lila raised her voice.

"Don't say that," I said.

"That is what people think," she said. "Why are you putting your neck on the line?"

"His mother took care of me." I knew what people thought, what they said. I mumbled, "Eli said it was the right thing to do."

Lila cupped my chin and tilted my face to make me look her in the eye. "What in God's name were you thinking?" Her voice shook.

"I don't know," I said.

Lila touched my purse. "What are you going to do with this?" She knew nothing of the money in the trunk.

With the palm of my good hand I wiped the condensing water from the counter. I took a deep breath, held it, until I could hold it no more.

"You can stay with us if it comes to that." Her eyes turned to Sophie and the harsh lines around her eyes relaxed as she took in her child, asleep on the floor, her tap shoes still on, her head resting on folded arms and her legs tucked beneath her body. "Bless her heart," she said. "She's worn out."

Sophie was Lila's breath, her blood, her love made real in the flesh. She loved the child without abandon, maybe because she'd been thirty-seven when Sophie was born and she had more wisdom than a young mother. Seeing Lila look at Sophie made me hurt for what I had withheld from Marina.

"Put her on Marina's bed." I walked unsteadily across the room. The drink had gone to my legs.

"I should take her home," Lila said.

"Stay here. It's late." I did not want to be alone. "Unless you're afraid to stay here."

"I'm not afraid of those people." Softly she gathered the girl, and her muscled arms flexed as she lifted.

I believed her.

Sophie's head rolled on Lila's shoulder. Her mouth fell open. "Help me with her shoes," Lila whispered.

My knees were numb from the liquor, so I sat and unlaced the tight knot of the black ribbon. The shoes slipped off, and the smell of her warm, sweaty feet drifted up.

"That is how those shoes come off after every dance lesson." A smile lingered on Lila's lips. She had forgotten my troubles, so taken with the beauty of the still child. "We'll stay. I'll call Gus after I lay her down." She climbed the stairs.

When Lila returned to the kitchen, she poured more whiskey, this time without the ice or Coke. "We'll hide the money. The last thing you need is somebody walking off with it. There will be Ivie and Nelly here and a house full of people." Lila had grown up hand to mouth and she trusted no one.

"Put it over the icebox." I stood and my head spun. "In plain sight, isn't that the best place to hide something?" I tossed the bag on top of the refrigerator. My father's money, enough to buy a house, to start a business, enough to live on for a long while.

Lila raised her eyebrows, a smirk on her face.

"I won't need his money." The whiskey gave me false bravery. Also, I had the money from the store hidden in the trunk, but I did not want to confess I had taken it. "I'm not going anywhere."

"I need to call Gus and tell him we're here." She took a drink from her glass and strode across the kitchen. She dialed the phone.

"Hello." She spoke low into the receiver. "I'm at your sister's." She wound the cord around her hand. "Good, considering." She looked at me and stepped through the doorway into the hall. She stretched the cord its full length.

I busied myself putting Lila's food in the refrigerator.

"Yeah," she said. "I know." She paused to listen. "You did?" She stepped back into the kitchen, slipped off her sneakers, and rubbed a foot with the other. "Well, I know." A few deep breaths later, she said, "We're fine here . . . Sophie's asleep . . . No, no, stay there . . . Okay. I'll tell her." She hung the receiver in the cradle.

"What did Gus say?" I asked.

"Gus and your father went to get Eli, but Eli and Washington were gone. They left together."

"Where did they go?"

"Gus thinks they drove to the seminary."

I imagined Eli driving and the hum of the highway beneath his tires. I wondered what he and Mr. Washington would say to each other, and I marveled at Eli's bravery, his willingness to put himself in the middle of another man's problems. I had not helped Mr. Washington for only noble purposes. Part of me did it to anger Elias and those who had always looked down on me and treated me like an outsider my whole life. I had helped him because he was Thea's son, not because he was a man created equal. But Eli had come to Mr. Washington's aid simply because Eli knew what was right. I was proud of my son's conviction, but I was still afraid for him and myself. "What if the people looking for Washington come here for Eli or me?"

"They won't come here." Lila sounded certain.

"They're liable to come here and burn a cross." It would scare me, if they did that.

"I've got a pistol in my truck says they won't burn shit." She took the whiskey bottle by the neck.

I turned off the kitchen light and followed her outside. She was barefoot and the soles of her feet flashed white in the dark, one step after the other. Her shoulders and hips moved with a swagger. The whiskey had loosened her. I took note of her stride. I would have to walk with confidence like that, in front of Nelly, Ivie, my daughter, down the aisle of the church where I was baptized, confirmed, and married, only this next time, for Elias's funeral Mass.

A small sip of drink moved down my throat and it felt as if a match had been struck inside me.

Lila strode across the grass to the driver's side. The door slammed and she came back, gun in her hand. "We'll be safe and sound."

The rain had cooled the night air. The river frogs chirped and groaned. The ever-present noise of the cicadas vibrated my ears. The clouds were gone, except for some wispy trails, and a sliver of moon hung bright. The smell of rain reminded me of fall and of the geese soon to land and make their home for the winter. I wondered if I would be here to see them.

Verna's porch light flickered on and then off. She was watching my coming and going.

Lila spoke low. "Your father told Gus you're leaving town." She emptied her glass. "'Going on a long vacation,' that's what he said."

The words made me drink mine down. I gagged at the bitter taste.

"Gus thinks you can go and things will settle down. Then you come back." She refilled her glass higher than before.

"He said that?" The whiskey had numbed the pain in my hand.

"He's angry," she replied. "He said this is some crazy business with you and Eli and that mailman."

"Is he angry at Papa or me?"

"Hard to say." Lila poured another inch into my glass. "Both, probably."

With each sip, I felt more off balance. I thought Gus might take my side. He had known Orlando Washington his whole life. Gus had served Negroes, first in Papa's store and then on his route. He had relationships with individuals and knew families and their hopes, but he saw himself in a higher position. Papa had taught him to be humble and gracious, always defer to the customers, no matter the color of their skin. It was the way to build trust and profit, and Gus was hospitable by nature, always happy, welcoming. He moved easily among whites and blacks, but Gus was no crusader. He would not go to a lynching, but he would not sit vigil for Orlando Washington either. If he thought my honor was at stake, he'd protect me—he'd blame Orlando Washington or Ivie or whoever wanted to hurt me. The whiskey made my thoughts swirl like a stick caught in an eddy.

Lila stared at me. "I told you when this started, that it would turn out bad," she said. I felt uneasy under her gaze, but then I realized the whiskey was affecting her too.

"I've had enough," I blurted out. "I'll tell them what I think." I stood as if there was somewhere to go.

Lila's eyes followed me like a cat watching a bird. "You're going nowhere." She waved her hand, dismissing the idea. "Your father is asleep. Nelly is too."

I stumbled toward the door, aiming to get my car keys. I tripped and hit the stone porch with my cut hand. The blood flowed and wet the bandage. Lila walked over and held out a hand. I looked up at her from the cool stone floor, comforting after the heat of the day.

"I am so filthy." I was disgusting, still in the stained dress, no stockings. "Do you know what Marina did?"

She drained her glass. "What?"

I took her hand and got to my knees. "She's having Mitsy's shop send over summer suits with sleeves. She thinks I don't know what to wear to the funeral and she doesn't even know about the marks her father gave me, or that I need to cover them up."

"Why don't you show her?" Lila pulled me up.

"I'm afraid she'll blame me." Seeing the bruises might change her mind, but Marina could dismiss them as easily as she had dismissed her father's misdeeds against Mr. Washington. Marina saw me as the troublemaker, the petulant child, and her father was the keeper of order. He had been expert at hiding his brutality.

"You've risked everything for nothing." Lila's tone was unforgiving.

"Lila," I said. I let go of her grip. "People did not want Papa on their front porch when he first came. He talked funny and looked different. He's Catholic. Not even coloreds were sure about him or what he was." I thought she should understand, after what my father put her through—threatening to take Sophie, treating her as if she did not belong because she wasn't Catholic or Lebanese, or because long ago as a teenager she ran off with that guitar player. "What about you? You married one of us and we are strange to folks."

"That's different," Lila said. She came from poor whites, and she did not look down on Gus or me, unlike the people who claimed to be descended from nobles—people whose families had held slaves and big land. She rationalized loving Gus, because he looked like a picture of Jesus, but she saw herself above Orlando Washington.

"You don't know." My words slurred as they left my mouth. "You couldn't know. You're so pretty and strong."

"Whether I belong or you belong, that's not the problem now." She spoke forcefully. "If Nelly says he was in this house, people will believe you messed with him." She leaned on the porch rail and took another drink, this time straight from the bottle. "And if she starts whispering that you had something to do with Elias, people will get suspicious."

The conversation would be the same with Marina. Worse. My ribs squeezed tight around my heart. I knew in my gut, Nelly would not keep it from her. Nelly suspected I'd done harm to her son and she would not stop until she punished me.

"Anna, you know better." Her voice was harsh. "If it gets out he was in the house with you, whether or not you did anything, your father or Gus is as likely to have him arrested to save face."

The words sent a chill down my spine. I had not expected Papa or Gus to take action, but I had not taken into account what was at stake for them. My stomach turned to think I might have to leave.

She looked me square on. "You should say you were wrong to let him deliver your mail." She lit a cigarette. All the clouds had blown away. The sky was littered with stars. "Say he came in against your will. Say you had to defend yourself."

"No," I said. "That would be cruel." Saying that was tantamount to murder.

She let go of my arm. "What's cruel is giving him hope." She was agitated, as if my standing up for him was beyond all reason. "He should stay gone."

175

"He took that job for a reason." I stared at the sliver of moon and my eyes watered. She did not understand. "He won't run from it."

"He already has." She sat back in her rocker and it creaked.

My throat ached. I could make out the Big Dipper and Orion's Belt. The stars were brighter with the waning moon. My mother and I had sat, both of us wrapped in a quilt, looking up at the stars, and she whispered how they had been her comfort on the voyage to America.

"You are asking for trouble." Lila chastised me the way she would Sophie.

I had wanted trouble for Elias, not Mr. Washington.

"The way I see it, you have to lie if you want to hold that grandbaby." She poured another glass for herself.

"That would be murder." I walked down the porch steps into the damp grass in my bare feet. I stepped over the fallen limbs. Stars peeked through the crown of the tree. Less than twenty-four hours before, I had stood at my window looking down into the branches, thinking to climb out my window and into the tree, to get away from him. I took a deep breath. I was drunk. "You don't know how I've lived with Elias."

"I reckon I do." Her words slurred. She leaned forward in her chair and the rocker squeaked. "You can live with us."

She came into the grass. She tossed a limb out of her path. When she got to me, she put her arm around my shoulder. I leaned on her. "I'm no good to live with anyone," I said.

"Probably not," she said.

"You know that day I came to you with the letter." The cicadas droned. "Gus came out as I was leaving. I was happy for the two of you, but I was jealous too. I wanted someone to love me the way Gus loved you."

A whippoorwill called out and another answered. "You were reading Papa's letter and you looked like you were about to lose everything. That's how I feel now. I looked at you, and for a minute I felt glad, because misery loves company. But then I saw what it said and I couldn't catch my breath and then I looked at you and I was ashamed how I treated you."

"It's okay now." Lila balanced against the tree. She lit another cigarette.

"You have everything." I held her arm to keep myself upright. "I'm glad Gus has you."

"You had a long day," she said.

"When I drove home from your parents' farm, there was a full moon. The brightest I ever saw, shining on the fields, bright and clear like day. I could see the green in the fields, the moon was so bright and low. I felt hopeful. My brother had you and together you had Sophie. I came into town and the moon gleamed off the water. I wanted to drive away and I did. I crossed the bridge. I thought I could leave Marina and Eli. They were old enough to take care of themselves. I was almost to Birmingham before I lost my nerve and turned around."

"Anna," she said. "You're tired."

"I got home and Elias was drunk here on the porch waiting for me. He yelled at me for running Papa's errands. He cussed you. He dragged me upstairs by my hair and shut my door and hit me with his belt. I did not cry out or fight him off. They were sleeping down the hall and I did not want to wake them because they had school." I felt sick from the drink and the memory. "How could they not have heard him?"

"He was a bastard." She hugged me. "A goddamn bastard."

"He stopped slinging his belt, and he said, 'I'm sorry. I'm sorry. I'm so terrible to you.' And then he started undoing my clothes and then he laid me down. That's how lonely I was for someone to touch me, that I'd take his hate if it meant I wasn't alone. I could smell Sophie's baby powder where I had held her, and he smelled of cloves and whiskey. I had wanted him to love me." My throat squeezed tight.

"Shit," she said.

The whiskey had loosened my tongue, and words poured out. "The next morning I got up and started the baking and made the kids' lunches. They came down and they looked sullen and tired like teenagers do, and I thought, 'They did not hear it.' They slept so sound. Then Marina put her head on my shoulder and it was not like her to show any affection, least of all in the morning." My eyes burned. "Elias breezed in and he kissed her head and then mine. And I thought I did the right thing to come home, because at least I had her and Eli."

The sounds of the night—the birds, the tree frogs, the cicadas—soothed the rough feeling in my chest. "I should just go now. Save everyone the trouble."

"You had too much to drink," Lila said.

"I have the money to go."

"Let's get you to bed." Lila tugged at my shoulder and we balanced each other as we climbed the porch stairs.

"Look at those goddamn roses she bought." I pointed to the white wreath. "Must be thirty heads on that." It bespoke how Marina loved him. "She shooed me out of her house. Ashamed for Michael to see me."

"She shouldn't have done that," Lila said. "Come on." I slowed the shutting of the screen door, so as not to disturb the wreath or wake Sophie. We stood in the living room, looked over the rows of chairs. She said, "Tomorrow will be hard."

Using the wall as my guide, I staggered down the hall. Lila walked behind me, in case I might fall, in case I might lie down on the hard, wooden floor.

"After you rest, we'll figure this out." Her voice sounded like a mother's, gentle, like she was talking to Sophie. Her fingers touched the small of my back, guiding me, prodding me up the stairs.

"Okay." I sat on the edge of my bed. My bare, dirty feet hung off the edge of the mattress. I smelled my sweat and the blood. I never went to bed dirty. The room spun. His room was empty. There was some comfort in that. Maybe I could rest like Lila said, and then in the morning, things would be better.

She brushed the hair back from my face. Her touch soothed me. "You need to sleep."

I undid the buttons of my dress and felt the air move against my skin. I would have to face Marina tomorrow.

Lila left the room and returned with a cool rag. "Here's a compress for your head." She placed it above my eyes.

"What will I say to Marina?" I was sad to think she knew what her father did to Mr. Washington, that she could condone it, that she felt so superior to Mr. Washington, to me.

When Lila heard Marina's name, she stiffened. Lila did not like how snooty she could be, how she never stood up to her father. Lila moved away from the edge of the bed, took a few steps to the doorway. "I'm not sure," she said. "It will be hard for her."

"What part, me leaving or me staying?" I was drunk. I had never been drunk. My body gave in to the soft bed. The starlight sent shadows of the slender, pointed pecan leaves across my walls.

In a small, tight voice, she said, "You'll cross that bridge when you get to it." She stood outside my bedroom door to get her bearings, then walked down the hallway toward Marina's room, where Sophie slept. The vibrations of her steps traveled through the floor to the bed to my body.

Bridges, burning bridges, crossing bridges. The Riverton Bridge appeared in my mind's eye. There had been a ceremony when I was a child to open the new bridge for traffic. Before, there had been the ferries and the railroad bridge. The whole town came, white and black, two separate, unmingling groups, to see an actual cat let out of a bag, the superstition being that if it crossed without harm, the bridge was safe. A fat tabby tumbled out of a burlap sack, and when it saw the crowd, it ran south across the bridge. The people followed. The cat paused, looked back, and ran, scared for its life. I walked across with one hand in my father's and the other in Mama's.

I wondered if I would cross the Riverton Bridge in the days to come. I wondered where I might go, if I had to. I had stood in front of the train schedule after Zada left. I had wanted to go to the far edge of the continent to a small town where no one would know me. Somewhere near Seattle or New York or Los Angeles. As far as I could go. I could say my husband died in an accident, and it would be as good as true. Elias would never find me or even lift a finger to look for me. I could raise the baby alone, maybe better without him.

After Marina was born, I told myself she would be better off without me. But now, twenty-three years later, the thought of never seeing her panicked me. I resolved in my mind, if I had to go, I would not go far, to the next town or the next, hovering near like the old Gypsy woman of my mother's stories from home.

I sat up in bed and pulled off the black dress. The cool air hit my body. I tossed the dress on the floor, and my head spun. My head hit the pillow and the room was spinning too. Instead of easing, the whiskey's effects grew stronger. I smoothed the black slip down over my legs. Lila's footsteps sounded in the hall again, coming from Marina's room. She had checked on Sophie and now the gentle night air or the whiskey bottle must be tempting her. She went downstairs for more, or maybe she was going to get the pistol and set watch, ready to protect me from what was coming.

I thought of Marina. She did not know what I knew, no notion of the bruises on my arms or the whispers that had followed me: *The Arab girl who lives in Blacktown,* and later, *That Anna Nassad works like a nigger in her yard—she could get help, but she doesn't know better.* That's what I remembered when it came time to decide whether Thea's son should deliver the mail or not. When he stood outside my screen door, I thought, here is one of God's creatures, the same as me, and I could hear it in his tired voice when he thanked me. But he was gone already. He knew the danger he was in. How stupid of me to think I could help him. I was nothing to him or his people.

I drifted in and out of sleep numbed by drink. I felt the same as I had after Mama died, sick in bed with the Spanish flu, coming in and out of a fog. Thea sat above me, pressing cool rags onto my forehead, running ice against my lips and tongue. Then Aunt Elsa came and she poked and prodded, having had no child of her own and being more practical in her method than Thea.

Elias came into my dreams, young and handsome. I felt hopeful, like the times I was half-asleep and woke to his body, warm and encompassing, on top of me. I would put my fingers in his hair, and I could believe, half dreaming, that this was love. Then the pressure in my chest surfaced like a buoy on the river, and I sat up, wondering if the last day was true. Yes, he was gone. All the feeling of when he'd been drunk or angry and found me alone, when the children were asleep or at school or outside, and he pushed or slapped me, that feeling came down like a heavy brick. When he cried and said he was sorry, he was not apologizing to me. He cried for himself, what he had become, what he had never wanted to be, an ogre like his father who had lorded over Nelly and Ivie and him.

Sophie came into the room and stood at the foot of the bed.

"Where's my mama?" she whimpered.

"She's not with you?" I felt a chill.

"No," she whined, unsure of her surroundings.

The rain had turned the summer night as cool as the day had been hot.

I perched onto an elbow. My head was dizzy from the drink. Lila must have been passed out on the couch, too drunk to hear Sophie or climb the stairs. "Come in with me," I said.

Sophie snuggled close like a cat. I remembered watching my children sleep. If Eli woke in a nightmare, I would hold him and comfort him. When he was little, I would say, "Sweet, sweet boy," and his warm face would nuzzle my neck. I sat with them, and when I got tired, I'd curl up on their floor. Elias would not come for me if I was with them. I was happy to hear their breathing and thankful to be close.

I wished I could go back in time and hold Marina more, hold her until she understood my love for her, hold her until I understood better what I should have been for her, so that now, when it came time for her to make a choice, she might choose me.

The sliver of moon hung in the window. I pulled a sheet over our legs and ran my fingers through Sophie's hair, the way I remembered my mother doing for me. Soon, Sophie breathed deeply, sleeping as only a child can.

Mama

Sophie's small body emitted heat. If I moved, she inched over until we touched again. Marina had never cuddled so close. It had been a long time since I held one so dear, even longer since someone had held me. I was eight years old when Mama came to me on her last night. The nights after her death, I held my brother with the same closeness as Sophie and I shared now. I had clung to Gus, who was three years old and sound asleep, dumb to the fact that our mother was gone forever.

The last night, Mama came into the room I shared with Gus. She sought refuge in me as her pain mounted, knowing her labor had begun. She propped herself on pillows on my bed and told me story after story. She knew it could be her last chance.

I thought of Marina's notion of me, and now Sophie's, and how these next few days might be their last chance to know me. Sophie had heard from my lips, *They think I killed him.* If I stayed or if I left, there would be lies and truths and mixtures of both. What they would remember of me, I did not know.

I remembered my mother saying that night, "The babies are talking to us." We knew she was having twins because a crease ran down the middle of her stomach like a cleft in a peach, with a baby on each side.

My ear was pressed against her belly. "What are they saying?" I asked.

"What do you hear?" Her fingers combed my hair, and her nails passed lightly over my scalp, sending goose bumps down my body.

I heard gurgles of gas, rumblings, not unlike what my own stomach said when I was hungry. "They say they are coming."

Being the woman she was, from the place she came from, she took my words as a prophecy, and to ease her nerves she told a story I loved.

"Every year, an old Gypsy woman came to my village, pushing a cart with a *diib*, a *wolf*, tied to the wooden handle like a dog on a leash. She came in the spring, lit a fire, and kept camp on the outskirts of town. She stole from the village, but she was tolerated out of charity, for she had no family, and in our tradition, you must be generous to the needy or you bring shame on yourself and your family. This Gypsy, she doted on the wolf as if he were a lapdog, and for years, her arrival was believed a good omen, for if an old woman could tame a wolf, she could spread her charms over the soil and crops of the village.

"Our Gypsy looted from our gardens, from the market bins, the henhouses, and the butcher's pile of bones. She took a bit from one household, and then another, so her pilfering did not upset one over the other. Still, the mothers of the village warned us to stay away, because Gypsies stole children and this Gypsy might give us to the wolf."

Mama squeezed my arm, my leg, and then reached for my ankle. I asked if she wasn't mistaking a big dog for the wolf.

"No, *binti*. It was a *wolf*, a huge wolf." Mama narrowed her eyes. "We doubted my mother, though, and so we took turns climbing an ancient olive tree, not far from the old woman's camp. My sisters climbed high, but I climbed the highest, and I saw the Gypsy stirring her pot and the wolf gnawing a bone stolen from the butcher's alley.

"The sight of the wolf frightened me, but I was proud of how high I could go. My sisters said, 'No, Vega, come down. She'll see you.'

My sisters panicked and they chided me, 'We should have listened to Mother and stayed away.' Then the Gypsy laid eyes on us. With a toothless grin, she wiggled her finger, motioning me to come to her. The wolf sensed us, stopped gnawing, stood on his four tall legs. He sniffed the air with his wet black nose."

At this point in her story, my body tingled, as if I were the girl in the tree facing the wolf. The cadence of Mama's words slowed.

"My mother's warnings came back to me, 'Stay far from the Gypsy.' My sisters pleaded, 'Vega, come with us.' Mayme tugged my leg, but I gripped the high branch for dear life. I cried. Elsa jumped from the lowest branch. She yelled at Mayme, 'She's under the Gypsy's spell. I'll get Mama,' and ran toward home.

"The wolf pulled on his rope. The old hag waved her hand to me, as if to say, 'Come here, little girl.' I was numb. The wolf grinned, showing his white teeth. If I obeyed the old woman's beckoning, I feared I would be his dinner. If I touched the ground, I believed the wolf would break his tether and chase me down."

I squeezed Mama's arm, so happy that she escaped the horrible fate, so happy to know the story's end.

"The wolf licked his muzzle, and suddenly, my body regained its power. I jumped and hit the ground and ran home with Mayme at my side. Elsa and my mother met us halfway. So afraid she had lost me, your grandmother's face was streaked with tears. She cried and cried, thinking what an awful death I had escaped. That night my father and some village men went with torches to clear out the Gypsy and her wolf. The beast bared his teeth. He sprang to the length of his tether and attacked the arm of a man. But another caught hold of his leash, and with a second rope, they looped his hind legs. They tore the wolf in two. The old Gypsy cursed them as they slayed her wolf, and she wept over the corpse as if she'd lost her only son. Her curses angered the men, and they chased her into the dark night. On their return, they burned her cart and the body of the wolf. Hidden in the darkness, she watched all her possessions and her companion go up in flames."

The story left me tingling, and I knew if ever I had the choice, I would remember to obey my mother completely. She was silent and her eyes had a far-off look, but I waited patiently for her to speak.

"Your Aunt Elsa cared for you when you were a baby." She stroked my hair. "She is coming to help me and Thea after the birth." Her temples beaded with sweat.

I waited. My skin tingled, knowing with the mention of Elsa what story came next.

"I had a hat-and-finery shop in Nashville with my sisters, and our father treated us like sons, so much that he did not worry about our mingling with men in our store or in town or at church socials. We could not have done that at home. We were strong together. Independent. A new kind of Syrian girl.

"One day, my sisters and I bought a mockingbird in a cage. We fed it apples, and its songs reminded us of the songbirds back home, but now our home was here in America. I thought the bird was the same as all the birds before it and all the birds after it, and I wondered if my sisters and I were the same as our parents and if our children would be the same too, all of us doing the same things and singing the same songs, repeating life again and again, or if each of us had our own path to take. My thoughts puzzled me, but I was sad the bird was trapped in the cage, so I let it fly off. And that was days before your father came into the store.

"He was handsome but big and oafish in a store of ladies trying on hats," she said. "When I asked if he would like to try one on, he turned red." Her face glowed. "I pretended not to like him so he would like me more.

"He had traveled south from New York, peddling down roads, other times taking a train. Our family store was a station. We Syrians were spread all over, and one family would take a newcomer in, feed him, offer advice, and send him toward his next stopping point. That's how my family went from New Orleans to Nashville, where we settled by the river, because it reminded us of our river in Zahlé.

"Instead of sending your father on, I married him. We decided we were Americans, and to marry for love, not as our parents arranged. Of course, his parents were in the old country and mine loved the match, so we were already free. We lived above the hat store until you were born."

I loved the next part of her story.

"When you were inside of me, like these babies now," she said and touched her swollen belly, "I knew you were a girl. No one believed me. Your grandmother prayed openly for a boy." She crossed herself and kissed her fingertips. "In the old country only boys are celebrated. Your father bought a baseball glove. 'What can a baby do with this?' I asked. It was for his son, he said. I warned him of his pride." She arched her eyebrow. "As soon as my laboring began, my sisters and mother began cooking a feast to celebrate." Mama paused and seemed to smell the air. "The food, oh! The savories roasted and stewed. The aroma of fresh bread and the rice pudding for a boy, all of it wafted in where I was. They were laughing and singing and I begged them to stop. It was bad luck to celebrate before a baby's birth.

"I asked for your father and told him, 'They are tempting God with their pride! Make them stop until the baby is born.' Your father stormed the kitchen and the women teased and prodded him until he had a fit: 'You are upsetting Vega. You must stop.' And they hushed. You finally came and your lungs filled and I was happy to see a strong girl." She touched my face. This was my favorite part: "You tricked everybody, smart and wily, like a girl should be."

I wondered how I was wily and smart. Most days I felt clumsy, uncertain of my words and movements, unlike her, graceful and beautiful. I wanted to trust she knew something I had yet to discover, and that one day I would be as she saw me.

"The news went around the house." Her eyes were deep and dark like a well that has no bottom. I wanted to fall into them and gather all she knew. "Everyone grew quiet. Back home, the birth of a girl was met with silence and prayers for the next child to be a boy. Your father looked at me and said, 'So, Vega, you give me a feisty girl?'

"I was not afraid of him. My sisters and I had come to America and supported ourselves without husbands—something we could never have done in the old country. I defied the old notions that boys should be more celebrated than girls. I answered him, 'Yes, I give you this girl. She is a strong spirit to face you fools waiting for a boy. Such a brave girl will handle your future sons with ease.'

"Your father held you and said, 'You heard Vega.' And everyone laughed, cut the meat and the bread, and finished the rice pudding. We celebrated you." That was the end of her story. She seemed content with the telling of it.

I sat near her until she fidgeted. When I moved, I saw her skin was ashen. She held her belly, and the blue veins of her hands were thick. "I feel sick," she said. It seemed she spoke to the walls, for she would never worry me on purpose. Before I could ask what was the matter, the pain seemed to pass and she spoke again.

"My Zahlé was a beautiful place. The river flowed out of the mountain and down through town. From the promenade we watched it tumble over the rocks, and when the river was low, we waded in the cold mountain water."

Mama bent over in pain, but then the pain passed, and she continued talking about her old life. "When it was time to harvest the olives, we camped in the orchards and ate plums and pomegranates from the trees all day. At night, a lamb would be roasted and flatbread baked over the fire. We unrolled our carpets and ate and slept beneath the stars, never covering our heads with a roof for days. The leaves of the olive trees were soft like velvet, the trunks were gnarled, and I imagined figures twisted beneath the bark. I asked my father, 'How old are these trees?' He said, 'Maybe five hundred years, or maybe one thousand.' Oh, *binti*, I wish you could see the olive groves." Her fingers combed through my hair.

She went on about the tiled marketplace and the oldest street in the city, where travelers came from all over Syria, Baghdad, and Palestine to trade their goods. And then her warm house with green shutters and high ceilings, goose-feather beds and cool tiled floors, her mother's oven and the hot flatbreads, spread with oil and *za'atar*, or the warm *ma'amul*, date cookies, she would eat when she came home from the nuns' school.

From my doorway, Papa whispered, "Vega, it is midnight. Let the child sleep."

"A moment more," she said. His steps sounded across the hall and I listened as he settled into bed. My mother and I cast our gaze on sleeping Gus. I was amazed at his stillness, what a tiny, gentle creature he appeared to be when no longer spinning and churning through the house and yard.

She radiated moist heat, but I clung to her mountainous body, sensing this would be the last night she could afford me her undivided attention. Her silence lulled me and my eyelids grew heavy, though I fought to keep them open, aware of her presence.

I woke in the dark. The bed was wet. I moved slowly toward the foot, sniffing to see if I had peed, but my gown was dry. The wetness had come from her. She perched upon the edge of my bed. Shadows replaced her eyes, and deep lines creased across her forehead and around her mouth. Her hands dug into the mattress. She told me, "Get your papa."

I looked to sleeping Gus, then ran to my father.

He sat up quick from the bed, as if he had not been sleeping at all. "Your mother?" He rushed past me to her.

I stood silent in the hall as he guided her out of my room into her own. She moved as if her bones were broken and each step shot pains through her body.

He passed me again, without a word, only stomping feet into his boots as he stumbled out the door.

"Binti," Mama's voice called. "Come here by me." I ran to her, not knowing what was happening. The lines on Mama's face looked like a tangle of knots. But her voice was calm. "Soon the babies are coming." She ran her fingers through my hair. "Papa has gone to get Thea and the doctor." To the priest after Mass and to anyone who would listen, Papa had bragged that the doctor would attend this birth. He had struck a deal with Dr. Walker in trade for free groceries delivered to his house for a year.

Her gown was soaked through. A tincture of blood stained it. Mama sent me for towels and a pan of water. I turned on the overhead light, but Mama complained it was too bright. I lit the oil lamps she kept on either side of the bed, and the amber light softened the edges of the room. It made my eyes sleepy, but there would be no more sleep. I wanted desperately to return to the quiet nest we had shared earlier, when she was mine alone.

She told me to wet the cloth and drape it on her neck. She leaned forward, her feet on the floor, toes curled under. Her thin nightgown stuck to her skin, and with some effort, she pulled it off. Her breasts were full and dark. Blue veins, like rivers on a map, curved around her engorged tummy. As she rounded her back, I rubbed the wet cloth across her skin. Drips of water rolled down the ridges of her spine. I ran my fingers through the path of water and pressed her flesh against the bone. She moaned and I knew I had given her comfort. I rubbed until my fingers went numb. She had recently cut her hair and it stuck to her neck like velvet ribbons. I asked did she want me to comb it.

"No, *binti*." She tried to smile, but her lips emitted a whimper that turned into a long, painful wail. It was almost five o'clock, the sky was still dark, and my father had not returned.

"Stand in front of me."

She held onto my shoulders, and with her feet spread apart, she squatted near the edge of the bed. She pressed her weight on me and moaned. Her face was a tight knot and turning a terrible red, her temples throbbing as she bore down. I thought she might push me through the floor, no longer my gentle mama, but a writhing, twisting creature that oozed liquids and groaned in pain. I looked away from her face and that's when I saw the crown of the baby's head, but then it disappeared into her again. Blood fell in large drops onto the floor. I looked at her and was afraid. She let go of me and sank on the bed.

"Get a sheet, Vega," she said. Thankful for any means of escape, I ran to the linen closet for the sheet. She covered herself. "Will you pour me a glass of water?" She gave a weak smile. I sensed she did not want me to see her suffering. I walked down the hall to the kitchen and drew the glass of water. I stood frozen to the spot, unable to will my feet to return to her. I waited for Papa and Thea and the doctor. I listened to Mama's whimpering. A terrible battle raged in my head whether to stay put or go to her, until finally my father's clomping feet sounded in the store below. He burst up the stairs and through the kitchen. "Your mother?" he asked.

I nodded, not knowing what to say.

He bounded down the hall. Thea turned the corner from the stairs. In her arms she carried a stack of sheets and a satchel. She had delivered Gus three years before.

"Where is Dr. Walker?"

"He'll be here directly," she said. She walked toward me. "Go on, now. You go to bed 'til I come and get you. It's early yet."

Thankful Thea was there to help Mama, I drank the water and went back to the room I shared with Gus. My bed was wet and so I lay down next to him. Morning light peeked through the curtains and I could see the stained sheets on my bed. Not sure what to do, I put on my day's clothes and sat next to Gus. He snuggled close to me. I could see her across the hall, moaning, propped up on pillows with her eyes closed. Her black hair was matted to her head. I wanted to go to her and wipe her face and comb the tangles out with my fingers, but knew I could not get to her. Thea attended her—wiping down her body, wrestling the sheets from beneath her, changing her gown. Thea caught my eye and shut the door to my mother's room. I turned away and cradled Gus in my arms.

I listened to the mournful moans and the coaxing for hours, until Thea burst in and roused Gus. "Get up." She saw I was already dressed. "Help your brother with his clothes and come eat breakfast."

"Yes, ma'am." There would be no dawdling whenever Thea used that tone of voice. She fried two eggs and served them with cornbread from supper the night before. Thea pointed to the door. "You children go outside and play. I don't want to hear from you." She spoke to me, for Gus cared nothing about the indoors. "You watch your brother. Keep him away from the river. Thea has no time for a drowned boy today."

She opened the balcony door and ushered us outside. The store would be closed for the day.

"Let him dig worms for fishing, pull weeds in the garden, play. Get food from the store when you're hungry. But don't come up here." She shut the door on us. Gus heard "worms" and already had a bucket of empty tobacco tins and was headed out to the garden. I sat on the black iron steps and watched him dig with the persistence of a hound. He held up worm after worm to show me his success. I walked out toward the garden and stood a few feet from him. A sailboat tacked back and forth to make the curve of the river. A barge pushed slowly past. In the time I waited, two trains blared through town and then rumbled over the bridge.

I fixed my eyes on the brick store and on the second-floor corner window where Mama was. The sky was crisp blue. It was a warm fall day and the clouds sat like cotton balls over the dark river.

Dr. Walker drove up. Papa must have been watching from an upstairs window. He ran down, talking quickly at the doctor about her pain, her effort. Dr. Walker followed Papa and calmly listened. Soon they were inside. A formation of geese landed near the water's edge. They honked to each other as they waddled onshore.

Thea walked carefully down the stairs. Her arms carried a load of stained sheets. She said, "Good girl," noting all was well with Gus and me. At the water pump, she dropped the sheets on the grass and filled a large washbasin with soap and water, piling in bloodied sheets and rags to soak.

She hurried back in. I turned to check that Gus was occupied. Gus was building a castle of mud, rocks, and sticks. He paid no attention to me and I knew he would not venture by the water, because he was afraid of the geese. I opened the back door to the store. A feeling flurried in my stomach, and I was certain I would be punished for going against Thea's orders, but worry for Mama made me brave.

I stepped in the door and slipped off my shoes. As I climbed the staircase, the house was eerily quiet. I was careful of every step and cringed at each sound. I moved so slowly that I thought I'd never make it to the top. But then Mama screamed, and the doctor said, "Bear down, Vega. Bear down." His voice was calm, but she was not. She screamed, more horrible than I remembered from Gus's birth. And then my father asked, "What's happening? What's happening?" His voice sounded like a child's.

I held my breath and ran up the steps, not caring that noise would give me away. At the top, I ducked under a table with a lace cloth that hung low. Through the lace, I saw my father moving from room to room. He rubbed his forehead, and his shirt was marked with sweat rings at his armpits. He went downstairs into the store. His office door opened, then shut.

Bright light flowed through the hall windows and onto the wooden floors, making a grid of light and shadow. Mama cried out for Papa but he did not return to her. She needed me. If she saw me, I thought, that would help her, but if I went, Thea or Papa would punish me and I'd be sent away. She cried out again. The late-afternoon sun poured through the windows and cast long shadows of the windowpanes on the wood floors. I eased out from under the table and moved toward her cries, down the hall through squares of light.

Her voice was low, chanting, *"Kyrie, eleison." Lord, have mercy.*

Downstairs, Papa's office door opened. His steps fell on the stairs, and I slid into my room as my father rushed past me.

"What can I do?" he asked.

I crossed the hall, and from the doorway of Mama's room, I saw Thea behind her, holding Mama's knees close to her chest. Thea's face was slick with sweat. Mama's sheet stuck to her body. Her hair stood up in all directions. Her face was gray and her eyes darted like an injured animal's.

When she saw my father, she cried out his name. With her hands tense and her fingers splayed, so that I could count them—one, two, three, four, five—she reached out to him. She grabbed his arm. She could not sob, for it seemed she could barely breathe.

"Can't you help her?" Papa asked.

The doctor's hands were between Mama's legs. He did not answer. His sleeves were rolled to his armpits, and I could see his muscles tighten as he pulled. I motioned him to stop, but he did not see me.

The doctor yelled, "Push," and Mama's face seemed to fold in upon itself.

Papa held her hand and as she pushed, her face and her knuckles went white but my father's face turned red.

"Thea, keep her up." The doctor's voice was strained, like he was lifting a hundred-pound weight. "Mr. Khoury, step out."

My father hesitated. He stood beside Mama, looking back and forth from her to the man who had his hands inside her womb.

"Step out," Dr. Walker said. "Now." His voice was harsh.

Papa jolted and tripped. I leaned back against the wall. I was not supposed to see his confusion or her pain.

He walked past and took no notice of my presence. His footsteps stopped at the back window. I followed him. He watched Gus dig in the garden below.

I moved swiftly in my bare feet down the hall. Thea cradled Mama's head and prayed in a low, steady voice. "Be with us, Lord."

The doctor did not look up, but said, "Thea, I need you here." His voice growled like a bear's.

Thea laid my mother down gently and took her place beside the doctor, pressing Mama's knees apart. Mama let out whimpers. She was too weak to do anything else. The doctor pulled and there were sounds of heavy breathing and strain. "Get the warm blankets," he said.

In his hands was one baby, small and blue, with a cord of flesh wrapped around his neck. In a few swift movements, Dr. Walker unwound the cord, wiped his body, suctioned his nose, his mouth, and slapped his bottom. No sound came. I felt sure the doctor had broken him. The doctor placed the still baby in Thea's arms and she rubbed him for what seemed a long time. Mama was not moving, except for her eyes darting between the ceiling and Thea, who stood near her feet.

Thea's face looked pinched. "He's gone to heaven."

"Put the baby down and help me, Thea."

She did as she was told in a most solemn manner.

"This one is breech." His face contorted, he seemed to be wrestling with Mama's insides. She appeared to wilt away, but Thea tried to prop her up to help push it out. When it seemed the baby would not come, the doctor took large metal spoons, what I later learned were forceps, and put them inside her. I sank down and squatted on the floor. My palms were sweaty and what I saw sickened me. But then, there was a sound, like a late-night cat. "A boy," Dr. Walker said.

Mama smiled weakly, and at least she had that moment of happiness.

Thea said, "Praise the Lord."

I ran to the kitchen to give Papa the news. He rushed past me, and I followed, but in the short time I had left my watch, Thea's face had turned grim. She rubbed the baby with warm towels and patted his bottom, all the while begging, "Little man, come on, now. Cry. Come on now, fella." The baby gave tired whimpers, but he never mustered the cry Gus once had.

The doctor tended to Mama. He sewed stitches and packed her with compresses to slow the blood that flowed from her. Papa knelt beside her head. Her eyes looked wild and her breathing sounded strange.

I stood in the door. The light was dimming, and with each passing minute, I felt certain my life had changed for the worse. It was dusk outside and the room was dark. Dr. Walker and Thea kept on working as if they were blind moles digging a tunnel. The oil lamps had been snuffed out at some point in the day. I moved into the room and switched on the pink glass lamp on Mama's dressing table. The rosy light that had once seemed cheerful burned my eyes.

I fingered the bone-handled brush that lay on the dresser. The tortoiseshell comb that once pinned her hair in place was propped against the mirror. It was a useless thing, now that she had cut her hair. I gripped the comb and thought if I squeezed it hard enough, she would stop bleeding and the baby would cry. Her hair would grow long, she would laugh again, and the baby would come back to life.

I turned to see Thea cleaning the babies with a sponge. Her apron dark and smeared with blood. The edges of her lips turned down and her eyelids seemed heavy. The babies did not cry or move or breathe. One was deep blue, almost purple in the dim light. The other, who had lived only moments, was pale in comparison. Thea saw me watching. She did not shoo me away, but gazed at me as if she wanted me to understand that life could be cut short, that blessings were special and rare. She wanted me to prepare myself for what she must have known was coming.

I remembered Mama's warning that God might take babies for his own purpose, but I did not feel better knowing they were with God. Papa stood and walked past me as if I was not there. With purposeful steps, I followed him down the hallway, outside, and down the stairs where Gus sat on the bottom step, forgotten and surely hungry. Papa picked him up and carried him to the truck. He never looked back at me, nor told me where he was going, but I knew he was going to get the priest.

I returned to Mama's room and stood in the doorway.

Thea saw me. "Come by your mama." My feet were heavy. I felt that if I stepped across the threshold, my life would forever be changed. Mama's weak eyes looked at me. She tried to lift her hand. I took it in mine and squeezed, but it was clammy and feeble, not her normal warm and strong hand.

The doctor was still working on her. "Thea," he said. "Take the child out. She has no business in here." He spoke to her sharp and angry.

Thea ignored him. She went about her work with Mama. There was lots of blood and Mama was pale. Her breath shallow.

The doctor told Thea twice more, "Take the girl out," before she finally scooted me into the hall. She did not shut the door, and for the next thirty minutes, I watched him pull blood-soaked bandages from her and replace them inch by inch with clean white ones. A needle glistened in the dusky light. He gave Mama a shot in the arm and when my father returned with the priest, Mama's eyes were closed and her breath shallow.

The priest was tall and thin and very pale. His voice had often lulled me to sleep in the hard wooden pews at Mass. His long, thin hands had placed the communion wafer on my tongue, had tousled Gus's curly hair and shaken my father's hand as we left church. I did not want him there, leaning over Mama, praying in his droning voice as the doctor worked on her, as my father wept, as Thea finally covered the babies with the blankets meant to bundle them.

The priest switched off the pink lamp on her dressing table near me and lit the wicks of the oil lamps on either side of her bed. The light from the flames danced on the dark walls and illuminated the priest's pale cheeks. His dark clothes blended into the night. His face seemed to float above Mama. I watched his lips move and realized he was giving her last rites. Mama was dying. The sheet beneath her was blood-soaked. The men standing over her were as pale as she, though she had lost most of the blood from her body and they had lost none.

The doctor sent Thea for more clean bandages. I followed her and found Gus huddled in a corner of the kitchen. He was covered in filth from his day of digging. I took his hand and led him to the tub, where I bathed him as best I could. I dressed him in his nightclothes, brought him a glass of milk and some bread and butter, and put him to bed in our room.

When I returned to Mama's room, she had stopped breathing. I stood in the doorway and watched the priest and my father kneeling beside her and praying. The doctor had left his post. I could hear the water in the kitchen as he scrubbed her blood from his hands and arms. Thea went around the house covering mirrors and stopped the pendulum on the tall clock in our family room. But all the fuss did not change a thing.

Thea made the praying men leave, so that she could clean the body and strip the bed. She had to push Papa out, and I followed him down the stairs and into Mama's baking room, where he sat on a wooden bench. I stood beside him and rested my hand on his arm. He said nothing. The priest knelt and prayed while holding our hands. Papa's face was the color of ashes. He said, "What a horrible death," as if the priest could undo her dying.

Thea tended to Mama until late and then solemnly stood beside my mother until her husband came to get her. He had to take her by the arms and lead her out. Only then did I hear her cry.

I tried to sleep next to Gus. No one had changed my bed, and I could not bear to do it myself. I took the pillow where her head had laid and breathed in her smell. This pillow had been the last thing she touched when we were a mother and her daughter.

All night Papa paced the floor, and once, I rose from my sleepless bed and followed him through the kitchen to the sitting room, down the hall past the flickering light of the oil lamps in her room and back to the kitchen again. He stopped and leaned against the doorframe with his face buried in his strong arms. I stood in the dark shadows of a corner and watched him. His breathing was regular and I detected no signs of sobbing or crying. He mumbled something. I looked closer. Wrapped around his hand were glittering beads. Mama's rosary. He was praying for her soul. I wanted to grab his leg, lift my arms so that he would pick me up and hold me close. But I was afraid he would walk away from me, if only because of his own grief.

The thought of him denying me, the grief for my lost mother, the loneliness of it all, let loose in me, and I cried as I never had before, nor ever would again. My wails startled him from his prayers, and in a few long strides, he swept me up into his bearlike arms. *"Binti, binti."* He held me for a long time until my crying stopped and the sobs and hiccups passed. He carried me to my dark room.

I refused to go into my bed. "She was there," I said.

A sigh from his lips and he tucked me in with Gus and kissed my forehead in a sorrowful way. "Your Aunt Elsa will come." He touched my hair before he walked down the hall to the kitchen. A wooden chair creaked as he sat.

Across the hall, her body lay still, dressed in her sky-blue dress. I went to her. Her hair was no longer wild; Thea had brushed it softly around her face. She looked clean and peaceful, on a new mattress brought late in the evening to replace the one soaked in blood. She lay on the best linen sheets we had, the ones that took a whole morning to iron. The oil lamps burned on either side of the bed. The soft light glimmered on the walls and reflected in the mirror and shimmered on the ceiling. It was as if dancing spirits lit her room. The sight was oddly beautiful and terrifying. I left her to see if the light affected Gus, but he slept soundly, and I envied how he didn't understand what was happening. I lay next to him again, but could not sleep for the flickering light bouncing across the hall. I took my pillow on which she had laid her head. It still held her scent.

I returned to the room of dancing light. I would keep vigil over her. My chest felt hollow, like her empty birdcage in the corner of the room. I touched her things. The silver mirror, the bone-handled brush and tortoiseshell comb. I watched her still body as I neared her closet, wanting her to turn and invite me into bed. Her ten silver bangle bracelets were strewn carelessly over the dresser. One of them had been engraved with my name and birthday. I found it and ran my fingers over her name and mine—*Vega*. I placed the bracelet on my wrist.

I lay down beneath the window closest to her bed and dozed on and off, waking to what seemed bright bursts of light but were only the small flames of the oil lamps. Deep in the night, the lights seemed strangely peaceful and soothing, and I pretended that Mama slept soundly and that when morning came, she would rise and all would be hopeful. I dozed once more, but jolted awake to the grim reminder that she was not asleep but gone forever, like the *forever and ever, amen* of the Lord's Prayer.

I opened the closet door and breathed in the familiar scent of Mama. I touched the fabrics of her dresses and made myself remember the occasions that she had worn each one. The fine silks for church, made from fabric Papa sold in his store. The one the color of summer grass was my favorite. The plain cotton dresses for everyday and the dark wool skirts for winter. In my hand I cradled her black dress shoe, with its pointed toe and leather-covered buttons and curved heel. With the soft leather next to my cheek, I breathed in the clean smell of talcum powder left behind from her foot. I feared I would soon forget the details of her—her clothes, her hair, the way she smelled of lemon verbena after a bath. So I pulled her dresses, one by one, from their hangers, and made a nest of them on the floor of her closet to sleep the next few hours wrapped in her scent.

The Mail

After a short and fitful sleep, I woke to the sounds of Lila cooking in my kitchen. Sophie did not stir. Lila clattered pots and pans. Grease popped and the smell of bacon filled the house, making me hungry. Sophie inched closer as if she sensed I was about to leave. There was a ribbon of sweat where she touched me. I slid away from her and sat at the edge of the bed. I listened to the house shift and creak as Lila moved around the kitchen.

The sky was still dark, but light was coming soon enough. This was the time I usually woke, took out my bowls, the salt and the flour from the pantry, and began baking the day's loaves and flatbreads. That part was over.

Sophie scooted closer. I touched her curls. Sleep and the bad taste of whiskey lingered in my mouth. I wiped the film from my lips. Memories of my mother's last night worried me. Marina would need me today.

I picked up the black dress, caked with dried blood, and tossed it into my closet. I took the housecoat from its peg. The cotton felt cool on my skin. I snapped the gold watch Elias gave me for our twentieth anniversary onto my arm. It was after six when I left Sophie curled and sleeping in my bed.

The smell of incense lingered in the hall from Elias's room. I shut his door. In the bathroom I undid the bloodied bandage on my hand. Cold water stung the angry red cut, but the sharp pain was useful to prepare me for what was to come. From the medicine cabinet, I took two aspirin and put the bitter pills on my tongue. I drank from the tap and swallowed. I wrapped my hand in fresh gauze and tried not to look in the mirror at my frizzed hair and the circles under my eyes, dark as night. I had never looked so tired and old.

Downstairs in my kitchen, Lila stood at the sink smoking a cigarette and sipping a cup of black coffee. The bacon cooled on a plate. Lila held the cigarettes in my direction.

"No," I said. "Thank you."

She poured steaming coffee from my percolator. "Did you rest?"

The giant coffee urn sat on the dining-room table. Piled around it, the cups, the plates, the neatly pressed linens. My house was soon to hold his coffin and then the house would fill with people.

I held the cup close to my face and breathed in the warm steam. "Sophie crawled in bed with me last night."

I wanted to tell her what she meant to Sophie. *Take nothing for granted*, I wanted to say. *Do better than me.*

Lila turned and looked out the window to the pale-gray morning. "Your garden has gone wild overnight."

It may not be mine anymore, I wanted to say. Weeds had sprouted. I had not tended it in three days. "It can go to the birds," I said. I was worried about my son and the postman. "Orlando Washington is gone," I said.

She winced and took a last drag off her cigarette.

"I'll be fine, but he won't." The coffee was warm and gritty, better than the whiskey the day before.

"You are thickheaded." She ran water over her cigarette butt. "He is nothing to you." If she'd had a horse whip in her hands, she would have cracked it to get me in line.

"Mama used to tell me a story about a Gypsy woman who was run out of her village in the old country." I wound the cuckoo clock over the sink. "A mob chased her out because she frightened my mother and her sisters. Do you think that's what will happen to me?"

"It damn well might if you keep on." Her eyes scoured my face.

"If Mr. Washington comes back—"

She cut me off. "He's gone. Gus says he's gone."

"I don't want to burden Eli with this."

"He'll be all right." She shook her head. "He's a grown man and he has the Church on his side. They can protect him."

I wanted to believe she was right, but I didn't trust anything.

"You've got nothing to protect you." She scowled. Sophie's feet padded across the floor above us. "You might have been better off with Elias alive." As Sophie's steps sounded down the stairs, Lila's expression softened.

"Mama," she said. The quiet of Lila's day was over. I was envious for such a distraction.

"Look who's here," Lila said. "My sunshine, my only sunshine," she sang softly.

Sophie's leotard twisted around her waist and the skin of her chest was exposed. She had wrestled it down to go to the bathroom. Lila helped her straighten it.

"She slept so sound," I said.

The pale-gray sky brightened. With Sophie hanging on her leg, Lila turned up the gas on the stove. The bacon grease popped, and she cracked three eggs into the pan. She took the biscuits out of the oven and fixed three plates of food. We sat and ate in silence.

When I finished, I reached for the canvas bag of money atop the refrigerator and went outside to my car. The mockingbird perched on a low limb, his gray-and-white-striped tail flicked up. He called out to me, flew down to the grass, and unfolded his wings. "You'll have to wait a minute, old man," I said. The wet grass was cool on my feet, but I could taste the heat surfacing in the air. The noise of cicadas thrummed like ocean waves—gaining, crashing, rolling back.

The pebbles of the drive cut into the soles of my feet. I opened the trunk of the car and shifted the grocery bags of money. I placed my father's money beside them and covered it all with a blanket. The money would not be safe inside the house, not with all the people coming and going.

Inside the front door, I called out to Sophie. "You want to feed the bird?"

"Oh, yes," she said and came running down the hall. Her face was bright. She smiled and her baby teeth showed. Soon she'd lose them and the big, awkward adult teeth would come in. I wondered if I would be here to see it.

I got the raisins from the cabinet and put a few handfuls in my pocket.

Outside, I gave her some, and she tossed them one at a time, high in the air, and the mockingbird flew up and down. Sophie flitted around the yard in her bare feet. The bird pecked at the ground and searched.

Lila came out with two cups of coffee in her hand. We sat on the porch steps and sipped the coffee while Sophie played. I was happy to have them with me and grateful that nothing else needed to be said.

The phone rang, and Lila patted my shoulder. "I'll get it. You sit while you can."

I hoped it was Marina calling to say she was headed to the hospital.

A car door slammed down the street and I saw a mail truck parked in the shade a few yards from my drive. It was not Orlando Washington; he did not have a mail truck. A man stepped from the shade of the tree. He was white. He clipped a ring of keys to his belt as he approached.

I walked barefoot across the dewy grass and gathered the collar of my housecoat together.

"Sophie," I said. "Go in and get your mama."

"But why?" she asked. She continued to run loops around the tree.

"Go, now, I said." I spoke sharply. I wanted her out of earshot in case the man said something she should not hear, but I knew by the look on her face that I had offended her with my tone.

She ran inside.

The postman's shoes crunched the gravel drive. "Ma'am," he said as he approached. His face was clean-shaven and fresh, his hair hidden beneath his postman's cap. He extended a handful of mail, probably sympathy and prayer cards.

"Good morning," I said. With my bandaged hand, I took the envelopes—at least ten. "Mail's early today."

"First on the route today," he said. "Catching up from the snag we hit yesterday." His eyes scanned my face, and he scowled at what he saw. I felt exposed and gripped the collar of my housecoat. This was why appearances mattered, why money made up for strangeness. I needed my nice clothes, my makeup and jewelry.

"What happened yesterday?" I asked, as if I did not know.

"Your friend left town." He smirked. "He left, like we knew he would. Can't count on an unreliable race." The hateful look on his face made it clear that all of Riverton was against Mr. Washington, not just Elias, not just Ivie. They were against me too.

The screen door slapped shut. Lila stood on the top step of the porch with Sophie in her arms.

His eyes left me and rested on Lila. "Ma'am." He tipped his cap in her direction.

He stared too long, and I turned to see what captured his attention. The child's dark, bare legs hung beside Lila's waist, and the head of brown curls rested on her mother's shoulder. The contrast of Lila's fair skin against Sophie's rich olive color struck me as peculiar, out of place, even though they were my people. The mailman's cold gray eyes returned to me.

My stomach churned. I had no nerve to ask more questions, but he offered the information anyway.

"His house caught on fire." He stepped away from me. "Strangest thing. Your son can tell you all about it."

The air felt trapped in my chest. "Eli?"

"What's that, Anna?" Lila said. "What about Eli?"

"He said Eli can tell me about Washington's house catching on fire," I said.

"Well, of course he can. Eli can tell a lot of people about a lot of things." Lila's voice was assertive, like it was when she commanded her horses in the ring. "He's a smart young man. Recognizes people. Remembers names."

I turned to look at her. She was not afraid to stand up to anyone. She could stare down a thousand-pound charging horse. She squinted and shaded her eyes against the glare of the morning sun and white-gray clouds. I moved toward her and the house. She walked out into the yard and put Sophie down beside me. Sophie grabbed my legs. I had been forgiven for snapping at her.

The postman said, "Never know where lightning will strike." His eyes narrowed and the smirk disappeared from his lips, leaving a hard, thin line. "Never know when you might be next."

"What do you mean by that?" Lila asked. She stood straight, unafraid of his threats.

"Oh, you know, every day is a blessing." He took a step back toward the road. "We never know when our time comes."

"That is true." Lila took deliberate steps close to him. "Something to think about."

He seemed startled by her proximity. She stood tall. She was not timid like most women.

"I know you," Lila said to the postman. "Robert, right? Your mama and daddy are down the road from mine."

"Yes, ma'am," he said. "I know you too."

They sized each other up. The mockingbird mimicked a crow cawing nearby.

He said, "Let's just say, that old boy won't bother you no more." The ever-present cicadas sent vibrations through the air.

"Well, that's good news," Lila called out. "Now everyone can go on with their own business." I could not see her face, but she sounded friendly, as if she were smiling. She disguised her tone as light, gay, but he had to know she meant for him to leave me alone.

The postman grinned and heaved his bag to his other shoulder. The keys on his belt jangled as he walked away. "Y'all have a good day, now."

"You too," Lila called back. She turned and faced me, her back to the street. "Good God," she said. "That was Gus calling. Eli is with him. Eli drove that colored man to the seminary and then came back to get something for him and saw a bunch of men lighting his house on fire." She spoke low so her voice would not carry. "You are going to need protection from town, and Eli's going to need protection from Marina. She's bound to skin you both alive." She looked down at Sophie, still sleepy and leaning against my legs. "Stay here with Aunt Annie and I'll get your tap shoes."

She climbed the porch stairs. The outline of the pistol lay beneath her clothes in the small of her back.

The mailman crossed Poplar Street to Verna's porch. Behind her house, in the tall oak trees, a streak of blue and white, a blue jay, flew up and disappeared into the green. Her front door opened and I glimpsed the bright pink of Verna's dress. The postman cackled and she peeked around his shoulder—a half grin, a flash of angry teeth.

Lila emerged with the ribbon ties of Sophie's tap shoes and tutu in her hand. The shoes swung and clapped together with her every step.

Vibrations from the cicadas crawled over my skin. "He said you never know where lightning strikes." I looked to Lila for reassurance. "What do you think he meant?"

"Maybe Washington will stay gone," she said. She put a hand on my shoulder. "One less thing for you to worry about."

"He's a person," I said. "Not a thing."

"You know what I mean."

I looked into her blue eyes. "Do you think Eli is safe? Do you think they'll come here?"

"Who's coming here?" Sophie's voice was husky with sleep. She leaned on me and rested one bare foot on top of the other.

"Nobody, honey." Lila went to the truck and put the gun under the seat. She came back and lifted Sophie. The girl's face nestled into Lila's neck. "Eli is safe. He's a grown man. He's smarter than all of us put together."

"That poor man," I said. All Mr. Washington had worked for was finished in one night. I knew him only as Thea's son. Did he have anyone else? Of course he did, he must have friends from school, from his time in the army, from New York. I had been in the house they burned, when his mother was still living in it, before she died. Papa had gone to visit her, and she had asked for me, so I went. She said, "That day at your daddy's, after your husband had hit you, why wouldn't you let me help you?" I had no good answer for her. She peppered our talk with her disappointment in me, and I accepted it, because I deserved it.

"Anna." Lila's voice was stern, full of warning. She put her hand on my shoulder and pressed. "What happened to him was bound to happen with or without you." She kissed my cheek. "He knew what he was getting into."

I touched Sophie's warm arm. I had taken a chance too, but I did not want it to cost me everything.

"We'll be back this afternoon," Lila said. "Gus will be here for the wake and the Rosary tonight." She walked to her truck and placed Sophie on the passenger side and rolled down the window. "If Nelly gives you any trouble, you come to me. You get in your car and drive."

"I'll be okay." It sounded brave, but the old woman's name sent waves through my stomach. I wanted to see my son's face, touch him, make sure no harm had come to him. "Where did you say Eli is? With Gus?"

"Yes," she said. "He's with Gus." Lila shut Sophie's door and walked around to the driver's side. Her door shut, and Sophie's head fell out of view as she lay across the seat. The engine rumbled. "I left the pint under your sink, in case you need it," Lila said out the window. "We'll be back."

I called out, "I will be fine." But I had to admit, I wanted Lila with me. She backed out slowly and the pea gravel popped. She turned off Poplar Street, and my stomach was queasy.

The mockingbird sang his normal call, two long trills and one short. I laid the mail on the porch step and tossed the rest of the raisins from my pocket. The bird flew down, impishly pecking the ground and flaunting the white and gray bands of his feathers.

The yard was littered with fallen branches from the heavy rain. I moved some to make a path. Marina's voice chimed in my head, telling me to go inside and change, not to be out in the front yard in my housecoat and bare feet. *Get a man for this work,* she would say in a motherly tone, authoritative, guiding me not to take a wrong turn. But I did not want to be inside where he had died.

A trickle of warm blood seeped from the bandage. If not for Marina, I would have left then and there—Papa, the store, the house, Riverton. I would have gotten in my car and driven away. Eli would be loyal, but if I left her to bury her father alone, she would never forgive me. A large branch blocked the path I'd been clearing and I rolled it away. It was heavy, but not so cumbersome as Elias's body.

Louise

Louise's black Buick pulled in the drive. I was happy to see she was alone, without her sister Nelly. She found me sitting on the porch steps with a fallen branch in my hands. The faint cuckoo sang ten times from inside the house. Louise's short, thick body stooped to lift a stack of cake pans from her floorboard. I went to help her, but she shook her head, *no*, and mimed a kiss to me. I cleared branches from her path so she would not trip.

"Go sit," she said. "Don't worry."

The mockingbird flew up as Louise passed. When she was inside, it hopped close to me and stood with its head cocked to the side like a begging dog.

I gathered the mail from the step and followed her inside. The house smelled of Lila's bacon and cigarette smoke. I had not cooked in two days, not since Elias returned from Orlando Washington's house. For Elias, I had made gravy, warmed some flatbread, greens, purple-hull peas, and ham. I had sliced a fresh tomato from the garden. After that, I had made nothing with my hands, no bread or pies, no food for myself, nothing to sustain life.

I laid the mail on the table and told myself, *This will pass.* Very soon, I hoped to make bread for Marina and prepare a *mezze*, a *table full of food*, around which my family would sit, and I would watch them eat while I held my grandchild.

Louise opened the mail, all of it prayer cards. She arranged them on the buffet for people to see. "So many cards so soon," she said. Then she scuttled around the kitchen, going into the cupboards and pulling out cake flour, sugar, salt, baking powder, orange-blossom water. The soles of her black lace oxfords brushed the floor like a worn-out broom. The refrigerator door opened and closed. Glass dishes rattled as she lined them up on the counter. There was too much food and no place to work.

"Where do you want these?" I asked her.

She shook her head. "I don't know."

My kitchen had become hers, my routine upended, all because of his death. I had been foolish to think life would go on as normal.

I moved tins and pans of food onto the kitchen table. Marina would direct us all soon enough.

Louise lit the oven and began measuring flour. She had cooked all of yesterday, and she was starting again.

"Louise, you want to bake a cake?" I put on an apron. "I will do it."

"No." She wrapped her thick arms around me and squeezed. She led me to the hallway, where heat from the kitchen and heat from outside had begun to collide. She returned and clanked around the refrigerator until she found the eggs. I entered the kitchen again to help her.

"No," she said. Her warm, thick hands settled on mine. "No. You do nothing." For some reason, she loved me—maybe because she had known me as a girl before my mother died. She had watched me grow up and had seen how Nelly and Elias treated me. I sensed Louise was happy for me that I was free of him.

"Marina wants a cake. But I tell her, nothing sweet at a funeral." She shook her head. "She says she will buy petit fours. I tell her, too expensive from the bakery, but she says, we need a sweet. So I tell her, and now I tell you, I bake a cake." She patted my arm.

"I'll help you." I started to enter the kitchen. I wanted something to do.

"It doesn't have to taste good." She winked at me and smiled. "So, I can do it." She noticed my hand. The bandage seeped fresh blood. "Go. Change it." She untied my apron and put it on herself. The ties barely met around her thick middle.

The doorbell rang.

"Go, now." She shuffled past me to answer the door. "Take care of yourself."

From the hall, I saw a delivery boy behind a large wreath. Louise opened the door wide and pointed to a corner in the living room. He positioned a tripod and hung the circle of fat white mums. "There's more," he said. Five more trips and six wreaths crowded the fireplace. He said, "Good day, ma'am," to Louise and was gone.

The house swam in a thick perfume of lilies and mums. The hot stove let off a metallic smell. Louise returned to the kitchen and measured sugar and baking powder.

I turned on fans and opened the windows to let hot air escape. I looked at the cards and who had sent them. Michael's parents, a few customers, church ladies, Father McMurray.

I wanted to be near Louise, near someone who cared for me. I sat in the corner near the telephone. I dialed Gus and Lila's house and hoped Eli would answer and say he was okay. I wanted to see Eli with my eyes. I wanted to know he was safe and that Orlando Washington was safe too, but no one answered.

I watched Louise move about my kitchen. I had walked the same circles—from the icebox to the sink to the stove. I could have been watching myself. Soon Marina would be here, setting things right. Earlier it had been Lila feeding and caring for me. All of us tied to the stove and the sink and the work to keep life moving forward. Nelly had done the same.

Soon his body would be back, and I feared my house would hold the sickly odor of embalmment and smell like a funeral home. The stove ticked up the heat. The pendulum of the cuckoo clock swung. *This will pass,* I told myself. Soon Marina would arrive. I needed to bathe and dress before she saw me. She would hate the sight of me and the state of the house. There was the yard to clean and the table to set before people came. I had to get through this day and the next. I thought of my mother as a girl crossing the ocean, looking at the stars and sleeping on the deck, hopeful, counting the minutes and hours and days to get to where she was going. That was all I had to do.

Wedding Day

Standing in the church before the altar, Elias and I said our vows and I placed the gold ring on his finger. His green eyes were drowsy from the long Mass. He lifted my veil. His aftershave, a concoction of cloves and oil, flooded my senses. My hand brushed the fine wool of his sleeve. I thought, *This is my husband, and I am his wife, to serve and obey and carry his children.* I knew he would make me his wife that night, but I did not know the physical process of how it would happen. I knew nothing past the romantic play, the emerald ring and the beautiful dress. No one had ever told me. Nelly mewled in the front pew. His dry lips grazed over mine and I felt sick that we would share a bed later that night.

Outside the church, Elias asked me if I minded riding in the back seat of his new Buick. He whispered, "I don't think she can fit in the back." He gestured toward his fat mother and looked embarrassed. The back door was narrow, so I agreed and waited while he and Ivie flapped around Nelly. Finally she eased into the front seat and Ivie scooted in next to me.

Elias drove toward our new house, and Nelly bawled. "My sweet boy is gone," she said.

"Mother," he said. "I'm not gone anywhere."

She tilted her head and said in a schoolgirl voice, "You are a good boy." She touched his hair. "You will always take care of me."

Ivie kicked Elias's seat. "Shut up the titty-baby routine."

Nelly sucked her teeth at Ivie.

At the stop sign, Elias looked back at me with moon eyes and mouthed, "I'm sorry."

Ivie grunted and I had to look out the window to keep from bursting with laughter. When Elias pulled into our new drive, I hurried away from them, through the crowd of distant cousins and Syrian businessmen from other towns, to the kitchen to find my mother's sister Elsa, who had been cooking for three days. We received the guests in our new house, because the rooms above my father's store in Mounds would never do, and Elsa was too proud to let Nelly prepare the wedding feast and lord it over her.

With the skirt of my wedding gown gathered in my arms, I clung to Elsa as she moved about the busy kitchen. I tried to bury my face into her soft neck. "It was awful in the car," I whispered. I told her how Nelly had carried on and how Ivie had insulted Elias and their mother. "I'm not sure what I've gotten into."

Elsa sucked her teeth in disdain. "Too late now," she chided. "He's got you." The corners of her eyes curved up with her smile. "And you've got her."

I wanted to pull her away from the stove to ask her what would happen on the wedding night. She was practical and pragmatic, and surely now that I was married, she could tell me what to expect or do—that is, if she knew.

Elsa patted my arm and dismissed me. "Child, I'm busy." She looked frazzled. She was not in her own kitchen and this was the largest number of people she had ever cooked for. She had Thea and two other women helping her, but that made her anxious too. I was the bride, so

I could not help, and she didn't want Nelly, because Nelly would have taken over, and if anything, Elsa's pride and honor rested in her cooking.

I turned to Thea for comfort, and she looked at me with kind eyes. She'd had a son. She had been a midwife and knew the ways of nature. She would tell me, I thought, better than Elsa could, but every time I got close, Elsa barked, "You are in the way. You cannot interrupt Thea right now." Thea was doing two jobs at once, stirring a pot of rice pudding and displaying the pastries on a tray.

Thea smiled at me. She whispered, "Your mama would be so proud."

I wondered what I had done that would have made my mother proud, but Thea had known her best. Thea was the one to hand her Gus when he was born and the one who held the dead babies, the one who prayed for Mama's soul the moment it left her body. I accepted Thea's words as truth. I would bide my time and find a way to ask her.

Elsa motioned me closer. Her breath was warm and smelled of mint. "They think I don't know what they do. But I am watching." Maybe she would comfort me now and give me a chance to ask my questions. "One of them put a spoon in her dirty black mouth and back into the pot. I sent her home. No pay."

Thea's lips drew tight. She knew Elsa and her prejudices. Elsa wouldn't let Thea work in the house, except to do laundry or the floors. I wanted to stand near Thea to shield her from Elsa. I could get my information and help Thea too, but Elsa prodded me toward the hall.

"Go and change your dress," Elsa said. "You will have a daughter to wear this."

I would have a daughter—children were the duty of marriage. I panicked. I was not ready to lie next to him, and I worried I should have heeded my father's warnings. He had tried to tell me I was too young, but I was too naive to understand what he meant.

I wanted to cross the room to Thea and thank her for her words about Mama, and then pull her away and tell her I was terrified of what was soon to happen. But Elsa did not relent. "Go on." Elsa pushed me out of the kitchen, and guests began streaming in to see Elsa and the food she was preparing. Louise and Joe, Elias's cousins, Nelly, Papa's brother and his wife, their grown children and their little ones—all of them coming to fuss over Elsa's food and to kiss my cheek as if I were a sick child.

When Aunt Elsa announced the food was ready, the women prepared plates for the men and then fed themselves. I was too nervous to eat. I was about to go upstairs and change as Elsa had instructed me, when Gus called from the living room. "Open your presents, Anna!" So young, only fourteen, he thought the presents made the occasion. Gus smiled and his white teeth beamed across his face. He was happy for me to be married to Elias. He liked him. Gus looked up to us because he saw us as adults in charge of our own lives. Gus was happy that I had a new, big house on the white side of town, and I supposed he hoped the same for himself one day. Seeing Gus so happy eased my nerves. I smiled back at him, but then I questioned his glee. The boy in him must have thought about it, the act that was to take place. I was angry that he probably knew, had probably discussed it with other boys or men, and I had had no one to tell me and had been too ashamed to ask or give it much thought until now, when I was faced with the impending act. I shuddered to think that everyone in the room knew what was to happen between us, except me.

I tried to calm myself and notice the beautiful things in the living room. For days, Aunt Elsa had sat in the house waiting for each piece of furniture to be delivered. Papa chose the carpets himself. My eyes fell on him in the corner. His food sat untouched on a side table near him. He ran his thick hands across his large, balding head. He looked at me and then averted his gaze to the floor. I felt a wave of shame, because he knew I would not be his innocent girl anymore. I was another man's wife.

Elias stood near, and I felt his warmth as I opened Gus's present first—a mahogany box filled with silver. I ran my finger over the pattern, a delicate etching with our initial, *N*. Papa must have paid for it, and the jeweler would have helped Gus choose it. I kissed his warm cheek and wanted my brother to remain close, but he dashed to the other side of the room in his excitement. I opened gifts of plates, dishes, crystal bowls, and a camera from Ivie. From the corner of my eye, I saw Papa's bowed head. Maybe, I told myself, he was sad and thinking of my mother or the fact that this house should have been built for her, but I knew it was more than that.

The last gift was Nelly's, a woven tablecloth worked with lace around the edges. "It was my mother's. I brought it from the old country." She smiled, close-lipped, with tears in her eyes. She wrapped her arms around me and whispered in my ear, "I did not want him to marry you, but he decided on his own. I pray you will be a good wife to him." She released me. She smiled and revealed the dark edges of her tea-stained teeth. She wanted everyone to see that she wished me well, but the tone of her voice sent chills down my back. I handed Elias the tablecloth to admire and I left the room to go upstairs.

Elias followed me into the hallway. He grabbed my hand and I started to cry. "What is wrong?" Elias gathered me in his arms, closer than he had ever held me before.

So much was wrong, I was not sure where to start. My nervousness, his mother, my father. "Your mother has a strange way of wishing me well, and my father acts like he is at a funeral," I said.

Elias groped my sides and his thumbs brushed against my breasts. He whispered, "It is a hard day for them."

I looked into his face. Soon, he would do something to me, something I did not understand, and suddenly he seemed to be leering, and I felt like a lost child.

"They are getting older and we are moving on." His words rang true. He hugged me once more, and I liked the warmth of his arms around me. I liked the way he smelled. I thought maybe he was nervous too, maybe I was putting too much worry into a natural thing.

I wanted to say that I wished my mother were alive to see us. I wanted to tell him, *She would be happy for us,* but if I said those words, *my mother,* I knew I would not stop crying.

He lifted my chin and said, "You should be happy. It is our wedding day." He looked to see if anyone was close. He whispered, "It's soon to be our wedding night."

I nodded and forced a smile.

He wiped the tears from my cheeks.

The men were calling him from the front room. My uncle had brought home-distilled arak and now the men were drinking and talking loud.

"It has been a good day." He let go. "I'll check on the guests."

He left me and I pulled the bridal veil from my hair. The pins fell to the floor. I looked into the kitchen and a host of women chattered as they cleaned dishes and put away food. I saw the top of Thea's head across a sea of ladies. To get to her, I would have to swim through cousins and churchwomen. I would never make it to her, for each woman would stop me to wish me well and offer a piece of advice, and even if I did, the likelihood of Elsa giving Thea leave from her post was not good. I imagined grabbing a random woman, pulling her upstairs to make her explain to me what should happen. But that would send everyone into a frenzy and I would look like a fool.

I walked upstairs to my new bedroom and listened to the party carry on. White curtains hung beside the gleaming new windows, and outside, the green pecan leaves filtered blue sky. A dark four-post bed was made in a linen coverlet, starched and smooth. The sun began to sink and shadows of leaves danced across the ceiling.

I decided to change and return to the party, but I was trapped in the wedding gown. The buttons ran down my back, and every effort to undo them was foiled. That morning, Aunt Elsa had buttoned me into it. She had said, "I could have married, but I did not want it. A lot of trouble. Look what it got your mother." She had made a sign of the cross at the mention of my mother, but I had been distracted by the veil and the emerald ring and the cloud of silk I wore. Alone in my new room, her words nagged me: "You remind me of Vega, how intent she was on Faris, and you are as focused on this one."

I did an inventory of my body, of the parts and the whole, the regular and the private. I worried about the place from which I bled each month, and thought of my poor mother bleeding her life out through that place. I knew babies came from there, and that it must be the place the seed entered. I wondered which of my parts he would want to touch. I knew what he had. I had changed my brother's diapers and given him baths when he was a small child. But I did not know what that became on a man or how awful it would be to see it so close and for so certain a purpose. My skin was on fire with indignity. I lay across the bed in a heap of white silk. I had never been in such a beautiful house or worn such a beautiful gown or felt like such a little girl playing dress-up in shoes that did not fit.

The screen door opened and closed. I heard voices on the porch. I sat up and looked out the window. Papa, my brother, the priest. Behind them, my father's brother and his family, Ivie, and the others trickled out onto the lawn, the street, and into their cars. My lanky brother looked back up at the house with curious eyes. The sun sat just above the horizon.

Leather soles scratched like sandpaper on the stairs. Then, Elias stood in the door of what I thought was to be our room, but was mine alone. "So, what do you think?" His voice was low. "The house is beautiful." There had been a great effort by him, Papa, and Aunt Elsa to make sure the house was finished and furnished for our wedding day.

"Yes," I said. My dry lips stuck together.

He spread his arms in the doorway like branches on a great tree.

I was trapped in the room. I was not ready for what he wanted.

The sun was setting and the room seemed to be lit with fire.

"Thea, make sure those gals get the dishes dry," Elsa's voice, harsh and direct, jolted up the stairs. "We have to take them back to the church."

Nelly spoke to Elsa in Arabic. The two women cackled. I felt certain Nelly said something about me with my dress off, something about her son having his way, but I did not know.

"Come here," Elias said. It was an order—kindly spoken, but still an order. "I will help you out of your dress." He leered like a wolf, his head down, his intense eyes grazing over me.

I wanted to run downstairs and go home with Elsa, back to my father's store. My face burned.

The sun dipped below the horizon.

He walked toward me, sitting on the bed, when I did not obey. This would be the price to pay for crossing the railroad tracks, for this house, for his name, for what I wanted. My mouth was dry and I could not swallow.

He said, "Anna, don't worry. I'll be gentle."

"Your mother and my aunt are downstairs." I could not look at him.

"They will leave soon." He touched my shoulder.

He would want me to remove my clothes and he would see me naked. What came next I imagined would be humiliating.

"They're not paying us any attention," he said.

Dusk settled into the room. The white lamp glowed weakly.

"Want me to put out the light?"

Unable to speak, I nodded. He walked to the other side of the bed and switched off the lamp. The room was gray except for the slight glow of the coverlet and my gown.

I moved toward a corner. I did not undress. I prayed he would have mercy and leave.

"Do you want help?"

"No," I answered.

"I'll leave for a minute if you like." He crossed the room and reached out as if to a cowering dog. He leaned over me and smelled of the anise liquor and cloves.

I pressed against the wall. Dishes clapped as they were stacked in the kitchen.

Voices carried upstairs. "You will take these to the church?" Nelly said to my aunt.

He worked his hands between me and the wall and then his fingers nimbly undid the buttons down my back. "Turn around," he said.

I cringed, but I did as he said. I pressed my forehead into the wall and prayed it would collapse on me.

"Thea will help me," Elsa said.

"I can do it for you," Nelly said.

"No, you won't." Elsa did not want to be obligated to Nelly. The two women chided each other in Arabic and laughed heartily.

I held my breath and hoped to pass out and save myself the humiliation.

"You are too modest," he said. "It's okay. This is supposed to happen."

The buttons were undone and the air hit my skin. Shivers ran through me.

"The wedding was nice." His long fingers ran down my back and he pulled me near. "Everyone had a good time." Goose bumps rose on my skin.

"Can we wait?" I mustered. "Until they leave?"

He undid the last buttons and pulled my arms from the sleeves. He slid the dress off my shoulders. My heart beat fast—like a flock of blackbirds taking off.

"I've waited," he said.

Today, or for his whole life—I did not understand his meaning. "Not yet." I gripped the bodice of the dress to guard against him seeing me. I was near tears.

"Don't worry," he said. "I will be gentle."

"What's going to happen?" I asked.

He laughed a quiet laugh, and my skin burned with shame.

"You will see," he said. "It's not bad."

I wanted to know how he knew, if he had done this before, but the idea of his experience mortified me.

"Take these to the car," Elsa's voice drifted up. "Be careful."

The screen door slapped shut and Thea's steps could be heard across the porch, through the pea gravel, and back again into the house.

He took his shirt off. His chest thin and lean, but strong. He was a handsome man. I had wanted to marry him. I had seen his naked chest on a hot day when he was doing heavy work at his store.

"You have to calm yourself." Elias pulled my wrists away and broke my grip on the bodice. The dress fell in a cloud of silk to my ankles. "Or this will be no good." He guided me out of the long skirt. "There is no reason to be so upset." He gathered the long slip and brought it over my head.

I lifted my arms as he wanted.

He kissed my neck with dry lips. "You are shaking. Don't be afraid." He undid my brassiere and pulled down my stockings and underpants. He ran his hands up my sides and over my breasts. He touched me gently and I began to breathe more slowly to calm myself.

"I am leaving," Nelly yelled to the house. The screen door slapped shut.

Elsa shouted, "Thea, let's go."

"Get on the bed," he said.

He took down his pants and underpants. For the first time, I saw him and what it was. It seemed unnatural and unkind to put that inside me, and kind of terrible that he and all the men I knew had to be burdened with such an appendage. I closed my eyes and got on the bed as he said. My jaw chattered as if I were naked in the cold winter wind.

"You will be fine," he said. "There's no reason to worry." He pushed me backward until I was flat. He opened my legs and lay on top of me. He placed my arms around him and nuzzled my neck with his stubble. To him I was a frightened animal being prodded and coaxed.

The bed was hard with his weight on me. It had never been slept in and the starched linen scratched my skin. The porch light flickered outside the window. I lay motionless and repeated his words inside my head, *You will be fine.* The pecan leaves made shadows on the ceiling. I held my breath against his weight and counted the leaf shadows on the ceiling and tried to ignore the unfamiliar pressure between my legs.

The front door shut. I heard Elsa outside talking. "Everything was nice," she said. "The food was good."

Thea replied, "Yes, it was. Hard to believe Miss Anna is married now." Except for the kind words she whispered to me, Thea had been silent all day. She had said Mama would be proud of me, and the idea of my mother helped me calm down for a moment. Car doors shut and the engine started.

He pushed between my legs and his weight spread my hips wide. There was pressure and a sharp pain. My face burned with ignorance. I had not known how to comply. I held my breath as he moved for what seemed a long time. He clutched and groaned and then warm moisture took his place, and my thighs itched with dampness, and what had happened was over.

He left the room and water ran in the tub. I did not want to interrupt him, so I cleaned myself with his undershirt that he left on the floor. I dressed in the satin gown Elsa had bought for my trousseau. I shivered on the edge of the bed and waited. A light clicked on and off. In the doorway stood his dark shadow of strong shoulders and thin waist. He ran his fingers through his hair. I lay my head on the pillow.

I could have said, "Are you coming to bed?" He seemed to be waiting for an invitation, but I did not know what to do. I was nineteen, barely older than a child and not any wiser. I expected he would return, because we'd never discussed sleeping in separate rooms. If he had come back to my bed, maybe we would have laughed at my ignorance and felt close, but when he entered the other room, I did not call after him. Part of me felt relief to be alone.

The house was cool and dark. I wound myself in the damp coverlet and sleep came fast. In the early morning, I woke before sunrise. I put on a new dress and listened to him snore in the room across from mine. I lay on the bed and looked out the window at the dark morning. I wondered how often he would come to me, and how long before I would be with child. I wondered if he would want to do the act again that night, and I felt certain I would not be so scared. I was embarrassed how pitiful I must have seemed. I planned to swallow my pride and tell him that he had been right, that I should not have been so worried.

I noticed the smell of coffee and heard footsteps in the hall.

Nelly appeared in the door of my room.

I popped up and straightened my dress.

"You are up before the sun," she said. "Good."

In the dim morning light, she saw the wedding dress heaped on the floor. She whipped it above her head and hung it on a padded hanger. "Elsa waited on you like a maid. You are the woman of the house now, not a child." She made the bed and tidied the pillows.

She strode across the hall and barked at Elias. *"Haaze kaslane,"* she said. *Don't be lazy.* She flipped on his light switch and slapped his bed. "Get up now," she said. "You have the store to open. The honeymoon is over." She laughed at her joke.

She motioned to me. "Come. I'll show you how Elias likes his eggs." She waddled down the hall toward the stairs. One last time, she called out, "Elias. Get up."

Nelly poured me coffee and cracked two eggs in hot olive oil. She slid the greasy eggs onto his plate and then made mine. Elias walked into the kitchen in sock feet, a blue tie draped around his white button-down shirt. I cast my gaze to the floor, so bashful to look him in the face. I wanted to tell him privately that I was fine, that I had been silly to have been so scared. If I told him that, he might hold me as he had in the hallway the day before, but Nelly sat between us. The sun peeked on the horizon. He looked at his plate of food without a word to either of us.

"Don't get used to this," she said. "Tomorrow, I will not cook you breakfast." I wondered if she had a key. I wanted to ask if she would be coming and going as she pleased, but dared not. She talked fast, and everything she said seemed important to her. I was to help her with the homemade goods for the store, stock the house with groceries, and that afternoon, I was to meet with the best dressmaker in town. She said, "You should look like something, now that you are my son's wife. You're not in colored town anymore."

I was starving and ate, even though the eggs fried in olive oil were not to my liking.

"I am glad you are eating. You are too thin," she said. "You need meat on your bones to have babies."

Elias coughed and his face turned red with embarrassment. His mother noticed too.

"She must eat." She waved her hands toward me. "Look at her. She is a scrawny bird. Having a baby will break her in half. If you don't break her first." She cackled and my skin flushed.

"I have to get going." Elias kissed his mother's cheek. I was surprised when he stopped and kissed mine too. His lips were warm from coffee and he smelled of cloves.

I wanted to follow him outside to have the chance to speak to him, but Nelly grabbed my wrist and stared at me with hawk eyes. "Do you bake?"

I told her, "Only a little."

"Your mother was a good baker. You would like it?"

"I can try," I said.

All day long, I prepared my words for Elias. I had not known what to expect, but now I did, and now I would do better. The words felt embarrassing inside my head, and I would blush as they left my mouth, but I was sure he would treat me kindly and calmly, as he had the night before.

On the second night, his mother stayed late. She talked and talked. I went to bed, and after she left, he came into my dark room. Elias said, "Anna." His voice was gruff. "Turn over. Get on your hands and knees."

His words did not register because I was rehearsing what I had to say to him. "Can I tell you something?" My heart pounded in my chest.

"No." He undid his belt and took off his pants. "Do as I said. Hands and knees."

I obeyed, but I said, "I wanted to talk about last night."

He stepped out of his underpants and climbed on the bed behind me. "We talked enough last night." His voice was all business. "You are my wife. This is your duty." He kneeled and grabbed my waist. "I don't want to discuss it." He lifted my gown and yanked at my panties. He pulled me backward and put himself inside me.

My jaw clamped shut. It felt unkind this way. I could not breathe. I thought that last night had been the worst of it, but each time he thrust and hit a new depth, I felt sick.

He held tightly to my sides, and then my hip bones became his grip. I could not hold myself up against his weight and I collapsed beneath him. When it was over, an intense sensation spread down my legs and up into my chest. It was all I could do to breathe. He left me facedown on the bed without a word. He washed himself in the bathroom and slept in his own bed.

I crawled onto my pillow, embarrassed by what had happened, by what I felt. I was sore from the thrusting, and yet it was not horrible. I wanted to be alone, but then I did not. If he had come back, I would have let him hold me. I lay wondering what he felt for me, if he felt more than a dog mounting another.

My skin burned. I prayed morning would not come, and that I would not have to show my face. I was more than ignorant. What other ways might he humiliate me? I prayed that the earth and sky would be still and for it to always be nighttime, after he had left me alone. I was a stranger in this place, without Elsa, without Papa or Gus.

I had begged my father to let me marry. He must have thought this was what I had wanted. Did Gus know? Or Elsa? Was this the reason why she never wanted to be married?

Nelly knew. She had two sons, so when she looked at me, she knew what had happened. Maybe that was why she stayed so late. She must hate me for knowing her son in this way. Thea should have told me, but it was not her place. My mother was the only one who could have prepared me, and I had to trust she would have warned me what to expect.

At the thought of waking and cooking his breakfast with Nelly to teach me, followed by the chore of baking for the store with her at my side, of coming home again to cook his dinner while she tortured me with her wisdom, to sit and eat with them both, only to be used and left once again upon my bed, I wanted to run. But I was married in the eyes of God, of my father, of all who knew me. I was spoiled. Maybe that was why Papa would not look at me the afternoon of my wedding, knowing what was to come.

In the night, my stomach cramped with worry and I grew sick. I did not wake Elias as I switched the lights in the hallway or when I retched over the toilet. I rested on the cool bathroom floor of black-and-white marble, clean and new, unlike the scarred linoleum in my father's home. This room held beautiful things—a large white sink with thick chrome legs, a mirror etched in leaves and flowers, a claw-foot tub and a wall of gleaming white tiles. My father built it for me—this house that should have been my mother's.

I stumbled back to my room past his door. His body stretched the length of his bed. His black hair against the white pillow. The sheets draped like a tent over his toes. He stirred but he did not wake. I went to my bed and listened as he slept. The sound of his breath was like a wave washing on shore and rolling back out, not a care to his soul. I thought, how wonderful to be him.

What Is Real

Marina's dark figure filled the doorway. She wore a billowing black dress, and her face and arms were more swollen than the night before. She looked like a hot-water bladder, full of fluid, ready to burst at any moment.

"Hello, Aunt Louise." In her arms she held a Mitsy's dress bag.

Louise shuffled across the kitchen and nudged Marina toward the table. "Sit."

"I'm fine. Don't worry about me." Marina touched her dark hair, pinned in a neat chignon. She looked at me. "You're not ready."

Louise moved back to the stove.

My hands shook. "I was remembering."

"Really?" She squinted and shook her head. "I can't believe you're sitting around, daydreaming, with everything there is to do." Her lips were painted pale pink, her cheeks rouged, and her skin heavily powdered. The heat would melt her makeup. She did not need it anyway. Her beauty was striking—the pale olive skin and the bright eyes, as bright as spring leaves.

"I sat in this spot, watching Elsa and Thea on my wedding day," I said.

At hearing Elsa's name, Louise stopped stirring a pot and gave the sign of the cross.

Marina shook her head. "Why must you keep on about this Thea?"

"She was my mother's friend. She helped raise me," I said.

"I know who she is." Marina's ire was up. She kneaded her temples. "She's the reason we're in this mess."

"She was here cooking for my wedding party, and then the next morning, your grandmother was here, working and working me. Now Louise. Now you are here too."

Marina scanned my housecoat, my bare feet, and my hair. She draped the dress bag over the chair. She asked, "Are you okay?"

I looked out the window.

Marina said, "There is so much to do. So many people are coming." I imagined who was going through her mind: Junior League women, church ladies, and Michael's colleagues. She said, "I need you to get ready."

All she cared about was my appearance, the surface of things. "Have you seen Eli?" I asked.

"He's at the paper." She sat, and her eyes winced in discomfort. "Going over the obituary."

I felt a wave of relief. He was safe, though I could not help but worry for him and for her. She was too headstrong to know the danger her body was in.

She breathed out slowly. Her time was near. "He went to Mounds last night." She sounded like a scorned wife. "The two of you will be the end of me. I have to live here," she said. "And everyone thinks you have lost your minds."

I ignored her reprimand. "You shouldn't be driving," I said. "You should have called me to get you."

Marina huffed. She would not be slowed down.

"The baby will come soon," Louise said, bringing Marina a cup of coffee. "Be careful."

"She's right," I said. "You need to take it easy."

Louise nodded in agreement as she moved back to the stove.

Marina sipped the coffee and pushed it away. "It's too hot to drink coffee."

I looked past Louise and out the window at the sky. The sun had burned off the last of the clouds. I joined Marina at the table.

Marina's swollen hand pressed my forearm. "You need to get dressed." She shifted toward me and touched my tangled hair. The heat in the kitchen was melting her makeup. Beads of sweat rolled down her temples. "I smell liquor. Is it you?"

I said, "Lila made me a drink last night."

"Of course she did." Her voice had a sharp edge. "Lila would make you a drink."

I said, "You might excuse me, this once."

Louise studied us and tried to determine the trouble.

"That's all Lila's good for." Marina's voice was indignant, small and tight. "I guess y'all drank one to Daddy's grave." She raised her eyebrows and her temple throbbed.

She must have known I was relieved he was gone.

"You should have been the one to talk to the undertaker." Marina crossed her arms above her bulging torso.

"I don't mean to upset you," I said. "It was a drink."

"You should have been the one to choose the casket and his suit." Her voice at a low boil, controlled. "You just disappeared yesterday."

"I'm sorry," I said. I felt guilty I had burdened her.

Louise's head tilted toward us. She was listening to every word.

"You should be at the paper now. He was your husband." She closed her eyes to shut me out. Her face flushed. "But you're too busy drinking with Lila."

"No," I said. She did not want me to be the one to do any of those things, but I bit my tongue. Anger swelled in me like the heat ticking up in the kitchen. "Your father drank a lot, but you never said anything to him."

"I am burying my father," she said.

"I never had the choices you've had. By the time I understood what marriage meant for me, it was too late." I had said the wrong thing. I should not have fueled her frustration.

Marina's voice wavered. "I am about to give birth, Mother. I don't want to bury him, but it has to be done." She seemed near tears. "You should be helping me with the details."

I could not stop myself. "I was nothing but his servant."

"I won't discuss this now." Marina stared at Louise. "This conversation is private." Her dark brows knit together and made a long line across her forehead.

"You know what he did," I said. My face was hot. "You know where he went." The cut seeped warm blood. I wanted to detail his wrongdoings, but she would hear only bitterness in my voice. I looked at my cut hand. "You make excuses for him."

She averted her eyes. "We've all done things we regret." She spoke low and controlled. She wanted to protect him. I supposed she wanted to protect me—and herself too.

My head throbbed and my stomach pinched. I had the urge to slide my arm out of the housecoat to show her the green and purple bruises he'd left. But she would defend him. She would say, "You let that colored man come to the house." It was like riding a wave whenever we argued, up and down, storing away new injuries and bringing up old ones.

Louise peeked in the oven and opened the door to pull out the sheet cake. The room filled with the warm smell of butter and eggs and flour. Louise's eyes met mine, and she shook her head as if to say, *Stop arguing.*

Marina stood slowly and patted her Aunt Louise's arm. "I need to call my gardener to clean that mess out front." Like that, she was back to business, her tone as smooth as a glass surface. It seemed Marina did not want me to see her real emotions, nor did she want to feel them. She passed me to get to the phone. "That storm was bad here." She held the receiver in her hand and dialed the rotary.

She spoke to her man in a singsong voice and my blood boiled. She had learned this from her father—swift, manipulative movements from anger to kindness to get what she wanted. She had his eyes, his ways. She was his daughter, and I wanted to argue with her, knock Elias out of her, but I held back. That was the wrong way. She was my daughter and too much was at stake. She hung the receiver in the cradle and turned her attention back to me.

Marina tugged at my housecoat. "Let's don't fuss. Give me a hug, Mama." Her touch felt false. She was readying herself to be the hostess and be seen. She wanted me on my best behavior, but I did not want to be judged with Elias in mind.

I hugged her, and like the morning before, she pulled away almost as soon as my arms were around her.

"I want pictures of him," she announced. "To put out."

"Isn't the portrait on the mantel enough?"

Her face puffed like rising dough. She braced herself to stand. "Isn't there a box of pictures in the china cabinet?"

"I'll get them. You sit still." In the dining room, I opened the bottom door of the china cabinet and pulled out an old hatbox, one from my mother's store. Flies buzzed around the room. All the windows were opened and more would fly in. I did not have the energy to shut them, nor would Marina or Louise have allowed me. I imagined I would be ridding the house of flies for days.

Marina followed me into the dining room and left Louise alone in the kitchen, rattling at the sink.

I opened the lid, and the fusty smell of chemicals and old paper escaped. Three olive-skinned girls looked back at me. Mama and her sisters. They wore coarse linen and leather sandals. A train of camels far behind them walked across the sand near the water. Seashell necklaces hung around their necks and crowned their long, black hair. They looked like they belonged in a fairy tale.

"Elsa gave me this picture. Mama is the youngest, Mayme, then Elsa, the oldest."

She looked at the photograph with wonder. "Look at them."

"They are in Beirut, visiting their aunt and uncle. Elsa said those necklaces were their souvenirs." Elsa, Papa, and Mama said everything in Lebanon was more beautiful—the greenest sea, the bluest sky, the sweetest air. And everything tasted better—the fruit, the vegetables, the roasted meat, the olives, the spices, everything. "Elsa thought Elias and I should go for a honeymoon, but he had no interest in going back or a honeymoon."

"You can travel now." Marina sounded as if she wanted to be rid of me. She placed the photograph on the table. Any interest she had shown in it was fleeting. I put the photo aside. I would take it with me if I left.

"We could go to Lebanon together," I said.

She looked up from the pile of photographs and grimaced. "Mother, I am in no position to travel across the world. Look at me." She was exasperated. "No one tells you how bad the end is."

"People try to forget." I wanted to warn her that carrying a child was easier than labor, and labor easier than raising it. Loving a child was the most bittersweet joy, maybe the most difficult thing in the world. I wanted to tell her, she could do her best and her child might see it as all wrong. She would know soon enough, this terrible chain of love, from mother to child, how the love was not always returned in the same measure, how it can hurt as deeply as it could be sublime. But I did not want to sound discouraging, because I loved her and I did not want to disappoint her.

"Maybe we could go to the old country one day, I meant," I said. "When you've had your children and—"

"I don't care about going there. My life is here." She was matter-of-fact. She held up a picture of her father on a steep dirt road on a mule's back. "Just look at this landscape. It's rocky and dusty, all mountains and ravines. People must work for the smallest comfort."

She returned to the careful study of the photographs, one by one. "Who is this?" she asked.

"That's me and you." The crown of my head is in the upper corner of the photograph. There is a glimpse of my forehead, the tip of my nose. I am looking down at her. She is one or two years old, and pushing against my arms, trying to free herself from me. I am studying the baby in my arms, the baby whose eyes burrow into the camera. Her expression is serious, neither happy nor sad, the same as she looked now sitting at my table. "We are at the store. You wanted to be put down to get into something. You were a terror."

"So you've said." She fanned herself with a handful of photos.

"I chased you up and down the aisles. You loved to spill over boxes or fruit or whatever mischief you could find." I remembered the feeling of dread, chasing her around, and wished I could go back and enjoy her antics. "When you were three, your father made you a crown of cardboard and tinfoil. You would sit still for a few minutes if we pretended you were the princess ruling us from your throne. Do you remember?"

She nodded and a smile crossed her lips.

"You would be satisfied for a short time, and then I'd have to take you to Nelly because I couldn't get any work done."

She frowned and her eyes accused me. "Work was important to you," she said. "You always had work, until you had Eli, then you had work and Eli."

She thought I loved Eli more than her, but she had been an independent child, seeming not to need me, and he had been like a helpless bird. For some reason when he was born, I knew how to care for him. "I'd do it differently with you if I could," I said. "You'll do better than me."

She rolled her eyes at my words and then stared at the pictures.

I was making her uncomfortable so I changed the subject. "Have you thought of a girl's name?" They would name a boy after Michael.

She placed a photograph of her and her father on the table. "A few."

"My mother's name was Vega," I said.

"That's your name too." I was surprised she remembered. "You want me to name the baby after you?" She arched a dark eyebrow but did not raise her eyes from the photographs. She sorted another picture of Elias and Ivie in store aprons under the Nassad Grocery sign.

"Not if you don't want to," I said. "There's Elsa's name and Mayme."

She grimaced. "Those sound like colored names."

I shook my head. "Not true." But I knew those names sounded low and foreign to her friends, to her husband and her husband's family.

"We were thinking Katherine or Marilyn," she said.

Louise stuck her head out the swinging door to check on us. She gave a nod, signaling that she was glad we were not arguing. Louise was right. I knew I must appease Marina so that when her father was buried and the baby was born, I could tell her of Nelly's accusations and calmly deny them, and she would choose me.

"There's a picture of my mother and me somewhere in Grandpapa's house. It was taken when I was close to Sophie's age." I wanted to find it and show her who she came from. "You look like her. My mother. I want you to see that picture."

"You remember what she looked like?"

"Yes," I said. "I remember her."

"You can show me later." Her hands shuffled through the photographs. She frowned at me and gave me an impatient look. "Right now, I want some of Daddy when he was young."

I watched her expression as she searched for a photo of him. She wanted something tangible to show her love. I was jealous, and I wanted her to feel close to me. I wanted her to see that I loved her more than I begrudged him.

"Let me look upstairs." I went to his room to the drawer where he kept the things he loved, the things he looked at when he was alone. In a shoebox in the drawer, he kept the old letters from Zada. I had read them when I wanted to know what was between them, what spark she had that I did not. I held the picture of the two of them in Mobile Bay. The wedding ring on his hand gleamed in the sunlight. I was tempted to take the box to Marina and prove what I had endured, but I dug beneath Zada's letters and found the pictures she would want—one of him as a boy with his father, one with her as a baby, another of him and his lion.

At the bottom of the pile was the newspaper article with the picture of him and me, the cedar trees and the hydrangeas behind us. He'd kept it because of the award, not because of me. His arm around my shoulder was for show. As soon as the shot was taken, he let go of me, and that smile on his face, the one so similar to the smile he wore next to Zada, receded.

I left behind the pictures of Zada and the article and took the other pictures to her.

Marina sat where I had left her, still looking through pictures.

I handed her the photos and immediately she latched onto one. "The lion," she said. She held up the black-and-white photograph. "It was real."

In the picture, a young Elias fed a cow bone to the lion through the bars of its cage. The lion stood on its hind paws. Its front paws wrapped around the black iron bars. Its face was a blur, but the muscle, the paws, the teeth spoke to its power. "Why have I never seen this?" She looked amazed. "I thought the signs were a gimmick." She meant the porcelain sign with the image of a lion that hung over the counter and another one over the sidewalk.

"What did you think that cage was behind the store?" I asked.

Astonishment fell across her face.

"Why did you think we called the store the Lion Grocery?"

"I thought he was teasing me." Tears welled in the corners of her eyes. "He used to call me his little lioness."

"It died a few summers before you were born," I said.

"I thought it was make believe." She took a cloth napkin from the table and blotted her damp face.

I told her, "When it was alive, the lion would grunt and cry in the middle of the night and it could be heard for miles. And then, when you were a baby and you howled at night, so loud, he'd hold you and whisper, 'You're the little lion come back to keep us awake.'"

"You should have told me." She shifted her weight and drew a painful breath.

"I didn't think you'd care." I never told her a lot of things. Like the bruises on my arms, or the way he made me feel for so many years, but as much as I hated her father, I did not want to shame her. "I thought it would embarrass you."

She tensed in pain and gripped her belly.

It seemed her time was near, and a twinge of excitement flashed through me. I went to the kitchen to wet a cloth. Louise patted my shoulder. I returned and Marina held the rag to her temples. Her body stiffened.

I felt sorry for the physical pain that she was about to endure. I wanted to warn her, but I did not want to scare her. "There's a lot you don't know." I crossed my arms and touched the bruises. She must have known something. How could someone so bright not know what happened under the same roof?

She tried to compose herself. She groaned, and under her breath she said, "You never talk."

Memories were hard and I didn't like to look at pictures. "What do you want to know?" I could see the baby moving—an elbow or knee raking across her stomach. "Ask me."

"How'd he get a lion?" She moved her feet to brace herself. Her belly constricted.

"The circus had come to town. Ivie traded groceries for her, and then he dumped her on your father. Elias didn't want her, but he couldn't get rid of her. He couldn't kill her."

She held the rag to cover her face. When she took it away, no trace of makeup remained.

"After I married, I was the one to take care of it." When the lion went into season, I hosed down the cage. If it rained, I pulled a tarpaulin over the cage. When she was hungry, I fed her. "I liked her. I did not mind the work, because when I had seen her after my mother died, I felt she held my mother's spirit."

"He had it that long?" Marina brought the photograph close to her face. "He looks so young. He looks like Eli."

"Yes." I had taken the picture with the camera Ivie gave us for the wedding. "In that picture, your father's twenty-nine, not much older than you." Elias grins in the photo. The lion is moving, excited, a blur of muscle, fur, claw, and teeth. "The lion's about eleven there, but the first time I saw it, it was a cub. Seeing that lion was the first thing that made me happy after Mama died."

"How old were you when you first saw it?" She was greedy for the story.

"I was eight when he got the cub. My mother had died, and I had taken to bed. Papa thought I was stricken with grief, but he learned I had the Spanish flu. Papa begged me, 'Vega, wake up and we'll go see the lion.' I thought it was a dream."

Her eyes did not leave the photograph in her hand. We never discussed this sort of thing.

"Thea dipped me in ice baths to break the fever. Then, a different woman came. I thought she was Mama. She and Thea coaxed me to rise. 'Get up, Vega. We'll go see the lion.' In my haze I dreamed my mother had risen from the dead and brought a lion with her. Then one day, the fever broke. I sat up and the woman said, 'So you have decided to join the living?' Her voice sounded like Mama's, and her face was similar, but different, and I thought dying had changed Mama. It made perfect sense. I started to say *Mama*. Then she ran her cool fingertips over my forehead. She said, 'You are just like Vega.' She was my Aunt Elsa, Mama's sister. She had come to help with the babies, but they were dead, and so was Mama. I snapped my mouth shut like an iron gate and I never dreamed of saying *Mama* again."

Marina breathed heavily. Her green eyes were intent on me. She placed the photograph on the table and gripped her belly.

"Do you want me to call Michael?" I asked.

"No." She took a deep breath. Her face was white.

I touched her back.

"No. I'm too hot." She pulled away from my touch. "Just tell me about the lion."

"Mama told me about a people in her homeland, the Druze. They believed, she said, that when a person died, his soul, if it had been good, would transform and be born a baby in China, because their prophets believed China to be the promised land. So coming out of my daze, I decided that Mama, because she was so good and so kind, had earned the right to will her soul into this lion cub to make her way back to me."

Marina's lips were drawn tight. The oven door creaked as Louise worked. Soon there would be people here. They'd bring his body back. If Marina's water broke, I could rush her away and call the funeral home and tell them to keep him.

Marina took my hand. "Tell me more," she said. My story seemed to help her pain.

I went on. "Papa drove us to your father's store. It was Sunday and the store was closed. Elias knew we were coming," I said. "He was eighteen, just a boy, but grown to me. He was building the cage. We got out of Papa's truck and Elias turned off his welding gun. He went in the store and brought out two quarts of milk and a nipple to feed the lion.

"Elias said, 'Glad to see you're well.' They had all worried that I would die, and that if I did, my father would crumble."

Sweat beaded on Marina's forehead.

I patted her forehead with the rag. "Your father held the cub and handed me the bottle to feed it." One reason I married him was because I thought he was that person—that young man who showed me kindness when I was hurting.

"I wish I had known this." Sweat rolled down her temples.

"It was a long time ago." My skin crawled at my foolishness. I did not understand my life with him, nor had I thought through my life without him. I left to dampen and cool the rag again. I knew Marina thought that if I had shown him compassion, our life would have been better.

In the kitchen, Louise sat with her head bowed. She was resting or praying. She looked up. "You are good?"

I nodded and ran cool water over the cloth. I took it to Marina. I turned up the fans as hard as they would go and the whir filled the room.

"Tell me more." Her lips pinched together as if she was in pain.

"Gus and I took turns with the bottles. The milk dribbled down our arms, and she licked us with a sandpaper tongue. When she had enough milk, she lay down in the sun, with her belly exposed. Your father sent us in for Coca-Cola and candy before he went back to welding."

Marina relaxed. The pains faded and she blotted her neck and face with the rag.

"Papa watched me like a hawk that day. Elsa and Nelly talked in Arabic, and usually he'd clamor on with them, but he kept his eyes on me." He thought he had lost me too. "I turned away and pretended Elsa's voice was Mama's."

Marina stacked the pictures she wanted to display and put the others back into the hatbox. "I can't believe the town let him keep a lion in a cage all those years."

"People thought it was interesting. When it was young, he drove it in his truck like it was a dog, and then he kept it tied on the backside of the store. But once it got big, he welded it in. He was afraid some crazy would let it loose. I could hear it grunt and call all the way at Papa's store."

"I'm going to have this picture run in the paper—tell that story," she said. "How people came to see the lion. How the store got its name."

The clock ticked. The house bloomed in the heat. The cuckoo began its litany of chirps. Marina looked at me, and then at her watch. "It's twelve already."

"Are you okay now?"

"I'm fine," she said. Her mind shifted gears and she sounded impatient. "Mama, it's time to clean up. We need to set up for the visitation."

I did not want her to be ashamed of me. I wanted her to know I stayed in my marriage to be with her and Eli. I could have run away and left them. I wanted her to know that she and Eli were the loves of my life, but it sounded too strong, so smothering that it would repel her. I wanted to prove my love, that I wanted to care for her and her baby.

I could see the pains had affected her, and her expression looked harsh in the bright light cutting through the window. "Time to get busy," she said.

I had felt close to her, but her words pinched. Her loyalty lay with him. I wanted to be the kind of mother mine had been—patient and forgiving—but he made me something else. I said, "Marina, I did not choose to have your father laid out here. I don't want all those people here."

Her tone was all business. "Whether you like it or not, you have to mourn him." Whenever she happened in on his yelling, he stopped and she darted out, both pretending like nothing happened. "We have to bury him with some semblance of respect."

"He was good at hiding things from you." I wanted her to know, but if I showed her the bruises, the bit of comfort we'd had together would vanish and we'd be back where we started.

She looked at me hard, her eyes and mouth at jagged angles. She let out a shuddering breath. "I know the two of you struggled. I know he was angry." She covered her face with her hands, and when she looked at me again, her gaze was soft. Her tone changed. "You'll feel better after a bath." She sounded like a child planning a tea party. "It's time to get ready. I need to get the big percolator going. Eli is coming with my silver. I want to put out those few pictures." Her eyes scanned the room where Louise had not yet tidied. "First the visitation. Then the Rosary."

"This is not necessary," I begged. "Let's call the funeral home. It's not too late to do it there."

"It is," she said without mercy.

I lingered too close and she shooed me with a wave of her swollen hand. "Mama, go upstairs and freshen up. People will be here around four." She pushed me into the hallway and retrieved the dress bag from the kitchen. "I'll help you get ready."

I did not want to get ready. I did not want to go through with this pageant for Elias. If I did not change, she would have no choice but to send everyone away.

But I followed her upstairs. She hung the bag on my closet door and pulled out two day suits with three-quarter sleeves. She laid a navy one on the bed. "For today," she said. She hung a black one on the closet door and said, "For tomorrow." The pale skin of her neck met her dark hairline. So beautiful, even from behind, even in her swollen state.

Growing up, she had asked questions—how I met her father, if I'd had other beaus, what was my wedding like? She wanted the romance and the love story, but there was only a one-sided story to tell. I gave her paltry details. The wedding was at the church, Gus gave us the silver, and her grandfather built the house on property he had purchased for my mother. Then I would remind her, in a harsh tone, how I grew up in Mounds over the store, working when I wasn't in school, no mother to dote on me. She would frown, sad or appalled at the poverty of my girlhood, so different from hers. She never worked a day in the store and she had anything she wanted—friends, piano lessons, dresses, ribbons, bicycles.

When she was twelve or so I discovered her in the attic in my wedding dress, and the sight angered me. "Get out of that now." She looked surprised at my temper. "Get out of it now." She gave excuses. "I'm playing. Why can't I play?" I told her to get it off and she argued with me until I grabbed her arm and ripped at the dress. I slapped her backside, a girl almost as tall as me, and she looked so full of hate. "This dress is not your plaything," I yelled. She had no idea why I was in a rage, but I wanted nothing of the lie of my marriage to touch her. I didn't know if she ever told her father what I had done or if she stole it away, like a hot brick in an oven, always there to remind her of what I was capable of.

"How's this one?" She held up a pale-gray blouse with a bow at the neck.

"That's fine," I said. I should have created more happy moments for her when she was a child, seeds of joy to grow on. Elias had given her so many. But I was stingy and too bitter to share what little hope I had stored away. If I had given her something more, she would have that now. She would see me differently.

I wanted to weep as she pulled out another blouse, this one cream, otherwise identical to the gray one. She was dressing me up like a plaything.

"Go, get your bath, Mother." She zipped the dress bag. "They are sending a hat and some gloves later today."

I wondered if she knew that the mailman's house had been burned and that Eli had driven him to the seminary. She might know, too, what Nelly accused me of. She might be hiding her knowledge to keep me in line, to save face and get through the ordeal of burying her father. Maybe she could handle only one crisis at a time, and my leaving was secondary to her father's death. Maybe she did not know. She was a mystery to me, keeping her emotions locked safe away, buried deep below the surface.

If Nelly whispered in her ear, *"Your mother murdered him,"* I feared Marina would harbor too much doubt not to convict me. It would be easy enough for her to wipe her life clean of me.

She busied herself making the bed and then sat on it. "I'll rest here 'til you're out. Then I'll help you with your hair." She held her belly and breathed out a long sigh.

I turned on the fan above her and widened the opening of the bedroom window. The mockingbird's song broke the quiet lull. His noise filled the room.

"Mother, you only have a short time." She flicked her hand. "Go, clean up." She wanted me ready and on stage.

I walked from the room but stopped and peered back through the open door. Her forearm rested across the mound of belly. A mournful expression fell across her face.

Her skin glowed. No trace of makeup was left, just the flare of life flowing through her. Good, that she was still and resting, perched like a precious bird in a cage. Marina was mine, if only for a few minutes more, if only for the time it took me to bathe. She was contained there, still, my daughter.

The Lion

After I married, I baked early in the morning and worked the rest of the day. I liked getting up in the dark and feeling the oven warming against my side as I drank my coffee. After the sun and the loaves had risen, I opened the oven to put them in and the heat rushed out like a warm sigh on my face. In the beginning I was clumsy with a hot rack or a pan and touched them to my forearm. I collected a row of tiny burns, stacked one on top of the other like a miniature white ladder running up my arm.

I was happy working. The radio played low and the sounds of the clock and my breathing were peaceful. I liked it all—the kneading, the folding, the flattening of mountain bread between my palms, the smells of yeast and fresh baked bread, the slick of sweat between my clothes and skin. I remembered my mother doing these same things, and this was enough to feel good.

The baking kept me going, especially later in the day, when I became Cinderella of Nassad Grocery. I cleaned the plate-glass windows, scrubbed the floors, discarded the ruined food, and anything Elias or Nelly asked of me. I also cared for the lion, Leona.

The creature watched for me. Her large golden eyes fixed on the back door of the store and waited until I came out. I believed she remembered my smell from my childhood and from when I was a teen-ager and came to her on the nights she rumbled and called and I could not sleep. I snuck into Papa's store and wrapped bits of meat to take to her. I ran as fast as I could down the river trail, not because I was afraid to be alone at night or that my father or Elsa would be angry with me for going. I ran because I was happy to be alive, to be running, to have the blood rushing through my veins and nothing but the natural world around me. It was like swimming through air and darkness under the trees. I was part of the landscape and no one looked at me to figure out what I was or where I was from. There were only my feet against the dusty trail as I ran beneath the bridges and past the old courthouse. I was anonymous.

As I got closer to the grunting lion, she stopped her noise and paced the cage, sniffing the air in the direction from which I came. I gave her the scraps of meat and she licked my palms where the meat had been. She lay down and she quieted. I sat with my back pressing against the bars and she scooted her weight close. She could have killed me one way or another, by clawing though the bars or severing my hand when I gave her the meat, but she seemed happy to have another living creature near. I pretended she held my mother's spirit, and beneath the quiet, dark sky, I told her my thoughts on books or boys or the mean girls, until her head lay on the concrete pad. Then I walked sleepily back home.

When I married and became her caretaker, she waited for me, like a sphinx, her head intent and high, her hind legs beneath her, her fore-paws in front. She jumped to standing when she saw me coming, waved her tail high, and paced her cage. The sight of me signaled food and water, relief from her loneliness. I hosed down her cage, lugged meat and bones for her, and gave her fresh water each day. I was the one to touch her and scratch her side. She purred from deep in her chest and it sounded as if it came from the center of the earth.

I never talked about the lion to Marina because that animal lived in constant misery until she died. A big cat, five feet long, she paced the cage, and her black-tipped tail constantly swatted away flies. Her tongue lolled out of her fleshy mouth and over yellow teeth. People came to buy a Coke, candy, or cigarettes and to have a look at her. She smelled, marking the corners of her cage and lying inadvertently in her own foul. There was the stink of the meat too. She went through a hundred or more pounds a week, most of it bits from the slaughterhouse or the hams or shanks about to spoil in Elias's cooler.

It was a nasty job, but I did it because I cared for her. She lay on the concrete floor with no shade on the hottest days and no protection from the wind or rain. I did what I could to help her, because when the lion saw me coming, she softly grunted as if she were saying "Hello." Her greetings were gentle compared to the great noise she was capable of—her grunting could be heard five miles away. I dreamed of saving her, but there was no place for her to go. The sight of her caused my heart to swell like a bruise, but it cheered me, too, when she looped her tail high and rubbed her flesh against the bars of the cage because I was near.

I persuaded Elias to rig a tarpaulin above her. "She's been fine all this time without a drape," he said. But I insisted, and he did as I asked, maybe to humor me. I rolled it back on nice days to give her sun, and when it rained I pulled the tarp over the roof and down one side of her cage.

Nelly chastised me for wasting my time, but Elias shushed her. "What is the harm?" he asked.

"She's wearing herself out taking care of that beast. She can't conceive." Nelly berated Elias that I was not yet with child, and she whispered in my ear, "It is a sin to interfere with God's work." She was greedy for a grandchild to hold, for someone to love. For my failure to produce a child, she looked down on me. She said, "When I was your age, I had borne my sons, had come to America, and was running my husband's business."

She told Elias to take me someplace nice—a vacation. Nelly said if I relaxed from work, I might conceive, but I did not want to have a baby. The idea that I might die as Mama had made me lonelier than ever. I had no mother to help me or teach me. Nelly would take over and the child would be as much hers as mine.

Elias wanted to get away, whether we created a child or not. He told me to pack a bag. We left the lion and the store in Ivie's care the next day. We had been married a full year when we drove toward Gulf Shores on a clear, blue spring morning. The dogwoods bloomed white and pink, and the redbuds had popped open their purple blooms. Easter was near, and that meant a big production with Nelly. I was thankful for the coming week without her and her constant questions.

As we drove toward the Gulf, I thought of my parents' crossing of the sea and the start of their new lives. I hoped the beach trip would be a new start for us. We were escaping Nelly and the store, but I worried about the lion in Ivie's care. I worried I had abandoned her.

Elias had not yet turned bitter and hateful, not yet raised a hand against me or called me ugly names. As we drove, I listened to him talk and realized he was like me, uncertain of his purpose. He hated being a grocer. He complained about the constant smell of rotting produce, the bloody butcher's aprons, the loading of boxes and crates, and most of all, the "kissing the asses of all the asses"—his customers. He hated being under his mother's thumb, but he said that when his father had died, "I had to keep things going. I had to keep them fed."

For one stretch of the drive, Elias talked about how his father had had little tolerance for Ivie's pranks, stealing cigarettes or getting caught with moonshine. Their father beat Ivie for every transgression—when the teachers said he didn't pay attention in school, or when he did not finish a job at the store, or when he broke down and cried for no apparent reason. Elias's father had other punishments too, like running laps in the heat or holding books with arms outstretched for long periods of time. Elias mostly avoided his father's brutality, but Ivie always stepped into trouble. Elias said, "I felt sorry for him. I want to help him for Mother's sake." He worried, too, about leaving Ivie in charge. "He's been sober for months," Elias said. "I hope it sticks."

For the first four days at the beach, it rained. We stayed in the cabin and nervously shifted around each other. Elias seemed pleased enough to be free of the store and his daily duties. He chain-smoked and drank coffee as he read paperbacks and newspapers in a soft chair in the corner. He did not shave and his beard grew in dark and handsome. At night, a lamp glowed near his face and he looked peaceful in the dim light.

I made coffee all day, and out of habit, I made the round discs of mountain bread, but without the rush of Nelly pushing behind me. We'd brought a crate of groceries and a cooler of sandwich meat, and he waited on himself according to his own hunger. I wore my hair loose, no jewelry or dresses. If our eyes met, he smiled and nodded, but he did not bother me in any way, no touching or climbing on top of me in the night. We were free from the roles we played at home and at his store. In the beach cabin, we were two polite strangers sharing a space.

I sat inside a screened porch overlooking the beach and watched the rain pelt the white sand and the wind blur the gray line between sea and sky. Each day, as the light dimmed and the gray line of sea and sky went black, I felt the disappointment of a child missing the circus. I had expected more—the excitement of my mother's Beirut, the exotic seafood, the octopus, the oysters and shrimp that tasted of the sea, and throngs of people, cafés, grand hotels, the lights of the city, sandcastles—or her excitement of seeing New Orleans when she came to America. I suggested we drive there for the day and spend the night, but he said, "No, we'll be battling weather all the way." There was only endless rain, sand in the sheets, Elias's cigarette smoke, and the bland food we had brought from home.

On the fourth morning, Elias woke me and said, "Let's go out." We drove in the rain down a strip of cabins and red *Vacancy* signs glaring against the wet, gray atmosphere. There was a Ferris wheel at the end of the road where we turned right to go into town. Elias said, "You couldn't pay me to ride that contraption."

"But you could see the ocean for miles." I tried to convince him. I wanted to go high like my mother, who had climbed the tower in her hometown. I wanted to see far away. "Maybe we could see whales or sharks."

"One loose screw and you plummet to your death." He lit a cigarette and pulled into the diner's parking lot. "I don't like being high."

We ordered our breakfast. The waitress moved slowly with the coffee and I watched the rain pounding the sidewalk outside. Elias lit a cigarette, and instead of opening the morning paper, he said in a pensive tone, "You make me nervous." I had seen that look on his face when he came to talk to me at my father's store, his green eyes bright and a small curve on his lips. I had wanted him to look at me like that again. He was flirting.

"What do you mean?" I asked. I wondered how I could make anyone, much less him, nervous. He was ten years older, my husband and boss. He was the one who came into my bed and did as he pleased.

He shrugged. "I worry," he said. He looked at the cigarette between his fingers, then his green eyes fixed intensely on me. His dark hair was thick and slicked back with the rain. "You work so hard, like a mule tied to a plow."

I felt a chill run down my spine, and my cheeks burned. "And you don't?"

"What I mean is"—he paused—"I don't know you very well." He held the cigarette between his thumb and middle finger and rolled the tip around the ashtray. He opened his mouth as if he were about to say more, so I waited for him to explain. "I'd like to know you better."

"What do you want to know?" I could not help but smile.

He touched my hand. "What is your favorite flower?"

I looked down at his long fingers over my palm. He had never asked that sort of question.

"Peonies," I said. "They start out small and boring. Just a tight ball. Then they open and never stop changing until they are this big glorious thing."

"Okay." Elias smiled at my answer. "We will plant peonies." He shifted in his seat and scratched his chin. He seemed nervous. "But what makes you happy?"

It was a hard question to answer. "I don't know."

He said, "I see you walk the path by the river."

"I like it there," I said. "It's a nice way to go to Papa's."

He nodded and touched my hand again.

"My mother used to take me walking there every day," I said. "Even if it was raining." I looked out at the gray rain hitting the cars. "We took umbrellas and we went. She looked up into the trees in the rain. She'd say, 'Look how very green the new leaves are against the gray light.'"

"Your mother was an artist." He lit another cigarette. "Or a poet." His cheeks blushed and an awkward silence fell between us. We had been married a year, and for the first time, we were having a meaningful talk.

"Why are you sad now?" he asked.

The waitress slid plates of eggs, sausage, and biscuits in front of us. He removed his hand and began to eat.

He had asked what made me happy. I did not know. I was young and newly married and I should have had some joy. He was right—I worked too hard and I seemed sad. I wanted to be happy, but the kind of happy I wanted was a mystery to me. I felt blood in my cheeks. I looked out the window. I said, "I'd be happy to go swimming in the ocean." For some reason, I felt I wanted to cry. "But the rain."

Elias heard me, but he continued putting jelly on his biscuit. "If you asked me what would make me happy, I'd say that I want to drop this mom-and-pop stuff. Do something else." He took a bite of eggs and thought for a moment. "I'd live on a farm, or in a big city, for that matter. Anything different than what I'm doing now. I don't want to make small talk with customers when there is nothing to say. I want to build things. Work with my hands." His face looked soft and hopeful.

I understood. "I loved English in school," I said. "I always liked reading and I thought one day I'd open a bookstore."

He laughed at my suggestion, and I felt the truth of how he saw me, young and naive. "Anna, you don't need to sell books to read books." He motioned the waitress for more coffee. "People who read go to the library. Anyway, you'll be raising children soon." He slurped from his cup and then lit another cigarette.

I clenched my jaw. Why did he ask what I wanted and then tell me how I was wrong? He assumed I wanted babies, but I did not. He knew nothing of my fears, that I would die in childbirth, or if I survived, that something would happen to the child. How could I tell him my morbid thoughts? I swallowed down my feelings, because I could not stomach being laughed at again. I told myself that he was trying in his own way, and I had to forgive his clumsiness.

"Travel." I sipped the hot black coffee. "I'd like to go back to the old country and see what it is like there."

"Ivie and me went after Papa died. Beirut, the big city, was okay. The cafés were fine. The coffee was good." He scratched his beard and looked out the window. "But I like flat ground. We rode on donkeys over narrow roads in the mountains. I looked down into a ravine, and the donkey's hoof sent rocks falling. I thought it was my end." The rain had slackened to a gray drizzle.

"Didn't you feel anything? Being there?" I was disappointed that his version of the old country was opposite my mother's.

"I felt hot and dirty," he said. "The *shluq* blew in—this hot, dusty storm from Africa—and I could not cool off. It was worse than the rain here."

"If it would stop raining, I'd like it here," I said. I poked at my eggs with my fork.

"I'm tired of sitting around." He swallowed his last bite of eggs, pointed his fork at my plate, and said, "You finished?"

I pushed my plate across the table. He opened the paper and read it while I drank coffee and watched the rain through the window.

At our cabin, he let me out and drove on. The rain was letting up to a sprinkle. I strolled down the beach not caring that I got soaked and cold. He came back after dark and I pretended to be asleep but he did not notice. From the smell of him, he'd been drinking. The next morning he lay in bed and asked me to make strong coffee. I floundered in the kitchenette until I noticed the quiet. The sound of rain had stopped. With the coffee percolating, I quickly dressed in my bathing suit, gathered up a blanket, a hat, the rubber inner tube, and before he could ask for anything else, I was gone.

For an hour, I floated far from shore. The sun was hot, beating down on my skin. I dipped in the cool water until I had a chill and then I climbed back on the inner tube and lay across it, covering my face with my hat. At times I worried the tide had taken me out too far, but then I did not care. My hair dipped into the ocean and I felt my curls weighed down with water and streaming out in all directions.

My eyes feasted on the sea and how it kept going and going, how deep and strong. The sea had rolled in and washed out for eternity and it would keep on forever. My mother must have known this, and Papa too. They had watched the land disappear for weeks and the distance of blue sea as far as their eyes could see. That was why she insisted on settling by the river—the reminder of water, of their home and the larger world.

I looked out from under my hat and for a moment could not see the land. Then the water bobbed me up, and there it was, the white sand shore and dark cabins. The saltwater beaded on my skin, already a deep olive from one morning of sun. The rolling motion of the sea soothed me, so far away I was from my responsibilities. I was alone and I felt peaceful.

The days of rain had calmed the tide, and the sea was tranquil. I took the inner tube in and then swam along the shore and past jellyfish and sand dollars. I saw rays scooting along the sandy floor. The Gulf was clear and golden green, and the white sand reflected light through the water. I turned on my back and floated. My eyes were drunk on the blue sky, the single white cloud, hanging as if from a string. I never wanted to leave the beauty of that morning. After I swam, I took the inner tube out again and floated on the quiet bobbing current.

I felt comfort in my smallness, floating on the sea, like one of the stars in the sky or a grain of sand on the beach. If I disappeared it would make no difference in the great scope of things. The idea did not make me sad. I felt calm to know the world was greater than myself. There was comfort to think about a world without end, like we said in church, or like the Druze beliefs my mother told me about. That a soul did not die, but was born another soul, that my mother's bird was a bird without end, that life would go on with me or without me, like the ocean rolling onto the sand. It made me happy, really, to think the world was big and my life small. It did not matter if I drowned, or if I ran away, or if I trudged along cleaning up after Elias and bearing his children. My life was part of a larger scheme and one day my life would end, but life would go on. I wanted to tell Elias my thoughts and see what he would say, if my ideas would make him laugh or angry or if they would pique his interest and start a debate.

Between the seconds the water splashed and my body flew in the air, I held my breath. I was certain a shark had found me. But it was Elias. I came up, my hat floating near him. He laughed and tugged me on the inner tube to shallow water, where he catapulted me into the air. I tried to swim away, but he grabbed my ankles and pulled me to him. The sand gave against my feet and he wrestled me back into the water. He was strong and playful and I could not stop laughing. My nose was cleared by saltwater and my throat was scratchy and dry. But I was having a good time.

He smiled at me with his handsome, bearded face and green eyes, and I felt like he saw me. So when he said, "Let's go inside," I gave up the beach and followed him. I expected he wanted lovemaking. He had not touched me the entire week and we were leaving the next day. In the shower, we rinsed off the salt and sand. As I twisted my hair into a towel, he lay in bed and greedily finished off a pack of cookies. He sucked down a Coca-Cola and belched.

"Come here," he said and patted the mattress. He wore a clean white T-shirt and a pair of boxer shorts. He rubbed his feet together and I took it as a sign of contentment. He stretched his legs and pointed his toes. "You looked too peaceful out there." He grinned and looked at me from the corners of his eyes. "I had to rile you up."

His chest expanded deep with breath. His legs were white as paper, unlike his dark face, neck, and forearms. He closed his eyes. His lips parted and he yawned big and loud. He seemed altogether boyish, lying there, as exposed and harmless as the lion often seemed to me on a cool fall day when the sun beat down on her flanks and dark-brown belly.

He opened one eye and lifted his head from the pillow. "What's taking so long?" He slapped the bed with his open palm. "Come here." Wrapped in my housecoat, I sat on the edge of the bed and combed out the tangled curls of my wet hair.

"Don't worry with that," he said. "Come here."

I felt attracted to him. For the first time in our marriage, we had been ourselves. We had laughed, and there was no one pushing. I felt as if I was in my own skin. I'd had time to think thoughts of my own. I had done something I wanted to do. Content, Elias had joined in, and we had a good time, a good day. More than anything I wanted to stay. I did not want to go back to the store or his mother or his aging lioness.

"Let's stay here," I said as he pulled me close.

"That would be nice." His voice was sleepy. He draped his heavy arm over me. "But we have to go back."

I listened to his breathing. "Not if we don't want. We can go somewhere else. Do something else, like you said."

He snickered. "Don't be stupid." He put his finger to my lips to hush me. "Be quiet now. I'm tired."

In a short time, he was snoring. My shoulder ached from the deadweight of his arm. My exhilaration vanished, and I knew after the long, quiet car ride tomorrow, my life would resume back to the long, lonely days. I felt with certain dread that I would soon become pregnant and our lives and duties would be cemented under the pressures of the store and family and what we were supposed to do.

I pushed him off, and for the rest of the afternoon I let the sun bake my skin as I sat on the shore and the waves washed up over my feet. My skin got so dark from one day at the beach that two days later, in our store, a man would call me "gal" in an unfriendly voice. When I faced him and he recognized me, he had blushed and begged my pardon.

My senses were fixed on the sea, the warm wind blew my hair, and the gulls dove in and out of the water. A woman walked past me with her three young children. I listened as their chatter, like chirping birds, drifted toward me and then away. I could hear happiness in their voices, and I envied them. I thought of my mother and her stories of Beirut. I thought of the photograph Aunt Elsa had given me on my wedding day, of those three young girls smiling, the sea behind them. I thought of my mother and my father and their crossings. I had never done anything so bold. Nelly was right about me.

I had the notion to pack my bag, take the remaining money in Elias's wallet, and sneak off. I could take the car, but then he'd surely find me. Papa and Gus would worry, and so would Elias. I knew of no one in the world to run to, and what kind of life would I have alone? I looked at the beautiful water and reminded myself not to be grim.

There would be more good days and there was hope to build on. Elias seemed happier than I had ever seen him.

The sun set, and I went in. Elias buttoned a starched shirt. "Hungry?" he asked. "Get dressed and we'll go out."

We drove to a steak house and he ordered his meat rare with fried potatoes. He ordered me the same and I did not argue, even though I wanted something different. On the boardwalk, he bought ice cream and I held his hand as we strolled toward the garish Ferris wheel lit against the night sky. The music of the Ferris wheel whizzed and droned in my ear. I wanted to ride it. I watched it go up and around. I was twenty years old and my life felt like a law laid down outside of my reach.

"It's been a good day," Elias said. He'd said the same on our wedding day. His tone was hopeful, prodding me to stop sulking, to find the good in the moment.

I smiled and agreed.

He kissed me by the Ferris wheel. His beard, the kindness in his voice, the soft expression on his face—I felt I was kissing a stranger, not the man I kept shop with in Riverton.

Elias made love to me that night and fell to sleep. I could not close my eyes for the burning feeling I had in them. After midnight, I walked out expecting darkness, but the night was lit with the full moon and stars reflecting on water. I remembered Mama, and I wondered if this salt air was what she'd breathed on the ship. Was this the smell of Beirut? My eyes burned with longing. I stayed in the same place until morning. Elias found me sitting on the beach and staring at the tide.

"Let's get a move on." He looked at his watch. His beard was gone, and the sight of his clean-shaven face saddened me. "We have a whole day's drive and the store to open tomorrow. Knowing Ivie, he's screwed something up."

"Okay," I said. It felt as if a rock were lodged in my throat.

"Are you okay?" I heard concern in his voice. He thought I was sad because we were leaving. I was, but for different reasons than he thought, reasons I could not explain then, maybe not now, except that I had rushed into marriage, not aware of what marriage could be or what troubles we would face. I had decided on a life before I knew the possibilities. I had jumped blindly in with someone I did not understand.

"We can come back," he said.

I nodded. I thought it was generous of him, but even if we did come back, the reprieve I hoped for would be beyond my grasp.

It rained on and off on the long drive home. Elias's body grew tenser with each passing mile. His shoulders tightened and his expression fell. As much as I'd wanted to stay away, I missed the lion greeting me and my routine of working the dough, the smell of yeast on my hands, the heat of the oven, and the trip to the store with the loaves and rolls packed high in boxes. I had given Nelly my starter to feed and she would have taken good care of it. I would feel relief to have my mind and hands busy again.

The sky was dark and misting when we arrived home in Riverton. "I know it's late," he said. "Is it okay if we check on the store?"

"That's fine." I was surprised he had asked my permission. Lightning streaked far off. We had driven through spring storms all day.

He wanted to size up the mess Ivie had made. He pulled into the alley and around to the back of the store. The car lights shined on her.

"Oh, no," I said. "Oh, no." She lay, a heap of fur, no movement, no rising or falling of her sides. Guilt flashed through me. She had given out from the loneliness and boredom of the cage.

"Stay here," he said. He ran toward the cage.

I stepped out of the car. The mist hit my face and a cool wind blew.

He saw that she was dead. "I just want to go home," he said. "I don't want to deal with this shit." He hit the hood of his car with the palm of his hand. He wasn't talking to me, because I had no power to change things, but having a corpse to greet morning customers would not do. He threw his arms up and cursed. The headlight beams shone on him and the misty rain. He yelled, "Go in and call Ivie. Tell him to get his sorry ass here."

I fumbled with the lock.

"She's been shot, Anna." Grief was in his voice. "Someone shot her. I should've known better than to leave Ivie in charge."

He fired up his blowtorch around ten o'clock at night. Elias was digging in knee-high mud when Ivie, drunk and stinking, arrived.

"It was sick," Ivie said. "I had to put it out of its misery."

"Maybe you need to be put out of yours," Elias screamed. "What's wrong with you?" Ivie shrugged. Then Elias sent him to round up some men to help bury it.

I held an umbrella and a lantern while Elias dug. When Ivie stumbled up with men to help, Elias sent me in. I watched from the open door of the storeroom. The lantern sat on the earth beside them. They dug until the grave was shoulder deep. Then the rain started to pour and the lantern flickered to nothing. I ran out and held a flashlight over the grave.

I did not think of my mother the night we buried Leona, but my body remembered the smell of opened earth and what it meant—life and death, living and dying. The lion that I had met shortly after she died was gone. Elias looked up at me. The temperature had dropped. It was a cold snap, but a feeling like hot water washed over me. His eyes worked my face, as if he was thinking, *What next?* He was as lost as me. Neither of us knew what we were doing or why we were doing it.

The helpless look lasted only a second. The rain began to fall harder. His expression went cold and he yelled at Ivie, "Let's get this damn thing in the ground." He threw the shovel and lifted himself out of the earth. It took all five men dragging her from the cage to the grave. They pushed her in, and she fell, heavy and loud.

Cause of Death

My foot left the bottom step, but I went no further. Nelly and her sister bickered in the kitchen. The dining and living rooms were empty of people, but in the living room, the polished mahogany box sat like a sailboat cupping his body. His salt-and-pepper hair was combed and pomaded in neat waves. His nose jutted toward the ceiling and his cheeks sank into the hollows of his mouth. The makeup on his skin had an orange tone, unnatural against the casket's tufted white silk. A rosary wrapped around his folded hands. His gold wedding ring caught light and gleamed. I wondered what he had felt the day I slipped it on his finger.

The time since his death seemed long and wide. He had been a daily fact of my life. Unexpected feelings of grief and guilt welled up and my legs went numb. I sank to the bottom stair and sat where his face was no longer visible, only the tips of his shoes, the silver crucifix that hung from the white silk of the open lid, and Nelly's portrait of him above the fireplace.

The night before last, Elias left me lying on the floor and drove away. He came back after dark and sat in the car for an hour. He killed the headlamps, but the dashboard glowed green on his face. The silver bottom of a flask flashed each time he tilted it. By the way he hung his head, he was drunk. I left the window and locked myself in the bathroom and tried to wash away all that had happened that day—the heat, the sweat, the sewing of the baby clothes, Orlando Washington stepping over the threshold, Elias in the doorway and then over me and then on top of me, trying to press the life out of me.

When he entered, he hollered, "Anna," again and again. His shoes clapped through the house, up the stairs, and stopped outside the bathroom door. It was locked, but Elias, drunk and determined, jimmied it open.

He loomed over the tub.

"Leave me alone." I pulled my knees to my chest to cover my body. My heart raced.

He grabbed the meat of my arm, tender from earlier. He was strong and anger made him stronger. He pulled me from the water as easily as a mother lifting a child from a bath.

I told him, "No," but he shoved me and lay on top of me on the cold, hard tiles. I tried to get out from under him, but he pinned my spine against the unforgiving floor. Sliding, pushing, flattening. He had not touched me in so long. I thought he was done with me or was impotent or had someone else.

I could not fight him from my position, wet and cold on the hard floor, so I turned my head and let my mind wander. I looked at the underbelly of the tub, the beautiful claw-foot tub I had once been so impressed by, that I had bathed my children in. I would bathe Marina's baby soon.

He pulled my hair so tight my eyes felt they would pop out of my head. "Look at me," he said. "Pay attention." He told me with his eyes that he hated me, that he wanted to kill me, that he was stronger and meaner, and that I was nothing to him. His eyes said, *Stay in your place.* He had been to Orlando Washington's house by then, but I did not know. He left me on the floor and I washed again. I dried the wet puddle where I had lain. I dressed and went to my room.

"Make me something to eat," he bellowed from the kitchen.

Downstairs, he was sitting at the dining-room table. I took my car keys and went out the back door. I could have driven to Lila and Gus's, or to Marina's to show her the bruises forming on my arms, but I knew he would follow me wherever I went and this would go on until I was dead. I felt a weight in my chest as I stared at the black night sky. I felt paralyzed, stuck to that very spot, as if he were holding my feet to the ground.

When he came to the back door and repeated his demands for food, I said, "I will be right there." He accepted my answer. He must have believed, after the night's events, that he was in control of my actions, that I had been put in my place. But before I returned inside to cook, I walked to the shed and then through the garden for a ripe tomato from the vine.

The swinging door was propped open and I could hear him in the dining room. Even his breathing sounded drunk. I made some quick gravy, warmed peas and flatbread, and cut the tomato from the garden. I sliced some ham and took him his plate. His chair creaked as he shifted his weight. He said, "Do you know where I've been?"

"I don't care," I said. I did not want to know.

He cackled. "You would care."

He sneered and I thought it was because of what he'd done to me. I left him at the table. I wanted to get out of his way as quick as I could. In my room, I pushed the highboy dresser to block his entrance. The feet of the dresser left scratches on the hardwood, but it no longer mattered. If he tried to break through the door, I would climb down the branches of the pecan tree outside my window. I was resolved he would not touch me again. His smell hung in my nostrils.

An hour later, I heard him mount the stairs, and then his nails scraped across the door. The sound was soft, soothing even, the way a lover might run his fingers across his beloved's back. His voice, low and hushed, said my name. "Anna." He paused. "I need your help." The curled telephone cord was in my pocket. I would have to remember to put it back.

I studied the pecan-tree limbs, like sweet arms reaching toward me. I could scoot out on the roof and grab that one. I'd rather fall than have him go at me again.

I listened to him breathe until his breath caught. After a silent moment, a quiet moan escaped him. His dinner did not agree with him. His voice, angry and low, seeped through the door. "You trying to kill me? You want to be with that ape?"

From the hallway, Nelly entered the living room shrouded in a black veil and a long black dress. She looked like she belonged in the last century. Intent on his body in the casket, she did not notice me sitting on the stairs. She pulled a chair near his head. Her gnarled hands worked rosary beads and her body swayed. Her prayers sputtered like hot grease through the thick air.

I hugged my arms and squeezed the bruises beneath the suit sleeves. From the kitchen Louise asked, "Coffee?"

A man answered, "No, thank you." I did not recognize the voice.

"No," I heard Marina say quietly. "I won't have it."

Through the screen, twenty yards away, Marina and Michael faced each other by the lamppost and the clematis her father had trained.

Michael's wide shoulders filled his seersucker coat and his hands dug into his pockets. He stared down at the ground, as if studying the grass blades beneath his shoes. I heard him say, "We need to . . . you need to . . ." But I could not make out the rest of his sentences. His back was facing the house.

A pained expression covered Marina's face. Because of Michael she was bona fide. That is what Marina believed. His family bragged that they had settled this land when there was only a ferry to cross the river, that they had once owned slaves and their plantation had been one of the biggest and most prosperous in Alabama. He was Catholic, neither of them could escape that, but his family had old money.

Marina stood tall and erect, despite her massive belly. "Easy for you to say." Her voice was muffled. "This is my family." She was a fighter, and I saw the fight on her face. Her cheeks were red from the heat. Marina scowled and her lips moved slowly as if she were solving a difficult problem. Her hawk eyes stared in my direction, but the bright sun was above her and I did not think she could see me through the shadows of the porch or the screen door. I wanted to help her.

He held out a handkerchief and she took it. The river breeze rustled the bright-green leaves of the pecan tree. The wind settled and I heard her clearly. "What do you want me to do?" She used his handkerchief beneath her eyes. "She's my mother."

I could hear in Marina's voice that she was rattled. I wondered if Nelly had made good and told her I had been alone with Mr. Washington, or of her suspicions that I was behind Elias's death. I wondered if Marina believed I could be capable of killing her father.

Michael's lips moved close to her ear, counseling her, telling her what to do.

"No," Marina said. "No." She knew my faults better than anyone.

He touched her face and tried to fix her rumpled hair.

She batted his hand away and pulled the pins from her hair. It fell in black waves.

An old truck drove up and the driver waved at Marina. Her gardener, come to clear the branches and storm debris.

"Mother." Eli stood before me at the base of the stairs and held out his hand to help me stand.

"You are okay." I stood and hugged him. No smell of smoke from a house burning, but I wanted to know what he had seen and how Orlando Washington was.

Eli's face was grim and his eyes were dark-ringed from lack of sleep. "The coroner is here."

I touched the new bandage on my palm and had a sinking feeling. "What does he want?" I touched Eli's face and arms. He was whole. No trace of harm, but my eyes watered.

"He wants to talk to you." His voice was solemn and he held his shoulders erect. "He's waiting in the kitchen."

"All right." Worry lines across his forehead made him look older. "I want to know what happened with Mr. Washington," I said. "Is he safe?"

"For now, he's safe." He seemed changed, more focused, less anxious, than when I saw him the night before. He took a handkerchief from his pocket and blotted my cheek. "The details can wait." His handkerchief smelled like his father. So did he—his breath, his clothes.

In the kitchen, a man in horn-rimmed glasses and short-cropped hair stood by the table. He was younger than me, tall and straight, stiff in his clothes, like he belonged in the military. "Mrs. Nassad?"

"Yes."

"I'm Martin Dupont, the county coroner." I recognized his name from past ballots and elections. "I examined your husband yesterday. I'm sorry for your loss."

What to say to that? *Thank you* did not seem right. "Yes," I said again. Today would be the visitation and later the Rosary. There would be people saying *I'm sorry*, but I wasn't sorry and I did not know the words of a grieving widow. I tried to remember what Papa said when Mama died, but I could not remember words, just hollow-eyed grief and the low, painful sighs.

Eli held a chair for me to sit.

"Let's go over the findings," Mr. Dupont said.

Nelly hobbled into the kitchen. She mumbled in Arabic to her sister Louise and noticed me sitting with Mr. Dupont. She spit out, "Who is this?"

The coroner turned his head in her direction. He stood and held out his hand. "I'm the coroner."

Nelly fell into a fit of wailing. She looked ancient in her black-lace veil.

Louise turned from the stove and took her sister into her arms. "Nelly, Nelly." Her voice was a sea of calm. "Hush, now."

"No." Nelly pushed Louise away. "He should know. I will tell him what she did." Nelly pointed her cane at me and then to Mr. Dupont.

Eli rushed to Nelly's side. "Hush, Grandma. No more of that today."

"You should be ashamed," Nelly said to Eli.

"Calm down," Eli said. No longer did he sound like a boy talking to his grandmother. He sounded forceful yet patient, like a loving parent who knew best.

"You should defend your father." Her voice rose to a shriek.

Marina would disapprove of the scene in front of this man, and I wished she'd come inside and gather Nelly up.

Mr. Dupont removed his glasses to clean them. His eyelashes were as thick as a baby's, and his eyes seemed gentle as he stared at her. He put them on again and watched Nelly chanting one of her grief songs. He clearly did not know what to make of her. Mr. Dupont returned his gaze to me and pushed the dark-rimmed glasses to the bridge of his nose. His eyes magnified. "I have a few questions," he said.

"You will ask her?" Nelly demanded. "She never took care of him."

Mr. Dupont squinted at me. Wrinkles at the corners of his eyes fanned out across his temples. He was not as young as he first appeared. "Can we speak in private?"

"Eli, please?" I motioned for him to take her out of the kitchen and was glad the coroner had asked for privacy.

"I don't need your help." She flapped her hand at Eli. "I want to hear what she says."

Louise gathered her sister's arm. Eli took the other and they steered her out of the kitchen. "Come with me, Grandma."

"No, I should be here. This man needs to know the truth."

The coroner looked at his black clipboard and wrote. The pen scratched the paper. His glasses slid down the slope of his nose.

"That's enough," Eli said. "Let's go outside."

The screen door shut behind them. From the porch, I could hear Nelly whimpering. "I will not leave him. I will not leave my boy."

"Nobody wants you to leave," Eli's voice trailed in.

Over the rims of his glasses, the coroner's eyes followed the voices, then turned to rest on my face.

My palms sweated and the bandage slipped.

Her wailing sieved through the screen door. "I want Ivie. He will listen to Ivie. Why you don't hear me, Eli?" Her words were like ants crawling over my skin.

"I'm sorry," I said.

"Grief hits everyone differently." He jotted a note on his paper.

"She doted on him her whole life," I explained. "He was her first-born son."

"I see," he said. "It is never easy to lose a child."

"No." I held his gaze. "I can't imagine." But I could imagine. I was losing Marina, with each moment that I did not make my case with her. I needed to tell her I had done nothing wrong in helping Mr. Washington, and if I must answer Nelly's accusations about her father, I would deny harming him until my last breath. My eyes were hot and my heart beat high in my throat.

Nelly quieted. Marina must have been with her.

He laid his writing pad on the table and leaned toward me. "Questions are hard at a time like this." He cleared his throat.

I gripped Eli's handkerchief.

"Your husband—you found him?"

"Yes." I had listened to him die.

"About what time?"

"Nine in the morning," I said, but it had been one thirty when he ceased his commotion. For thirty minutes, I had waited in the stillness.

I listened at the door for sounds of breathing or movement. With shaking hands I pushed the dresser out of the way. I looked out. A crowbar lay on the ground near my door.

"Is that your usual waking hour?"

"No." I shook my head. "Usually Elias is up first and then me to cook his breakfast and start the baking for the store. But I overslept when he did not wake me."

He scribbled and I wondered what was useful in those details. Looking up, he said, "I wanted to say, I have enjoyed your baking over the years."

An unexpected kindness. "Thank you," I said, but I wanted him gone and Elias's body gone, the flowers, Nelly. I loved Louise, but I wanted her out of my kitchen, out of my sight. I wanted to put him in the ground. Once he was buried, I would be free. I wanted peace and quiet. I wanted the baby to come.

"Did you notice anything unusual the night before?" He twirled his pen between his fingers.

"No," I said. "No." I squeezed the bruises on my arms. What did this man know of the postman, about the threat of lynching, about his house burning to the ground? I tried to search his face for clues.

Michael pushed in through the swinging door, and the smell of expensive cologne entered with him. His clothes were crisp and his wavy blond hair fell just so. I wondered if their baby would have blue eyes like him, like Sophie. Marina must have sent him in, and I imagined she was hovering on the other side of the door and listening.

"Good afternoon," Michael said to Mr. Dupont. He stood close behind my chair. "I'm Michael Matthews. I'm Mrs. Nassad's son-in-law."

The coroner nodded, but returned to questioning me. "Did you notice any tossing or turning, him getting out of the bed?"

I cleared my throat. "We did not share a room." I held Eli's handkerchief over my eyes. My heart stirred like a startled bird. *What does it matter?* I wanted to ask. *He wanted to kill me. If it had not been him, it would have been me.* The bandage slipped.

"What happened to your hand?" He gestured to the cut.

"I cut it on a piece of glass yesterday."

Michael shifted his feet.

"Did you hear him call out?" Mr. Dupont asked.

"No, nothing." It was a lie. Elias's noise kept me sitting on the edge of my bed. The light of the waning moon reflected in the mirror and bathed the walls in a wash of lilac. In the mirror, I looked ghostly. I listened to him gag and bellow. I wanted it to be over.

Mr. Dupont wrote on his pad. "And why was his body moved?"

I had picked up the crowbar and stepped carefully into the hall in case he might be lurking, waiting to flush me out, and then I saw his body, facedown and sprawled across his bed. I had watched for a movement and listened for a sound. When his chest did not rise or fall, I turned him over.

The coroner's small, childlike eyes searched my face.

"What do you mean?" I asked.

Nelly, on the porch, started up again. "Let me go in, Eli," she said, and I could hear Marina shushing her too.

"He was on the dining-room table when the funeral home came," Mr. Dupont said.

"Oh," I said. "I did not want him moved, but his mother, she is from the old country. Syria then, Lebanon now," I said. "She wanted to lay him out and mourn him at home." I wondered if he could read a liar, if he could get the truth from a person.

"I see." Mr. Dupont noted this.

Michael's warm body hovered. He touched my shoulder as if to comfort me.

My shirt was wringing wet, but if I removed the suit coat, the green bruises would peek from the hems of the short sleeves and more questions would follow.

Nelly sputtered inside the screen door and sobbed in the next room.

"Had Mr. Nassad been complaining of chest pain, weakness, nausea?"

"He had heartburn, he said." That night, after the soft scraping of his nails across the door, he shook it and the lock rattled in the jamb. He banged and I prayed the lock would hold and the dresser would not topple. I opened the window and looked down through the limbs of the pecan tree to see if there was a way for me to descend. He was sick in the bathroom, and then he stumbled back to my door and rattled it again. "You have poisoned me, you witch." Then begging, "Have mercy. Take me to the hospital, and we can make peace." There was stumbling down the stairs and a rambling through the kitchen. I squeezed the phone cord in my pocket. He would not find his keys either. I had hid them in the back of the silverware drawer. Then he made a slow climb up again.

"That will do." Mr. Dupont gazed over the rims of his glasses at Michael and me with a mournful smile. He saw me as a grieving widow.

I bowed my head and held Eli's handkerchief to cover my eyes. Michael patted my shoulder, as if to say *Good job*, and left to report to Marina. My temples beaded with perspiration and I blotted my face as if I were blotting tears.

That night, when I had struggled to turn the deadweight of his shoulders and body, his mouth gaped open and bile spilled out. His eyes, the color of green glass, did not blink.

"Just one more question, ma'am."

I looked up.

He took off his glasses and folded them into the palm of his right hand. His heavily lashed eyes searched my face. "I'm duty bound to ask." Without his glasses balanced on his nose, he looked ten years younger. "Do you know of anyone who would want to harm your husband—an employee, a customer, a family member?"

I swallowed my breath. "No," I said. "His family loved him. His mother is devastated. His children too. He was a good man."

The screen door slapped shut. Michael must have gone outside.

With a flick of his wrist, he settled his glasses on the tip of his nose and wrote again. "Your mother-in-law, she suspects you harmed him?" He looked over the rim of his spectacles and waited for my answer.

"She is angry that I helped Mr. Washington." That was my best excuse for Nelly's behavior, and it was true.

Mr. Dupont nodded as if he sympathized with the situation. Maybe he was someone who would have allowed Mr. Washington to deliver his mail had he been assigned to his street.

I cast my gaze to the floor. "She's never cared for me, for our marriage." I squeezed my eyes shut and worried what she might be saying to Marina. "She wanted him to marry someone else."

That early morning, I did not turn on a light. The stars were bright, but the moon was waning, almost invisible. In the dark, early morning, in my nightgown and bare feet, I walked across the cool, dew-kissed grass to the shed and returned Elias's crowbar to the wall and the can I'd removed earlier to its shelf. I tracked blades of wet grass into the kitchen and plugged the telephone cord back in. From the drawer, I took his keys and hung them on their hook. Upstairs I began to clean around his body, in his room, in the hall and the bathroom.

Mr. Dupont placed the lid on his pen. "Usually, when a question of foul play has been brought, there is an investigation. We send the deceased to the medical school in Birmingham for tests that we can't do here."

I wiped the vomit from his mouth, and with my nightgown tied between my legs, I scrubbed the kitchen. All of this I did in the dark, so Verna would not notice lights on in my house.

I watched Mr. Dupont read his notes. I bit my lip to keep calm.

After I had wrestled new sheets on his bed, I got a rug from the attic that I had put away for summer. The carpet was bulky and the rough backing scratched my skin as I dragged it down the stairs, past his room, and into mine. I kicked it into place and covered the scratches on my floor. My gown was soaked with perspiration. I stopped to drink water from the bathroom sink, took a cool bath, and changed my gown before lying down again.

I thought I could live in peace—I would soon be a grandmother, run the store, or sell it. I thought I could help Mr. Washington. I thought I would be safe. I lay in bed with the window open. The breeze from the river flowed inside. I slept hard until the heat of the morning woke me.

Mr. Dupont looked over the rims of his glasses. "I'll speak with your son, and then I'll sign the death certificate."

"Okay." I stood. I hoped Nelly's silence meant she had dozed off, or better yet, she might be dead.

In the living room, on the sofa pushed against the wall, I found Eli with his grandmother propped in the crook of his shoulder. Her glasses were folded and placed on his knee. Her withered hand lay cupped in her lap. Her mouth fell open in the shape of an O. Her carrying on had worn her out.

Marina stood against the wall nearest the kitchen where she'd been listening.

"Eli," I whispered. "He wants to talk to you."

We maneuvered Nelly from his arms. She was light, gaunt, insignificant in my hands, barely the weight of a child. She'd been such an enormous woman, and now she had so little flesh around her bones. I propped her onto pillows and stood near to keep an eye on her should she wake.

Mr. Dupont asked Eli similar questions. Eli said he had been away at seminary, so he could not speak to any changes in his father's health. "But Mother would know," he said. "She's stood by him all these years."

A turn of the truth.

Marina stared at me and a chill raced down my spine. If her eyes could spit darts, I would be dead.

"Do you know of anyone who would want to harm him?"

"No," Eli said. "People liked him."

"What about that business with the colored mailman?"

"I can't imagine." Eli's voice trailed off. "We were only trying to help him."

We, he had said, *we*, as if his father had been party to it all.

"Neighbors, angry customers?"

"No. No one wanted to harm him." Eli sounded resolute.

"And what about your grandmother—she doesn't trust your mother?"

Eli said, "Grandmother has never been kind to my mother, and it's worse now. She's looking for someone to blame." Eli cleared his throat.

Marina left her spot and stepped onto the front porch.

"People her age," Mr. Dupont said. "Keep a close eye on her. Grief can weigh hard on the older folks."

"I imagine so." Eli's voice strained.

There was a pause. A scratch of pen to paper. "Would your mother want to cause your father harm?"

"No. Absolutely not." A rush of certainty filled his voice.

"I'm sorry to have to ask, but it can be difficult to see much difference between a heart attack and poisoning." Mr. Dupont's tone was light, conversational, like he was letting Eli in on a trade secret. "Similar effects, but I've always detected it. The doctors in Birmingham haven't disproved a case of mine in sixteen years. I suspect your father had an overwhelming stress event that caused his heart attack. He had all the signs—the skin color, the enlarged heart, the gastric distress."

Eli cleared his throat.

"I apologize for talking shop." Mr. Dupont's voice returned to its somber inflection. He shuffled papers and scooted his chair. "Let's give this to your mother."

The men stepped into the hall. On the sofa, Nelly began to rouse and groped around for her glasses.

Mr. Dupont handed me the paper, the heading *Death Certificate* in plain black letters across the top. The official-looking paper with its embossed stamp said the cause of death was massive myocardial infarction. He whispered to me, "I'm sorry for your loss."

"Thank you." I handed the certificate to Eli.

Eli wrapped his arm around me.

I looked at the floor because I could not look my children in the eyes. My knees felt numb.

Mr. Dupont handed Eli his card. "If you have any questions, contact me."

Nelly got her glasses on and pointed at me. "Are you taking her now?"

Mr. Dupont raised his eyebrows. "My sympathies to you, ma'am," he said to Nelly. If I were to go to trial, he'd take the stand. He'd answer questions about today, about Elias, about the things Nelly said.

Mr. Dupont shut the screen door softly behind him. "My condolences," he said to Marina on the porch. Michael stood near the street, where the men were nearly finished clearing the yard.

I started out the door toward Marina.

Nelly used her cane to stand and pounded the wood floor with it as she moved toward me. "Where are you going?" Nelly's voice whipped through me and I froze.

"Grandma," Eli said. "Leave her be." His voice was authoritative, like a teacher scolding a student.

"Quiet," she snapped. To her, he was a child, the same as her sons. She pointed at me. "Marina will disown you." Her voice was cold and calculating, not senile as Eli had made her out to be. "You were never good enough for my boy. You were a white nigger then and you still are."

Marina shot through the screen door. "Grandmother!" she said. "Enough." Marina would go toe to toe with Nelly, with me, with any person. "I don't want to hear that kind of talk. Not today."

A holly bush rustled near the porch rail. The mockingbird alit atop the bush. Michael shook Mr. Dupont's hand as he passed. Michael's crisp white sleeves were rolled to his elbows, revealing a golden shade of skin. He took a drag from his cigarette and looked back at the house.

I had done what I had done to be with Marina. I had to get through this day and the next.

Nelly's gnarled finger poked my arm. "You leave or I will bury you alive."

"Stop it," Marina said. "What if Michael hears you?"

"He should know the truth." Nelly grasped Marina's swollen arms with withered hands. "Your father worked to give you everything."

"What about me?" I squeezed my hands into fists. The cut throbbed. "I worked beside him. Everything we have is from me too."

Marina's face was red. She shot me a look.

"If she had her way, she would have left you," Nelly screeched.

Marina had heard this her entire life and the story was part of her. "Michael's partners will be here in an hour." Marina kept her voice low, measured.

"You have your father to thank for your position." Nelly lost her icy tone. "Your grandfather opened the store here, not in Mounds like your mother's people, but your father made the store what it is. People respected him. They knew he was a good man. She has brought you nothing but shame."

"Michael thinks we're crazy, and I don't blame him." Marina rubbed her forehead. No trace of makeup remained, but she would fix that before people arrived.

Nelly's hands clamped together like the priest at Mass blessing the Eucharist. She turned toward Elias's dead body. "I told you what she was." She moved easily, like water rolling across the living-room floor. She laid her head on his chest. "Heaven forbid this!"

Marina leaned against the wall for support and traded glances with Eli.

I reached for her and she jerked away.

"No," Marina shouted at me. Her temple throbbed. "You asked me if I knew what my father had done. Ask me if I know what *you* did." Her eyes bore down on me. Her face was broken into sadness, anger, disbelief. "You let that man in this house. You put him in more harm than you could ever help him out of. What was Daddy supposed to do when he came in and found you alone with him?"

Eli pulled Nelly off the body. "You both have to stop this," he said to Marina and to Nelly. "Helping him was the right thing."

Nelly pushed Eli. "Go! Go! Get away! You should be ashamed." She balanced on her cane and took up wailing. "Your mother is a shame!"

Eli closed the lid of the casket, and Nelly hobbled into the kitchen to her sister.

Sweat beaded on Marina's temple. She glared. "Because they found out you let him in, they put a brick through the grocery window."

"Who are 'they'?" I asked.

The men outside were finished cleaning the branches from the yard. Michael crossed the lawn toward the pickup.

"What does it matter? If it's the whites or the blacks." Marina held her stomach. "We are still the talk of town."

"The window is already being replaced," Eli piped in, impatient with her. "You care more about your reputation than a man's life."

"What about our father's life?" Marina asked. "All of this craziness killed him."

Eli took a deep breath and looked down at us from his height. A car door shut. He glanced outside. "Father McMurray is here." Eli went out to greet him.

Out on the lawn, Michael took a money clip from his pocket. He counted cash and handed the men payment for their work. The old beater truck, filled with branches, pulled away. Those men would go back to Mounds. They knew this was the house Orlando Washington delivered mail to, where Elias Nassad had lived, and that I was Faris

Khoury's daughter. How careful they must be to come here, do a job, and act like nothing was wrong.

"It's half past three." Marina looked at the watch strangling her wrist. "The visitation is at four. We'll have the Rosary around six."

Michael strolled to meet Father McMurray and Eli under the shade of the pecan tree.

Marina groaned and made her way to the dining-room table.

"If you're having the baby, let me take you to the hospital," I said.

"No." Marina perched on the edge of a chair, her eyes closed, her pale olive skin gleaming with perspiration. "No."

"No, you're not in labor, or no, you won't go to the hospital?" The old ache in my chest tugged the same as when Elias was near. "I'm worried about you."

"If you are worried, that is your own doing. I can't clean up your messes any longer—not yours, not Daddy's."

Female voices carried in through the open windows. Marina turned her head. "The church ladies are here. I have to get things ready now."

How very much she was like him. I could do no right. He had seen me as a burden and now she did too. But I knew what she felt, in that moment, the pressure in her back, her abdomen, her legs, that constant physical weight, and the weight of fear before the baby came. She did not know what came after. She was ignorant of having a child, caring for her, aching for her. She was ignorant of all the complications, how you could love a child and resent her too.

The Vigil

The Catholic church ladies flowed in, one after the other, arms laden with dishes. "Oh, Anna," they said. "Your house looks so beautiful." I knew they had always been curious to see inside our house, not a factory worker's house or a farmer's.

No, I wanted to say. We had money when others did not, but I did not host parties or teas. I had no interest in opening myself up to their judgments.

"Isn't it wonderful he can be here?" one of the church ladies asked.

I did not nod or answer the stupid women.

"Where is Marina?" they asked.

"She'll be down in a minute," I said. Marina had gone upstairs to primp.

When Marina appeared in the dining room, no longer did she look perturbed. She wore a simple face of grief, powdered and pretty. Her hair was swept up in a perfect French twist. The church ladies swarmed to show her what they had brought. She smiled at the macaroni and cheese, the chicken casserole, the fruit pies. I knew she wanted some bland American foods for herself and her husband's family and colleagues. Marina called to Louise, "Do you think we should put out the cold dishes?"

Louise peeked around the corner of the door. "You sit. I do it. Okay?"

Marina nodded and Louise disappeared back into the kitchen.

"Tell me what you want me to do," I said.

The church ladies placed their dishes where Marina pointed. She treated me as if I were one of them and I followed her orders dutifully, arranging plates and servers, writing on the cards, placing the casseroles, the pies, the pitchers of lemonade and tea. "Put the silver to the left." Marina's voice regained its edge. "That server is too small."

I moved the plates and forks and napkins as she directed. Louise, the church ladies, and I filled the bellies of the chafing dishes with hot water and lit the Sterno beneath. Marina kindly asked them to help Louise straighten the kitchen, to fix the rows of chairs, and to start the giant percolator. We shuffled back and forth as she wanted.

A steady stream of perspiration rolled off my neck and down my back. I would not take off the suit jacket. I would spare Marina that. I kept my back to the coffin, the rows of white chairs, the huge wreaths crowding the casket.

Father McMurray and Eli murmured in the corner. "You've done what you can," I heard Father McMurray say to Eli. "We can't right all the wrongs in one fell swoop." They spoke about the mailman and his safety, about where he could go and what he could do. Father McMurray scowled in my direction, as if to say, *Haven't you caused enough trouble?* I could hear him say, "If we do any more, we risk angering the parish over a Negro who is not even Catholic."

Marina stood by the screen door to receive the visitors.

Eli touched my shoulder. Someone had opened the casket. I could avoid the day's purpose no longer. My son sat me near the head of the casket. The mingling smell of embalmment and sweet flowers turned my stomach.

Nelly slept, propped in the wingback chair. Louise brought me water. The church ladies filed by and touched me with their warm hands. Surely even they had gossiped about me letting the postman walk up our front steps. "Tomorrow will be hard for her," they said, casting their eyes in Nelly's direction. "Marina too," they said. "She was her daddy's girl, and he was so proud of her, always bragging about her latest accomplishment."

"Yes," I said as politely as I could. I was as proud of her as he had been. Who did they think we were? They had no idea the misery that happened within these walls.

They brought Marina a chair. "Sit, Marina." She would obey for a moment, then stand again and move the chair away.

The masculine voices drummed—Michael, Eli, Father McMurray.

Marina remained standing, nodding, talking softly to the visitors, the Catholics from the parish, then the Lebanese from neighboring towns as far away as Birmingham and Florence, then Michael's parents and the businessmen Elias knew. Electric fans whirred. The windows were wide open, but the air was stagnant, unbearably hot, weighing on us all, hanging like the black veil I would wear this evening at the Rosary and tomorrow at his funeral Mass.

Marina used her chair to prop open the screen door. More flies buzzed in.

"Shut the screen, Eli," I said, but he did not hear.

With Michael and Eli beside her, Marina stood with her sorrowful face and her hand resting on her belly. To those who questioned it, Michael explained in his lawyer's tone, "Grandmother could not bear the idea of the funeral home." He sounded official, authoritative, like the mayor of the town.

No one blinked at his answer. "Terrible heat today," they said, but they spoke in code. They meant the funeral home would have been cooler.

Like a statue of Mary, Marina stood, long-suffering but certain of purpose, receiving all who came to pay their respects. Her face was wan.

All the blood in her body would be pooling around the baby and into her swollen ankles. Gravity pulled. It pulled and pulled. I wanted to cry for her. She would see. I brought her another folding chair, a glass of ice water, and without a glance or word to me, she sat for a moment and drank.

She must be exhausted, I thought. *Her head must ache with worry for all of us and the baby inside her.* How could she hold court, reign over his death so expertly, with a child in her womb? I closed my eyes to remember when she was inside me, the feeling, the beautiful flutter, like a bird's wings in a flash of blinding sun. The baby moves, like swimming through water, only the water is inside and the swimming comes from the inside out, a joust of an elbow, a leg, or a knee and the pressure on the pelvic floor, persistent like a soft wet weight pushing down, down, down. How beautiful to get lost in a moment that only a mother and child have. This burial would be done tomorrow, and we could move on. We could put this torture past us.

A fly buzzed near my face. "Michael, please shut the screen door."

"No, Mother." Marina's eyes met mine. "I need the air."

"The flies." I crossed the room to shut the door. "The food is out."

"Leave it open." She whispered to me. "Go back to your place."

When Sophie and Lila came, Marina picked the girl up. Lila looked alarmed. "Be careful," Lila said. But I thought, *Let her. Let her lift the forty-pound child and her water will break and then we can take her away from this miserable business.*

Behind Marina, Lila stood, watching and waiting to catch her if she fell. Soon Marina's baby would be here. Marina held Sophie, despite the discomfort she must feel. She would be a good mother. I felt elation inside, like a spring breaking though ground, to watch my daughter and the love she had to give. I was biding my time to get to the joy.

Marina put Sophie down and Sophie ran to me. She wrapped her arms around me and hugged sweetly.

Marina resumed shaking hands, nodding, thanking every person for coming. She told them how much her father would have appreciated it and motioned them into the house. People circled. Their voices rose like steam from a hot bath, lifting to the ceiling, veiling everything. Their dry lips moving over teeth, a nod. *Yes.* The frown to acknowledge his death. *Thank you for coming.* Eyes shifted to the dining room and the blanket of food over the table. The excess seemed grotesque. Marina's silver forks and spoons flashed in the afternoon light moving from plates to mouths. The Catholics would stay for the Rosary. The others, the Protestants, would leave, appalled to think we prayed to Mary.

Nelly wanted to say a Rosary for each decade of his life, but the priest and Marina convinced her one Rosary with meditations would suffice. *Why*—my skin crawled, as if ants marched up and down my legs, biting—*why had I let Nelly have the visitation in my house?* I reminded myself: to get to the better part with Marina.

People stood about on my carpets, staring at him and then averting their eyes to the small plates held beneath their chins to catch crumbs. They had come not for me or him, but to attend to this morbid ritual. Or maybe they had come for her. Marina could sway people to her way.

Sophie's weight on my lap felt good. Her eyes stuck on him, the juts and crags of his forehead, the hollows of his cheeks. A fly landed on a lock of his pomaded hair. I did not shoo it off. She turned away and buried her warm nose into my neck. My eyes landed on his shoes, polished to a high shine, without a single crease or scratch. Marina had bought him new shoes. She had bought me new clothes and him new shoes. She had dressed us up for the show. Heat swelled off of Sophie. She was like a quilt thrown over me on a hot day, but I did not let go.

Lila touched my shoulder and I felt comfort. I imagined that was how her horses felt, her calming presence, that everything would be okay now that Lila stood beside it.

"Gus will be here soon," she said. "Everything going okay?"

No, I wanted to say, but I bit my tongue.

Her blue eyes scanned my face. "Your papa is outside."

I looked out the window and saw my father standing in the front yard. I put Sophie down to go to him.

Cars lined Poplar Street. Low gray clouds had moved in. The sky threatened more rain. A snapping, hot wind blew off the river. The neighbors' houses were dim and quiet. I could hear the chatter flowing from my house. The clink of coffee cups and plates. Verna sat on her porch. Her eyes followed me. I did not wave or speak and neither did she.

The lights glowed and the colors of the garden burned bright against the gloomy sky. Papa's hat jutted over his eyes as he stared into the rambling branches of the fig. Perhaps he was tracking the branches, like the past, one year after the other, hoping to find the moment when things had gone wrong with me. This tree sprawled ten feet wide and ten tall. He had brought a shoot from his yard and he and Elias planted it before Marina was born. *Figs for prosperity.* The branches hung heavy with fruit. He pulled a fig and ate it like a disinterested bull chewing grass in a field. Papa picked another one, peeled the purple-brown skin, sucked the garnet-colored flesh, tossed the remains, and began again. The mockingbird flew down and strutted toward him. Wary of my father, but wanting the remains of his fruit, the bird opened and closed his wings and flashed the white bands of feathers. He filled and emptied his chest like a tiny bellows. Papa did not notice. He took a white handkerchief from his pocket and wiped his hands. He adjusted his hat to the crown of his head.

I walked through the grass, the earth claiming the heels of my shoes. "Papa," I said. My fingers glanced the back of his suit, damp with perspiration. He shrugged at my touch. "Did you walk here in this heat?"

"Down the path." He did not look at me. "Isn't that what you do?"

"Yes," I said.

"A shame these will go to the birds." He reached into the tree and pulled another. "You should take what you can with you. Or a shoot and plant it. Stay rooted to where you are from."

"You look pale." I did not want to discuss my leaving so freely. He looked confused and tired. If I left, I would not be able to look after him. "I'm worried about you."

"Worried about me?" Papa would not look me in the eye. He wiped his hands on a handkerchief. He grunted. He looked out at the street. "I am old. I've lived my life. But what are you going to do?"

I looked down at my shoes and stepped out of them. My stocking feet sank in the warm grass. I took a fig leaf to wipe the mud from the heel. "Come inside and get a cold drink. It's too hot out here."

The screen door slapped. Sophie stepped onto the porch stairs. She and Papa locked eyes for a moment, then she cut back into the shadows by the rocking chairs.

"When you were a girl," Papa said, "you took pennies from the drawer and slipped them under the back door to the kids and they'd buy candy and then you'd slip them another. Around they'd come again."

Lila came out to the porch to retrieve Sophie, but Sophie refused. "No. I don't want to go in there." She did not budge from her spot.

"I couldn't figure where they got more money." Papa looked at the ground and scratched his head. "She had died and I didn't have it in me to punish you."

I picked a fig and held it out to him.

Papa coughed. When he caught his breath, he cast his eyes up to the light glowing around the edges of a gray cloud. "I should have said no. I should have been stronger when he came asking for you." Papa would not look at me, as if he would turn to salt if he did. "I thought maybe I was wrong about him. And you were so stubborn . . . It doesn't matter now."

My skin prickled.

"Do you remember her?" He took the fig from me.

"Yes." I looked for the face of the young man that was my father. He had grown thick and bald and pale. I wanted to hear his stories.

Gus walked up the drive. He saw Sophie and Lila on the porch. He looked at Papa and me talking. "Go inside," Gus said to Lila and Sophie. "I'll be there in a minute."

"You heard Daddy," Lila said, and Sophie knew that meant business.

Lila eyed me, as if asking, did I need her to come stand beside me? Gus headed up the porch stairs to usher them in.

"We'll be there in a minute," I called to Sophie. She reluctantly went in with her mother. But I agreed with Sophie: I did not want to go inside. All I wanted was to send people out of my house and go in the garden and work at the weeds, pull the ripe tomatoes, the okra, the runners of mint that had strayed outside their limits.

"You're like her. Your mother." Papa wiped his forehead with the pink-stained handkerchief. He might as well have told me he loved me. He rarely mentioned her. "You work hard like she did."

Gus lit a cigarette and stood on the top step of the porch. He was like a muscled bulldog, short and stout, keeping a watchful eye on the road and the people coming and going. He saw Papa and I were talking and he gave us space.

"But she had joy." He stuffed the handkerchief in his breast pocket. "He stole that from you."

"I won't leave Marina." I felt a stubborn refusal. "Or the baby."

Papa stared at the house buzzing with people. "Marina won't have you when Nelly is finished." He shook his head. A look of disgust crossed his face, maybe because of Nelly or maybe for what he thought I had done to Elias.

Sophie broke free of the house, past Gus's reach. The screen door slapped shut in her wake. She landed against my legs. She held tight. "I don't want to go," she said. "I want to stay with you." She held on until Lila came for her, and then she darted around the tree.

Lila gave chase to Sophie.

"Why can't I stay with Aunt Annie?"

"Little vixen," Lila said with a smile on her lips. The chase had become a game and Sophie giggled and ran past us to the backyard.

Gus stood on the stairs as the Protestants began to leave. He looked apologetic for his wife and daughter's gleeful play on such a somber occasion. He did not want to embarrass me or Marina.

"Nelly won't stop if you don't leave." Papa's eyes were wet from heat or worry. "She wants you to suffer."

Sophie screamed from the backyard. "I don't want to go. You can't make me go."

I felt as if I had stepped into a trap, unsure how to escape the danger I was in. I wondered if this uncertainty was what Elias had felt when he knew that he was dying, or what Mr. Washington felt leaving Riverton, or later, when he learned that they had burned his house.

"Have you heard any news about Mr. Washington?" I asked.

Papa shook his head and flung an uneaten fig on the ground. The mockingbird flew down and pecked at it. "A damn shame he tried to rise above his station."

Papa's words angered me, because there was some truth in them. Orlando Washington was driven from town because he wouldn't stay in his place, but I envied that he had taken a chance and acted on his own. Thea would have been proud of him, but that was a bitter consolation because he'd never set foot here again. I'd caused him and myself trouble. Thea would be angry with me for asking him in. Why had I thought I could sit at the table with Thea's son and no harm would come? If I had turned Orlando Washington away, as everyone else did, if I had ignored my feelings of kinship to his mother, if I had left well enough alone, maybe Elias would never have hurt me again, and he would be alive, and we would be waiting together for the phone to ring, Michael on the other end telling us Marina had delivered a healthy child.

I looked up into the fig tree. Hundreds of figs hung on the branches. It would be a shame to let it all go to waste. I had let so much go to waste.

"Some customers came by today on account of Eli helping him." Papa's collar was wet. Circles of sweat spread through his suit on his back and under his arm. Papa began to cough and he bent over when he could not stop.

Gus bounded off the porch toward us. He put his hand on Papa's elbow. "Come in and get some water," he said.

Papa spit into his handkerchief and let Gus support him. The coughing had sapped his energy.

Lila flushed Sophie from the backyard. The girl ran screaming into me. "I don't want to go." Her cheeks were red.

Gus put an end to Sophie's antics by swooping her up and handing her to Lila. "Just take her home."

"No," Sophie wailed.

I don't want to go either, I wanted to say to her.

Papa watched Sophie. "It's my fault I raised you there," he said.

Lila mouthed *Goodbye,* and I felt sad, how the sight of Lila and Sophie made me wish for those years with Marina, if only I could have focused on Marina and not the store, not Elias, if I could have been patient like Lila. I wanted them to stay here with me now.

Papa raised his voice. "I let you grow up there. She died and I couldn't leave." His face was ravaged in worry, as though he could change history if he solved the riddle of what went wrong.

"That's over now," I said.

Gus prodded Papa toward the porch, but he did not budge.

"Elsa told me to move you—to build the house I had promised your mother." Papa's words were frenzied. He looked pitiful, as if asking for my forgiveness. "Elsa said you shouldn't be in Blacktown."

A steady stream of townspeople, Marina's friends, and Elias's Rotary and business folks stared as they passed us. Michael's parents left too, even though they were Catholic. Marina must have convinced them to go home.

"After he hit you, I should have put you all in a car and driven you away." Papa moaned and the pain in his voice sounded like Nelly's.

"That's enough," Gus said. He was aware how odd we looked standing out in the heat and how Papa's words were garnering attention. "It's time for the Rosary." Gus put his hand on Papa's shoulder.

Papa shook Gus off. "I should have killed him myself. But I was too afraid I'd never see your mother again." Papa would never risk a mortal sin. "I saw what he did. I told you to stay with me but you had your mind set." Papa had worked himself into a frenzy.

"You need to cool off." Gus tried to steer Papa to the house. In my brother's face, I saw the little boy who had looked to me for direction.

"This heat is getting to you, Papa," I said. "Let's get you in the shade."

Papa's eyes, pale and weak, searched my face. "Vega would have stopped him. She would never have let harm come to you."

Warm tears fell on my cheek. I wanted Papa to be sure of me, to believe me innocent—I wanted to *be* innocent, for his sake, but I had disappointed my father, and no denial of mine could erase his doubt.

Gus managed to move Papa toward the house and I followed.

Gravel crunched in the drive. We turned to see Ivie. His shoulders hunched and his walk was crooked.

"He's already drunk," I said.

At the sight of Ivie, Papa spit on the ground and Gus stood taller. Their bodies tensed.

Ivie ignored us and ducked into the house as the last of the Protestants left.

Papa said, "I told Ivie you could live with me."

"Why would I do that?" I would not go from being Elias's wife back to my father's daughter.

"He said you can't." Papa's cheeks flushed red with anger. "That drunken ass said you have to leave." Papa shook his head. His eyes brimmed with tears.

"It's not up to Ivie what I do or don't do."

Gus tugged at Papa's arm. "Let's go in."

"I will not pray for his soul." Papa clenched his jaw. Sweat or tears rolled down his cheeks. "I won't go in."

"Come sit in the shade, then." Gus led him up the stairs. "Under the fan."

Papa relented. He said, "My prayers will be for you." He squeezed my arm and hobbled to the chair where Sophie had been.

At the door, I slipped my shoes back on. I stepped inside with Gus and hoped it would be over soon.

"He is so angry," Gus said. "I don't blame him."

Dishes of food covered every surface and the house smelled of a high holiday—maybe the last this house would see with me in it. Gus parted the churchwomen to get water for Papa. When he returned to my side, he handed me a glass of water too. He said, "It is going to be a long night." The cold glass felt good against my wounded hand.

My house was no longer my own. Had I ever loved Elias, the presence of Father McMurray and Sisters Hilda and Agnes might have comforted me. I might have found solace in the thirty men from the Knights of Columbus and their wives packed into my living room, but I was nauseated by the smells of sour breath mingling with hot wax from the burning candles and the altar boys' relentless swinging of the censer, filling the air with sweet-smelling smoke.

The air was burdened. We were too many fish in a bowl and the air could not support us all. Father McMurray's pink face streamed with sweat. He droned on about "a good man" and "love and grief for Elias," and how he was "a pillar of the community, a good Catholic," and on and on. My chest constricted at how Father could lie so openly in God's name, knowing Elias had gone to intimidate Mr. Washington. I gripped my brother's sleeve.

The sun set. A chorus of solemn voices repeated: "Hail Mary, full of grace, the Lord is with Thee. Blessed art Thou amongst women. Blessed is the fruit of thy womb, Jesus. Holy Mary, Mother of God, pray for us sinners now and at the hour of our death. Amen."

People whispered, "Do you want to be closer?"

"No." I stood one foot in the room, the other on the porch. "I need the air." I would have drifted outside, past my father, to the road and then walked away if not for Gus and his thick, warm palm gently holding my bandaged hand, keeping me put.

Cars passed slowly to see the vigil—the Catholics praying to Mary, windows open, candles burning, the rhythmic prayer flowing out to the street.

If men appeared tonight, as they had the last two nights at Orlando Washington's place, no one would be surprised. They could come because of my faith or because of their suspicions of me and Orlando Washington or because they blamed me for Elias's death. Few would flinch if they carried me off or burned my house or lit a cross.

As a child, I had seen a cross burned after Midnight Mass on Christmas on the lawn of St. Patrick's. Papa carried us. Gus in one arm, me in the other. "Don't look. Close your eyes," he said as he hurried to his truck. Gus gripped my hand against Papa's back. I looked over his shoulder, so strangely beautiful it was to me, the flames in the sky, the popping wood, the smell of smoke. It reminded me of Mama's oven. We knew already, but Papa told us, "You are Christian children, if anyone asks—never Catholic—just Christians."

I grieved to see my children suffering. Eli's mouth twisted in earnest prayer. His face was slick with sweat. I wondered what he prayed for, if it was for his father's soul, or Orlando Washington, or me.

Every so often, Ivie turned to glare at me and I could make out the scratch I had given him at the store. Michael knelt behind Marina and kept his hand on the small of her back. All of them crowded up near the casket and swayed to the rhythms of prayer. If one of them fell, they would go like a row of dominoes.

I stared at the veiled heads of Nelly and Marina and realized I had been preoccupied with my father and forgotten to wear the veil to show respect for the dead. There would be tomorrow for that. We were not in church and I felt I was drowning in the thick air.

Nelly clung like a tick on Marina. All evening the old woman had been whispering in her ear. I didn't need to be able to hear her words. She was dropping seeds of doubt:

Why was the colored mailman here?

Why is your father dead?

He was healthy.

He was young.

She killed him.

For that mailman.

I knew Nelly's accusations rang like a bell in Marina's ear between breaths of prayer.

Marina's face sank with every word from Nelly and each passing prayer. Marina's labor was coming. I could see the discomfort in her face and how she held her belly. She was too stubborn to admit it.

She'd placed photographs of him on every surface. When I looked away from his corpse, my eyes fell on photographs of him and his children. And ones of him in Lebanon, at the church in Tyre, and another on a donkey's back, another beneath a pergola covered in grapevines. Even one of us on our wedding day. There was the porcelain sign from the store. She'd made Eli fetch it and she'd taped the photograph of Elias and the lion to it.

I rested my head on Gus's shoulder and breathed his lime after-shave. The last prayer for the dead ended after eight. The priest said, "Go in peace. In the name of the Father, the Son, and the Holy Spirit. Amen."

Marina and all gave the sign of the cross. The priest offered his hand to help Marina stand. She levered herself up on her own. Michael motioned to make way and declined any company. The room held its breath as she hobbled to the kitchen, but when she was out of sight, whispers grew to full voices.

Nelly sat like a stone, her large, wet eyes fixed on Elias. The mourners stood and began to file slowly out the front door.

Gus led me out ahead of the crowd. The night air was heavy and humid, but a welcome retreat from the trapped heat of breath and bodies and incense. We stood on the top step of the porch, shook hands and said goodbye to the people spilling out. The men nodded solemnly. The church ladies squeezed my good hand and touched my arm. "Peace be with you," they said.

"Peace be with you," I responded.

On the porch, Papa sat like a penned bull, moaning and snorting as thoughts passed through his mind. I had never seen him so agitated, even worse than yesterday when he told me to leave town and gave me money. Was he thinking of the day that he gave in to my pleadings and told me I could marry Elias, or the day Mama died, or the day I returned home to Elias? As I told people good night, I watched Papa and looked past him at the windows blazing in candlelight, as if the house were on fire.

The Scene

When the last church member left the vigil, Gus and I stayed put beneath the pecan tree. Father McMurray remained inside with my family, whose restive voices spilled out onto the lawn. Neither Gus nor I wanted to be inside with Nelly, Ivie, or the corpse in the casket, so we hid in the shadows with the cicadas thrumming and Papa rocking in the chair on the porch.

Marina stared out of the window, but I felt sure she could not see us, because it was a new moon and the night was darker than usual. I was on the outside looking in, where I had always been, and where I would be from now on. Marina crossed the room to the priest and Nelly, who looked shriveled and small next to them. They guided Nelly into the hall and they disappeared from my view. The thought of Marina so close to Nelly made me sick. "I want this to be over," I said.

"Yes, I know," Gus said. He sparked his lighter and lit a cigarette, and clouds of tobacco smoke hung in the air.

"Two things in my life I did on my own," I said. "I married Elias and I helped that man. Both turned to shit."

"You didn't know any better when you married him."

"Papa knew, and I didn't listen." Candles glowed in the window and the warm light seemed to flood the house. The only spot of darkness was the end of his casket.

"You stay with us if it comes to it." Gus inhaled and the orange tip of his cigarette lengthened.

"Thank you," I said. Lila had offered already and they were generous to want to take me in. If I stayed, the awful heat would be gone in eight weeks' time and the migrant birds would be back—the geese, the cranes, the herons, and the ducks. The baby would be sleeping through the night, and with some luck, I would have ridden the swell of Marina's anger and the town's outrage.

Gus took a long drag and slowly exhaled the smoke. "I know you didn't do anything to Elias." His tone was hopeful because he believed the best of me. "If you go, you'll go for a few weeks, a month, then come back home."

Papa's chair creaked as he leaned forward. He was listening as he had when we were children. Back then, he pricked his ears to learn what we were up to, and then only if necessary did he interfere.

I plucked a fig from the tree, turned the skin inside out, and ate it. "Is that what you think I should do?" The fruit was sweet and ripe.

"For now." Gus's Adam's apple rested above his collar and tie. He took one last drag and tossed the butt out into the grass. "All this will blow over," he said, but he did not sound convinced.

I touched Gus's sleeve and pointed to Nelly passing in front of the window. "What makes a person so hateful?"

Gus snuffed out the butt with the sole of his shoe. "I don't know why people do the things they do. I just do what Lila tells me." The outline of his smile showed in the dim night. He was good at making light and putting me at ease.

In the window of the house, Father McMurray returned to view. He stood above the corpse and lowered the casket lid. Nelly was no longer visible. She was somewhere near Marina, unfettered by the priest and saying what she pleased.

"What will Mr. Washington do?" I wanted to talk to Eli and learn Mr. Washington's plans, but talking to Eli meant going inside with Nelly and Ivie.

"The man fought in a war." Gus loosened his tie and took it off. "I don't suspect this is much different." He rolled the tie and put it in his pants pocket.

"What's going to happen to him?" I wanted absolution from Gus for my part in Mr. Washington's troubles. If Gus said that I had done the right thing, and that asking him inside was an innocent mistake, I would feel some vindication.

Across the street, Verna's porch light flickered on and then off.

"You need to worry about yourself." Gus flipped his lighter and slapped it shut again, then took out another cigarette and lit it. He fidgeted when he was nervous.

Papa coughed and the rocker creaked under his weight. He was still listening to everything we said.

"They burned his house," I said. The night was muggy and hot, but a chill ran over my skin in rhythm with the cicadas. "They took away his home. His livelihood."

"They may come after you." Gus took a drag and he looked up at the sky. There was no moon, and the sky was littered with stars.

"He was your friend and you don't care about what happens to him?" I stared at the windows where the candle flames danced and my eyes burned.

"Not my friend."

"Of course he was," I said. "And don't you remember Thea taking care of us?"

"Papa paid her," he said. "It was her job."

"You were little and don't remember, but she was with Mama when she died," I said. "We should look after her son."

"If he was going about things as normal, yes." He blew out a line of smoke in the darkness. "But he's threatening a way of life."

"One man doing a job does not threaten anything." I searched the outline of his face for some understanding. His face pinched in a scowl.

"That's it," Gus said. "You don't see. It's not just him. There will be more like him breaking up the order of things and there will be more violence." Gus spent his life mixing on both sides. Negro farmers were most of the customers on his route. He worked in Papa's store in Mounds. "That crew that burned his house may come after you."

"You grew up with him, and you don't feel some compassion?"

"I am not one of them." His voice was filled with frustration. "Neither are you. It's not your fight." Gus saw himself and us as white, I knew. He grew up in the middle of Mounds, but he felt above everyone there, even though the Riverton kids heckled us. He didn't think about the people we came from. He wanted to squeeze into the white world as best he could.

"Nelly will say you let him in your front door, and Elias is dead twelve hours later." Gus's words sounded like a sentencing, and in his voice I heard his frustration. He did not believe I could go away for a week or two or a month and return.

"Nobody knows the truth," I said.

"Well, what is the truth?"

I felt his eyes on me. "I gave the man a glass of water. Then Elias came in and nearly killed me, and left me on the floor to go intimidate him. That is the truth."

He took another drag, then snuffed it on the sole of his gleaming black shoe and tossed it away.

"When Elias got home, I was already asleep and he had a heart attack." I was glad for the dark, so that my brother could not see the heat on my skin. I did not want to lie to him, but there was no other way to stay and know my grandchild. "That is the truth."

"I'm on your side," Gus said. "And all I want is you to be safe and to do my work and take care of my girls. I don't want you run out of town." Gus touched my arm and I felt some relief, hearing his words.

"There she is, the grieving widow," Ivie called from the porch. We looked up at him raising a silver flask in the glowing doorframe. His dark silhouette looked like a devilish figure. "I thought maybe you were hiding from me."

"I need a drink," Gus said under his breath. He took a handkerchief and wiped the sweat beading on his brow. "God help me I don't kill that bastard."

"Hey, Gus. Did I hear you want a drink?" Ivie stumbled down the stairs. "Well, here I am."

I bowed my head and hoped Ivie would walk on, past us and back to his shack behind his mother's house. What else had he heard between Gus and me?

Papa rose from the chair. His shoes scuffed across the limestone porch and he leaned against the rail.

"You truly are good for nothing," Gus said. Gus was not as tall as Ivie, but he was stout and compact in the shoulders and legs. He was sober, too, and could run over Ivie if given the chance.

"Me?" Ivie reeked of whiskey. "I'm good for a drink." He slapped Gus's shoulders.

"Don't touch me," Gus said.

Ivie held his hands up in mock surrender. "Trying to be hospitable," he said and took another swig from his flask.

"Go home, Ivie," I said. I grabbed Gus's arm and hoped to lead him inside.

"It's not me that's going anywhere," Ivie said.

"Let's go in, Gus." I tugged on Gus and tried pulling him toward the candlelit house, but Gus's feet were planted.

"Mama tried to tell Elias all those years ago. But he fought for you." He tipped the flask to his lips. "That's funny, ain't it?" he jeered.

"If he'd just left you alone, he'd be alive, and you'd be where you belong in Blacktown."

Gus stepped close to Ivie. "Go back to your hole and crawl in it."

"You're the one can't control your women." Ivie stooped to put his face level with Gus's. "Not your wife, not your sister."

Papa took slow, careful steps down the porch stairs. I wanted to stop him from lumbering toward us, but I needed to get between Ivie and Gus.

Ivie smiled, wolflike. "In two days, my store will be running like nothing ever happened."

Gus puffed his chest out and knocked Ivie back. "Now is not the time to talk about the store."

"He's drunk." I pulled on Gus. "Let's go in."

"You worried I'm going to shut you out, Gus?" Ivie slurred his words.

Gus smirked. "Not at all." He poked Ivie's shoulder. "You won't last. Your mama's too old to roll your drunk ass out of bed and drive you to work every morning."

"That's enough," Papa said. He stood behind Ivie and put his hand on Ivie's arm. "Go on, now," Papa said with authority, and at one time, out of respect or fear, Ivie would have obeyed him.

Gus put himself between our father and Ivie. "Go home."

Ivie wiped his mouth with his sleeve. "This is my brother's house. You leave."

The three men shuffled around each other. Papa's movements looked slow and painful. His back hunched and his knees and arms bent at jagged angles. Gus bobbed back and forth, trying to get around him at Ivie, and Ivie staggered around trying to grab at Gus.

"Stop this nonsense," I said. "Let's go inside." I tugged at Gus and Papa. "Leave him."

"Listen to her," Ivie said. "She's smarter than she looks. She pulled the big black wool over all of us."

Gus's nostrils flared. "You are nothing but a drunk."

"You should know about that. Being married to one." Ivie cackled.

"Show some respect." Papa got his feet under him and gave Ivie a solid push.

Ivie rocked on his heels.

"Sober up and act like a man." Papa's voice sounded strong and young.

Gus butted up against Ivie to punctuate Papa's words.

The hairs on my arms stood up. I could not get between them. "Michael!" I called for help and tried to separate them, but their bodies were mixed together. "Gus, stop this," I said.

"Go home, old man," Ivie said. He looked at me and jabbed at my shoulder. "And take this nigger-lover with you."

The train let out a long blare near the river bridge. Then the wheels, metal against metal, and a steady hum of engine noise filled the night.

Ivie grabbed my bruised arms and pulled me into him. His whiskey-soured breath landed on my cheek. "Funny how you and Elias always shit on me, but you're no better than me."

"Let go of her." Gus jerked me in the hopes of freeing me from Ivie's grip.

Ivie let go and reared back to swing at Gus, but the blow landed in Papa's face and he fell to the ground in a heap.

I screamed for help. "Michael! Marina!"

Verna's light switched on.

From inside Marina yelled, "Mama?"

Papa lay like an ox stuck on his side and could not put himself right. Gus and I labored against Papa's weight, and when we got him up and saw his bloody nose, Gus barreled into Ivie. They fell to the ground and rolled in the grass punching and pounding. The porch light came on and Father McMurray appeared over them. He yelled in his Irish brogue, "What's going on? For heaven's sake!"

Like two schoolboys, Ivie and Gus separated at the sound of Father's voice. Ivie staggered and then bowed like he was on stage. "It's all over, Father. A family misunderstanding, that's all."

Gus touched his bleeding lip and brushed off his clothes. He went to Papa's side and tried to offer his handkerchief for the bloody nose, but Papa refused him.

Ivie grabbed me up and whispered in my ear, "If you don't go, I'll have a mob at your door."

Eli rushed down the stairs toward Ivie and gripped his uncle's shirt. "Get your hands off my mother. What's wrong with you?" His voice sounded harsh and deep like his father's.

Ivie whipped out of Eli's grasp and stumbled backward. "Simmer down, Nephew." Ivie snickered and tipped the silver flask to his lips. With a flick of his wrist, he screwed the cap back on. He lurched toward the street.

Nelly, a dark stick figure among the others, knocked her cane on the stone porch. "Go home, Ivie!" She did not want the priest seeing him drunk and fighting, so she waved her cane at her son as if he were a cur dog.

Marina's tall, rotund body pinched out the light in the doorway. She put her arm through Nelly's and said, "Come in."

Papa staggered toward the dark street and mumbled under his breath.

"He can't walk home like that in the dark," I said to Gus.

"I'll get him." Gus pulled his keys from his pocket and put his handkerchief to his lips. "I'll be back after I take him home."

"You don't have to come back," I said. "I'll be all right."

He hugged me and the familiar smell of sweat and lime came from his warm skin. "No," he said. "You're not safe here alone." He jogged off after Papa, and soon his dark clothes blended into the night. Down the street, his red brake lights came on, then the headlights, and soon the rumble of his truck faded in the distance.

Marina

In the moonless night, Nelly wailed, "I want to go home." Her voice held the bottomless sorrow of a mother who had lost her child. She reached for Marina to steady herself and called out for her sister. "I am sick to death. I want to go home, Louise."

Father McMurray's eyes rested on Nelly in the window. Then he looked at me. He touched my arm. "Anna," he said, "do you want me to mediate between you and Marina?"

"No." It was a stubborn refusal of the one thing that might have helped. She would be mortified if our troubles came out to him. "No."

Nelly caterwauled, "Take me home. I cannot look at the casket another minute."

The two sisters scurried back and forth. Louise complained, "There is too much to be done, Nelly. You have to wait."

But Nelly persisted. "I am dying of grief."

"I'll clean up," Michael said to silence the old women. "Eli can take you home." He called out, "Marina." His voice, patient and deep, said, "Tell me what to do." Marina listed the chores for him: do the dishes, put away the food, wipe the counters, sweep the floor, empty the coffee urn. He told her to sit and rest, but as soon as he was in the kitchen, she fluttered around Louise and Nelly to help gather their things and usher them out.

"Anna, you have the opportunity to right your wrongs," Father McMurray whispered in my ear.

I studied the pale old priest and wondered what Nelly had said to him, if she painted me as a hateful wife or an unfit mother, or maybe he blamed me for the town's upheaval over Mr. Washington. "What wrongs are you speaking of, Father?" I asked.

Father McMurray spoke quietly: "Anna, your children are suffering at your absence. I watched you and you did not pray for Elias's soul. You must attempt to reconcile your feelings about him for their sake," he said. "I know the two of you had troubles, but the burial of the dead is a corporeal work of mercy and it is your duty as God's child to forgive Elias." His words buzzed like radio static. *Do your duty,* that's what the church would have said if I had gone to them the first or second or thirtieth time he beat me.

"How can you say that when you know he went to Mr. Washington's?" I asked.

"People are imperfect," Father said. "But I can help you do your Christian duty. His burial is the chance to forgive him, to right the wrongs that you may have done to him and he to you. No marriage is faultless. Jesus turned the other cheek, and now you must for your children. You must open your heart." A sermon he must have given before. He took a handkerchief from his pocket and wiped the spittle that had gathered in the corners of his mouth. Then, words gentle and unpracticed: "I can see Eli and Marina are suffering from your absence in mourning their father."

What he said was true. I managed to say, "Thank you, Father," but my throat stung as if I swallowed a jar of bees.

Father McMurray patted my shoulder. "There is no fear in love," he said and walked to his car. He meant to admonish me for my lack of piety toward mourning Elias, but I took it differently. I loved Marina and she loved me. I could have hope. I should not be afraid to hope for her love. We could work past her frustration with me.

Eli and Marina helped Nelly down the stairs.

When she saw the priest was gone, Nelly said to me, "You deserve to be in the coffin. Not my son."

"Let me talk to Marina," I said.

"You are a good girl, Marina. You are my love." Nelly spoke sweetly. "You are a good boy too, Eli. You will take good care of Grandma now that your father is gone."

I reached for Marina. She was my child, not Nelly's, but my hands fell on the old woman by mistake. The heat coming from her skin surprised me.

"Don't touch me." She sucked her teeth. "You are a shame."

"Enough." Eli stood tall with his shoulders back. He took charge of Nelly and tucked her into the back seat with Louise. From the car, Louise chided Nelly in Arabic.

"That's all the excitement for tonight, I hope." Eli's eyebrows pressed together with worry. He said to me, "After I take them home, I'm going to the seminary to check on Mr. Washington. I'll be here early tomorrow."

"Can't you make a call? Have someone else look after him?" I did not want Eli in harm's way.

"No," he said. "It's my responsibility."

"I want to know you're safe," I said. "I want to know what's happening."

"Tomorrow," he said. "I'll tell you everything." Nelly and Louise bickered in the back seat of his car. He hesitated to get in with them. The chirping of their irritated voices trailed as he drove away.

Marina and I stood in the dark yard. A waxy smell came from her. The priest must have blessed her with his holy oils in preparation for birth. I touched her arm.

"Please, don't." She shuddered, and I knew that Nelly had made good with her threats.

"No," I said. "I love you." I tried to put my arm around her shoulder.

"No." She broke my grasp and took a step toward the house. "I want Michael. I want to go home."

"Listen to me one minute." I grabbed her shoulders like she was a child.

"Let go of me." Marina twisted out of my grip.

"Talk to me." I wanted to grab her and hold her.

"Grandmother told me what you did. Nothing you can say will make that go away."

I saw no trace of love or compassion on her face. My heart pounded in alarm.

"You're the only one to let him deliver. I begged you to stop."

She was talking about Mr. Washington. My pulse still pounded in my ears, but I could draw a breath. "Marina, the man was just doing his job."

"Then you let him in the front door. And God knows what else." She moved toward the porch.

I blocked her way up the porch steps. "No, nothing like that happened."

"Grandmother says you and that man—"

"No," I said. "That's not true. I only gave him a drink of water." They had latched onto this idea and could not see past it. "I was trying to help him."

"It might as well be true. The idea will ruin us."

"It's not true at all." I was exasperated that she could not see past petty gossip.

"Let me by." She tried to push past me, but I did not budge. She stared at me coldly. "Daddy's not here to protect you anymore."

"Protect me?" I tried not to get flustered so that I could convince her, but I could feel him on top of me trying to press the life out of me. "He never protected me."

Her swollen red hands clamped the porch rail like a vise. "He defended you, when people came in the store saying all kinds of things."

"If he told you that, he lied," I said. How many times had he forced himself on me?

Her fingertips turned white from her grip on the rail. "He told more than one person, 'She's being a good citizen in her way.'"

"No." I shook my head. "Maybe you said that?"

Her eyes were as sharp and as keen as a hawk's. "I heard him say it."

"Maybe he said it in front of you. To please you." My heart raced with panic. "You didn't know him the way I did."

"You are unbelievable." She crossed her arms and her lip trembled, the same way it did when she was a girl and didn't get what she wanted. "I will soon have a child to raise, and that's hard enough without this."

"Without what?" I asked.

"Grandmother said you killed him." She tried to pass me again, but I did not let her up the stairs.

"You believe that?" My breath had left me again. I was shaking. I touched her warm arm to try and calm myself, to try and calm her.

She recoiled from my touch.

"Your grandmother is hysterical. You can't listen to her."

"Michael," she called toward the glowing doorway, then turned to me. "He was fine night before last. It doesn't make sense." She turned away and called once again, "Michael!"

Michael could not hear her back in the kitchen.

"If that were true, Nelly would have me in jail." I felt the horror of losing Marina's faith. If I did not have that, I would have nothing. "Marina."

"You don't understand." She clenched her jaw and slapped the banister. "I am the reason you're not in jail."

I took her hand. "If Nelly loved you, she wouldn't burden you with her anger for me."

"If you loved me, this would never have happened." She jerked her hand away. "After he's buried, you are dead to me."

My voice rose. "Why won't you believe me? I did not hurt him."

She stared me in the eye. "I don't know if you did. I'm not sure I want to know, but even if you didn't, you wanted to. You never loved him." Not loving Elias was the worst thing I could do in her eyes.

"I did," I said. "I did love him. Do you think he ever loved me?"

"You never let him." Her voice was thick with anger.

"He beat me. Just two days ago." I wanted to go on: *What could you know? You were a child. You saw him without flaws.* Instead, I said, "He loved someone else, never me. He stayed with me because he had to, and when he got angry, he hit me because I wasn't her. When he touched me, he was thinking of her."

Marina stepped backward away from me. "That's not for me to know."

"He told me. He said it," I said.

She shook her head as if she thought I was pitiful. Marina said, "I was a child. I had no power over what happened, and I can't change it now."

"But what he did was wrong."

She held my stare. "You were a grown woman and it was between the two of you."

I bit my lip. "You will disown me? Do you think I'll just leave because she tells me to? I've lived through hell with him so I could be with you and Eli."

Her green eyes stared at me, unwavering. "Michael," she called again.

I lowered my voice. "No matter what happens, I love you. I am your mother." *I gave you life,* I wanted to say. *I stayed with you. I never left you.* When she was born, I wanted to hold her, but my body was weak, my mind a mess. Nelly took her and she quieted down.

"You're right. I can't change that." Marina's eyes flinched in anger.

"Please hear me out." I reached for her again. I was begging, grasping for straws, anything to hold on to. The cicadas vibrated sound in the air and I could feel the sound bouncing off my skin.

"Michael," she called out.

"Don't turn your back on me."

"Really?" She stopped and faced me. "You turned your back on me." Her lip quivered. She took a deep breath and her green eyes teared up.

I placed my palm on her damp, warm cheek.

Her head, heavy and tired, pressed into my hand. It was as if she wanted me to hold her, as if she wanted to forgive me. Marina wiped the corners of her eyes.

She lifted her cheek from my touch. "I have my own family to think of." Marina wiped her eyes and looked for Michael over my shoulder.

"Your grandmother is not your family. I am. I am your mother, and you are soon to see what that means."

"She was *his* mother." She took an exhausted breath. "But I'm not talking about her. I have a husband and a child on the way."

"You are my child," I said. "And you will see when the baby is in your arms, how nothing mattered before and nothing else will again. Only that child. That is how I feel about you."

"I've never been important to you." Vanished were the emotion on her face and the anger in her voice. No longer did her eyes tear or her lip protrude. She held her head high and her neck stiff. "I know what he did. I tried to distract him by playing the piano or talking to him. I stayed up late, I got up early, and you never noticed. You never knew I was watching out for you. I tried to take care of you." She looked practical and resolute, like a lawyer making an argument. Nothing but reason. "Now you have to take care of me. You have to go, or this will ruin my life and this baby's."

I was frightened that she believed what she said. My body shook. I took off the suit jacket I had been sweltering in all day. "See what he did."

She stared at the green and purple marks in the shape of his hands, ugly in the glare of the porch light. "I came to you and told you to stop the business with Washington, but you had it in your head."

"I did it for good reasons." I was about to lose Marina.

She stared at me with her intense green eyes. She waited for me to speak.

"His mother, Thea, stood by Mama when she died. She told me, 'Remember your mama,' when no one else spoke of her. She called me by my given name and no one else would. She was witness to my mother's life. She did not let me forget, and I could not stand by and abandon her son."

Marina's eyes were wet. She looked away and wiped them dry. "Cover up before Michael sees that."

"I stayed because I loved you and Eli," I said. "I could never have left you. I lost my mother and I knew how that hurt. I was never as good as her, but I loved you more than I loved my life."

"Almost done," Michael called from the kitchen.

She covered her eyes. "Even if I want you to stay, they won't let you." She walked up the porch stairs past me and stuck her head inside the door. She called out for Michael again.

"They?" My knees felt weak and I realized I had no power to change what had happened and what was to come. "You mean your grandmother and Ivie. You can make them be quiet. They will listen to you."

"There are others." She wobbled to the rocking chair where Lila and I had sat the night before. "A lot of people want you gone."

"Let me stay with you." I hurried after to support her, but she shook off my touch. "I am not afraid of anything, if I can be with you and the baby."

311

She lowered herself into a chair. My stomach lurched at the sight of the casket through the window.

"When you were born," I said, "I held you, so small and warm."

"That's not what Grandmother says." Her eyes twitched. "She said you refused to name me. Refused to hold me."

"At first, that was true. I wasn't strong like you." I touched her hair. "But I did. I did hold you and I loved you, but I was confused. But you won't be. You are ready. I see you with Sophie and with Michael. You have something I never had."

She let out a tired sigh and composed herself. "Please, cover your arms before Michael sees."

I put on the suit coat. "She wants to poison you against me."

"She only wants to protect me." She looked at me, cold and unforgiving.

Elias had sat on the side of the bed in the hospital and asked me what I wanted to name her.

I could have answered him—*Vega*, after my mother. He was trying. I knew that. I could see love in his eyes, but it was not love for me, and I was sad and jealous. He loved what I had given him. He loved the baby girl. In my anger, I turned away from him and that anger turned to loneliness and then bitterness. I did not answer him except to say, "Go home." I had once hoped he would love me, but after she was born, I understood my situation clearly. I told him, "Let me rest while I can."

Marina's eyes were tired and her skin dark beneath them. "I can't talk anymore."

"I was afraid," I said. "When I had you." My mother had died when she was not much older than Marina.

Her perfectly groomed eyebrows arched high on her ivory forehead. "Afraid of a baby?"

"Yes." A relief to admit it. "I was afraid of what I would feel if something happened to you, like what happened to my mother. If I lost you, I could not bear it."

"That's an excuse," Marina snarled. She wiped her wet cheeks and looked at Michael blowing out the candles in the living room. He could hear us through the open windows and the screen door.

"Your father and your grandmother never said no to you," I said. "Now you have Michael. I had no one to love or help me."

"You never let anyone close to you. Not me. Not Daddy." Marina closed her eyes and rested her head against the rocker. "Maybe Eli. Maybe you loved him."

Elias had come, freshly shaven, smelling so good and clean, of soap and cloves. He wore a starched shirt, and I was lying in a hard bed, cold and smelling of blood. I did not want him to see me like that. His hand touched mine. It was warm, gentle pressure against the coldness of the sheet. "Tell me a name. Whatever you want." I was silent. I rolled over and left it to him and Nelly to name my daughter. I listened to his footsteps on the tiles and then the door shutting behind him.

"I've not been a good mother," I said. "Let me try to do better."

"It's too late."

Michael stepped out onto the porch. "Marina, you ready to go?"

Slowly, she lifted herself from the rocking chair. He stooped to support her.

"You don't remember the good," I said. "Remember when I taught you to swim. Remember the treats, and the times we went for walks."

"What you've done has destroyed the good." Her voice was dispassionate. "I want you to leave."

Michael said, "Marina, stay calm."

"I'm fine, Michael."

"You never walked across the railroad tracks to go to school. You never worked a day in your father's store or helped me bake one loaf of bread." The bitterness in my voice weakened my argument.

"I was in your way," Marina said. "If I made a mistake, you let loose on me and sent me to her so you could work in peace."

Michael took a deep breath.

She was right. It had been easier to give her to Nelly than to risk losing her without warning.

"Say what you want, Mother. Cry at his funeral for everyone to see." She ratcheted herself to standing. "But I know what you are."

He put a hand on her forearm. "Let's talk tomorrow," he said, trying to temper her words.

"You are upset." I straightened the sleeves of the suit. Michael's blue eyes watched me. "I know how you feel. My mother was gone when you were born. I had no one."

"We'll have that in common. My mother will be gone too." Marina and Michael locked eyes, and I felt the price I would pay.

Michael crossed between us. "Anna, we will see you at the church." He was ending the conversation. His wide forehead wrinkled above cool, blue eyes. "Is there anything else I can do before we go?"

"No," I said.

"You'll excuse us, then?" His hand on my shoulder was gentle, but he was dismissing me. "It's been a long day and I need to get her home."

I stepped out of the way. I could tell he knew everything Nelly had whispered in Marina's ear.

"I hope you can rest." His words, kind in tone, had a physical effect on me—like Elias's knee in my chest, pressing the air out of my lungs. Like my father doubting me. I would not rest knowing how Marina felt.

Marina wobbled to their car. She was out of my reach, like long ago when she was sixteen and marching, twirling a baton in the Fourth of July parade. I saw her first and pointed her out to Elias. The parade headed down Main Street, past the store, toward the old courthouse and town square. Marina threw the silver baton and it flashed in the sun. Her dark hair fell and bounced about her shoulders. Her green eyes were striking, even from a distance. She caught the baton like there was nothing to it. She had grit and worked hard to be good at what she wanted. Another toss behind her back, she spun around, and the white skirt filled with air like the dome of a bell. The baton landed in her hand.

Elias's hand rested against the small of my back. He felt proud like me. I shifted from his touch, but the heat from his body shrouded me. As he took a deep breath, I could feel his chest expand. For a moment he held his breath, and his shirt brushed against my back. The sight of her paralyzed him, made him forget to breathe. He loved her. That was true. He exhaled, and the hot air from his mouth rushed past my shoulder. His body was so close, and I wished his touch was true.

I was surprised to see, at a certain angle, my likeness in Marina's face. She was graceful like my mother. She moved toward us as the bass drum pounded the marching beat. The next moment, it was Elias that I saw in her features.

She turned and twirled, jumped in the air as the baton rose higher and higher and then fell into her grip. She was neither of us. She was her own person, moving gracefully, purposefully, solidly onward. She tucked the silver baton under her arm and waved to the crowd flying small American flags on sticks. She marched near us, and I wondered if she would afford me the same jubilant smile she gave the crowd or if she would offer me more—a special wink or an intimate nod—because I was her mother. Then, I feared she would look past me, around me, as if she did not recognize me at all.

"Beautiful girl," someone said to us.

Elias's hand automatically returned to my back. The other hand squeezed my arm. "We're very proud," he said. His touch was kind, and his voice was true, honest, loving when he spoke of Marina.

She passed. Her legs pumped up and down in the short white boots. She must have seen us in front of the family store, but nothing changed in her demeanor—the same smile, the same heartfelt wave, but no special recognition—no wink, no kiss blown into the air, no greeting muffled by the beating bass drum. So close, I could have taken a few steps to touch her flushed cheeks or to swipe aside the strands of hair stuck to her face, but I feared her smile would disappear if I crossed the boundary between us.

And then she was gone, out of sight, followed by the marching band and a shiny, red convertible with Miss Jubilee sitting high and blowing kisses. Elias went back inside. The parade was over. I stood in the same spot, listening to the droning beat of the bass drum and longing for another glimpse of my daughter.

The Hospital

I stood on the porch and listened to the night birds warble and the cicadas thrum. I did not want to be alone inside the house with his body. Gus would be back soon, and his presence would help cool my thoughts after the burning exchange with Marina.

A bright-green leaf as large as my hand fluttered past my head. I watched it float inside, toward the candle near the casket. It was not a leaf, but a golden luna moth with wings shaped like ginkgo leaves. The moth was looking for a place to lay its eggs and it landed in a spot of candlelight on the golden wood of the casket. I followed it inside and blew out the candle, then scooped the luna in my palm and released it on the bark of the pecan tree.

Outside in the dark, I was happy, away from him, away from the confines of the house, and I slipped off my shoes to spread my feet on the cool grass.

The phone rang and I hurried to answer it in case it was Marina or Eli calling.

Gus's voice said, "It's Papa. I found him and brought him to the hospital."

Cold ran through me like Elias's ghost. "Is he okay? Are you there now?"

"He's had a heart attack." Gus sounded frantic. "They put him in a room."

I drove toward the hospital, and the cover of night cooled and lulled me as if no badness lurked. Surely he was fine. Surely it was the heat, the worry, the scuffle with Ivie. I had never known my father to be sick. I parked and locked the car with the money still hidden in the trunk. Papa wanted me to go, but I was here, tied to Marina, to him, to this town.

Inside the hospital, my eyes had to adjust to the bright lights. The sharp smell of alcohol burned my nose. I followed a nurse in a white uniform to Papa's room and my footsteps echoed down the green-tiled halls. He lay, a mound of flesh covered in a plastic tent, and his stillness frightened me.

Gus sat on a cushioned bench and he sprang up when he saw me.

"What happened?" I looked at Gus's swollen lip.

"I found him sitting on the curb. He was screaming, 'Vega is gone. Vega is gone.' I told him, 'Mama died a long time ago.' He said, 'We have to find her, tell her to go to my people up north.'" Gus's sleeves were rolled and the veins in his forearms bulged.

"He didn't know me," Gus said. "Didn't know my name." He looked scared. "He tried to hit me. He said, 'You took Vega.' I told him, 'No,' and got him in the truck, but he started again. He jerked my arm and I almost drove off the road."

"Vega is my name." I led Gus to the bench and we sat. "He was talking about me."

"I know." Gus looked at me with sad eyes. "I tried to calm him. I told him she's not going anywhere, and he said, 'I should have killed him.' I told him not to talk like that and he got angrier. He said, 'Who the hell are you?'" Gus pulled out a pack of cigarettes and knocked a single out. He could not smoke for the oxygen in the room and he put it back in the box.

I went to Papa's bedside and he looked at me through the plastic sheet. His eyes were big and frightened like a deer's.

"Ivie did this to him." Gus stood and paced the tile floor. "I didn't know what to do so I brought him here."

"You did the right thing," I said. "Did you call Lila?"

He nodded. "After I called you."

Papa's eyes followed the sound of our voices as if our words were clouds floating above his face.

Gus added, "Papa kept saying, 'My heart is breaking.' It was more than just him being upset. I told him to show me where it hurts. He couldn't lift his arms and then his eyes rolled up and all I could see were the whites of his eyes. So I came here. They gave him some fluids and a shot so he could rest and they put that tent on him."

Papa brushed his fingers against the plastic and moaned when he could not touch me.

"I'm here," I said.

His eyes were like small pools of dark water. Gravity pulled the flesh of his cheeks toward the pillow. "Where am I?" he asked, sounding as though his tongue were heavy and thick.

I could not tell him he was in the hospital, because he thought hospitals were where people went to die.

His eyes searched my face. "Vega," he said. "Vega."

"Yes," I said. Hearing my name, I felt how tiresome the name *Anna* had been for so long, that refusal of who I was, my mother's daughter. I was Vega, not Elias's wife, not after twenty-seven years, two children, and countless nights. My father knew me. He had known me before I had known myself.

"A big dog got in my way on the route." Papa spoke slowly, his words choppy like the river on a windy day. "I had to stand my ground and wait for it to back down. Then it left and I went to the next place."

"You're dreaming, Papa," I said. "From your peddling days."

319

"No, no," he said. He tried to sit up, but he could not get his arms beneath him. "I came round the bend and the river. There was your mother. Little children around her." His words slurred with the palsy in his face, and I had a sinking feeling he was dying.

I reached beneath the curtain and made him lie down, but he was feeling agitated and restless. I touched his pale forehead.

Papa was still trying to sit up when the nurse came to check him. "Lie down, Mr. Khoury." She told me, "Leave the curtain down. He needs the oxygen."

I stepped away and Papa lay patient and quiet while she took his vitals. He looked small, a bald head floating on a bed of white. "He's very sick," she said to me. "He's had a heart attack."

His eyes searched the ceiling, the nurse's face, my own. "Vega," he whispered. "Vega. Vega." The name tumbled from his lips like pebbles dropped on the road. "Vega, I'm sorry," he said. "Will you take me home?"

The nurse tucked the sheets tightly around Papa's legs and then wrote on his chart.

Gus paced and his dress shoes clapped against the tile floor. The noise agitated Papa, and he knocked the plastic as if he were knocking on a door. I told Gus to be still.

The nurse said, "If your father doesn't settle down, we'll give him more medicine in an hour. The doctor will see him in the morning."

Papa wrestled beneath the sheets the nurse had tucked and tightened.

"You need to rest," I said. "You are okay." I held my hand against the plastic and he tried to place his shaky hand on the opposite side.

The nurse saw the stained bandage on my hand. "Let me see that."

I held it out to her. "He's confused," I said. "He doesn't know where he is. He thinks I'm my mother."

"The medicine should settle him down soon." She unwound the bandage with a gentle touch.

I looked at Gus, half dozing on the bench. I could sleep there and he could go home.

"That's a nasty cut," the nurse said. "I'll stitch that up while you're here."

"Is it that bad?" The wound oozed clear liquid from the split flesh. I thought of Ivie pushing me into the broken glass and his drunken insistence that I must leave.

"If I don't stitch it, it'll get infected. I'll be back after my rounds, and we'll fix you up." She gave me fresh gauze to hold over the wound. Her rubber-soled shoes made almost no sound as she crossed the room and closed the door behind her.

I sat next to Gus. I watched Papa's breathing and whispered, "He looks bad. I'm afraid he could die."

"We are all going to die," Gus said. "But not yet." Gus patted my knee.

"Look how shallow his breathing is."

"The medicine is doing that."

"I made him sick to death," I said. "Papa told me to leave, but I can't go with him like this."

Gus opened his eyes. His temples throbbed. "Elias was a goddamn bastard, and Ivie is too. They are the ones who did this to Papa."

I looked at Papa's chest rising and falling. He'd slowed down with age but I had never seen him on his back. Always, he was busy in the garden or the store and he never sat except to do the books. "Ivie won't rest 'til I'm gone."

"You're not going anywhere." Gus rubbed his eyes. "You'll stay with us or we'll stay with you."

"For a day or two." My bones felt tired.

"Listen," Gus said. "Ivie will never open the store, and if he does he'll go off on a bender after a day of hard work."

We sat quietly for a long moment, and then I said, "I have always envied birds, how they can pick up and go where they want."

"You can't go anywhere with Papa like this." His voice broke. Gus would fight for me until he could not fight anymore. When we were kids, he came out swinging if anyone was mean to me, and I had played the little mother and loved him, read to him, and sat with him all those nights when he woke up afraid and wanting her. We had taken good care of each other.

"I won't go with him like this. I want to stay to be with Marina."

"I won't let them hurt you." He leaned his head back, closed his eyes again. "You're my sister."

"You can't fight Ivie every time he comes around," I said. A thin line of blood rose in the cleft of the cut. The truth seemed as heavy as the casket in my house. "Marina is angry with me. I have so much to repair." I felt scared for Papa's life. I felt scared for her. I remembered well now how it felt to lose a parent, and I had done so little to comfort Marina.

Gus stood and stretched. "I need a coffee."

"Okay," I said. "Go, while he is resting. Get me one too."

Gus left, and Papa moaned from beneath the plastic tent. I went to his bedside, and he turned his head and blinked as if his eyelids were weighted.

"I want you to know." He cleared his dry throat.

I shushed him. "You need to rest."

"She was afraid." He blinked and swallowed and shook his head. "The doctor told me to stay away from her. No more babies." His words were slow and cumbersome, muffled by the plastic tent. "I thought she was strong. I thought that doctor was just worried. But he was right." He had lived all this time blaming himself.

"You need to rest," I said.

With a trembling hand, he touched the plastic between us. "There is more."

I shook my head and tried to shush him.

"I remember," he said, "when you were a girl, you and your mother fed the ducks. This crow watched and followed you and you tossed it some bread. The next morning, he left you a present on that spot. You fed him and for weeks and he brought you little scraps of things—a piece of tin, a mussel shell, a marble, a broken piece of jewelry, a ribbon. You kept the treasures in my peddler's box."

I did not remember the crow or the treasures. I wondered if the medicine was making him dream.

His hazel eyes searched the tent for someplace to rest his gaze. "My brother and I peddled all different places. We passed through the valley, the hills." His speech was slow, slurred.

"You need to rest," I said.

He said, "The sun will come and go. The moon will change."

"Please rest, Papa."

"The sky will rain and rivers will rise. You will be hot one day and freezing the next." He shut his eyes and swallowed. One side of his face drooped. "It will pass. God willing." His voice trailed off.

"Rest." I wanted him to get stronger, to get better. I did not want to hear deathbed talk. "I know your peddling stories," I said. "You and your brother migrated south like a pair of birds not knowing where you would land and roost. You passed the cougar drinking from the mountain stream, and you saw a black bear stealing honey from a beehive, both of them too busy to notice you. You slept in barns and did odd jobs for money or dinner. That's right?"

He blinked open his eyes. "You draw your breath, do your work, and pray to God. Troubles will pass. That is what I thought. We were young. We were not afraid."

I wanted to hold his hand, but I was scared to lift the tent.

"We were too young to know fear." Papa's hazel eyes fixed on me. "But I am old now and I know too much." He closed his eyes.

A moment later, Gus walked into the room with two Coke bottles and two packs of M&M's in his hands. "I went looking for coffee, but this is all I could find."

I said, "Should we call Father McMurray?"

Gus sat and I joined him. "Not yet." He handed me the bottle of Coke and the candy. It tasted so sweet and good and reminded me of all the days Gus and I drank sodas and ate candy from Papa's shelves.

Gus ate his candy and drank in long gulps. "I could use a real drink."

"Do you remember after Mama died, when Papa took us to visit his brother in Connecticut?"

"No." Gus shifted in his seat. His eyes were tired and I could see exhaustion setting in.

"We came into the city at Grand Central Terminal, and before we took the train to our uncle's, Papa wanted to show us where he started. We walked down Fifth Avenue and got a taxi."

"I don't remember." He threw the candy wrapper away and began to pace the floor.

"You held my hand tight and your eyes were big, looking at the people and buildings. We got to Washington Street and the Middle Eastern bazaar. Papa said, 'This is where I first came,' and he pointed to this window and that shop and he took us down into a cellar of a building and spoke Arabic with a man. There were women at tables sorting boxes under flickering lights." They sorted all kinds of things: lace, hair pomade, shoelaces, ribbons, Christmas ornaments, squares of silk. All the stuff he had started with in his peddler's box. "A woman gave me a silver thimble and you a rubber ball. You let go of me and grabbed her legs. Papa tried to pry you off but you started crying, 'Mama, Mama.'"

Gus repeated, "I don't remember."

"I thought he should marry her and bring her home. I thought that was why he had brought us there, to find a wife. Then we went upstairs to a room full of rugs piled high and you climbed to the top and jumped to Papa. He told you, 'No,' but you were so persistent and happy that he let you do it over and over again."

Gus yawned and leaned his head against the wall again. "I don't remember our mother or what she looked like. He took her pictures down. I remember that."

"There is a picture of her that he kept in his drawer that I used to look at when I wanted to remember her. I wanted to find it yesterday. I wanted to see her face. I wanted Marina to see it, but I could not find it."

Gus put his thick hand on my arm. "I'll help you find it."

"Do you remember her funeral?"

Gus spoke, dreamlike. "I remember Papa held me over the coffin and said, 'Look. This is your mother.'"

I had been afraid Papa would drop Gus on her and I tugged Papa's pant leg. "Put him down," I had said.

"Marina's baby won't know me," I said. I ate the last of the chocolate candy, a small comfort in that cold room. "Marina doesn't want anything to do with me."

"Remember when I married Lila, and I thought Papa would never speak to me again?" Gus had a wry smile on his face. "But he did. Marina will come around too."

"I don't know." I did not feel hopeful sitting in Papa's hospital room. "It is a different thing." The venom in Marina's voice hung in my memory. I had no place to go, not home with a casket waiting, not to my daughter who rightly thought the worst of me.

"Take it a day at a time." Gus stood to stretch. "Let's get him better. We don't know what's ahead."

It was practical advice, but I felt I stood on the edge of the bridge about to fall. "You go home to Lila. I'll stay here with him."

"No," he said. "I'm not leaving you here."

"Go home," I said. "No need for both of us to stay up all night."

"Do you want to leave?"

"No." I wanted to sleep. "I can rest on this bench."

I tried to imagine living with my brother or what would happen if I stayed put—if a mob or the police would come drag me out of my house with Verna gleefully watching. My heart felt heavy, but I was not scared. I would do whatever I had to do.

"Tell you what," Gus said. "I saw a couch in the waiting room. I'll lie down there and you stretch out here. Come get me if anything changes." His footsteps echoed down the hall.

I opened the window and looked out into the street. The night air was a balm to my senses. The trees were black. Crickets and tree frogs called. The pitch-dark sky was littered with stars. During the new moon, the stars shone brighter without the moonlight. Tomorrow or the next night, the moon would be a sliver of light in the sky and the stars would fade, if only a little, as the moon waxed. I wondered where I would be this time tomorrow night, if I would leave town, or if I would be here with my father, or someplace in between. The river was south in the darkness, not visible from this north point in town. If I drove home and walked into the river, I would surely sink to the bottom, how heavy I was with regret. But I could never leave like that, not willingly. I tried to think like Papa, *This will pass. God willing.*

I took off my suit coat and folded it like a pillow. I wanted to rest and forget the trouble. I cradled my wounded hand. I could not remember how small a baby would be, but soon I would be reminded, and the thought of Marina's baby comforted me.

The nurse nudged me on the shoulder.

I had fallen asleep. "What time is it?"

"It's two thirty."

I sat up.

She moved a chair next to me and spread a clean white towel over a silver tray and pulled a spotlight near. She took a syringe full of saline and washed out the cut. It burned. She poured iodine over the cut, the same as Marina had done the day before.

"How's he doing?" I tried to see his face, but his body blocked my view. Slight, shallow movements told me he was breathing.

"He's strong." Her tone was hopeful, but her eyes told me different. "He's a fighter."

A pinch, then a needle hooked through my skin. A tug, another pinch. "A few more and you'll be good as new."

I'm afraid I won't be, I wanted to say. I would never be good or new. I never thought I would feel the depth of pain I had known as a child the night I lost my mother, but seeing him helpless in the bed brought it back fresh. I would have no one who would remember me as an innocent child. No one who held me or watched me grow or remembered things I had no memory of. My father knew things about me that I did not know yet, and I needed him here to tell me.

She pushed the needle through my skin one last time.

I began to weep.

"It's okay. Sometimes a little physical pain makes the feelings come out." The nurse paused with the stitches and touched my arm to comfort me.

I wiped my eyes. "I didn't expect to see him like this."

She turned the light on my arms, bare because I'd taken off the suit coat, and shifted my sleeves. "Did he do that to you?"

"No," I said. "No. Papa would not hurt me. He never even spanked us."

She dropped my sleeve and removed her hands from my arm.

I sat straight and hoped the sleeves would fall an inch more to cover what Elias had done.

"Who did that to you?" A caring question that I did not expect. If she knew who I was, she never said, but if she didn't, she soon would. She would talk to her friends, her fellow nurses, and they would tell her I was the one that let the Negro mailman deliver. She would say she had taken care of me and my father. She would tell them about the bruises, about the cut, the weeping, and if it became common knowledge that Mr. Washington was in my house or if my family publicly accused me of my husband's death, she'd figure out the rest.

"He's gone," I said. "The person who did this is gone."

"That's good." She nodded. "Nobody should put their hands on you."

It felt good for a stranger to see what he did and say it was wrong.

"I'm going to be a grandmother," I said, trying to calm myself. I smiled to stop the flow of tears. "My daughter is due any minute."

"Well, that's wonderful." She smiled and folded the stained towel over the suture kit. "Maybe you'll be here visiting them in about a week. Come by and I'll take those out for you." She took the silver tray out of the room and returned with a pillow, a blanket, and a cup of water for me. "I'm Betty. Just ask the labor-and-delivery nurses to get me."

"Thank you." I cradled my throbbing hand in my arm. I did not expect the kindness she had given, and I did not know what to expect in a week's time, if I would be in Riverton or far away or in a jail cell.

She checked Papa's vital signs and moved around the room, adjusting his covers, wiping his forehead. "Is there anyone you want to call?" she asked. "Do you want me to get the chaplain?"

"Do you think it's time?" My heart beat fast at the thought of him dying. I stood to see the old man. He looked like a sleeping child, innocent and vulnerable.

"I don't know," she said. "But I don't expect him to get much better."

"I'll call the priest in the morning."

"Okay," she said. "Let me know if you need anything else." She turned off the overhead light, and a small lamp near his bed glowed faintly on the green tile walls. "The doctor will make his rounds in the morning."

She closed the door softly but he roused.

"Anna," he called out. "Anna."

I ran to his bedside, saddened that I was no longer Vega to him.

He looked frightened, like he was waking from a nightmare.

"I am here," I said. I wanted to lift the plastic to touch him and calm him.

Papa's eyes were large and wet. "There is no sin you cannot confess," he was yelling.

"I know, Papa." I pressed against the plastic and found his hand. "Settle down. I'm here." I felt sorry that my poor father was wrestling against my guilt, that he was feeling the burden of shame Nelly wanted me to feel.

"The worst sin is to deny God. You can pray. You can do penance. You can still save your soul." His words had energy and breath.

"You have to rest." I felt as if I were choking. "And get better."

"Promise you will confess. The sooner the better. The greater chance for forgiveness." His eyes looked wild and I feared he would overwhelm himself.

"I will, Papa. I will confess my sins." If he did not quiet down, his agitation would get the better of him. I wanted to set his mind at ease. I did not want him to suffer any more. "But I did not poison Elias. I did not." Already, I had lied to Marina, Eli, Gus, the coroner, and now my father. It was what I had to do. He closed his mouth and his eyes, and I felt relief he had stopped.

"Vega did not want to go." He spoke slowly, tired from his outburst. "She must have cursed God all the way. I pray she did not. I pray she calmed herself before her soul left her body. I hope she is safe." His words petered out and his face went limp.

I watched to see that he was breathing, and then I settled back on the cushioned bench. His stomach moved slower and slower, like the second hand on a clock about to lose its wind. I did not want him to suffer and I did not want him to go, but I feared that soon he would die. He seemed to be holding on, not wanting to leave because I was in trouble. I would be an orphan, no mother or father, no one to love me the way a parent loves a child. There was my brother, who had his own family, and my son, but he had his schooling, his life, his work before him and I did not want his future harmed by my misdeeds. All I had wanted was to live in peace and to love my children.

I should have called Gus into the room, or Eli or Marina on the phone. I should have called Father McMurray to give Papa his last rites, but I was so tired and I wanted no more buzzing around the dying or the dead. I needed Papa to rest and get better. Tomorrow I would bury Elias, and I told myself I would not have to bury Papa anytime soon.

I wanted to lie there one quiet moment and think of the water, of the river that was not far away, of what it was like on that summer night when I sat with Papa and the children and their jars of fireflies. I imagined walking by the water with Mama and feeding the ducks and the crow. I tried to remember the crow's gifts and I thought of Sophie and how she would be elated if a crow brought her gifts. I must remember to tell Lila that such a thing was possible.

I needed to sleep, so that in the morning I could rouse myself to face Marina and Eli and bury their father. I wanted to close my eyes and shut out the horrible, slow sound of Papa's strained breath. If we got him home, I would stay with him and nurse him back to health. I thought, *Damn Ivie to hell.* I would live where I wanted, and Ivie had no right to threaten me or my father. I thought of the chores awaiting me. The floors would need to be scrubbed, the drapes taken down and beaten. I would give away all the groceries and then burn the old boxes and papers, the old *Al-Hoda* and the indecipherable letters written in Arabic. I would find her things, the photographs, her silver bracelets and her hair combs. I thought of the brick oven in the back room of Papa's store. I would teach myself how Mama had made her bread, and I would make the house as simple and clean as she had. After the work and the scrubbing, I would sit on the back porch and think of her and breathe in the smell of the river in its different seasons—now, with the rotting leaves of late summer, to winter's cold, to the new grass and reeds of spring. I would look out at the water and imagine her with me. The river birds would land and take flight and barges would float past and the rich men from town would tack their sailboats back and forth.

As if my thoughts had conjured her before us in the flesh, Papa sprang upright, the last bit of life surging through his body. The plastic tent covered his face, his chest and shoulders. He fought against it and his arms flailed. The metal stands hit the floor with a clang. He grunted and struggled to untangle himself. The nurse rushed in, and when he fell back, he was gone.

The Grave

At the cemetery, I perched like a crow on the hill above his casket covered in white roses. From my vantage point, I could see the ink-dark river and a storm coming from the south. In his tenor voice, Father McMurray sang like a wild bird: "Lord our God, receive your servant, for whom you shed your blood. Remember, Lord, that we are dust: like grass, like a flower of the field." *We are like dust. We are like dust.* Elias is dust and so am I.

Marina knew that I'd be late, but she had not saved me a seat among the mourners. I did not want to walk down the gravel path and stand before them while he was committed to the earth. It was better to look over them from far away, up high, where they could not trouble me with their judgments.

I had spent the morning at the hospital, knowing Marina would seethe at my absence from his funeral Mass. I insisted to Gus that he go on to the funeral while I waited for the doctor's explanation that the commotion with Ivie, the heat, and Papa's age had taken a toll on his heart. While the doctor spoke and tried to comfort me, I blamed myself. As soon as I could, I drove from the hospital to the graveyard and did not stop at home to change into Marina's black suit or get the veil and gloves.

In the front row of mourners, Gus sat wearing yesterday's suit and the shirt he had slept in at the hospital. His beard was almost black after one day of growth, and I could be sure that Marina was irritated with his appearance. I hoped she could understand, but every second I spent away from her, I imagined her love for me splintering and Nelly's seeds of doubt sprouting and growing as fast as weeds.

Nelly, the crouched old crone, leaned on Marina. I wished that my father was alive and that death had taken Nelly instead. The moist, heavy air blew across the water and dark clouds hung low. The sky was soon to open and pour rain. The cicadas droned in the rising humidity. Soon they would lay their eggs, their vibrations would cease, and they would die. I did not want to be dead to Marina.

I sat above them, outside the circle of mourning, but Lila sensed my presence and turned her head. The kind look on her face and in her eyes steadied me. Under her arm was Sophie, whose hair seemed to dance in ringlets around her face. She peeked over her mother's shoulder to see what had Lila's attention. Sophie waved and shouted my name, and her voice carried over the stark quiet. All the heads, including Marina's, turned to gawk at me up on the hill. Lila covered Sophie's mouth, but she kept on, "There's Aunt Annie. Up there," and her voice was muffled only a bit.

Marina's body recoiled into Michael, and Ivie sneered with delight to see me cast out so far away from my daughter and my place among them. Lila shushed her one last time and Sophie hid her face in her mother's neck.

The priest's words rang like bells, and the mourners turned their attention back to him. "We commend the soul of Elias Nassad, Your servant. In the sight of this world he is now dead." Father McMurray's face streamed with sweat above his layered vestments. He looked as though he were melting into a puddle. "In Your love, may he live forever. Forgive whatever sins he committed, and in Your goodness, grant him everlasting peace." I clenched my jaw as my body shook in disagreement.

The graveside prayers were over, and people took quick steps up the hill to their cars. No one spoke as they passed and I felt as invisible as the wind. In six weeks, Marina's baby would be baptized and these people would be at the baptism. I wanted to be among them, not a migrating bird gone south for the winter or for always. As each person ignored me and passed without acknowledgment, I steeled my resolve to stay. I would stay to bury my father. I would stay for Marina and the baby's baptism. The deed to the house was in my name. Nelly and Ivie could not take that. He was in the ground and the death certificate had been signed, and though Nelly could raise suspicions, I had doubt on my side too. They thought they had me, that I was as good as gone, but I belonged here with my children.

Sophie, Lila, and Gus hurried up to me and Sophie's small arms wrapped around my legs. My brother and his wife hugged me too, and I felt consolation in their touch. "We're going home for a while," Gus said. His eyes were red from lack of sleep and crying over Papa. "Do you want to come with us?"

I shook my head *no*. "I'll stay with Marina." I hoped she would allow me to be in her presence.

Ivie helped Nelly up the hill.

Lila grabbed me and hugged me again. She did not let go. "I'm sorry about your daddy," she said. I felt a wave of grief wash over me, but I had to rein it in.

Ivie and Nelly were gone and I did not want to miss a chance to speak to my children. "I have to get to Marina and Eli," I said.

Lila loosened her hold on me. Her blue eyes teared and I saw she was hurting for me and Gus. "I'll see you later, then," she said.

A hard knot fixed itself in the center of my chest as I approached my daughter. Neither Eli nor Michael could move her from the spot. She clenched a handkerchief and hung on Michael's arm despite the muggy heat.

The gravediggers waited. They would not fill his grave with mourners present.

Marina's face looked more swollen than the day before, and I worried her body had reached a dangerous point. I started to sit next to her and take her hand, but the anger across her face stopped me.

The sky rumbled, and Michael said to her, "Let's get out of this heat so you can put your feet up."

Marina said, "A minute more." Her ankles had ballooned and I worried her body would burst from the pressure.

Michael, impatient with her, unlaced her grip from his arm. He said, "I'll wait by the car," and climbed the hill.

"Let's go with Michael," I said. "It's about to storm."

She stared at the coffin.

"Go ahead with it," I said to the gravediggers when I saw she would not be moved. They removed the blanket of flowers and turned the winch until the casket was deep in the ground. They took down the frame that had held the casket and began to shovel clumps of mud over him. The relief I had expected escaped me. Instead a deep ache resounded with each shovel of dirt that fell on top of him.

Marina bowed her head.

Eli waited patiently by. His fingers grazed Marina's shoulder to let her know he stood beside her.

"Marina," I said. "Let's go with Michael."

"You missed Daddy's funeral." Anger lathered on her tongue.

"I had to be with Grandpapa. I had to talk to the doctor," I said.

"You stood up there looking down on us," Marina said.

"There was no place saved for me and I did not want to disrupt the prayer," I offered.

Marina's eyes fixed on the gravediggers. She seemed to have turned to stone. "I've lost my mother and father in the same day," she said. "Now Grandpapa too."

"I'm still here, *binti*," I said.

She blinked and looked at me with red eyes. "What did you call me?"

"*Binti*," I said. "It means *my daughter*. That's what my mother called me." It was hard to believe I had never called her that. "Grandpapa reminded me of it."

The sky threatened and the funeral men began collecting chairs behind us. Marina labored to stand. I reached out to help her. My heart pounded with hope when she took my arm, but she gripped so hard that I thought she meant to hurt me. Her face told me that her body had seized.

"It's time to go to the hospital." My voice was tentative, mixed with hope and fear. I knew what was coming and she did not.

Eli saw the trouble and tried to bolster her up.

"Let me take you," I said.

"No." Another refusal, but she spoke in a civil tone. "Michael will. Eli, get Michael."

Eli rushed up the hill and screamed Michael's name.

The gravediggers stopped what they were doing to see if they could help, but I shook my head.

"Don't you see that I want to fix things?" I swallowed hard. If I just started to speak, the words would come. "Marina." I drew a deep breath. "I am sorry." It was true that I was sorry for the pain I caused her. I didn't know if she could believe me, but I would try to convince her.

"No." She cut me off. "No. No. No." It was all she could say. She could not catch her breath. She clung to my arm as if it were a rope and she were dangling from a height. She could not stand straight.

"I love you." I wanted her to know that. "I'm here for you." Michael and Eli were running; their heads bobbed at the crest of the hill.

She held up a trembling hand. "Stop talking."

"Okay," I said. My hands were shaking too. Another roll of thunder clapped.

She leaned into me with all her weight and I did not know if I could hold her up. "Oh," one long syllable, came deep from her core.

"The baby's coming," I said. "You'll be okay."

She looked me in the eye and I could see she was afraid. The wind rustled the trees at the edge of the cemetery.

I struggled to keep her upright. She'd been in labor for days, and now she could no longer ignore the pains.

"Oh." She howled a long and primal moan and then a gush of fluid washed down her legs.

Michael and Eli arrived, breathing hard from running. They wrapped their arms around her middle and I walked behind them up the hill, feeling useless as they moved in awkward jolts. She leaned on me as Michael pulled the car close and we eased her into the back seat.

"I'll go with you," I said.

Marina's eyes were shut. She could not hear or speak and I remembered how labor pain took over the whole body.

Michael said, "I've got it from here." He shut the car door and his tires spun in the gravel as he raced out of the cemetery.

Eli held my arm. "Let's follow them," he said.

"They don't want me there." My eyes fell below us on the statue of Mary, with her hands open and her gaze downcast, by my mother's grave, down the path from Elias's. Mama had talked about the icons of Mary from her home, and Papa must have chosen this large statue for that reason.

The gravediggers looked to the sky and worked fast to get ahead of the storm.

Eli watched the men working. "She loves you," he said. "They were arguing about you this morning. She doesn't want you treated this way." Eli had a better chance of saving the world than mending what was broken between his sister and me.

"I want to visit my mother's grave before I go," I said. We walked back down to Elias's grave and I took one of the wreaths meant for him and carried it to my mother's grave. Eli followed me down the path toward the statue of Mary. Two small headstones that belonged to the babies were on her left, and soon Papa would be buried on her right. Gus and I would bury him, and I wondered how much more I could take.

Eli's long legs strode beside me. "She doesn't want you to leave," he said.

"I think she does."

Thunder sounded. I touched the inscription of her name: *Vega Khoury. Beloved Wife and Mother.* On the baby boys' gravestones, their birth dates were the same as the day they died. I bowed my head and hoped that Marina and her baby would be safe.

"You need to have faith in her," he said.

"You're right." I did not have the heart to tell my son the truth of my situation and that I had lost my faith long ago. I worried he had too much stake in it. The smell of damp earth from Elias's grave carried in the wind.

"If you stay," he said, "I'll stay with you."

"My mother was so good," I said. "So gentle." I remembered her thick black hair, tied back in a white scarf, her flowing blue skirt, and the accent of her voice. Her bracelets sang as she moved.

Eli stood by me, close and patient.

"What will Marina remember me by?" I asked Eli. *Nothing so sweet,* I thought. "Mama was so young. I thought she knew so much, but she was not much older than Marina when she died." My Marina was soon to be a mother, and I prayed she would do better than me.

"I saw what happened to you, Mama." Eli meant what his father had done to me. "I'm not going to let it happen again."

"It's not your job to take care of me."

"Ivie and Grandmother are not going to steamroll you." He stood tall and his face was stern. He believed he could protect me from them.

"I was supposed to take care of you and Marina." I felt sorry for him that he trusted in me as much as he did. I did not deserve it, but I would take it, greedy as a thief.

"I've been thinking," he said. "I'll come home and go to the state school nearby. Then I'll apply to law school."

"Don't you change your plans, for me or for them." I ran my fingers over her name. *Vega.* "You don't know what people are capable of."

"I do." He raised his voice and I heard the anger in it. "I know what my father did and I want to do better."

"You don't have to pay for your father's sins," I said. *Or mine,* I thought.

Eli searched my face. Then he looked in the direction of the fresh grave. "I can't ignore what's being done."

"But it's dangerous," I said. "You can't change everybody's mind." I hated that I sounded like my family, how they wanted to dissuade me from caring what happened to Mr. Washington, how they wanted me to look the other way. "If I leave, then things can return to normal. You go on with your studies. All I care about is you and Marina and that you're safe and happy."

"If you stay or go, it's not going to change my mind." Eli sounded as stubborn as Marina. "You did the right thing by helping him."

I shook my head. "I should never have asked him inside." I could not reconcile my motives or my actions.

"You were being kind," Eli said. "Why should either of you suffer over a kindness?"

The men pounded the red dirt with their shovels to tamp it down and then placed the blanket of white roses over his grave.

"I'm afraid I helped him to spite your father." All of it mixed in my mind.

"You were not wrong," he said.

The gravediggers walked up the hill with their shovels and ropes in hand.

"There is right and wrong," Eli said. "Lives are at stake and I won't stand by and do nothing." He sounded like a man of conviction, but I saw the boy who looked at me with pity, who knew what his father had done to me. For what I had done to his father, there would be no redemption.

"You have a good conscience," I said. "You have grown up a good man." I did not have a good conscience. I had scraped by for so long that I had lost it along the way. The sky was dark and lightning flashed close by.

"Let's go see about Marina," Eli said. He led the way up the hill away from the graves.

I was tired of what waited for me—Marina's anger, burying my father, and leaving town—but my son had hope and he believed in goodness. I was afraid for him, afraid if he took his faith too far, that I'd bury him too.

"We'll have something to celebrate soon." Eli's voice was hopeful and he took my good hand.

"Yes," I said. "You are right." I forced a smile and thought of how Sophie had brought us all together. On the day of her baptism, we had sat around the table, Elias and our children with Gus and Lila, Papa, Nelly, and Louise. We had been so happy watching Sophie play and toddle in her white dress, and I had thought, *Now is our chance.* We held so much hope in Sophie, that one creature, and here was our chance again in Marina's baby, who was sure to be loved and adored and smart and beautiful.

I had made it this far and now Marina's baby was almost here. If I bided my time, if I had faith in my love for my children, maybe Eli would be right. The rain began to fall and the hot ground steamed. The water fell cool and clean on my face like a baptism washing away the past few days of misery.

The Trial

When Marina had been in labor eight hours, Michael bought his second pack of cigarettes from the waiting-room vending machine. It was late, and we were all tired. The rain had pounded the windows all day as Eli whispered his plans in my ear. He wanted to leave the seminary and enroll in the state school nearby, to be close and watch over me. He planned to volunteer for the Alabama Christian Movement for Human Rights at a Baptist church in Birmingham. The people running it had taken in Orlando Washington, and Eli wanted to do his part until he had a law degree and could work full time.

I was scared for him to take such a stand. I wanted him safe and whole at the seminary, where the ones who went after Orlando Washington could not get him, but I said nothing, because he was bound and determined and it was his choice to make.

Michael kept his distance from us and paced and smoked. His suit pants were wrinkled and his shirt was damp. I asked him if he'd like a sandwich from the cafeteria, and he eyed me with suspicion. He wanted nothing to do with me, and at one point, his vitriol spilled out onto Eli. "If you don't mind, shut the hell up. I don't want to hear what you're talking about."

It had been dark for an hour when I insisted Eli go home and get some sleep. He offered to go with Gus the next day to help with Papa's funeral arrangements so that I could take as much time as I wanted with Marina and the baby. He stood and stretched, no longer tentative in nature, but a tall young man answering the challenge before him. I was proud of who he'd become, and surprised too, that Elias and I had raised someone with the fortitude to stand up for others. Before he left, Eli extended his hand to Michael to wish him well and show there were no hard feelings from earlier, but Michael looked the other way.

When Eli was gone and we were alone in the waiting room, Michael crossed over. "You should leave too."

"I'll wait to see Marina and the baby."

"You're not going to see her or the baby." He sounded like a judge reading a verdict.

I did not protest. I remembered what Eli had told me, that Marina and Michael had argued and that she wanted me to stay.

He moved to the opposite side of the room, and I realized he was more dangerous to me than Ivie. Michael had Marina's heart, and I was a weight around his neck.

But no matter how angry she was, I was her mother and I knew she loved me. She was the same girl who stood by me while I baked bread, the same girl who looked at me with trusting eyes when I taught her to float on water, the same girl who spent her childhood watching out for me. I would not desert her because Michael told me to.

The baby girl was born at midnight, and in the early morning, Marina was brought back to a room. Michael stood gatekeeper at the door, and each time I tried to enter, he had a different excuse. At four in the morning, he said, "She's too weak. She lost a lot of blood." At six in the morning, he said, "She's not herself." The doctor had given her twilight sleep, and she was hallucinating, in and out of consciousness. At nine, a nurse wheeled a bassinet with the baby into the room. Michael followed her, and as I tried to enter, he stepped in my way and grabbed my arm. "There's no reason for you to hang around and stir things up."

I searched his blue eyes. The dark rings beneath were evidence of the long night and morning. "Take your hands off me," I said. "I want to see my daughter and grandchild."

He removed his hands and crossed his arms. "What I should say, Anna, is, since you are leaving town, maybe it's better to have a clean break."

"You're wrong about that." I thought about what Eli said. *Have faith in Marina.* I remembered what Father McMurray said. *There is no fear in love.* My stomach churned with nerves. She was angry with me, but she loved me. Blood was thicker than water, and I wanted to see my daughter and her baby. I tried to pass him, but he blocked my way again. His face was slick with perspiration. He smelled like earth and salt. "I won't leave until I see her." I wanted to trust his kind blue eyes, but I knew better. He was a snake in the grass, disguised by manners and a handsome face.

"The brick in the store window and the house burning are only the beginning." His voice was low. "There will be more trouble."

"I'm not afraid of bricks in windows or Ivie's threats." I spoke calmly.

"Aren't you afraid of a mob at your door?" His voice was disguised with concern.

"Let me see Marina." I didn't care what came after.

"I don't think you understand how bad this is."

"Eli says it will blow over." I wanted to believe Eli, that Marina loved me and she could forgive me. I would adopt the mind-set my parents had lived by so long ago. They had forged ahead and put on blinders to trouble and doubt. They got on a boat to a new world, and come what may, they built a new life and saw it through.

"Eli is an optimist, but I'm a realist." Michael's face was calm like the river on a windless day. He was unmoved by me. "Nobody likes what you did."

"I know you want me gone." The cold green tile of the hospital walls sank into my bones. The nurse left the baby with Marina and walked past Michael and me. I tried to see inside the room, to get a glimpse of Marina and the baby. The shades were drawn, but I could see the wildness of Marina's black hair fanning over the white pillow. "Eli said you two argued about me. He said that Marina wants me to stay."

He grabbed the meat of my arm and the bruises still hurt, three days later. He steered me away from the door and across the hall. "You need to understand something."

All night, like a good lawyer, he had thought through his case, piece by piece, laying out his argument for when the time came. "Your neighbor heard the commotion the day the mailman was in your house." So he'd talked with Verna or Verna had talked to him.

"Mama?" Marina's weakened voice called from the room.

His blue eyes were sharp and cold. He leaned in close to my face. "They'll take you to jail for fornication with a colored." His breath, stale with cigarette smoke and coffee, fell on my cheek and sent a chill down my spine. "Even if they can't prove murder, I cannot help you if you stay."

"Mama? Is that you?" Marina's voice rang like a shrill bell.

I tried to step around him. "Yes," I called out to her. "I'm here."

He blocked me. "We can sell your house for you."

"No, thank you."

"We can send you money if you don't have enough." He was bargaining now.

I tried to pass, but his arm shot across my way.

"We can visit you wherever you decide to go." He was offering false promises. "I know you have your father's money and money from the store."

Marina cried out, "Mama." Her voice was flat, plaintive.

"I'm here, Marina." My voice ramped up with emotion. "I'm not leaving her. Not when she needs me."

A nurse leaned over the desk and stared in our direction. "Everything okay?" she sang out.

Michael gave a smug smile and a wave. The nurse went back to her work, but Michael did not like the attention we were drawing, and he softened his voice. "You are on the wrong side of this."

My heart beat faster than it should. "His mother cared for me. I wanted to help him."

"That's how these people work." Michael stared past me, down the hall, to see if the nurse was still looking. "You are the victim here. He preyed on your ties and your kindness."

"I don't believe that," I said.

"It's reprehensible what he did to you. They go against every tradition and structure." He blocked Marina's doorway again, gesturing as if he were before a jury. "Even if you did not have relations with him, he put you in a bad position. He knew better than to go inside your house, and now your fate is no better than his."

"I've lived my life on both sides of this town, and I don't see it that way." I was tired of arguing with him, when what I had been waiting for was across the threshold.

"That is precisely the problem." He touched my sleeve faintly with his fingertips. He could see I was upset, and his softer touch was an attempt to calm me. "Nobody will believe you, Anna."

"I don't care." I was not frightened by him or the possibilities, because beyond him, in that room, was my hope, my daughter and hers.

"Listen to me." His tone was all business. "You are now finished with your part of civil rights. They burned his house, and if you keep on, one of you will be dead." He looked at me and he saw trash. All the time he had been with Marina, he had hidden his disdain, or else I

345

had been blind to it. "You need to save what little pride you have and move on."

"I have no pride." I stared into his cold, crystal-blue eyes. "I have a daughter and a son and a grandchild. That's what I have." I was not afraid of being alone or leaving town, but I did not want to leave. "One day, I hope you will lose your pride, for the sake of my daughter and yours. Now, I want to see the baby."

I tried to push past him, but he braced his arm. Michael, this blond father of my grandchild, my daughter's husband, was attempting the same thing as Elias, trying to control what I said and did. I looked at his arm, barring my way, and thought Marina had married a man like her father, his way or no way. But then, she called out, "Michael, let her pass," and I knew Marina would not be held back by him. She was a force of her own.

At her demand, he swept his arm aside, motioning that I should enter, as if he had never intended to block my way.

Marina's black hair sprang wildly around her swollen, ruddy face. She looked crazed, not beautiful or glowing but bedraggled, like my mother on her deathbed.

"I almost died." Her speech was slurred and the darkness of her eyes swallowed me up.

"No, no, you are fine." My heart danced to see Marina nestling the baby.

"I died for a minute," she said. "They tied me down and ripped her out."

"But you are okay." I walked toward her and thought every woman feels close to death giving birth, but Marina was safe now. The ordeal was over.

"You are a ghost," she said. Her eyes were like black coals and she did not blink. The medicine was still active in her body and playing tricks on her mind.

"No. I'm right here." I stopped, afraid if I got any closer she would ask me to leave. The baby was swaddled, and a tuft of black hair peeked out.

"I can see you, I can hear you, but if I touch you, nothing will be there." Marina's face seemed frozen in a frown. The medicine skewed her mind.

"You are dreaming," I said.

"No." She shook her head calmly. She looked at me with wild, black eyes. She seemed not to notice the weight of the baby in her arms. "You are dead to me."

"You're not feeling well." I wanted to go to her, to touch her and hold the baby, but I was afraid she would lose her wits and do something horrible. "I understand." My confidence in her love diminished with each word and doubt crept in.

"He's here, waiting for you," she said.

I wanted to ask, *Who?* But I dared not, because she might have said *Daddy.* I said, "The medicine they gave you makes you have bad thoughts."

"I've always had bad thoughts." No emotion showed in her face or in her voice.

Of course she'd had bad thoughts. How could she have escaped my sadness or her father's? We had shared it from the beginning, before she was ever born. I'd withheld from her or been incapable, and she, an innocent child, watched and waited for me to be better, but she could not fill the gap and make me whole. Marina had, like me, lived without a mother.

She said, "If they don't get you, he will."

Whether she meant Elias or Michael or Ivie, her words sent shivers down my back.

"You said you wanted me." I hoped to change her line of thinking. "I heard you calling me."

"I did. I called for you when they strapped me down." She looked at her wrists. "You didn't come."

"They wouldn't let me. I was here the whole time waiting for her and praying for you." I inched closer and when she did not protest, I stood by her bed. The room was the same as the room her grandfather had died in.

"There was lamb's wool on the wrist straps that held me down and I thought of the lambs Grandmother fed all summer before she led them to slaughter."

"I'm here now." The room Papa had died in was on the floor above and looked out over the same view.

"You disappointed me again," she said. The truth was spilling out like a flooded well.

Maybe this was motherhood, longing for a person who would out-grow you, longing for a love outside your reach.

"You should have warned me about giving birth," Marina said.

I tried to swallow the tears. "You'll forget all of this when the medi-cine wears off." She would forget this conversation and the labor.

"I will never forget." The pupils in her eyes, big and black, cut out all the green. If anyone had the will to overcome medicine that blocked memory, it would be Marina. I wanted her to smile at the baby, even if she stayed angry at me. "I don't care if you stay or go," she said.

I wanted to give her comfort and touch her face or comb her hair. I wanted a glimpse of her newborn.

"Michael says if you stay we'll leave Riverton."

The baby's crop of black hair peeked out from the swaddle. "Do you want me to leave now?" I would go if it would end her suffering.

"No. I want you to see what you're missing." The deliberate cadence of her words felt cruel. "Take her. I'm tired." She held the baby at arm's length. "Go on, take her."

She was weaker than she knew, and I scooped the baby, afraid Marina might drop her. I held the light, warm bundle, so much lighter than Sophie. For all the sadness weighing on me, for the bile Marina wanted to spill on me, I felt immense joy to look at this new face, the pink, scoured cheeks and eyelids curtained in thick eyelashes. This baby had come late, I could tell by the fullness of her cheeks, her thick hair.

There was no proportion to the joy I felt, or what I had ever felt, good or bad. Holding my grandchild, I had a glimpse of what love could be, and I lost my breath, as if all the bad did not matter. That moment with Marina's baby was all the good of the past and the future. "What did you name her?"

"Eliza," Marina said. Her eyes drooped with sleepiness. "I named her Eliza Anne." She rolled over, with her back to me, and fell asleep. The medicine, the birth, all of it had worn her out.

The baby rested in my arms and the warm bundle soothed my heart. I looked out the hospital window to a brilliant blue sky with none of the clouds or rain from the past few days. The sun glared white hot off cars parked below. The world was bright and clear, but I could barely grasp what there was to see. In that small room, my daughter slept and I held her daughter named after Elias and me. The truth was the bundle in my arms, and I could feel it, a fleeting glimpse, that love had come too late and all in a jumble. All love and loneliness, and I had only a short time to sort it out.

My mother's Gypsy came to mind. Mama had tried to tell me how she had been lonely in her new world, an oddity to most people she met. She had been the Gypsy on the outskirts and now I was the same, never to be trusted or let in, scorned and cast out by my daughter and family. I watched Marina sleep, and I felt her love and her loneliness too. She would be as lonely as I had been without a mother or the father she loved. He had been a different man to her than the one I knew, and I realized one person could be many. My mother, brave and wise in my memory, was young and frail and worried to my father. I could not know them any better than I could know if Marina would change her mind about me.

I did not want to put the baby down, because when I did, I would be without a purpose, drifting like a raft in the middle of the river. I was not afraid of being alone or staying or leaving. I was afraid I would not know this child, Eliza Anne, breathing, soft and quiet, against my cheek. She opened one eye to peek and her lips moved in a sucking motion.

Marina mumbled in her sleep, "I don't want to choose." She opened her eyes, serious and deep, the pupils like a black lake with a fringe of green. Her breath shuddered and she closed her eyes again. With the baby in one arm, I wet a rag with cool water and placed it on Marina's forehead. She did not stir.

The baby's lips parted and closed as she dreamed of suckling. I pushed the call button for the nurse to bring a bottle and it was a powerful feeling to hold her. Marina would love her and do better than I had. "This will pass, Eliza Anne," I said out loud, and as the words left my lips, I felt a rock in my chest. How many babies did one get in a lifetime? I had had four, Marina, Eli, Sophie, and now Eliza. I had wasted time being angry and passed my anger on to Marina. All I could hope for was a chance to show her better now. I could not dare to hope for more.

My arms cramped, and I was tired from not sleeping, worry, and emotion, but I knew it was my chance, my beautiful chance to hold her. The baby squeaked and let out a newborn's wail. I changed her diaper, and when the air hit her naked body, she howled. I swaddled her, and in the warmth and tightness of the blanket, she stopped fussing. I picked her up and felt calm, despite the knowledge that very soon, I would bury my father.

Michael stood sentinel in the hallway. He coughed and looked in and I knew he was counting the minutes until I left. The nurse brought a bottle and I fed the baby, rocked her, and watched Marina sleep for two hours. Her fingers were still swollen, and I wondered how many days before she would be slim again and fit into her smart clothes. I wondered if the baby would change her, if she would soften in her dress or in her attitude or if she would see the world in a gentler way. I felt a thickness in my throat—a cold, hard lump that I could not swallow. The heaviness traveled through my whole being, and I worried I was too late in my understanding. I should have been more patient with her, more giving and loving, and I should not have begrudged her for being her father's child.

Michael stepped inside the door. "Are you done?"

"No," I said. "Not close." It was folly to have thought he would help me. "The baby is hungry again. Would you have the nurse bring a bottle?"

The nurse came in at two thirty with another bottle. I said, "Let her rest."

Marina continued to sleep through the afternoon.

At the five o'clock feeding, the nurse offered to take the baby to the nursery, but I said, "No. Leave her with me."

The baby ate again with vigor and burped louder than I remembered a baby could. I changed her again, swaddled her, and breathed in the smell of her scalp. I languished in the warmth of her small body.

"I know you," I whispered to Eliza Anne. "I love you." Both of them slept and the baby was a beautiful weight in my arms. She was fed and content. The nurse checked Marina's pulse and listened to her heart while she snored.

I put the baby down in the bassinet and tried to tame Marina's wild hair. She did not stir as I ran my fingers through the waves of hair, as she had loved for me to do at bedtime when she was a girl.

I peeked through the blinds. It was near five thirty, and the haze of white heat had burned off and the sky was softening toward sapphire blue. In less than three hours it would be dark. Warm sparks of sun bounced off the cars below, and mine sat on the street with a trunk full of money, a thief's dream, hiding out in the open.

Part of me thought I should go south to the Gulf of Mexico, to a room or a cottage on the beach, and make a home for myself. If I went far away, Eli would feel no obligation to protect me, and Marina would be free of me. I would cross the Riverton Bridge and see the old courthouse in my rearview mirror. I would look back until the river, the bridges, the town were gone from sight and the pain would trail behind. But when I looked at Marina sleeping, I knew better. I could not leave.

I looked at Eliza Anne's sweet face and tried to remember what I had wanted when I married Elias. I had wanted him. I had wanted love. I had wanted to be like my mother. All I knew for certain, I had wanted more than what I had or what I got. That was when regret washed over me like cold water. I had waited too long to stand up for myself, for others, for Marina and Eli, for this baby girl, and I had gone about it the wrong way.

Marina stirred. "You're still here?" She reached out for me or the baby.

I left my post at the window and tucked the baby next to Marina. Marina rubbed her eyes. "Aren't you afraid?"

"No," I said. "It breaks my heart to go."

I buried my head against Marina's neck. Her scent was mixed with sweat and blood and hospital soap.

"Mother." Marina nudged me. "Get up. The baby is fussing."

I stood back and looked at them.

"You should go," Marina said. "You should go tonight."

I sat on the edge of her bed. "I have to bury my father. I have to do what is right."

"I'm afraid for you." Her pupils had shrunk, and the bright-green color of her eyes was visible again.

"Don't worry about me," I said. "You are a mother now. You worry about her and I'll do my best."

Michael, who had been listening in the doorframe, came in. "It's time you go, Anna."

Marina stared at me with wet eyes. I prayed she would never know what it was to sacrifice love or feeling in order to survive, to finally have a chance, to have it so close, as close as I held baby Eliza, and to feel it slipping away. She would never trust me. Seeds of doubt had been planted in her mind, in Michael's mind, and nothing I could do, no denial, no words, could change that.

"I'll follow you home." Michael was civil in Marina's presence.

"No need for that," I answered.

"I think there is." He spoke with a kind and fatherly tone, for Marina's sake, but I knew his true feelings. "There could be trouble." Michael was as liable to drive me off the road or throw me in the river as anyone else.

"I'm not going home," I said. It was half truth. "So you don't have to worry about me." He could think I was leaving town, that was fine—I wanted nothing from him. I kissed Marina's forehead and then touched the warm baby's cheek. I whispered in Marina's ear, "I'm not leaving you."

She did not flinch or protest. She did not give me away to him.

I walked through the cool, sterile halls of the hospital where my children and my grandchild were born and where Papa had died, and out into the heavy, humid air. The sun hung low, bright and hot, and the air was thick with light. This was my home and I would not leave Marina and her baby. I would not be run off.

Home

The mockingbird shrieked from his perch in the tree as I walked up the porch steps. The coffin was gone, my furniture had been righted, but the table remained cluttered with servers and chafing dishes. No second round of food had been warmed for a funeral reception, because we had gone to the hospital for Marina.

In the dim house, I emptied the pantry of dried fruit and nuts for the neglected bird. I tossed the treats for him and the leaves rustled as he swooped down. He sang and flitted around his bounty, and I thought, *Let the old bird gorge himself.* His handouts from me would soon be over. He could eat from the garden for the rest of the summer, but in two months' time, the geese would come, the leaves would turn and begin to fall. Maybe by winter the mockingbird would forget our arrangement.

I took off the suit Marina had bought me and put on a loose-fitting dress. The sleeves were short, but it did not matter who saw the bruises and who did not. I packed my clothes and jewelry, some sheets and housewares. Downstairs, I gathered the *rakweh*, the spices, and my recipes. I found the picture of my mother and her sisters, the one of Marina and me and the ones of my children. I checked the money in the trunk of my car, and then filled it with my things. Then I began to load my baking supplies, the bowls and pans, the baskets, my measuring cups. I took my bread starter from the icebox and carried it like a chalice to my car. It smelled slightly of vinegar, but I would feed it to bring it back.

Verna stood on her porch watching me. I turned and smiled and raised my middle finger to her, in case she didn't know how I felt.

She said, "Well, I never," loud enough to carry across the street. She turned on her heel and went inside, but still I felt her eyes on me as I packed my car.

I was so tired that I could have gone inside and slept, but my old life stopped me. I would never live there again, not where he breathed, not where he died, not where I had scraped by. Nor would I leave this town, Marina and her child. The sheriff or a mob might still come for me, but I would face whatever I had to for Marina and Eli. I was not leaving. I would rather live on Marina's fringes, like the Gypsy of my mother's story, begging for scraps, an outcast, waiting for glimpses of them and their love, than run away to nothing.

Verna sat in her window and she must have been happy, thinking, *That Arab is finally gone.* The sun dipped, and the horizon was a line of pale green and the sky a deep sapphire blue. I marveled at how quickly the sky and the world could change. In the dark, I picked enough figs to fill two baskets and put them in the front seat of the car. "Figs for prosperity," I said to keep from crying. Like a bittersweet prize, I ate them and tossed the skins on the road as I drove across town to my father's store.

It was eight thirty when I locked my car behind Papa's store. I put the starter in Papa's drink cooler and took a Coca-Cola. I dialed Lila and told her where I was so that she would not worry. She asked about Marina and the baby, and I could not help but smile.

"You sound happy," Lila said.

"I'm at peace," I said.

She told me Eli and Gus were with Father McMurray, but they'd be back later, and she'd let Eli know where I was. I hung the receiver in the cradle and I snuck out the back door.

I took the towpath by the river and headed east toward my house on Poplar Street. The sun was gone, and in the east sat a sliver of moon and a scattering of stars. My eyes adjusted to the darkness among the gray tree trunks, and my feet pressed into the dark earth, damp from the days of rain. I looked out over the river and felt alive. The noise of the cicadas and frogs vibrated in the air and bounced off the canopy and the silvery black water. The sounds, the water, my breath in my ear, my heart in my chest—all this comforted me.

I crossed beneath the bridges and past the loading docks. The thump-thump of cars drowned out any other sound. I remembered coming here as a girl, and as the train went over, the rumble filled my whole body and the flash of the horn deafened my ears.

I began to run. The old courthouse with its black windows, like dead eyes on a stone face, reminded me of Marina's black pupils, her hard labor, the medicine that made her feelings run over like a flood. Across the way was the corner of the post office, and I thought of Orlando Washington, and how my husband and Ivie and others, whoever they were, took Mr. Washington, to scare him and to show him they would do him harm if he tried to rise above his station in life. The frogs sang loud in my ear, the whippoorwill called. Ivie and the others would harm me too, if I gave them the chance.

I ran and a stitch pinched in my side, but I felt full of purpose, and pain would not stop me. I came off the path and stood at the back door of my house; it was dark and quiet. I was not afraid on the path in the night, but I was afraid in my kitchen, of who I had been and what I had done inside those walls. The smell of the house and our life together filled my nostrils. A wave of shame passed through me as the cuckoo clock ticked and the river frogs groaned and the night birds chirped.

My blood felt cold. If they came now, they would catch me. But Ivie was not here, nor were the folks Michael warned me about. I was alone and Verna's lights were off. In the drawer nearest my stove, I kept a big box of matches. I took them out and began.

In each room, first upstairs, then the basement, then the main floor, I struck a match and then another. The sulfur tip caught to an orange flame and I set it to paper, to cloth, to curtains, pictures of him or whatever would burn. The place felt eerie in the glow and lick of flames spreading around me. In the kitchen I looked beneath the sink and found Lila's pint of whiskey. I lit the stove and the oven and tossed a towel over the flame so it would spread. I poured the whiskey, lit it, tossed the last of the matches into the fire, and backed out the door.

Beneath the white mulberry trees, I waited for the fire to take hold and looked one last time at the garden Elias and I had planted together. The pole beans were his and the tomatoes mine. The eggplant hung heavy on the small bushes and the okra had grown taller than me. All of it gone to waste.

Smoke filled the windows. Marina's silver would warp and melt, the pictures of him would shrivel to ash, and all the walls and beams would burn in the night. I thought of the cuckoo, the furniture, Papa's rugs, the giant church coffeepot. The fire and the gossip would distress Marina, but she had a beautiful distraction to help her forget the misery of this place.

They had burned Orlando Washington's home, and I had burned my own, but the act was not the same. They had pushed him out on the threat of death. They might come for me too, but maybe I had bought some time. Ivie or some other fool would brag that they had burned my house. Maybe the others would be appeased.

The orange flames filled the windows. I'd leave it a place for birds and squirrels to nest, an eyesore to greet Verna daily. I was happy Mr. Washington was safe. I was happy the house would burn to ruins, save the stone porch on which he had stood.

I could see the flames growing and feel the heat rising, and in a few moments, the windows would pop. Flames would pour out the openings and scorch the brick. The noise of bursting glass would wake Verna and she might call the fire department or she might not. She might let it burn and gather a crowd to revel in my suffering. They would think I got what I deserved.

I hurried west along the path, past the old courthouse, and at the bridges, I looked back at traces of smoke billowing gray against the black sky above the trees. All of that sad life was gone, and I had been the one to do it, not Michael or Ivie or any of those who wanted to hurt me, the ones who had tormented Mr. Washington. They wanted to run me off, but every step I took was for someone: Mama, Marina, Eli, Papa, Gus, Lila, Sophie, Elsa, Eliza Anne, Thea, and Orlando Washington.

There were others who had made this path: the Indians first and then later, walking on their journey west, the ferrymen settling this outpost, the men and women working the land or floating bales of cotton down the river, the soldiers resting on the banks between skirmishes. Maybe Ivie now, coming toward me or coming from behind.

Many people shared the guilt I carried. A history of people made us what we were, this town, cut in half. All of us shared responsibility for the bad things that had happened to me, to Elias, to Orlando Washington, but most of us denied it.

The smell of smoke filled the air, and I could not see the stars above the trees where my house once stood. I was not afraid if they came after me. *This all will pass.* That is what Papa said. They had burned Orlando Washington's home, and I had burned my own. My heart beat high in my chest as the din of the fire truck carried through town.

Inside Papa's store, I flipped the light switch and the clutter of his life met me hard. I walked into my mother's baking room, and in my nervous energy, I started sorting Papa's things. He had stacked garden tools along the wall and I moved them by the back door to take out the next day. I tossed empty cardboard boxes there too. While I worked, I remembered the fire in her oven, the hot white ash and her baking bread and cooling pies. I looked inside the oven and tried to remember how she used the heat.

Baking in Mama's oven would be trial and error, but I would learn. Marina wanted bread and I would make it for her every day. Maybe Eli was right to have faith in her, because she had not given me away to Michael, nor had she refused me when I told her I was not leaving. Maybe Marina could forgive me and I would see Eliza Anne again, whether it was tomorrow or next week or in a year or in ten years. One day, I would give her my bread that I made in her great-grandmother's oven, but for tomorrow morning I would bake in the regular oven. I went to the front of the store to get my starter and some flour to feed it.

Ivie's face pressed on the glass door and I screamed. When he saw me, he swung a bat and shattered the glass. His long arm reached through the shards to unlock the bolt.

I ran to the back door to get out, but the boxes and the tools I had piled up were in my way.

He swung a bat in every direction, knocking groceries off shelves and busting the register and the counters as he strode toward me.

I threw the boxes at him and he batted them away. He leered at me and seemed to be enjoying himself, but finally he grabbed my bruised arm with one hand and yanked me close. He sniffed my hair. "You stink of smoke and you think you're going to pin arson on me?" He smelled of musk and whiskey and his face was drenched in sweat. He let go of me with a shove.

I reached around and got a hand on Papa's garden hoe. "Gus will be here any minute."

"I don't think so." He wore a rope around his waist. "He and Eli stopped at the fire at your house."

I moved away toward the kitchen. I lifted the hoe with the blade facing him. "Get out." I swung the tool toward his face.

With a feral look in his eye, he laughed at me threatening him. "You know all about that fire, don't you?"

Eli and Gus would be tormented watching my house burn and thinking I was inside.

Ivie lunged and I had no choice but to shuffle backward into Mama's baking room.

"I went looking for you and I saw what you did." He swung his bat and it grazed the hoe and sent vibrations into my arms. I would lose a battle of strength. "Put that down before you get hurt." His eyes were crazy, wild. He could bury me with his body.

"Get out," I said. "You're drunk."

"I'm always a little bit drunk." He swung the bat and knocked the metal shelves that held Mama's pans and the tools Papa had haphazardly laid there. The tall shelf rocked off balance and landed with a great clatter. The pans rolled around like tops spinning and gave off a ghostly noise.

"Why were you at my house?" He had gone there to hurt me. I held tight to the hoe, and if he came at me, I would strike him and run.

He swung the bat on my mother's worktable. The pounding of wood hurt my ears. "Why were you *not* there?" He drank from his flask.

"Because it was you who burned it."

"Don't do something you'll regret."

"I have no regrets." He moved stealthily around me. "Me and you have unfinished business." He lifted my mother's table and turned it on its side. Papa's papers fluttered to the floor.

The phone in Papa's store rang. I tried to step around him, but he blocked my way.

"I wanted to thank you." A dark smile covered his face.

"Why?" The ringing kept on. It was probably Lila, and I regretted not going to her house. I had thought I was above his threats. I had tempted fate by setting my house on fire, but the feeling I'd had holding Eliza Anne had overwhelmed me to be bold and start new and fresh.

He took a step closer and leaned in. "You did what I always dreamed of."

The phone rang and I jostled the hoe in his face. "Go away."

"Whoa, now." He moved closer, betting I did not have the grit to injure him. "My brother was a goddamn bastard."

"I want you to turn around and go." I pushed the flat blade of the hoe into his chest, but he was strong and the force of his body drove me toward the corner. The phone rang one last time, and I prayed Gus and Eli would leave the fire and come here before he hurt or killed me.

His face was slick and his eyes intense. He took a step away, and with a grunt he crashed the bat into the wall. It splintered and he threw it on the ground. "I came here in peace."

"Your brother loved you." I tried to think what he wanted to hear, anything to get away from him and what he planned to do. "And now you have the store. He wanted you to have it."

"Naw." His body inched toward mine and I did not have the strength to stop him. "He didn't give a rat's ass about me." He drank a long swig from his flask.

"Go," I said. "Go home and work in your store."

Quick and nimble, he grabbed the handle of the hoe and pushed me against the wall. He was close and I could smell the whiskey on his breath. "I came for you."

"Don't do something you'll regret," I said again. I held on to the hoe with both hands and kept it between us. The stitches burst and the blood ran but I did not let go.

"Like kill you?" His face sagged from age and drink but his eyes ran greedily over my face and neck. He lifted the sleeve of my dress and ran his fingers over the bruise. "He was awful to you." His words slurred and his eyelids hung heavy.

I pushed the hoe into his chest, but he did not notice the pressure of the tool. Either I was too feeble or he was too fixed on me. "Go home, Ivie. You are drunk."

"He was a mean bastard." He put his hands in my hair. The tool was between us, but his sweaty cheek pressed on mine. "I watched him hurt you and I watched him get richer and I didn't get nowhere."

I did not know if I had the strength to stop him. I pleaded. "If you hurt me, you'll never be good again."

"Is that how you feel?" His face hung over mine. "All you ever wanted was a man to treat you nice." He ripped my dress.

"Leave me alone." I could feel the old fear rising, but I pressed the blade into the meat of his chest as hard as I could.

"You don't want to do that." He grabbed the handle again and his brute force turned my weak arms. He looked like Elias, only where Elias had a keen eye, Ivie seemed bewildered. "If you do that, I'll have to hurt you."

"You wanted the store. You have it. You wanted me out of Riverton. At least I'm in Mounds," I said. "Now leave me alone."

"I had a new idea." His breath landed on my cheek. "You and me, we could work together. You ran that store as much as him. You can work and I'll take care of you, treat you nice."

His eyes were half shut, and in his reverie, he let go of the handle. I twisted it and shunted it into his flesh. He bent over in pain. "You goddamn bitch." His voice was gravelly and deep.

The blade had landed on his arm, and blood ran down onto the ground. I got around him, but in two or three steps, he had hold of me and threw me to the floor like I was a sack of potatoes.

I scooted toward the door. "Gus is coming," I said. "He'll kill you if you hurt me."

"Your Gus ain't coming." He stood over me with his foot on my arm. His blood dripped onto me as he took the rope from around his waist, to hang me or pull me or tie me. "Now you made me mad."

I thought of Eliza Anne, of Marina and Eli. I thought of their faces and how much I loved them. I could not move, but I screamed, "If you kill me, you'll have nothing,"

He barked at me. "What do you have? Huh? What do you have?" He fumbled as he wound the rope around my neck. He held it tight and crouched down over me.

I tried to hold him off with my arms, but his weight was heavy. "I have my children and my grandchild."

He pulled the rope tight with one hand and groped under my dress with the other. "Shut up," he said. "They don't want you. Nobody wants you."

"Forget about me. Forget about Elias. Just go," I begged. I could not move away without choking myself. It had been one thing for Elias to touch me. He was my husband and the father of my children. I had wanted to love him. But Ivie's touch made my skin crawl and I did not want to die at his hands.

"Lay there and shut up and maybe I won't kill you." He clenched the rope tighter and pulled at my dress with his free hand.

That is when I saw the shadow in the hall. I did not know if it was someone else come to do me harm, or if it might be Eli or Gus. Ivie was too drunk and too intent on pulling at my underclothes to notice.

When he reached down and fumbled with his pants, I shot my fingers into his eyes and dug my nails into his eyeballs to rake them out. They pushed in deeper than I thought they could go.

His body recoiled and I jerked my knee into his groin. He yanked the rope and choked me. A shot fired and the report filled the small room. He rolled over on his side. I crawled away toward the door and Lila stood above me. She gave me her free hand to help me stand.

Ivie lay huddled near a dark pool of blood.

"Did you hit him?" I coughed and could not catch my breath.

Lila shook her head. She pointed on the wall where the bullet had passed through. She had shot high to scare him. "Any damage is from you."

The blood on the floor came from the gash I'd given him. I felt weak-kneed and sick.

"Go call the sheriff." She kept her pistol pointed at Ivie. She sounded firm, but her hand shook.

Ivie whimpered. "I can't see nothing." He tried to get to his knees.

"Don't move, or I won't miss this time," Lila yelled as if he were a wild horse that she meant to tame.

His wits were slow from the drink and his eyes were swollen shut, but he knew she meant business, and he sat stone still.

I stumbled to the phone and dialed the sheriff's office. They knew Ivie and they would come, but I did not expect them to come fast, because of who I was and where we were. I hurried back to Lila through the wreckage of Papa's store.

"How did you know?" I asked her.

"Someone called and said your house was on fire. I knew you were here." I could hear the dryness in Lila's mouth. Her lips and words stuck together like tacky paper. I could tell she was afraid.

"Where's Sophie?" I asked.

"Asleep in the truck." Lila kept her eyes on him but lowered the gun. "Go sit with her until they get here."

I staggered to the truck where Sophie slept. I scooped the warm, sweet child into my arms and her weight reminded me of why I had not left.

The deputy arrived and he sauntered to where I sat with Sophie. He asked, "What seems to be the trouble here?"

As I told what had happened, his hands rested on his belt and he did not take a single note.

"Did you know your house burned?" He showed no concern that my house had caught on fire or that I was bleeding and in a torn dress with rope burns around my neck.

I answered, "Not until Ivie told me."

"And who discharged the weapon?" The officer looked back at the store and the shattered glass.

"My sister-in-law. She's inside," I said.

"Tell me where you were this evening." The deputy spit onto the gravel.

I held Sophie and felt calm. "I was at the hospital with my daughter and then I went home to get my things and I came here. My neighbor Verna saw me packing and I called Lila to let her know where I was."

"And why did you leave your house?" He looked at Sophie asleep on my lap.

"I was afraid for my safety." I stared at him and he spit again.

"You wait here, while I talk to the other parties." The deputy stepped through the broken glass into the store.

That's when Eli and Gus drove up. The deputy was out of sight. Eli jumped out of his car and saw me. "Are you hurt?"

"I'll be fine."

"Oh, God." Gus stared at me. "Is that your blood?"

I shook my head no.

"Is Lila okay?" Gus lifted Sophie from my arms.

"Yes," I said.

"Who did this? Ivie?" Eli tilted my chin to see my neck.

Sophie's legs dangled at full weight and her mouth parted against Gus's shoulder. I was relieved she had not seen or heard any of the commotion.

I hugged my son. "I am okay. He won't bother me again." Now I had proof and witnesses to Ivie's ill will.

"We were at the fire and heard the call over the police radio." Eli looked me over and touched my chin. "He's going to pay for this."

The deputy's voice carried from inside the store onto the street: "You want me to drop you in the river and put you out of your misery?" His steps crunched through the glass inside the store. He was coming back out.

Ivie slurred, "One almost killed me and the other nearly poked my eyes out."

The deputy exited with Ivie, who had free hands but walked unsteadily, tripping over level ground.

Eli braced like he would charge Ivie, but I grabbed his sleeve.

Ivie sat himself in the back of the patrol car.

Gus took Sophie inside. "I'm going to check on Lila."

The officer turned to me. "Do you want to press charges? In a domestic dispute, it will be your word against his."

"Of course she'll press charges." Eli's temples throbbed and his face was red.

The officer ignored my son. "There are extenuating circumstances to consider."

Eli barked at the officer. "You mean Orlando Washington? You're not going to arrest Ivie because she helped Orlando Washington." Eli leaned close to the officer's face and raised his hands as if to provoke him.

"Watch yourself." The deputy put one hand on Eli's chest and the other on his weapon.

"Eli, walk away." I jerked my son out of the deputy's reach and Eli slumped toward the damaged storefront. "You can go, sir. Get Ivie out of here."

The deputy tipped his hat as if he had been my knight in shining armor. "Don't worry, ma'am. I'll take care of him." I wondered what he would do, beat him or congratulate him.

The red taillights of the patrol car headed toward Riverton.

Whatever happened, I hoped Ivie would not bother me again, not with the suspicion of fire hanging over him, not after what the deputy and Lila witnessed. Nelly would drown him first.

I hurried over to Eli. "It's going to be okay."

Eli's jaw pulsed. "Look what he did to you, to your house, to Grandpapa's store."

"I'm safe."

Eli shook his head. "It's wrong. The roughnecks rule the world despite the law." He hit the hood of Lila's truck.

I wanted to reassure him. "I'm not going to be run out. I'm here for you and Marina."

"You can't stay here by yourself." Eli hung his head. He looked tired. "I'll have to open Dad's store."

"No, you won't," I said. "You and Marina will sell it and you'll go to school. You're not my caregiver. Not yet."

I wanted to say, *I struck the match that burned my house,* but I could not. I had bought myself another night and another day. I did not know how many days and nights it would take, or if I could ever win my daughter. If those who wanted to punish me thought I'd been served my due, maybe they would leave me alone and I could try.

I put my arms around my son. "It's been a hard week. Go upstairs to Gus's old room and sleep. We'll figure things out tomorrow."

I followed Eli inside, where Gus had swept the broken glass and cut cardboard to cover the door. Gus looked at me, worried. "How are you?"

"I'm okay," I said. "How's Lila?"

"She's shaken up, but she's resting with Sophie." Gus scratched his beard, which had grown in two days. His eyes were sad. "She's never fired a gun at anyone, but she loves you. She wasn't going to let him hurt you."

"Let's get some rest," I said.

Gus taped the cardboard over the window. "We can sort this mess later."

"We'll be okay," I said. "Help me pull out some rugs for a pallet." Papa's room was empty, but I could not bring myself to sleep there.

Gus rolled the rugs out, one on top of the other. He went upstairs to sleep and I changed into a fresh dress and washed my face in the dark. I lay down and listened to the still house and the sounds of the cicadas and frogs.

I wanted sleep, but my mind would not stop. All my loved ones were under the same roof, except Marina and Eliza Anne, but they were all safe. I would convince Gus and Eli that I could live here. I wanted to make bread in Mama's oven and work in Papa's garden and I hoped

Marina would accept me living in Mounds. At night, I'd sit on the balcony and look at the river and maybe Papa's neighbors would see me as my father's daughter and not as Elias's wife. Time would tell. If Michael's warnings came true, if they brought up charges or chased me with burning stakes, I would face what I had to, because there was the chance Marina might come around.

Across the floor, against the counter, my eye caught sight of Papa's *kashshi*, which had been under his bed a few days before. Papa must have moved it. I crossed the store and touched the soft, worn wood of the peddler's box. A tinker had made it in New York with only an axe and a hoe to plane it and a knife to notch the dovetailed drawers. The dry leather straps had scarred my father's shoulders. The large compartment held bags of sugar or flour or cloth, whatever was ordered or needed, and across the front the small drawers were labeled in Papa's handwriting: *cinnamon, allspice, cloves, black pepper, buttons, needles, nails, tobacco.*

Why had Papa moved the box? It had been all but empty when I'd searched it for Mama's picture. I flipped on the light and looked inside one drawer and then another. The old scents remained. Crumbs of cinnamon sticks. Cardamom. Oregano. Vanilla beans. A few stray bone buttons. Then, in a large drawer I remembered having been empty, Mama's ten silver bracelets, untarnished, shining silver in the dim light. Papa must have polished them. One was engraved with my name and birthdate and one with Gus's. They slipped on my wrists as if they had been made for me.

I opened the lid, and down in the deep bottom was a yellowed envelope. Inside it were locks of hair tied with ribbons and labeled in old-fashioned scrawl, not Papa's or Mama's smooth hand. The labels said, *Vega, Miss Vega, baby Gus, Nicholas,* and *Matthew.* The writing was Thea's. Mama must have whispered the twins' names into her ear, and because she knew the depth of Mama's love, Thea put us all together,

Vega and her children, in this simple way. I prayed I had done right trying to help her son.

At the bottom of the box, the picture of Mama looked back. I brought the frame close to my eyes to study her face and noticed the dark rings under Mama's eyes. She was beautiful, but not as calm and carefree as I remembered.

In his worst moments, Elias told me I was ugly and square jawed like my father, but there I was a child, beautiful and innocent. I saw myself in Mama's eyes. I saw Marina in her too, how similar we all looked, but the expression in Mama's eyes was complicated. Perhaps, that day when she called me to help her water the fig tree, she sensed a future sadness, as every mother does—but despite the worry, she held me with love and hope and smiled for my father taking the photograph. I recognized the same feeling in myself, for my daughter and son, my brother and Lila, for Sophie, and now Eliza Anne. Looking at my mother's face, I saw the love I had always wanted. I had always had it, but I had been too distracted by sorrow to see it.

I was a child then and she never spoke of her fears or loneliness to me. I wished I could have known Mama better. If she had grown old, I would have known her flaws and weaknesses. I hoped I would have forgiven her those, as I hoped Marina would forgive mine.

Papa had filled the peddler's box to give me because he loved me. He understood. I put the picture back in the box and shut the lid. I was unable to look at my mother's face any longer. I turned off the lights, lay down, and felt my mother's presence. I was home now. I could try to right the wrongs I had done, now that I was where I belonged. I would give Marina the photograph and hope there was time to make things right. I covered my eyes with my arm and the bracelets jangled.

I'd give Marina the picture at my father's funeral, and she would see the hope in my childhood face and recognize herself in my mother's image. She might see Mama's worry and her hope and her joy, and I would say, "What you feel for Eliza, I felt for you, but I had trouble showing it." I would tell her that I had wanted to be good and loving like Mama, and if she gave me a chance, I would prove myself to her.

If she turned away, I would keep trying. I'd bake bread in my mother's oven and carry the loaves to her. If she would not see me, I'd leave them on her porch and wait for something in return. One day, I would put these bracelets on Marina's arm and hope for an embrace that captured the feeling I had holding her child while she slept. That was the moment when love was clear to me, when I had a glimpse of truth, that pain and suffering were the right costs to have paid for my children. That was the moment when redemption was present, and I would wait for that to come again.

Acknowledgments

Thank you to Danielle Marshall, Jodi Warshaw, and everyone at Lake Union for your amazing support of this book. I am extremely grateful to Victoria Sanders, who encouraged me from our first conversation. I offer special thanks to Beneé Knauer and David Downing, both generous editors who gave me keen insights and cheered me on.

Thank you, William Whitley, for reading so many pages, for your humor and goodwill. I also wish to thank my dear friend Alana Booker, who has been privy from the first conception of this story to its final draft, and all the many friends, teachers, and family who have encouraged me along the way.

I am also grateful for the works of Alixa Naff (*Becoming American: The Early Arab Immigrant Experience*) and Philip M. Kayal and Joseph M. Kayal (*The Syrian-Lebanese in America*), which shed much light on the specific and the collective experiences of the early Arab Americans.

About the Author

Photo © 2016 Amy Gibbons

Cheryl Reid grew up in Decatur, Alabama. She studied art and writing at Agnes Scott College and earned an MFA in Creative Writing from Georgia State University. She lives with her husband and three children in Decatur, Georgia. *As Good as True* is her first novel.